THE
PRESIDENT'S
NEMESIS

MICHAEL BERES

Platinum Imprint
Medallion Press, Inc.
Printed in USA

Published 2006 by Medallion Press, Inc.

The MEDALLION PRESS LOGO
is a registered tradmark of Medallion Press, Inc.

Printed in the United States of America

Library of Congress Cataloging-in-Publication Data

Beres, Michael.
  The president's nemesis / by Michael Beres.
    p. cm.
  ISBN 1-932815-73-2
  I. Title.
  PS3602.E7516P74 2006
  813'.6--dc22
                        2005031450

10 9 8 7 6 5 4 3 2
First Edition

THE PRESIDENT'S NEMESIS

MICHAEL BERES

CHAPTER 1

THE PRESIDENT'S NEMESIS

AT PRECISELY THE same time on two consecutive nights, the large black vehicle moved slowly through the darkness of the parking lot below Stan's window. It could have been a Lincoln Navigator or Chevy Suburban. The headlights and taillights and side marker lights gave it a general shape, a large sport utility vehicle. He was certain it was the same vehicle both nights. If the vehicle appeared a third night this would be very curious indeed.

The first night, when the vehicle parked in front of the garbage dumpsters on the far side of the parking lot, Stan thought it might be a police vehicle, detectives on a stakeout. But why with the lights on? That first night he stood at his front window until the vehicle drove away. Slowly at first, until it got to the apartment complex entrance. Then fast, heading south around the curve on Elmwood Drive, taillights disappearing between the gas stations at the crossroads.

Stan saw the same vehicle again the next night, parked in the same spot with its lights on. As he stood at the window that second night, he saw two figures in the front seat. The passenger got out on the far side next to one of the garbage dumpsters. Only the top half of the passenger was visible moving toward the front of the vehicle. Small head, short hair, large shoulders, a man. The man lifted the lid of the garbage dumpster and placed something inside, or simply reached inside. Then back into the vehicle. No courtesy light on while the door was open, so Stan could not see faces. And like the previous night, the vehicle drove slowly out of the lot, then fast once it was on the road.

On two nights in a row at exactly one in the morning a vehicle had visited the garbage dumpsters in the parking lot and Stan's curiosity began to torment him. If he didn't stay up late every night he would never have seen it. But he did stay up late. Sometimes watching television—switching between the classic movie channels or the Biography or History Channels. Sometimes at his computer surfing the Web. If he didn't stay up so late and have such an idle mind he wouldn't have concocted dozens of reasons for two men driving up to a garbage dumpster at one in the morning and tossing something in.

Stan really hadn't seen much of the driver, only that there was one, but because of the police stakeout idea he assumed both were men, both wearing overcoats like the guy who had gotten out and gone to the dumpster. Maybe they lived somewhere else, one of those new subdivisions way south, and were too cheap to pay a scavenger service. But a more enticing possibility was FBI agents checking someone's garbage. So why hadn't he seen a flashlight? Last night the man with large shoulders opened the lid, reached inside, then closed the lid gently with both hands. No noise, no package visible, like the man was reaching in to touch the garbage, to see if there was garbage. Crazy.

Tonight, the third night, Stan had prepared for the vehicle's arrival. He'd switched off the television at twelve-thirty and turned his lounge chair toward the window. As he sat there he thought about kidnappers picking up a ransom. But if that were the case, the man would have snatched up the ransom package and jumped back into the vehicle. And if the man had been putting something into the dumpster, what would it be? Garbage. A guy from the apartment complex who works nights, rides in to work with another guy because they both drive gas guzzlers and want to save money. A disc jockey and engineer doing the before-dawn shift at a radio station.

"Hey, man. You gonna stink up my vehicle with garbage again?"

"Only 'til we get to the dumpster. I'm too lazy to walk it over."

Stan rose from his chair and walked to the window. Should be in bed instead of spying on guys who'd laugh like hell if they knew a crazy bastard was watching them. But he needed to see if the vehicle returned tonight. A large vehicle tricked out with oversized wheels and maybe some other gadgets. A vehicle for someone with money to burn, or a vehicle for official business. He stared at the rows of cars and sport utes and pickups in the lot. But all of these seemed too small. He leaned close to the window looking at the vehicles parked at the far end of the lot. One vehicle parked beneath a yellowish overhead light in the distance looked like a big sport ute, but the distortion of the window glass and the distance made it impossible to tell. He waited.

Then, although the back entrance to the complex was not visible, Stan could tell that a vehicle had driven in because of the dip of headlights. Instead of a black sport ute, a large black car appeared from behind the last apartment building and turned toward him. High beams on. He backed away from the window out of the glare and watched the car approach. Once inside the complex it did not stop until it reached the garbage dumpsters. The car had come from the road, had turned into the complex for one purpose—to park at the garbage dumpsters across the lot, not more than fifty yards from his second floor window. On previous nights it had been a sport ute, tonight it appeared to be a limo.

Stan hadn't realized he was backing up until his chair bumped against his calves. He stooped down, heard his knees crack, and watched for movement inside the limo. He knelt on the floor balancing himself, his hands on the windowsill. He thought about gangsters, hit men sizing up a hit. Or maybe terrorists hiding out in apartments nearby, preparing for an attack. He was about to reach for the phone on the end table when an orange glow appeared in his peripheral vision.

The big sport ute that had been parked at the far end of the lot beneath the overhead light had moved out and was coming this way, only its parking lights lit. Maybe the police were already watching. Maybe someone else had seen the limo and now there would be a sport-ute-limo confrontation. The sport ute with oversized wheels had a spotlight mounted on the driver's door. He waited.

The sport ute's parking lights lit up the bumper of the limo ahead. A foot apart, limo and sport ute stood motionless. Limo with headlights on, sport ute with an unlit spotlight.

A man got out on the far side of the sport ute and walked quickly to the limo. Big shoulders, small head, just like the man from the previous night. Still no courtesy light inside the sport ute, and now no courtesy light visible inside the limo as the man opened the rear limo door and a tall thin man got out and stood next to the big-shouldered man. The tall man raised his hand. Not like a stickup, not like a wave. Like the Pope giving a blessing. Then the big-shouldered man opened the dumpster and the thin man lifted something in. At first the package had been hidden by the limo. But as the man lifted it in, Stan saw the shopping-bag size of it for an instant before the lid was closed.

The tall man got back into the limo, and after the other man closed the door he returned to the sport ute. Then the two vehicles drove slowly out of the lot, and when they turned onto Elmwood Drive sped through the curve in one swift movement like a snake. Just before they disappeared between the darkened gas stations, the headlights of the sport ute came on.

Stan's footsteps in the first floor vestibule echoed through the stairwell as he walked past the building's mailboxes. He checked his left coat pocket for his keys and kept his right hand in his right coat pocket, gripping his .45 automatic, still warm and moist from having been held as he descended the stairs.

It was two in the morning, nearly an hour since the vehicles had gone. Stan had sat in his lounge chair for a long time deciding what to do. At one point he'd held the phone in his lap, lifted the receiver and listened to the dial tone until it changed to the recorded message saying he should hang up and dial again. He'd hung up the phone. He'd not called the police because of the conversation constructed in his mind.

"I'd like to report a strange occurrence."

"Is this an emergency?"

"Well, no. You see, these two vehicles parked over by my garbage dumpsters for a while and two men got out and threw something in. The strange part is that this is the third night in a row that I've seen one of the vehicles."

"Two vehicles, huh?"

Eventually, after making him feel like an ass, the police would come out to look in the dumpster. Then they would question him. Whether they found something or not they would question him.

"You always stare out your front window at one in the morning?"

"I was watching television."

"Out the window?"

"No, but I do glance out occasionally. Is there a law against that?"

"Does anyone live here with you?"

"No."

"Where are you employed?"

"I'm retired." He'd want the facts straight, he's not that old. "Early retirement."

"Your name is familiar. Aren't you the guy? . . . A long time ago . . ."

Stan did not want to be questioned unless there was a reason. He did not call the police. But there was still something in the dumpster, something about the size of a shopping bag.

Though Stan could hear the drone of night bugs from the swamp across the road, the parking lot seemed quiet compared to the vestibule. Inside there had been his echoing footsteps. Out here his footsteps died in the night air, no echo, nothing but the bugs across the road. As he approached the dumpster he knew he would run back inside if he heard a car. If a car simply passed by on the road, he would run. He considered turning around, but if he did he knew he would be up all night wondering what was in the dumpster.

Stan had reasoned it out back in his apartment, had selected a single answer from all the possibilities. It had to be something valuable. Perhaps money or drugs or a gun. If it was drugs he would simply put it back. But if it was a gun, or guns, he did know something about that. Of course the possibility of it being money was the strongest draw. Even if it was counterfeit or marked he might be able to get rid of it a little at a time in surrounding towns. Although, once he did find out what was in the package, he could then call the police. The main thing was to be certain it was something worth calling the police for. Because if he called the police on a false lead there would be questions to answer, questions that had a tendency to unearth the past.

Stan had memorized the position of the package when he saw it lifted in, front right corner of the right dumpster. He approached the dumpster enclosure quietly, recalling how sometimes it wasn't so tidy around the enclosure like it was now. Like when someone was moving out of the complex and they'd pile all kinds of junk out here rather than moving it. That's when the scavengers came out of the woodwork. Sometimes a scavenger would arrive late at night and load junk into the back of a pickup older than his old pickup. But there was no overflow of junk tonight, no one had moved out and left their crap behind.

The enclosure was made of wood, just tall enough to hide the dumpsters from three sides. Unfortunately the open side faced Stan's apartment building. Made for a great view. People hauling garbage, kids trampling the grass, and then at night . . . at night there was the occasional scavenger, and now this. As Stan stood before the dumpster he listened for rustling inside. Although he'd never seen rats, he once saw a raccoon jump in after someone had propped a lid open. He looked around, saw a light on in an apartment, but it was some distance away.

The lid of the dumpster was cool and wet. Although the lid was spring-loaded, Stan had to use both hands to lift it. Once the lid was up he was able to hold it with one hand while he reached inside and felt around with the other hand. There was only one bag down deep inside in the far right corner, its plastic feeling oily. He lifted the bag out, placed it on the ground while he closed the lid gently, then picked up the bag and walked quickly back to his building.

The bag bumped his thigh and shots of chills assaulted him from behind. If someone confronted him, would he pull out the .45 he hadn't fired in years? After finding the key to his gun cabinet and taking out the .45, it had taken him several minutes to figure out how to load the damn thing. Safe in his apartment he placed the .45 on the kitchen counter, the barrel aiming at the wall.

Stan stood looking at the black plastic garbage bag on his kitchen table. The overhead light glistened on it. It weighed about as much as a quart of milk. When he shook the bag he felt and heard another bag inside, a paper bag rustling. The bag was not full, not stuffed like a garbage bag should be. He recalled neighbors taking plastic bags with them to pick up after their dogs when they walked them. He thought about mobsters getting rid of a victim piece by piece. But he knew if he didn't look inside, the mystery would drive him crazy.

Had to be a pile of cash. Like winning the lottery. His retirement checks wouldn't support him much longer, and his meager Social Security wouldn't kick in for quite a few years. He'd have to move to a cheaper place, sell his guns, find another part-time job like the one he just lost at the grocery store. Or maybe if he reported his find, there'd be a reward. But with that would come the news coverage. Accepting a plaque from the mayor, having to answer questions about his find, having to answer questions about his past.

When Stan finally began untwisting the wire tape, he tried counter-clockwise but it only got tighter. Because his hands were shaking, the wire jabbed beneath the cuticle of his thumb. He sucked the blood from his thumb, wiped his sweaty palms on his slacks and tried again. Several turns in the clockwise direction finally got the tape off. Keeping his face at a distance, as if a raccoon or a cat or a rat might jump out at him, he opened the bag. Then he moved in closer and peered inside.

The paper bag inside was dark brown, stiff like the reddish-brown paper in the meat department at the grocery store. Stan recalled photos of fetuses he'd seen on an anti-abortion Web site. He thought of how his son's body had deteriorated in a shallow grave so long ago. He hadn't seen the remains. The police lab had verified the identification through dental records. He recalled his wife's face, the way she looked when he found her dead in the bathroom a year after they found Timmy. His wife's eyes open when he found her, her head facing the door, her head twisted against the bathtub by the force of her weight, her cheek smashed against the tile forcing her mouth wide open as though she had screamed before her death. As though she had screamed out his name and he had not been there to hear it when she fell . . .

No. The package on his kitchen table was too small to be a body. Even if it was part of a body, the only two people who meant anything to him were gone. There was nobody left who meant anything to him. If it was something grotesque, he could take it, had to take it because now his curiosity was overpowering.

With the paper bag still inside the plastic bag, Stan unfolded it and slowly separated layers of thick paper. At first he saw only a general gray shape, could have been anything. Then he opened the bag quickly to get it over with.

Eyes staring, gray, cloudy. Distorted mouth. Bloodless cheeks and nose. Blond hair matted down, glistening wet beneath the overhead light. Slice in the neck, color of boiled meat, folded back touching the chin.

Stan dropped to his hands and knees on the kitchen floor. Then he jumped up and ran to the bathroom where he knelt at the bathtub and bent his head under cold running water. Breathing, breathing until he choked, gagged, and vomited into the tub trying to erase what he had just seen.

CHAPTER 2

THE PRESIDENT'S NEMESIS

STANLEY JOHNSON LIVED alone, had lived alone since his son then his wife died. His wife had a sister in Arizona but he hadn't heard from her in years. Better that way. Less to remind him that his only son had been murdered and his wife, in her grief, had killed herself a year later with liquid drain cleaner.

Dr. Todd, sitting crossed-legged on the sofa visit after visit, tried to convince Stan it wasn't his fault. Stan had let Dr. Todd think he was cured, had made Dr. Todd believe he felt no guilt. He had fooled Dr. Todd. What a joker.

After his wife's suicide, Stan married himself to his job at the Joliet National Research Lab. He had practical experience that gave him an edge over engineers fresh out of college. But less than two years ago there were drastic cuts at the lab and he was given a choice. He could either take early retirement, or get laid off. So he retired.

Stan had sold the house after his wife's death and moved into a second floor flat in town. Then later, to save commuting time, he'd moved into the apartment complex where he still lived, where he had lived nearly fifteen years. The lab's main entrance was less than two miles north on Elmwood Drive. The limo and the big sport ute had sped south on Elmwood after dropping off their package.

The black plastic bag was back in the garbage in the same position he had found it. He had folded the inside bag without looking, careful not to bump against the head with his hands, even through the paper. He sealed the plastic bag as it had been and wiped the top of the bag with a washcloth where he had touched it. He took some of his own garbage and, wearing gloves, lifted the two bags together so he would not have to feel the weight of the head. He left his .45 automatic behind because he was more concerned with getting the head back into the dumpster than being attacked. He walked when he thought someone might be watching. He ran when he thought he heard a car.

Now he was in bed still wondering if he should have called the police. He still could. Tell them he could not bear to keep the package in the house. Tell them the truth. He was no longer afraid of what the police would say. He was an innocent bystander. Yeah, one of those innocent bystanders you see on television, either made to look like a fool, or hounded into saying things you maybe didn't want to say, especially when the men in the vehicles might be watching.

For some reason, he knew that if he reported anything to the police, the men would know it. They would find him and kill him. Maybe they were terrorists or gangsters. They'd seen him in the window those other nights, or tonight when the headlights blinded him as the limo turned toward his apartment. Although there were times in the past when he'd thought it might be good to die, to leave the memories behind and find out if there was anything better after this life, he felt differently now. Perhaps it all came down to survival. A living, breathing lump of flesh, food in one end, crap out the other end. A living, breathing thing that, when confronted with the possibility of death, does not want it.

But it wasn't only the fear of death that kept him from calling the police. There was the fact that it was too late to help the dead child. There was the fact that reporting his find might cause great anguish. He'd had plenty of experience with police investigations when his son disappeared. Better for the parents to have hope than to know.

Timmy would have been in his twenties now. Weekend visits to the old house. Grandchildren. But none of that was possible because of a perverted bastard who was never caught. Timmy had been missing nearly four months before they found his body. During that time Stan always had hope. Having hope was a job to be done. Someone had to do it. He tried to give his wife hope. He tried to convince her to see beauty in nature, to visualize Timmy there, in nature, among the creatures and plants. Trying to give his wife hope had taken on a religious zealotry. It was a difficult job, made even more difficult by disasters and war and terror in the world. Events that magnified the loss. But finally he did succeed at giving his wife hope, and in the end it was the hope that had killed her.

Too much thinking. Too much looking out the damn window. None of this would have happened if he had a job. And if he didn't get his ass in gear and get a job soon he'd have to move to a cheaper apartment, sell his guns. Yeah, guns. Lot of good they'd done him over the years. Taking the .45 out with him to the dumpsters like he's some kind of vigilante.

He'd bought the guns when he worked at the Lab. A lab guard named Sedgwick sold him six guns. The last one he shot was the .45, and that had been over ten years earlier when Sedgwick talked him into joining a group of survivalists at an outing in Northern Wisconsin. Paranoid creeps shooting the bark off trees and drinking gallons of beer. At the time, Dr. Todd had seemed quite interested in the group.

"Did joining the group have anything to do with your son's death?"

"I don't know. Maybe."

"Did you feel you could find the murderer?"

"I just thought if I was prepared and if I ever did come across him . . ."

"Just in case, then?"

"I guess so. Maybe I simply wanted to blow off steam. Or maybe your bills are getting too high."

"I like your sense of humor, Stan."

"Yeah, they say when I was a kid I was a riot."

Mostly, Dr. Todd wanted him to talk about his childhood. Poor little Stanley Johnson. Dad gets squashed between boxcars in the yards, Mom dies of pneumonia with Dad's Purple Heart around her neck. A stint in the orphanage until Aunt Lillian and Uncle Jack take him in. A "sore thumb" because they already have two kids. But Uncle Jack gets him a job hauling boxes of parts to women building televisions at the Zenith plant—women who call him "Little Stanley" or "Stan the Man"—and thus begins his illustrious career in electronics.

Home was a loft over the front porch of his Aunt and Uncle's bungalow, a loft accessible through the dark attic, hot in summer, freezing in winter. At night the bed his only comfort. Dr. Todd had made him talk about his childhood, his bed that he bought with his own money.

When he was a child he always felt safe in his bed. When he was a child his bed was a raft floating on shark-infested seas. Or sometimes he imagined his bulletproof bed floating in midair, men with automatic weapons shooting at him from below. Whenever he went to bed as a kid he always leaped in as if the bed were a bridge between his real and imaginary worlds. Once, when he sneaked his junior high girlfriend Tammy up to the room, the bed

13

really did float. It was his first time, but not hers. At least that's what she said. Even now, in his mid-fifties, he still felt a tingling sensation in his legs and groin when he climbed into bed. He never told his wife Marge about his old games, but she used to ask about the strange way he got into bed.

"Stan, how come you always jump into bed like that?"

"Because, my sweet, I'm anxious to be near you," he always said.

The bed was protection. If he had been in bed early the last couple of nights, and tonight, he would never have seen the limo and the sport ute, never have separated the dark brown paper and seen those gray eyes full of fear, that flesh the color of almost-cooked meat.

He pictured the limo and sport ute again, followed the action step by step from the time they parked at the dumpsters and the two men got out. Two men, the one from the limo tall and thin putting the bag into the dumpster, the other a big-shouldered guy going back to his sport ute after slamming the limo door. Faceless men, the color of their skin obliterated by darkness. Was it his imagination or did the big-shouldered guy pause before he got back into the sport ute? Did the guy pause at the open door for an instant and look up?

Stan got out of bed and went into the kitchen in the dark. He could feel bits of something clinging to his bare feet as he walked across the cold kitchen floor. He looked toward the door to his apartment, saw only darkness. Was the door open? He froze for a moment, staring at a dim pin of light at eye level. A single eye in the hallway staring at him.

No, idiot! The peephole! It was only the hall light shining through the fisheye lens of the peephole. He went to the door quickly, stubbed his toe on one of the kitchen chair legs, groaned, stood in the dark massaging his toe with one hand while he held onto the secured door chain with the other hand. Yes, the chain lock was in place.

He groped his way slowly to the cupboard, felt his way along the edge of the counter past the sink. Outside the window above the sink he could barely see lights in the distance flickering through the trees. He opened the cupboard, took out his bottle of cheap scotch and had a swig.

After he put the scotch away he paused in the hallway and stared at the living room window for a moment. Had the man paused to look at one particular spot, at a window, perhaps his? Was that the reason he had not called the police? Because he knew they'd seen him?

He felt his way down the hallway, dragging his feet to clear whatever debris the bottoms of his feet had accumulated in the kitchen. He approached the bed carefully so as not to stub his toe again, this time on a bed frame leg. He leapt into bed quickly so the sharks would not bite him and the men below would not shoot him as he crossed over from that world to this.

He centered himself in the bed, arms at his sides, feet together, knees pulled up. He laughed aloud at his childishness, then stopped laughing when he heard the raspy sound of his own voice.

Not funny. Not funny at all.

CHAPTER 3

THE PRESIDENT'S NEMESIS

STANLEY JOHNSON

NOBODY SEEMED TO know how the Three-Peat Club in downtown L.A. had gotten its name. Patrons speculated, figuring it was because of the Lakers' three playoff championships under Phil Jackson. But the club had been around a while and obviously had been named long before that. Perhaps the name was coined to give the Lakers something to shoot for. Maybe the owner of Three-Peat was from out of town and brought the name from Chicago where the Chicago Bulls three-peated back in the 1990s. When asked, the bartenders at the club claimed ignorance about the details.

It was one a.m. in L.A. A weekday night, which meant there was a pretty good crowd at the club. Because of its downtown location, weeknights were busier than weekends, the place humming with after-hours business. Like that up-and-coming exec over there with the high-class chick. Or that up-and-coming chick on the other side of the room with the high-class stud. Of course nobody called patrons at Three-Peat chicks or studs, especially not the bartenders.

Sheila, the redheaded bartender, was breaking in a younger bartender named Emilio tonight. Between rounds Sheila filled Emilio in on the comings and goings of the clientele. This included distinguishing daytime business professionals from nighttime business professionals. Knowing who was who would help Emilio maintain decorum in the club.

As Emilio topped off a bloody Mary under Sheila's watchful eye, he stole glances at a middle-aged man who had left a table and walked across the room to use a pay phone in the vestibule that led to the kitchen.

"With these customers in here being such high rollers," said Emilio, "I'm surprised to see one use the same pay phone the busboy uses."

"Perhaps Mr. Serrantino doesn't want to take a chance being overheard on his cellular," said Sheila.

"High rollers use phones with scramblers," said Emilio.

"Perhaps Mr. Serrantino is simply old fashioned," said Sheila.

After delivering the bloody Mary to the hostess kiosk at the end of the bar, Emilio returned to Sheila's side where they stood together polishing tumblers that had just come out of the washer.

"I'm impressed," said Emilio.

"By what?" asked Sheila.

"You knowing the guy's name. You know the names of all the patrons?"

Sheila smiled, nodded toward Mr. Serrantino as he left the kitchen vestibule and headed back to his table. "Not all their names. Just the important ones."

At the far end of the bar, the television that had been mute until now came to life. The TLC logo for "The Learning Channel" was in the lower right-hand corner and on the screen the Zapruder film was being shown. As had happened billions of times on countless screens since his death, John F. Kennedy's brains were again blown out onto the trunk of the limo. The hostess who had turned on the television motioned with the remote toward a table where two young couples watched attentively. The program, a special on the assassination, was just beginning and obviously the two couples had requested it be turned on.

"They say everyone remembers where they were when it happened," said Emilio. "Do you remember where you were?"

"Sure," said Sheila. "I was in first grade at St. Ann School. Sister Bernice started crying when an announcement came over the intercom and pretty soon we were all crying. I'm not sure if we cried because we knew what was going on or because we'd never seen bad old Sister Bernice shed a tear. Now, don't tell me you're old enough to remember where you were."

"Of course I do," said Emilio. "I was a stray cat on the streets of Mexico City. Mind you, that was in my previous life."

"Did all the stray cats cry?" asked Sheila.

"We howled," said Emilio, as he leaned to one side to get a better look at the blond woman sitting at Mr. Serrantino's table.

When the woman with blond hair sitting at Mr. Serrantino's table turned back from having glanced at the Zapruder film on the television, she said, "Do you recall what you were doing, Jake?"

Serrantino thought for a moment before answering, glancing toward the ceiling as if seeking heavenly assistance with the recollection. Then he said, "I was in junior high school."

When Serrantino did not continue, the woman said, "Tell me about it, Jake. Like, where did you go to junior high and how did they announce the assassination and all that. You tell me what you remember and I'll tell you what I remember."

Jake smiled. "Lena, you weren't born yet."

Lena smiled. "Like I said, you tell me what you were doing on that day and I'll tell you what I was doing."

"All right," said Jake, becoming serious. "We were in history class and Mr. Pajak was called into the hall. When he came back he said we should go to the auditorium for a special announcement. At the time I was having a childish spat with another boy, and circumstances being what they were, I sat off by myself. It was a large auditorium, you understand, much larger than was needed for the student body. We had to wait a long time for the principal to get his act together and get up to the lectern. By the time he finally did, I was beside myself because by sitting off by myself I was able to see everyone in school glancing back at me while stories about me spread through the auditorium.

"So that's how it was, Lena. I remember the day Kennedy was assassinated as the day I was humiliated in front of the entire student body. In fact, when the principal finally made his announcement, I recall being relieved and even somewhat delighted. A strange reaction. But that's how it was. Finally, the attention had been taken from me, sitting alone at the back of the auditorium."

"That's quite a story," said Lena, obviously moved.

"Thank you," said Jake. "Now you tell me your story. The true story. Were you a glint in your father's eye, or were you already in your mother's womb?"

Lena smiled. "No, I wasn't in my mother's womb. In fact I'd been popped out three years earlier. I can see the gears turning over in your head. Yes, that's right. I'm not twenty-nine or even thirty-nine like you'd thought."

"Your age doesn't bother me, Lena. Let's have the story."

Lena became serious. "We lived on a farm in Kansas. I remember being in the living room of the farmhouse standing on the sofa looking out the window. The reason I was looking out the window was because I'd heard the John Deere tractor outside. I knew something was up because it was parked on the lawn. When the front door opened I could hear the radio on the tractor. I was too young to interpret what was being said but I could tell by the voice of the man on the radio that something had happened."

Lena paused to take a drink, then continued. "He didn't come to me. He walked through the living room to the kitchen. We had a swinging door to the kitchen and he closed it behind him. He left me out there listening to the man on the radio. When he finally came out he went back out the front door like I wasn't even there. My mother came out of the kitchen, picked me up and held me and cried as we watched the John Deere drive back into the fields. I cried, too, but I wasn't sure why."

After waiting to see if she was finished, Jake reached out and put his hand on Lena's hand. "I notice you didn't call him by name."

"Who?" asked Lena.

"The man from the tractor. I noticed you had a name for the tractor but not for the man. Was he your father?"

Lena looked down at Jake's hand on hers. "Yes, my father."

"Is it significant that you didn't call him your father in the story?"

"Perhaps."

On television there was a pause for commercials and a campaign ad came on. At first it was difficult to tell who the ad was for because of the shared male and female voice-overs being used. The man talking passionately about family concerns and human rights and the environment, the woman talking equally passionately about economics and national security and world order. The voice-overs were played against a backdrop of wolves moving in slow motion in a snowy wilderness. The wolves brought to mind another ad in which the wolves became a threat and lunged toward the camera. However, in this ad the wolves busied themselves with bringing the result of their hunt to a den in which wolf cubs began feeding. Eventually it became clear that the ad was a counter ad designed to overturn stereotypes. After the shot of the wolf cubs feeding, a full headshot of the candidate appeared. As Rose Adams Haney, the New York Democratic senator challenging Texan incumbent Andrew Montgomery, went on about eliminating stereotypes, Jake Serrantino turned toward the television with a look of annoyance on his face.

Sheila walked quickly to the other end of the bar, picked up the remote and muted the television. When she came back she stared at Emilio who stared back at her, apparently waiting for yet another pointer about the clientele at Three-Peat this night.

Sheila glanced out at a table against the wall. "See the gentleman in the green shirt eyeing Mr. Serrantino's lady?"

"You bet I do," said Emilio. "Who wouldn't be eyeing her?"

"He's not a regular," said Sheila. "If he goes over to their table, you'll need to steer him away."

"Is that part of the job?"

"Yes, it is."

"Why?"

"Because Mr. Serrantino owns this place."

"The club?"

"Not just the club, the building."

"All forty floors?"

"All forty floors."

CHAPTER 4

THE PRESIDENT'S NEMESIS

BUD'S IGA WAS on the north side of town. A pretty busy place until the meat scare the previous spring. The papers said it was rodent hair. Bud said, "Sorry I can't afford to keep you, Stan." But Stan still hoped he could get his job back.

Evie Schneider worked behind the customer service counter. Evie was tall and thin, blue eyes and short boyish hair. Although she'd seen Stan, Evie had to take care of a few customers who'd been in line. Evie wore a short sleeve white blouse, probably a straight skirt, but he couldn't see it because of the counter.

He and Evie had dated while he was working at the store. She'd been divorced a few years. Her husband waiting until the last daughter married before he walked out. The ex lived in the city, an ad agency exec. Evie had pointed out some of the products the agency handled. Stan watched for the commercials for the agency's products on television and noticed all the ads had seductive women in them.

When Stan dated Evie they talked about their lives, their families. He wondered to what extent Evie felt sorry for him because of his wife and son. He wondered if that was why she agreed to spend the night with him. He recalled Evie saying, at one point during their lovemaking, that he was such a funny guy.

He told Dr. Todd about Evie.

"Does she makes you happy?"

"Let's not get carried away."

"Sexually satisfied?"

"I think so."

"Don't feel as though you're using her, Stan. She's a big girl."

"Hey, wait a minute. Have you been looking at my girl's tits?"

Dr. Todd laughed. At least he was good at that, making his shrink laugh.

After losing his job at Bud's, Stan stopped going to Dr. Todd because retirement health insurance paid only a small part of the bill. And he stopped dating Evie. Not because he couldn't afford it. He just felt tired.

The line at the customer service counter was gone. Evie smiled, adjusted her hair.

"How are you today, Stan?"

"Pretty good."

"Any luck job hunting?"

"Not yet. Is Bud in?"

"Sorry, Stan. Bud hasn't said a thing about hiring anybody."

"So business is still bad."

"I'm afraid so. Especially with the new Wal-Mart across town."

A very old man elbowed in next to Stan at the counter and Stan stepped back. Maybe he looked at men younger than himself the same way, a kind of defiant stare.

As the old man placed a tattered lotto card on the counter along with his bills, Stan noticed the torn lining of the man's coat. Perhaps he, too, would be buying lotto tickets with his last dollars in ten or fifteen years. His last hope for fame and fortune in this old world before they carry him away in a body bag.

Nausea, dizziness, gray eyes. At least in terrorist attacks the bodies are blown to bits or burned up or something. But a head cut off and put in a bag and thrown into a dumpster . . .

Stan got a cart and went up the first aisle to do his shopping. He stopped at the magazine racks in aisle four. Nothing refrigerated in his cart yet, so he stood in aisle four flipping through magazines the way he had years earlier in simpler more innocent times whenever he went shopping with his wife.

News magazines pumped up about the upcoming election between incumbent President Andrew Montgomery and challenger Rose Adams Haney. Gossip about stately Montgomery, bedrock of neo-conservatism, versus lovely Haney, rambunctious New York Senator. How the two campaign managers used the sex issue to fight it out for media attention.

When Stan was young and strong and full of spunk back in 1968, he was arrested in Grant Park during the Democratic Convention. The shit of it was he hadn't even been there demonstrating. He'd been working at a Eugene McCarthy office in the suburbs and when he came out of the office that night, thugs beat the crap out of him, drove him downtown and dumped him in the park. He should have realized then that his life and political life were a bad mix.

He gets his ass hauled down to Grant Park the night the whole world is watching. His and Marge's first date is the night Nixon is elected to his second term. He should have known better than to have anything to do with politics. But no, like a fool he continued being a loyal Democrat, even worked for Carter during his successful campaign. The last time he'd been in a polling place was the day Timmy disappeared. He'd voted in the morning and been called home from work because Marge could not find Timmy. Later that night, while news of Reagan's humiliating defeat of Carter amid the release of American hostages in Iran filled the airwaves, he and Marge waited in vain for word that Timmy had been found. Four months later, the day Reagan was shot, they found Timmy's body. As they say, and as he said many times during the weeks and months following Timmy's disappearance, "Screw Politics!" That was another part of the shit of it. Him. The way he reacted to Timmy's disappearance. Too much damn hope is what he portrayed. And now? Now he'd take to his grave the guilt of having driven Marge to suicide.

Car and truck magazines with dream machines Stan could not afford. Sport utility magazines with intimidating machines he did not want to think about. Motorcycle magazines with sinister looking machines. Young women in leather shorts and vests straddling throbbing phallic symbols. Wrestling magazines. The current crew slicker looking than the old Hooded-Demon and Gorgeous-George types from his youth.

Gun magazines. Ah, yes, gun magazines. Stan wasn't really interested in guns, but he still had the collection Sedgwick had sold him. A shotgun, a .30/06 with scope, a single shot .22 rifle, a .38 pistol, a .22 pistol, and his trusty .45 automatic that was home in his dresser drawer instead of locked in the gun cabinet where it belonged. A loaded gun hidden beneath his underwear. Stan the gunslinger. What a laugh Sedgwick would have had if he'd seen him running back from the garbage dumpsters like a frightened little boy.

Stan recalled Sedgwick's eyes narrowing in a display of genuine seriousness when he talked about how a man has to protect his family. But it wasn't Sedgwick who talked him into buying the guns. It was the remote possibility that some day he might have vengeance for the deaths of his wife and son.

Stan bought the gun cabinet from Sedgwick, too. He fired the guns in Sedgwick's barnyard. Sedgwick watched him fire each gun, told him how good he looked with the guns as if he were trying on suits at J.C. Penney. Stan joked that he should shoot at the broad side of Sedgwick's barn to see if he could hit it, but Sedgwick would have none of it. Sedgwick was that serious.

"Aim higher, Stan. That's it. Here, let me adjust the scope."

A couple weeks after Stan purchased the guns, Sedgwick invited him to the weekend outing with the survivalists. The survivalists wore camouflage clothing, some blackened their faces. Codes on the backs of traffic signs for the U.N. invasion troops and all that. With nothing else to do, Stan shot at mounted targets all day long, his shoulder aching from the kick of the .30/06, his wrist aching from the kick of the .45. Then, after too much beer, he was sick all night and on the ride home the next day.

Since the survivalist outing with Sedgwick, the closest Stan had come to firing any of the guns was when he loaded the .45 last night. He decided to unload the .45 as soon as he got home and lock it back in the cabinet.

At Bud's IGA the gun magazines were on a middle rack where any kid could get at them. According to Bud, who insisted he was born-again like the President, the higher racks were reserved for more dangerous magazines, the ones with sex in them.

Stan recalled Evie once saying that in the old days, long before he worked at Bud's, the top rack had been reserved for detective and murder mystery magazines with their lurid covers. But times had changed.

Evie collected old mystery magazines. Stan recalled how excited Evie was when she found several boxes of ratty old magazines at a garage sale. *True Detective, Real Detective, Murder Incorporated, Police Gazette, Police Facts, Crime Journal, Police Dragnet, Sensational Crime Stories.*

Stan left aisle four and finished his shopping. Ground beef—without rodent hair he hoped—cheese, milk, bread. Enough cholesterol to make sure he died of natural causes some day. He pushed the cart back to the customer service counter. Evie watched his approach, no old men buying lottery tickets, no baby-lugging women cashing checks.

"Finished shopping, Stan?"

"Yes. You didn't by any chance see Bud?"

"Oh, nuts, you wanted to see him. I'm sorry, but you missed him because he just left for lunch."

"Jesus Christ," he muttered before he could stop himself.

Evie took a step back from the counter, whispered harshly, "Jesus Christ yourself!" Then, less harshly, "Stan, you've gone from a funny guy to a mean guy in an awful hurry. Pretty soon you'll have bad boy stickers on your pickup."

Evie tried to smile, but it didn't seem like a smile to Stan. All he could think about was having to go home to his damn apartment and the fact that he'd really wanted to see if Bud might hire him back. Evie stared at him, her attempt at a smile failing miserably because of him.

A fat woman stepped up to the counter with checkbook open. The woman eyed Evie then Stan and he walked away before he had to acknowledge the woman's stare. He checked out without looking at the customer service counter. When he passed the counter on his way out the door, Evie was gone.

In the parking lot he accidentally bumped the shopping cart into the car next to his old Toyota pickup. The car had parked too close, right on the white line. On the way to his pickup he'd noticed that the car was emblazoned with American flag and yellow ribbon decals, as well as a bumper sticker that said, "God Bless Andrew Montgomery." It was an older Buick

LeSabre, probably belonged to the old man in the tattered coat buying lotto tickets after cashing his meager Social Security check. Stan threw his bags onto the front seat of his pickup, shoved the cart against the parking blocks, got into his pickup, and drove recklessly home, which was not all that dangerous because the pickup misfired most of the way.

"It's good to keep busy," Dr. Todd had always said. "As long as the activity is aimed toward your goals."

"I don't know what my goals are."

"Sometimes we tend to be blinded by pie in the sky instead of taking advantage of the day-to-day goals of life. A well-cooked meal, a satisfying book, a pleasant conversation, the shine on the hood of the car or the kitchen floor . . . these are the goals life is made of."

"I'll click my heels next time I wax the floor."

After the groceries were put away, Stan swept the kitchen floor, washed it and waxed it. Now he sat in his chair near the living room window, flipping through the newspaper he'd picked up at Bud's. Nothing about a missing child. No stories of volunteers marching abreast through local fields covering every square inch. That's what the newspapers had said about the search for his son.

Last night he wasn't sure whether the head was that of a girl or boy. Now he wasn't sure if it had been a head at all. Nothing but a bag of tricks. If he'd dumped it out onto his kitchen table would he have found other tricks inside?

He flung the newspaper across the room so that pages opened and fluttered like giant dying butterflies. He cursed himself for not having called the police. He was not certain whether he might still call the police, tell them the truth about his fear of the men in the limo and sport ute. But what good would it do the parents of the missing kid? He and Marge would have been better off if they'd never found Timmy. Damn it, Timmy! Why'd you have to be found?

Calm down, calm down. Garbage pickup tomorrow morning. Once the head is gone from the dumpster everything will be fine. Unless there's a sudden rash of child killings. That would change everything. Just like not finding Timmy's body might have changed everything.

Marge had been a sensitive soul, crying at movies and weddings, crying even on their wedding night as they sat in bed, he in his crisp pajamas, she in a black teddy. A sensitive soul, but she gave no warning that she'd commit suicide, that she'd drink a container of drain cleaner and await his return, her eyes open, lips glistening, overflowing with acid and bodily fluids.

During the week before her death Marge had seemed willing to start over. She made plans to repaint every room in the house, even Timmy's room. She read catalogs, folded down pages with colorful draperies and bedspreads. He felt as though they might start over, try to forget. Even though they were only in their early thirties, Stan knew they wouldn't have another child. It was unspoken. The same way their not going to church anymore was unspoken. He had never been religious, but before Timmy's death they went to church as a family. Marge so damn happy those Sunday mornings when they took turns holding Timmy during mass. When Marge died, her will—a new will—said no church service, no wake, no burial, cremation.

Timmy disappeared from the backyard the first Tuesday in November, 1980, the day Ronald Reagan slaughtered Jimmy Carter.

"Was he playing with other children?" asked Inspector Jacobson in his deep voice, his dark face always serious and seemingly emotionally uninvolved.

"No," said Marge, rubbing her hands together, trying to keep from crying.

"No, he was playing alone. He was pulling his blue tractor around the yard. I could hear the tractor. It made a clicking sound. When it stopped, I looked out the window after only a few seconds and he was gone."

Inspector Jacobson put his hand on Marge's shoulder when she cried and Stan put his hand on her other shoulder. Since her death he pictured Marge like that. Her crying, his shaking hand on one shoulder and Inspector Jacobson's calm dark hand on her other shoulder. Four months later, the day Reagan was shot, Inspector Jacobson stood next to Marge, his hand on her shoulder again, and told them that the body they found buried in a rural wooded area west of town had been positively identified as Timmy.

During the four-month wait, Dr. Steinberg, Stan's division director at the lab, gave him as much time off as he needed. Dr. Steinberg was the same man who, years later, told Stan there was no longer a job for him. When he was forced into early retirement he did not argue because he recalled how kind Dr. Steinberg had been when Timmy disappeared. Decades had come and gone and it still seemed like yesterday when he stood in Dr. Steinberg's office asking for time off to look for Timmy.

Dr. Steinberg looked at him with his dark eyes, eyes that carried so much expression because his full beard covered the rest of his face. Dr. Steinberg stepped around his desk and hugged him. Stan could feel the coarse beard on his neck. Before he left he saw tears in Dr. Steinberg's eyes. Dr. Steinberg understood pain. As an infant he'd been given to a cooperating German family minutes before his parents were taken away to Auschwitz.

Stan wondered why he should now think about Dr. Steinberg. Stanley Johnson wasn't a Jew. He wasn't anything. Vague mixtures of Slovak and Hungarian and French and British. Nobody knew who or what he was. Might as well be a damn head in a dumpster. Let someone else worry about it. He had nothing to do with it. And, like Dr. Steinberg, he had been burdened enough. Enough!

Stan went into the bedroom, sat on the edge of the bed facing the dresser. He opened the top dresser drawer and took out a large manila envelope. He dumped the envelope full of yellowed newspaper clippings onto the bed. He had collected the clippings after his son's disappearance. He had pinned his hopes on information gathered from newspaper clippings. He recalled telling Marge that perhaps the information could be pieced together in some way. Night after night he had searched for a pattern the police might have overlooked. Now he read only the headlines of several of the clippings spread before him.

"Johnson Boy Still Missing. Police Comb Joliet Woods for Missing Boy. Chicago Police Join Search. Parents of Missing Boy Still Hope. Have You Seen This Boy? Timmy Johnson, Age Five."

The yellowed and beady reproductions of Timmy in the papers did not do him justice. He had fair skin and light hair like Marge. He had her small nose. He would have been a handsome young man. Like any proud parent, Stan had imagined Timmy becoming President, becoming someone like Jimmy Carter. But when Carter disappeared from politics, Timmy disappeared from life.

Beneath the clippings describing Timmy's disappearance were clippings of other missing or murdered children. Stan had collected the clippings for several years in hopes he might help find the murderer. He wanted to believe the murderer had attacked other children, not just his son. Stan felt alone in his grief and in his hope. Marge had surrendered to despair and he had collected clippings.

Then, after Marge's suicide, a strange thing happened. Even though he'd never met other parents of missing children, collecting the clippings made him feel a kinship with them. It was before the Internet and Web sites and chat rooms on missing children. Collecting clippings was the only thing he had besides his lousy job and his gun collection. Perhaps he would have used one of his guns to kill the murderer if he'd found him. Not a her. A him. Vague images of a face he'd never seen but tried to construct.

Stan stopped collecting clippings after a visit from Inspector Jacobson. The Barrington Police had forwarded a letter to the Joliet Police. Stan had written the Barrington Police offering help in capturing the killer of a six-year-old girl. His letter insisted the murderer was the same man who had murdered his son. His letter said the man was short and fat and hung around alleys and playgrounds.

Inspector Jacobson wanted to know where Stan got the description. They went through the clippings together. He'd mistakenly clipped an article about a rapist in Chicago, a short fat man who lurked in alleyways around hospitals. Inspector Jacobson informed Stan that this man had been in jail during the murder of the six-year-old. Inspector Jacobson told Stan his letter had wasted their time. That's when Inspector Jacobson recommended that he see Dr. Todd.

"Why do you blame yourself for your wife's death?" asked Dr. Todd

"Because it follows."

"Follows what?"

"Marge killed herself after Timmy's death, and Timmy's death was my fault."

"Why?"

"Because I wasn't there when he disappeared. Because when Timmy was alive I knew that somewhere there was a little girl who would meet Timmy someday. Now she's out there alone and he's gone. Don't you see? It's my fault!"

At the time, Stan tried to explain to Dr. Todd that his having been involved in politics when he was younger had to do with Timmy's murder. Political events were omens. He made a chart showing all the so-called co-incidences. Timmy born the day Ford was shot at. Timmy kidnapped the day Reagan was elected. Timmy's body found the day Reagan was shot. But Dr. Todd did not understand. There were many things Dr. Todd, with all his degrees, did not understand.

Stan fell across the clippings of missing kids and wept, wishing for himself another life, another set of circumstances, another family. A family that would not have died in the middle of his life when he needed them most. Then he fell asleep.

CHAPTER 5

THE PRESIDENT'S NEMESIS

STANLEY JOHNSON

THE FIRST TIME Lena visited Jake Serrantino's "cottage" in San Clemente, he told her an elaborate story of how the sand for the enclosed Zen garden had been excavated at night from a local beach some years earlier without benefit of an excavation permit. The sand was particularly clean, Jake said, because the beach had been groomed quite often at the expense of Hollywood celebrities with homes in the area. Good enough to be considered virgin sand, Jake had joked several minutes earlier prior to their lovemaking. Lena stared at Jake's glistening body. Like her skin, Jake's leathery skin was coated with sweat. During their lovemaking the sun had moved high, turning the Zen Garden into a blast furnace.

Lena wondered if Jake was wealthy enough to beat skin cancer. Or wealthy enough to make a Zen garden out of smack. Enough white to keep her pleasantly, but carefully, high. Jake wanted her on methadone. Just as Jake did not have to fear overexposure from the sun because of his access to the best medicine money could buy, she'd no longer have to fear the horse inside her.

Lena was the only one who called him Jake. Walter called him Mr. Serrantino. The housekeepers here and at the penthouse called him Mr. Serrantino. The building manager and bartenders and health club workers called him Mr. Serrantino. Any time a phone rang, men, always men, asked if Mr. Serrantino was in.

This time of day, if the sand here were back on the beach where it belonged, they'd be able to feel a light breeze off the ocean. Moms on the beach with little kids, babies sitting in the sand, covering chubby legs with it. Moms clucking like hens in the noon sun. Business girls would also be on the beach, not business-business, her business when she was younger, before Jake came along. Back on the beach, before Jake and his buildings and condos and Zen garden, she could spot any hooker, even a Beverly Hills hooker, a mile away. Casual strut, beach-walking not john-hunting, but can't take that walk away. And pampering. Hookers always pamper themselves during the day. Plenty of suntan lotion, slow easy moves, ignoring everyone else, not wanting to strike up a conversation, no money in it, save it for later.

A jagged rock at the far end of the garden resembled a crooked rickety pier sticking out into the sea of sand. At the beach the pier would be crowded with old men fishing, one or two shirtless despite the risk of skin cancer. Jake was old enough to be one of those men. In his mid- to late-fifties, but he refused to say exactly. If Jake hadn't made the right connections he'd be a flabby brown-skinned fart fishing on the pier. But Jake had made connections. And now he *was* a connection, powerful enough to conduct business by computer and phone from the penthouse of the building he owned. Maybe he owned lots of buildings. Maybe he owned the city. Maybe he imported the stuff that kept her up, high, alive.

A few weeks ago Jake bought her a new notebook computer and she took a course at Cal State. She was on the legitimate side of the World Wide Web for a change. Unfortunately, you couldn't download white powder no matter how fast your connection.

Jake grunted and when she glanced over at him she could see the beginning of gray at his hairline, the undyed hair growing out of his scalp, threatening to display his age. Time for a visit to the hairdresser thirty floors below the penthouse. Hair not thick enough to hide the new gray, scalp tanned through thinning hair but not as tan as the rest of him. Keeping his California tan a regular ritual so that Jake's body would be golden on the satin sheets, golden except for his white little old man's butt and his red dick. For having an Italian name like Serrantino and an enclosed Zen garden at his San Clemente "cottage," she figured for sure his butt would have shown a little Mediterranean olive. But it was white as an Irishman's.

Jake grunted again.

"Getting pretty hot," she said.

Jake shaded his eyes with his forearm. "I fell asleep for a minute."

"Not good in this sun," she said.

"I get nightmares when I fall asleep in the sun. You were in this one."

"Me?"

"Yes. You were a little girl in a farmhouse, frightened to death of something I couldn't see. I was there, watching as you stood terrified on the sofa looking out the window, and I couldn't do a thing to help you."

Lena reached out and lay her arm across Jake's chest. "That's my life all right. Nobody could do a thing to help me until you came along."

"Funny thing about the dream is that I identified with you as a little girl. In all my life I don't think I ever identified with a woman, let alone a little girl. I think it had to do with our conversation last night."

"Recalling where we were and what we were doing when Kennedy was assassinated?"

"Yes. I also think it had to do with the fact that I had a bit too much to drink. I recall babbling on about boyhood days while Walter drove us down here last night. Just so I know, did I mention how I got my name?"

"Your last name?"

"No, my given name."

"Something about taking it from a guy who did you wrong in business. Taking the name of the enemy. I don't recall the details because I put down quite a few in the limo myself."

But there was more to it than that. Much more. Like sand in a Zen garden or on a beach. Always more where that came from.

"That reminds me, Jake."

"What?"

"You said last night that even though you don't go to church you consider yourself an evangelical Christian."

"Yes, and?"

"Isn't a Zen garden from Zen Buddhism?"

Jake turned and stared at her. "Trust me, Lena. Having a Zen garden doesn't conflict with Christianity."

In the back of the Benz on the drive from L.A. to San Clemente the night before, after telling her he was a Christian, Jake's conversation had quickly moved from boyhood enemies to adult enemies. From what Lena could tell, Jake had someone else named Jake killed because of what he knew. Jake didn't say what this other Jake knew, but he did say it had to do with his fathers. Two fathers. Strange, Jake said he had two fathers, but no mother. He mentioned a housekeeper who became a surrogate mother while he was a schoolboy. Something about classmates finding out the housekeeper was not his real mother and taunting him about the woman's sexual tastes. Eventually Jake's monologue meandered into power and politics, his accumulation of wealth in the blossoming computer industry, his close association with presidential administrations, especially the Reagan administration. But after his last drink and just before Walter pulled into the long drive to the "cottage," Jake returned to the junior high auditorium in which he was made fun of by classmates while Kennedy's assassination was announced. At one point, as he told about the incident in the auditorium the second time that night, Lena reached out to touch Jake's cheek and felt a tear.

Lena knew the Benz would be cold. She'd put on a sweatshirt and sweatpants. Jake wore a jacket. After they were settled in and Walter pulled the Benz out onto the highway, Jake pushed the button that opened the partition.

"Yes, Mr. Serrantino," said Walter.

"I've got to make a call at exactly twelve-thirty and I don't want to use a cellular. Take us toward the apartment but make sure you get to a phone at twelve-thirty."

"Yes sir. I'll stay off the freeway."

Lena did not speak as they drove back to L.A. She knew better than to speak to Jake when he was thinking about business. She knew better than to ask why not a cell phone. She had learned several weeks earlier that when Jake said he was going to make a call she should keep her mouth shut. Jake made lots of calls, some from pay phones, some from his study in the apartment. She once walked in on him when he was on the phone and he had simply covered the mouthpiece and pointed back toward the door as if she were a child. Afterward, Jake told her to always knock before entering his study. If he wasn't in the study she had no business there.

Well into her forties and sometimes Jake treated her like a child. But he had a right to treat her like a child. Part of the cure. And he'd come just in time. She'd been burning herself out, sometimes seven or eight "special" tricks a night, trying to support the habit Raphael started up again after she'd been off the stuff so many years. Goddamn Raphael slipping that stuff in her nose, under her skin. The stuff living in her like a cat, peaceful and purring sometimes, other times clawing her insides. Might as well grind up hundred-dollar bills and poke that juice into her arm, into her thigh, into her butt where it didn't show as much. She'd gotten off mainline, at least she'd done that. At least she'd done that, you goddamn big H!

She'd been fine supporting herself with odd jobs before Raphael came along. She'd even gone into cyberspace, her photos on Web sites dedicated to sexy women over forty. But then along came Raphael with his "special" tricks. Dudes willing to pay extra for "experience." And with these "special" tricks came the H to keep her going and there she was right back on the treadmill, just like when she was in her twenties and on the street.

Walter stopped at a gas station and they waited in the Benz while Jake went to the pay phone. Pay phones were hard to find, it seemed most of them had been ripped out. But Walter always seemed to be able to find one.

She stared ahead at Walter's thick neck imagining she could telepath a message into his thick skull. Not dumb. Just didn't talk much. Loyal as hell. Walter probably supporting an aged mother or something. All she'd ever been able to get out of Walter was that he had a black belt and had once been a wrestler. He said college, but he was more likely one of those W.W.F. guys. Could have had his blond hair long then, curled, crazy bastard grabbing the microphone and screaming his guts out. Now, with his hair short, wearing a suit, he looked like a Hollywood bit character.

She looked toward the rearview mirror. "Walter?"

"Yes, miss." Walter did not look into the mirror, but kept staring ahead at Jake who was using the pay phone mounted to the cinderblock on the outside wall of the gas station.

"Getting pretty hard to find pay phones these days."

"Miss?"

"Pay phones, they're going extinct."

"Oh, yes, miss."

"So, who's he calling all the time?"

"I wouldn't know, miss."

"A man in his position, he must be talking to important people. Is he part of Homeland Security or what?"

"I said I wouldn't know."

"How long have you been with him?"

"Four years."

"And in all that time you haven't figured out what business he's in?"

Walter turned slightly and stared at her in the mirror. "His business is none of our business."

"Why not? What's the big deal?"

"The big deal is that Mr. Serrantino doesn't like anyone prying into his affairs. When he wants you to know something he'll tell you."

Walter looked straight ahead again where Jake had turned toward them, holding the phone, not talking, listening, waiting.

Maybe if she found out what business Jake was in she could get in on it. Maybe then she'd feel secure. Maybe then she wouldn't wake mornings wondering if this was the day Jake would dump her back on Raphael and find himself a younger working girl to put on extended vacation.

H E ALMOST TUMBLES out of bed, grabs at the bed, handfuls of newspaper clippings. Phone ringing. Light from his window. He's fallen asleep again in the middle of the day, this time on top of newspaper clippings. He hurries dizzily down the hall to the phone in the living room.

"Hello."

A woman. "Mr. Stanley Johnson?"

"Yes."

"I have a collect call for you from Mr. Derek Washington in Los Angeles, California."

Derek Washington again, tried to call him collect several times before. "I don't know any Derek Washington. Are you sure he has the right Johnson?"

"Is this Stanley Johnson, forty-two Hickory, Apartment four, Joliet, Illinois?"

"Yes."

"That is the party Mr. Washington is calling. Will you accept the charges?"

"No, I can't accept the charges if I don't know him. And if someone

41

wants to call me, why can't he just use his free minutes, or whatever . . .?"

"I'm sorry, Mr. Washington, Mr. Johnson will not accept."

He listens for Derek Washington's voice but there is only a click.

While getting his mail in the vestibule Stan was careful not to look out the front door where the dumpster baked in the sun.

His mailbox was stuffed again, so full it popped open as soon as he twisted the dial to the last number in the combination. He pulled pieces of mail from the center to relieve the pressure, then carted the bundle up the stairs. The amount of junk mail in his box had increased steadily over the past few weeks. Some of it was from charities and political campaigners and gun groups and fringe organizations. But most of it was pornographic.

Early retirement was supposed to be a time for relaxation and travel, not spending the day going through junk mail. The government had saved a bundle retiring him early, and now they were wasting his time delivering this crap. When he was forced into retirement, he'd been pretty vocal, blaming representatives and senators and even the President. Probably sounded like an idiot, like the President had singled out poor Stanley Johnson for forced early retirement. Maybe that's why his mailbox was crammed with this junk. He'd been singled out. His name on idiot lists. He was probably the talk of the back room at the post office. Maybe he even had something to do with the fact that he'd seen so many different men and women delivering mail at the apartment complex.

Letter-size envelope, first class, addressed in free hand, no return address, New York City postmark. Inside, a three-page pre-printed letter that looked as if it had been photocopied and recopied thousands of times. "THIS IS

NOT A CHAIN LETTER!!" it said. So he knew it was. He had been getting chain letters almost every day. Some quoted the Bible. Some said "The End" was near. Most contained threats for those who dared break the chain. This letter began with its threat.

"A letter like this was found on the body of a derelict on skid row! John Kennedy, Bobby Kennedy, and Martin Luther King received this letter and failed to answer! Gerald Ford and Ronald Reagan both answered their letters, causing two assassination attempts on Ford to fail, and causing Reagan to recover from his wounds and go on to serve two full terms!"

Stan laughed out loud and threw the letter aside. Then he took a copy of a weekly weapons magazine from the pile and flipped through it. Deals on military surplus rifles, do-it-yourself gun models, knives, swords, machetes. Though he had not subscribed to it, he had been receiving the magazine for several weeks. He had written "Not Accepted" across the first issue and put it back in the mail, but the magazine still came, every week.

The next piece of mail said it was "sexual in nature." A sealed envelope inside the first envelope. Reading the warning message made him feel for a moment like an adolescent peeking through a bathroom keyhole. He remembered a joke one of the guys told at the lunch the lab gave for the early retirees.

A retiree staying with friends leaves his guest room late at night and sees a light coming from beneath the bathroom door and from the keyhole. His hostess, a young and beautiful woman, can be heard singing behind the door. There is the sound of bath water being drained and a shadow dancing beneath the door and at the keyhole as the woman sings a haunting melody. The retiree creeps to the door, stoops down, and puts his ear to the keyhole.

He recalled the laughter, the young guys laughing hardest. He looked at the envelope in his hand, at its warning about sexually explicit material. Instead of opening the envelope he thought of his shrink, Dr. Todd.

"Perhaps you should take risks, Stan. Go to a singles bar and see what happens. Times have changed. You don't have to be aggressive. If you meet someone, fine. If not, just head on home and switch on the tube."

"You make it sound easy."

"It is easy if you limit your expectations. Go for a drink, nothing more. Sit at a bar for a while instead of drinking alone."

"And this is supposed to make me forget about my wife and son?"

"Are you still worried about taking someone else's girlfriend?"

"What do you mean?"

"That Johnny Tate you told me about. I believe it was in junior high. You said you stole his girlfriend."

Dr. Todd got him to admit his childhood fear of Johnny Tate. He recalled the way Johnny approached him in the hall at school one day, looking away at first like nothing was wrong, then turning to him, telling him to expect a visit from someone. He couldn't remember the exact words but he knew he'd been scared, especially after he did get a visit on the way home from school one afternoon. A man pulled up in a Cadillac. A big guy who told Stan he'd better respect Johnny Tate or he'd have to answer for it. Here he was a fourteen-year-old kid, and a hood threatens him.

"Were you frightened?" asked Dr. Todd.

"No, I simply had old Uncle Jack call out the rest of the family and we iced Johnny and his mob pal. Of course I was frightened! I was a kid with no parents, no one to talk to, no one to protect me!"

"We can't minimize an event like this. We'll talk about it another day. In the meantime think about taking risks and we'll discuss it next time."

When Stan opened the envelope in his hand he saw no photographs but was shocked and disgusted by the headlines.

"Teenaged girls in bondage. Realistic-looking knife scene."

He pictured a machete from the weapons magazine being used on a young girl, a little girl, a child, the child whose head was still inside the bag of tricks in the dumpster. He felt perspiration on his forehead and knew it was hot in the apartment because he had not opened windows on the south side, the parking lot side, for fear he might smell something rotting in the dumpster.

He tore the ads that had come in the mail into shreds until his kitchen table was covered with pornographic confetti. He looked at his shaking hands and went to the cupboard for his bottle of scotch. He wished he was at work. He wanted to be busy doing something. He lifted the bottle, measured two shots in his mouth, swallowed hard, and put the bottle away.

Some of the pornographic confetti on the kitchen table had fallen to the floor and he got a broom from the closet and swept the kitchen floor that he had just waxed that morning. When he swept the confetti into the dustpan he noticed bits of something green mixed in with the scraps of paper. He examined the contents of the dustpan in the light from the window over the kitchen sink. Maybe he was rotting away, he thought. Maybe the heat in the apartment had given him a disease akin to leprosy, and his skin, gone green, was beginning to flake. He walked to the wastebasket in the corner of the kitchen and stood with the dustpan, staring at the green bits. When the phone rang, he dumped the dustpan out.

"Hello?"

"Mr. Stanley Johnson?"

"Yes."

"I have a collect call for you from Mr. Derek Washington in Los Angeles, California."

"I won't accept it!" he shouted, and slammed the phone down.

CHAPTER 7

THE PRESIDENT'S NEMESIS

For THE MOST part, George Domenico found his post as President Montgomery's campaign manager quite satisfying. But there was always some part of every job not to like. In this job it was the secrecy. Not secrets shared between him and the President, but the various factions of secrets that angled in from multiple directions during the months of the campaign. Domenico had always considered himself a straight shooter, a family man. The President approved of the family-man image. What the President did not approve of was Domenico's refusal to attend weekly Bible study meetings. To Domenico it was one thing to have beliefs, but an entirely different matter to share those beliefs in prepared statements based on Bible readings with those around him. It just didn't seem right in the White House. And now, as the end of the campaign neared, and as secrecy in Washington became ever more prevalent, Domenico had the feeling he was outside the loop. Not only had he refused to attend Bible study meetings, but now he looked forward to the day he could close the books on the campaign and move on.

Domenico had just returned from his luncheon meeting with the

President in the Oval Office. Because the meeting went on longer than expected due to complications surrounding a planned last minute stopover in
the Chicago area before election day, Domenico did not have time to prepare
for his three o'clock meeting with Charlie Thorsen, the Secret Service Director of Protective Operations. Domenico had called the meeting because he
wanted to be reassured that the Secret Service was on top of the situation
involving the so-called "Man in L.A." Although he'd been told time and
again that the "Man in L.A." was not a loose cannon, he wanted to hear it
again, this time directly from Thorsen.

But when Thorsen came into his office, Domenico knew he would hear no
such thing. True, he and Thorsen would address critical matters concerning
the election, but because Thorsen immediately placed his notebook computer
on the desk next to Domenico's notebook computer and pulled his chair around
to sit on the same side of the desk as Domenico, it was obvious the communica-
tion concerning the "Man in L.A." would not be spoken aloud.

Aloud, after the usual greetings and small talk, Domenico said, "I'm
concerned about the Chicago visit, Charlie. Since the final debate is the
night before, I'm concerned your men will be spread too thin."

On his computer, Domenico opened up the Notepad program and
typed, "What's Serrantino up to? No bullshit."

Aloud, Thorsen said, "We're covered in Chicago, George. Advance
teams at the airport, downtown, and in the suburbs. With three teams we'll
be able to handle any seat-of-the-pants last-minute campaigning Monty
wants to pull."

On his computer, Thorsen also opened up the Notepad program and
typed, "Nothing as far as we know. All we do know is he doesn't trust us."

Aloud, Domenico said, "With three teams spread across Chicago, you
should be able to protect the man, the symbol, and the office?"

"That's what we do," said Thorsen, looking up from his computer, an annoyed look on his face.

"Be prepared," said Domenico, also looking up from his computer. "I'm sure the President will want to do some media thing in the suburbs."

Both men smiled self-righteously, then looked back to their computers.

On his computer, Domenico typed, "If he doesn't trust us, we shouldn't trust him. You watching him?"

Thorsen typed, "The best we can. But we can't find out everything or control everything he does."

Domenico typed. "Why?"

Aloud, Thorsen said, "Whatever Monty wants to do, be assured we'll be ready, even if it's at the last minute."

When Thorsen failed to type on his computer, Domenico typed, "I said no bullshit! Why the hell can't we control the old fuck? Level with me! You want to talk? Want me to start asking out loud?"

Thorsen typed, "No. Not out loud."

Now both men simply typed, saying nothing aloud.

Domenico: "Again, why can't we control him?"

Thorsen: "Serrantino goes way back. We have no choice but to let him be."

Domenico: "Exactly why?"

Thorsen, after a pause: "Because of what he knows."

Domenico: "What does he know?"

Thorsen: "Everything."

Domenico turned to look toward his window where the drape was closed, looked at Thorsen, then looked back to his computer and finally typed, "Everything?"

Thorsen: "Yes."

Domenico: "Why wasn't something done about this years ago? Like those others?"

Thorsen: "Because he's gathered pros around him. They're good at taking care of him. Even if he goes, they blow it up so everyone knows."

Domenico: "Who are these pros?"

Thorsen: "Ex-CIAs all the way back to Iran-Contra."

Domenico: "Old guys?"

Thorsen: "Not that old. New recruits back then. Now, late forties and early fifties. According to records from Langley, could be as many as a hundred who graduated together. They're loyal as hell to S. He has finances to fund whatever he's doing until we're dead and gone."

Domenico: "So what do we do?"

Thorsen: "Watch him."

Domenico: "Let me know if anything changes."

As Domenico and Thorsen resumed their vocal conversation about plans for President Montgomery's Chicago visit, they both erased the text on their screens, exited the Notepad program, ran a program to erase extraneous temporary storage, and finally closed their PCs.

After Thorsen was gone, Domenico picked up his phone. He wanted to hear a reassuring voice. He wanted to talk about something else. He wanted to talk about plans for the future once this damn campaign was finally over. He wanted to get an opinion on whether he should tell the President he did not want an appointment in the administration's second term.

"Hi, honey."

"Hi yourself. Sounds like you're not having such a great day."

"What makes you say that?"

"I can always tell by your voice."

"Maybe we should communicate by e-mail."

Domenico's wife laughed. Not because communicating by e-mail was humorous, but because for years, in front of the kids, they'd used the term "e-mail" as a code word for sex, as in, "I'll e-mail you later."

"I'll e-mail you tonight," said Domenico's wife.

"I'm looking forward to it," said Domenico. "Maybe we'll also talk tonight."

"That important, huh?"

"Yeah, that important."

CHAPTER 8

THE PRESIDENT'S NEMESIS

STANLEY JOHNSON

EVEN THOUGH THE sun had long been down it was still stuffy in the apartment. Stan had suffered through it, not turning on the air conditioning, not opening windows on the parking lot side.

Most of the news on television that night was about the upcoming election. The candidates and their running mates campaigning all over the country. A newsman interviewed President Montgomery's campaign manager. The two men spoke of the President's plans to come to Joliet during his Chicago stopover on the way to Los Angeles next month. During the interview they showed shots of the President during another visit to another Midwestern town. The President walking toward a crowd of well-wishers. Waving and smiling as he always did.

Another commentator interviewed challenger Rose Adams Haney's campaign manager. The two women spoke of Haney's plans to speak at a conference of the National Organization for Women. Nothing about old farts who hadn't even begun collecting their Social Security yet. Nothing that had anything to do with him except for the fact that he, and guys like him, were left out of the picture. Then the commentator, referring to an evangelical conference Haney had spoken at, asked about Haney's Christianity. Haney's campaign manager replied that the candidate did not wear her religion on her sleeve. Stan glanced at his right forearm, at his wrinkled and dirty shirtsleeve. He imagined what folks at an evangelical conference would think of him. Dirty Old Man Stan would be an easy mark for them. Someone they can feel sorry for and pray for and, when they're honest with themselves, someone they can hate.

The news went on with coverage of the two running mates. Vice President Allan Nelson choosing to campaign in California, despite its history of going Democratic. Haney's running mate Senator Bill Ingersoll campaigning in his native South Carolina. The coverage playing clips of speeches in which both men obviously played the attack dog. Strong on the War on Terror and on support for the agencies involved in Homeland Security. Supportive of families and moral values. The clips of shouting and anger choreographed for the evening news reminded Stan of the many episodes of anger he'd experienced in his life. Could he identify with the anger? Sure he could.

But none of the news on television that night was really of any importance to him now. Nationally, the Presidential election dragged on. Internationally, war and terror raged. No, none of that was important right now. What was important right now was that there was no report on the news of a dead or missing child.

Stan recalled how he had gotten sick the previous night, down on his hands and knees on the kitchen floor. He'd been weak and vulnerable like a child. In many ways he was a child, a retired child living through experiences that could prove valuable later on. But when? When he was seventy or eighty? Perhaps tonight, with the help of binoculars, he'd get a license number. Then he could call the police and have facts to back up his story.

He turned the television off and sat in the dark in front of the living room window thinking about decomposition. At least the head was sealed in plastic. At least he did not have to think about worms in eye sockets, the invasion of the brain. Too bad he wasn't still visiting Dr. Todd. They'd have a grand old time, he and Dr. Todd, discussing how the presence of the child's head in the dumpster affected his every waking moment.

At exactly one a.m., his watch having been set at the ten o'clock news, he saw headlight beams in the parking lot. Taillights on parked cars reflected the light one after another as the two vehicles moved through the lot. They'd come in together this time, the black sport ute with only its parking lights lit following closely behind the black limo.

Stan knelt in front of his window to hide his body below the window frame. He watched the same two men get out, the big-shouldered guy from the sport ute opening the rear door for the thin man in the limo. The thin man raised his hand again very quickly. The big-shouldered guy held the dumpster lid open while the thin man took something out. Then they got back into their vehicles and drove off.

Stan thought he would have been able to see more with binoculars. But within seconds both vehicles were rolling away from him down Elmwood Drive. The license plate lights were out, perhaps purposely, and in the dim light he could see that the license plates themselves were obscured by dirt even though the two vehicles were shiny. They were gone and he knew they had taken their bag of tricks with them.

Why would they kill a child? Why would they put the head in the dumpster one night and pick it up the next night? A hideous practical joke meant for someone else? Maybe it really was a trick head in the bag. He hadn't touched it. And now, now that the head was gone, he could never call the police.

As he lay in bed, with sharks from his youth nipping at his toes, he tried as hard as he could to convince himself that the head had been a mannequin head, embellished with colored wax.

If he had been in bed the last three nights he would not have even known about the stupid trick. He decided he would not stay up the next night. He reached over to his radio, sharks or no sharks, and turned on his favorite all-night station. He lay awake in the stuffy apartment listening to strains of Gershwin's Rhapsody in Blue.

Outside it was much cooler. Dew had settled on cars and lawns and the dumpsters. A thumbprint remained in the dew on the top corner of a dumpster lid where a gloved hand had held it. A faulty spring mechanism had kept the lid from going all the way down and it was raised about three inches. From the side it appeared as though someone or something was inside peeking out.

A cat scurried across the lawn from the direction of the woods behind the apartments and made its way to the dumpsters. It sniffed along one dumpster then looked up at the partially raised lid of the other dumpster. After studying the opening for several seconds, the cat took three quick strides before leaping up into the narrow opening and disappearing inside.

Beyond the dumpsters, at the west end of the apartment complex, a vehicle with only parking lights lit drove slowly into the entrance. Once off the road the vehicle turned off its parking lights and moved very slowly, making its way to the building across from the dumpsters. When it passed beneath an overhead light, its sport-utility shape would have been obvious, had anyone been watching.

Instead of driving up to the dumpsters across from Stan's apartment building, as it had a short time earlier when it was here with the limo, the sport utility with oversized wheels pulled into a parking spot in front of the apartment building next to Stan's apartment building. The sport utility parked next to a white van where it was hidden from the dumpsters and from Stan's apartment building. The white van was a basic work vehicle, no windows in back, but it did have a ventilation flap on top, which was up. The van's roof, windshield, and front side windows were covered with dew.

The sport utility vehicle had parked very close to the passenger side of the van, and when the van's passenger window suddenly slid down, Jimmy Carter appeared inside. The man in the driver's seat of the sport utility spoke with Jimmy Carter who smiled like crazy from the passenger seat of the van.

"Time to go on in now?" asked Jimmy in a whisper.

"Time to go on in," said the man, his voice deep.

Jimmy turned toward the back of the van. "You all ready back there?" Then he turned back to the sport utility. "They's all ready."

"Thirty minutes," said the man in the sport utility. "No more no less."

"Right," said Jimmy.

The sport utility backed out and left the lot the way it had come in. It did not turn on its lights until it reached the road.

After the sport utility was gone, Jimmy, whose smiling expression had not changed one bit, raised the passenger window.

A moment later, three men in dark coveralls exited the back of the van followed by Jimmy Carter, who was also in coveralls. They closed the back door of the van quietly and walked up on the lawn between buildings. They each carried a satchel and walked quickly, disappearing into the darkness behind the buildings. Just before they disappeared, in profile against the dull glow of the night sky, it appeared that Jimmy Carter's head was significantly larger than the heads of the other men.

The cat that had been in the dumpster scurried out of the opening beneath the lid and leaped down. It stood for a moment, staring toward where the men had disappeared, then hurried off in the opposite direction.

CHAPTER 9

MORNING CALM WAS interrupted by the sound of the garbage truck, its diesel engine groaning as it lifted each dumpster, devouring its contents. Perhaps knowing the dumpsters were now totally empty would help him start over, get his mind off the black plastic bag, get his mind off the limo and sport ute.

Stan showered and shaved and skipped breakfast. He opened the front curtains and did some stretches. He put on a sweatsuit and went out for a walk in the crisp September air. When he got to Elmwood Drive he jogged, imagining himself running from a limo and sport ute, laughing out loud in the sun.

He jogged south on Elmwood Drive and turned into a neighborhood of expensive single-family homes. Several houses had campaign signs in front, Montgomery-Nelson signs alternating with Haney-Ingersoll signs. All of the signs were bright red, white, and blue. What other colors could they possibly be? A Hummer in the driveway of one house had a sticker on it that said, "Only Girlie Men Vote Democratic." A Honda in the driveway of another house had a sticker on it that said, "Rose Knows."

Back in the apartment complex there were no lawn signs. And as he jogged back into the complex parking lot he noticed that only a few cars had bumper stickers on them. At the end of his jog he did a few stretches, then popped the hood on his Toyota pickup and pulled the dipstick to check the oil, glancing at the dumpster enclosure from behind the Toyota's upraised hood. The enclosure opened onto the parking lot, but most of it was set back, taking up what would have been the lawn of the building across the way. The border of grass around the enclosure was worn to bare earth from people short-cutting with their trash, and from kids playing around the enclosure.

When Stan finished checking the oil he slammed the Toyota's hood and wiped at the dirt accumulated on its brown sides with his finger. Four buckets of water from his kitchen sink, four trips up and down the stairs, and his brown Toyota pickup was clean. A little rusty around the edges, but at least clean.

He washed up, put on a clean sport shirt, a wild tie he'd been sent as an enticement to help hungry children, new jeans, and his jean jacket. He drove to Bud's IGA, figuring he'd ask Evie out to lunch, apologize for his behavior the day before.

Dunn's Deli was around the corner from Bud's. A good place to grab a quick lunch and have a chance to talk. They both ordered Reubens and coffee.

"Sorry I spouted off yesterday, Evie. I wasn't myself."

"What's with the tie? You don't usually wear a tie."

"I thought I'd be a little formal to let you know I really am sorry for the way I acted."

"What the hell," she said, blushing a little. "We all have a bad day now and then. You and me, we've got to make the best of things in this crazy world."

The best of things indeed. Dr. Todd had been supportive of his romance with Evie, had wondered if he'd felt guilty. He told Dr. Todd that all the guilt he had in the world was reserved for Timmy and Marge. No, he hadn't felt guilty about his romance with Evie. And he did not feel guilty now as he pictured Evie in bed. In her late forties, and Evie still looked pretty damn good.

"Would you like to go out this weekend, Evie? Maybe dinner?"

"I'd love to. My ex wants me downtown to sign some papers, but the hell with it. I'll tell him to talk to my attorney. Call me tomorrow and we'll plan something. We'll make it Dutch."

"No, I . . ."

"I insist. Don't say anything more about it."

He felt a little embarrassed and ate the rest of his sandwich in silence, thinking about the last two nights.

"Say, Evie, are you still collecting old mystery magazines?"

She looked up, smiled. "Sure. Did I tell you I actually read the things? I like vintage cases. It's interesting to see how criminals were undone back then before all the scientific techniques they use today. If I had it to do over again, I think I'd go into law enforcement. Or maybe private investigation. My attorney hired a private investigator to confirm what my ex was doing after hours down at the old office."

"It must have been hard for you before the divorce. Anyway, I do know what you mean about investigative work being rewarding. I suppose that's why television crime shows never go out of style."

"Lots of variety in crime and mayhem," said Evie. "Keeps our minds off war and terror and global warming."

"Yeah, I guess so," said Stan, as he stared at Evie. "Everything from bodies in garbage cans to disappearing corpses, all designed to keep our minds occupied."

Evie smiled. "Disappearing bodies are a cliché in mystery fiction. In non-fiction there usually isn't a body to begin with."

"How about murderers returning to the scene of the crime?" asked Stan. "Another cliché?"

"Actually, it happens a lot," said Evie. "I read a story not long ago about a man who killed his business partner in his house and made it look like robbery. Years later, the killer goes back to the house after it's already sold to somebody else and starts asking questions. After his arrest he says he was curious about what his partner might have left behind. He got to the point where he figured the dead guy owed him something because, after all, he did kill him."

"He really thought like that?"

"When people commit murder they stop thinking rationally. Criminals end up being their own nemeses." Evie looked at her watch strapped high on her forearm, off her thin wrist. "I've got to get back to work. You'll call me tomorrow night then?"

" I will. And remind me to borrow some of your old magazines."

"Okay. What the heck. You might enjoy them."

After he dropped Evie at Bud's IGA, Stan drove around town for a while. Lunch with Evie had refreshed him. Maybe the head in the bag on his kitchen table had been a hallucination. No, he'd seen the head and he'd never be able to forget it. Maybe someday he'd tell Evie the whole grisly story. His own true tale of suspense and mystery.

He'd always wondered whether his son's unsolved murder years earlier had drawn Evie's interest in the first place. He'd been working at Bud's for about a month when his coffee break happened to coincide with Evie's one afternoon.

"My wife died some time ago," he said when she asked about his family.

"Did you have children?" She said, "did" instead of, "do you have children," as though she already knew.

"We had a son, but he died."

"I'm so sorry," she said, and seemed to make that unspoken agreement to never bring up the subject again. But Evie did bring it up again.

Stocking cans of peaches in aisle one. Monday afternoon, not many customers in the store, so the checkers were helping stock shelves. Evie, the detective, had worked her way near him. She stocked bottles of lime juice and lemon juice on the top shelf while he labeled cans of peaches and slid them onto the bottom shelf. As he stooped on the floor, the edge of Evie's work skirt was at eye level. The hem of her skirt raising and lowering when she stretched to push bottles onto the top shelf. As he stared at her legs he found himself bending lower, pushing cans farther back on the shelves than necessary.

They talked. Evie above, him below trying to look up her skirt. She asked about his old job at the lab, and he rattled on about it, probably boring the hell out of her.

Evie pulled another box of lime juice from the stock cart and put it on the floor next to him. She stooped down to cut open the box. Her faded work skirt, having been washed numerous times, stretched and rode back to the middle of her thighs. Her knees parted slightly and he could see the white of her underwear.

"How old was your son when he was . . . what did you say, killed in an accident?"

"He wasn't killed in an accident. He was murdered."

When he finished the story, including the details about Timmy's birth coinciding with Ford being shot at, Timmy's kidnapping coinciding with Reagan's election, and Timmy's body being found coinciding with Reagan being wounded, Evie seemed deeply touched. He recalled vividly that a tear fell onto a case of peaches he had not yet opened. He recalled vividly how this made him look from Evie's knees to her face. He recalled vividly the look on her face as she wept silently in the canned fruit and vegetable aisle at Bud's IGA.

He and Evie hung around together after that. First coffee breaks and lunches together, then out to dinner, finally spending the night at his apartment.

He told Dr. Todd about Evie. How he'd spent the night with her, how they'd dated for a month, how they shared coffee breaks at work. He also told Dr. Todd about the afternoon Evie found out about Marge and Timmy.

"What were you thinking about, Stan?"

"What do you mean?"

"The circumstances. A woman you find attractive in a somewhat revealing position, while you tell about your wife and son."

"Is it too obvious? Too pat? Have I put my foot in my mouth like Jimmy Carter saying he lusted after women? That was his problem. Too damn honest to be President. Nobel Prize okay. President? Forget it."

"Stan, just tell me what you thought at the time."

"Yes. I was thinking, 'Here I am telling about Marge and Timmy and I'm looking up Evie's skirt.' I actually thought that. So what do you think, Doc? Was it a turning point? Was I feeling guilty about it without knowing I was feeling guilty? Or am I simply a closet voyeur?"

"Moments of realization are similar to historically important events. We remember exactly what we were doing at the time. Like when Kennedy was shot."

"For me it's the day Reagan was shot."

"So you said. Tell me about it again."

He and Marge had driven to the police station in the rain. When they arrived, Inspector Jacobson didn't waste time, quickly telling them that the child's body they found had been positively identified. Timmy had been shot through the heart within hours of his disappearance. Marge wept as the news about Reagan's shooting spread through the halls of the station, uniformed policemen outside Inspector Jacobson's door speculating about Reagan's injuries.

He and Marge did not speak as they drove home that day. They listened to the radio. Reagan was injured, but he'd be okay. Timmy was not okay. Marge, who'd wept uncontrollably in the police station, sat next to him in the car with her arms clutched about her as if to hold herself together. Rain swept across the road as he drove.

But today the sun was shining. And as he drove around town, he thought about the good times he and Evie'd had together. He drove to the south end of town, passed Evie's brick bungalow with its closed-in front porch, its two huge pine trees symmetrically spaced on either side of the front steps. Maybe he'd go home with Evie Saturday night. They'd make love at her place this time. Maybe he'd get away from his apartment for a couple nights. Tonight he'd go to a show or something, and again on Friday night. Saturday night he'd stay at Evie's, maybe for the whole weekend. Forget about the men and the limo and the sport ute and the package that, by now, would have been crushed and buried in mounds of garbage at the dump, had the men not come and taken it back the night before the pickup.

As he drove down Evie's street, he decided he felt pretty damn good, despite what had happened the last couple of nights, and despite what had happened in his past. Even though he'd had only about three hours of sleep the night before, he felt wide-awake and alive. Maybe the coffee at Dunn's Deli had some extra shots of caffeine in it like they do at Starbucks. Yeah, maybe that.

After the brown Toyota pickup disappeared around the corner, a white utility van parked down the street pulled slowly forward and stopped in front of the brick bungalow. The van's windows were darkly tinted and the bright September sun made it hard to distinguish anything inside except that the driver wore a baseball cap and sunglasses. Had anyone been watching, they would have seen the driver's lips moving as he apparently spoke with someone through a thin microphone connected to a set of headphones.

After a moment, a man in coveralls, sunglasses, and baseball cap who carried a buried line detector and wore earphones, came out from behind one of the pine trees at the side of the bungalow's front steps. The man stared for a moment in the direction the Toyota pickup had disappeared before walking quickly to the van. The man got in through the van's sliding side door. Then, instead of driving off, the van's engine stopped and the driver turned to speak with the man in back.

"Middle-aged folks minding their own business," said the driver.

"Why do you say that?" said the man in back.

"Because we'll be there someday."

"Yep. We're not getting any younger."

"Think we'll get orders concerning their well-being before he gets in her pants?"

"Who knows what orders we'll get? And when?"

The driver of the van turned forward and stared out the front window as he spoke. "Maybe we should try different masks. Bush Senior, Clinton, George W., maybe even Montgomery."

"Jimmy Carter's better" said the man in back. "Got his attention like the doc said. Fits his anti-Vietnam-War profile."

"Was it that, or the hit we gave him?"

"Both. Next time, for a little variety, and so things aren't quite the same, you can play Porky Pig."

"I'm honored," said the driver.

Silence for a moment, then the man in the back of the van said, "Enough. I can hear the clock ticking in her living room."

"Back to the apartment?" asked the driver.

"No," said the man in back. "The warehouse. I want to make sure everyone's set for tonight."

"What if he doesn't go home?"

"That's what we need to plan for."

The driver started the van, and as he drove off, said, "I wonder if Social Security will be there for guys like us when we retire."

The man in back answered, "Better start putting money into that personal account."

CHAPTER 10

THE PRESIDENT'S NEMESIS

BEFORE JAKE CAME along and swept her away to the penthouse high over downtown L.A., Lena shared an apartment with Anita in West Hollywood. Close enough to the freeway so the moan and groan of traffic could be heard even through closed windows.

Lena did not take the freeway to the apartment. Jake said her Miata was too small for the freeway, said she needed something larger for the freeway, hinted he'd buy her a Hummer. "More sheet metal to protect that precious body God gave you," he'd said.

She took Wilshire Boulevard and side streets. She turned off the radio when the news came on, news about local small-timers getting ready for the election, brown-nosing with the big boys to get a few votes. The top was down and the Miata hummed, its paint and even the inside sparkling clean. When Jake said the garage man at the building would take care of her car, he meant more than simply making sure it wouldn't get ripped off. The gas tank was full and, before she got into the Miata at the garage exit, she was certain the tires looked new.

Even with Jake out of town, like he was today, she was taken care of. She could spend a couple hours a day at the health club, fiddle with her computer, do some shopping, eat at restaurants, and put the bills on Jake's tab. If she didn't want to, she wouldn't even have to leave the building, or the penthouse for that matter. The housekeeper would get her anything she wanted. Well, almost anything. She still had to go out at least once a week and get her stuff from Raphael. Maybe even that would change eventually. Maybe Jake would get a connection, a main supplier, enough smack for a year or two or three. Enough time to ease her out. If she had that much smack, if she had a stash of it to last her, she'd ration it out, ease down, come off it on her own.

Anita sat in front of the sliding glass door in her apartment air-drying her hair after washing it. So much hair, so curly, amber-brown glowing in the light from the window. Lena had always envied Anita's hair, had tried to dye hers once, but it came out flat, dull like reddish sand. So she remained a natural blond who was, nine times out of ten, pegged a dyed blond.

Anita wore gray sweatpants and sweatshirt. The shirt had UCLA printed on it, faded letters, one of Lena's old sweatshirts left behind that afternoon months ago when Jake—a UCLA alumnus—plucked her away from this place, from this life. Anita left behind to fend for herself, a working girl hoping for that bit part that would eventually lead to the big time. Yeah, right.

Anita was only twenty-nine, the closest thing to a younger sister Lena would ever have. In many ways Anita was more mature than her. When they'd met neither she nor Anita had been on drugs. Maybe that's why Anita chose to room with her instead of someone younger. Maybe that was the main reason. And now?

She could tell Anita wanted to talk seriously. Some French Columbard wine came out and they sat sipping it for a while before Anita started in. The sun's rays barely burned through the smog at the sliding glass door.

"You've got everything a girl could want," said Anita. "And you don't have to work for it. It's the stuff again, isn't it?"

"I've improved, Anita. Really I have."

"Sure." Anita put down her glass, folded her arms and stared at Lena.

"I'm working on it. I've stopped mainlining."

"Big improvement, still stickin' it to yourself, just not in a vein. We've been through too much for that bullshit. You're just as heavy into the shit as you were when you moved out. I can see it in your eyes."

"You don't have to believe me if you don't want to."

"Listen, Lena. If I didn't give a damn about you, I wouldn't ask. I'm just wondering how it is when the stuff's free. Free rides have a way of ending up at Forest Lawn."

Anita paused, expecting an answer, stared daggers at her, continued. "You piss me off, you know that! You start out on the street, looks like you'll die on the street, you get your shit straight . . . for how many years? How long were you straight before Raphael got to you?"

"I don't know, quite a few. I guess I'd pretty much hacked my way through my thirties on the straight and narrow."

"That, too. Way older than me and you look my age. And now you're going to throw it away?"

"I won't throw it away, Anita."

"With free stuff comin' in? Bullshit!"

"I won't O.D., Anita. I just won't! And the stuff isn't free. I still have to get it myself. It's not like Jake encourages me. He's talked about sending me to a methadone clinic."

"That's the first time you mentioned his name. Is this Jake character in the video business?"

"No."

"The Internet business? Porn Web sites?"

"No. He's a religious guy. Us being together has nothing to do with business."

"Religious, huh? I've heard that before. What business is he in?"

"I don't know. He goes out of town a lot. He's flying somewhere today."

"Have you ever gone out of town with him?"

"No."

"Have you ever gone to church with him?"

"No. He says he doesn't go to church, but that he's still an evangelical Christian."

"Yeah, I guess there's a lot of those. In fact, I bet if you asked half the johns in the city they'd say they were evangelicals. Maybe they talk to Jesus for pointers during their drive over when visiting hookers."

They were both silent for a moment, Anita staring at her sadly while she fluffed her hair.

"Jake," said Anita finally. "Nice Christian name. So what's your best guess about his business?"

"He owns a lot of property. Says his old man was loaded and he used his inheritance to make wise investments after he got out of UCLA. Computer business and real estate. Dot-com stuff before that bubble burst. Big money, big connections. All I care about is that he's there and I've got him."

"Still, a girl's got to watch out for herself," said Anita.

"I know. I've thought of that. When I first met him I thought he was a little quirky. But then I figured, what the hell, who isn't?"

"Any hints who he's played sugar daddy to in the past?"

"No. But I do know what you mean. Like, why is he being so good to me when he could have a younger chick? Something else that bothered me at first was thinking he might have picked me because he likes women he considers failures."

"You mean like he's looking for someone he can save?"

"No, not like that. He's never pushed the evangelical stuff on me."

"Maybe he fears or dislikes women who have power and he figures you won't overpower him."

"Yeah, that could be."

"Any hint he might be gay?"

"Not at all."

"Well, at least it sounds like you're thinking about all the things a woman needs to think about these days."

"Yeah, but I also think about my role in our relationship. Like, am I simply in it for the ride? Like, is it all about money and nothing else?"

"Think of it as a security blanket," said Anita.

"Yeah, a security blanket."

Except she didn't feel all that secure. Jake could drop her any time, seemed the kind of guy who could change his mind about her and never look back. Kept her on edge that way. If only she could get in on his business, whatever it was. If only she could make herself useful, indispensable.

Anita let the subject drop. Anita still on the street, playing catch-up, always playing catch-up, so of course she'd be wary. Couldn't blame Anita for not understanding.

Some things never change. Except for being more than a decade apart, they had followed pretty much the same path, her and Anita. Runaways. Both from the Midwest. Both with families who didn't give a damn. After the first few months out here age didn't make any difference. They weren't kids anymore. The dream that someday folks back home would see their sweet faces on the silver screen back in Kansas was long gone. Yeah, some things never change. More than a decade apart and both the same except Anita didn't have that goddamn white horse running around inside her. So who was more mature?

She ate lunch at Anita's, then left to go look for Raphael.

After finally getting through to Raphael on the phone, she waited at the usual meeting place near the Greek Theater in Griffith Park. The spot was secluded, far enough from roads through the park, a clear view on all sides. Nothing at the theater until evenings or on weekends, so the only people around were occasional joggers and tennis players at the courts in the distance.

The wooden bench was warm. The sun hung in the smog like an eye. Traffic sounds were distanced, filtered through the trees in the park. At the tennis courts the balls being whacked sounded like the clicking of tongues. When she was a little girl she would suck her tongue away from the roof of her mouth—thock—with that same sound when she pulled the play pacifier from her play baby's mouth. Her play baby was named Lena because her play baby always leaned on her pillow when she was away at school. When she ran away, when she came here, she changed her name to Lena. Elizabeth seemed too plain and carried with it too much baggage from the past for a girl who might star in a movie someday.

That was the whole reason for coming out here when she was fifteen. She and ten million others figured if they hung around the studios long enough they'd get a break. Just like an old-time movie. Except when she got here the first thing she had to do was find a place to sleep. Guy number one was a pusher, guy number two a pimp. After that she hustled on her own and found her own place. She never called home to Kansas, never told them where she was. Not a home really, just the place she lived as a little girl, and then as a teenager who couldn't get her mother to believe that, at thirteen, her father had raped her in the barn.

When she was in her twenties she got off the street, got a legitimate job at a photo studio in Santa Monica, started out answering the phone but moved up to posing the models, showing them how to smile and pout, helping with costumes. Worked there a few years until the owner made his sideline video business the main business. Then she was in the video business for a while. Off and on bit parts. But she refused to take it up the ass or let guys cum in her mouth. And so, as she once told Anita, "The video business petered out." After the video business she worked as a receptionist in a downtown law office. She was in her mid-thirties when she got a phone call from a cousin that her father had died. When she went back to Kansas for the funeral her mother wanted nothing to do with her. And so on back to the coast with its false promises.

Where the hell was Raphael? Said he'd be here by two and it was already two-thirty. Probably late on purpose. Gotten pretty smart-assed in the last couple months. Jealous because she's not on the street anymore. Pissed because he can't come around every other week and tap a piece off her. "Jus' for a good business relationship," as he put it.

Crazy half-breed, skin the color of imitation leather chairs in doctors' offices. Half black, half Mexican, maybe a little white mixed in. Probably the white in him makes him so smart-assed.

"Damn you, Raphael! I've been waiting here almost an hour!"

He sat on the bench next to the one she was on, sat in the middle, stretched his arms along the back and looked up to the sun. "Bea-utiful. Just bea-utiful." He was wearing loose-fitting painters' pants and a Hawaiian shirt. His shaved scalp was oiled and his mustache and goatee looked like he'd combed them.

"Yeah," she said. "Beautiful."

"My, oh, my," said Raphael. "Do I detect sarcasm?"

"Cut the crap, Raphael."

"You want me to play the tambourine for you?"

Always the tambourine man. Why couldn't he just call himself a pusher? "What the hell do you think I'm here for?"

"Don't be annoyed, Freud. You sound like someone just back from the cure. Or maybe you're mentally undressin' the bulge in my pants?"

"The only bulge I'm interested in is the one in your shirt pocket."

Raphael was still looking up at the sun. "I see, says the blind man to the deaf mute."

"You will be blind if you keep staring at the sun."

As soon as she took the money out of her purse the exchange went fast. Raphael grabbing the wad of bills and handing her the cigarette pack containing the stuff all in one motion as he walked in front of her.

"Supplies are down," he said as he walked away. "Next load'll cost ten percent more."

He walked to the tennis courts. Strutting, so sure of himself, hands in the big pockets of his painters' pants. She should get another supplier. Raphael hard to deal with now that he knows about her benefactor. Price going up every week. Must be a Beverly Hills supplier she could use. All business, delivery boy, the works. Maybe Jake could help. Maybe she'll ask when he gets back. With his connections Jake could call someone on the phone and the next day she'd have a new supplier.

Birds rustled in the tree she had parked under. Should have put up the Miata's top. Had to clean droppings off the seats. Given a choice, the birds choose the park, the sanctuary, away from the noise and smell and hype of the city. Given a choice, to be on the stuff or to be a bird, which would she pick? Taking a shit on some ex-hooker's car seats. What a ball.

She put her purse under her seat so it couldn't be grabbed at a stoplight and drove back into the city toward her penthouse sanctuary, a cage of stone and glass and conditioned air.

At L.A. International, a black stretch Mercedes Benz limo pulled up to the terminal drop-off area and the trunk popped open. The driver, a large short-haired man, got out, took a leather suitcase from the trunk, came around to the rear passenger door. When the passenger got out there were no credit card formalities. Instead, driver and passenger paused for a moment at the open door.

"Walter, I'm concerned about what you said in the car a few minutes ago."

"I wanted you to know, Mr. Serrantino, that I consider it part of my job to watch for these things. Especially at a critical time like this."

"Why is this time different than any other?"

"It seemed an important time because of what's coming up."

"All times are important, Walter. Past, present, and future."

Walter looked about uncomfortably. "I only meant to do my job. I only meant to keep you informed of her intentions, and of her weaknesses."

Serrantino put his hand on Walter's forearm. "I appreciate your concern,

Walter. Thank you for the information. We'll take things as they come. We've never had a problem changing course in the past, have we?"

"No," said Walter.

"Good. I hope the others remain as intelligent and open as you've been."

Serrantino touched the suitcase handle and Walter handed it to him.

As Walter was getting back into the Benz, a frenzied man and woman in business attire asked if he was for hire. Walter did not speak, but simply shook his head no and the couple ran off to another parked limo.

CHAPTER 11

THE PRESIDENT'S NEMESIS

ALTHOUGH THE HEAD of the child—if there really had been a head—was gone from the dumpster, Stan was still frightened the men might return. No reason to return because they'd taken the head away the night before. But just the same, he'd go somewhere, be out of the apartment until after one in the morning. And tomorrow night? He'd worry about that tomorrow. After that was the weekend. Saturday night and maybe the rest of the weekend at Evie's so that he would not be back home until Monday.

He'd driven around town after lunch with Evie, feeling pretty good, hopped up on caffeine. But back at his apartment he'd felt down again. He'd emptied his mailbox and sorted through junk mail at his kitchen table. He'd gone on his computer and erased all the junk e-mail. Then he'd gone on the Web for a while, but when a site devoted to voyeurism opened up one window after another when he tried to back out, his outmoded computer locked up and he shut it down in disgust.

He'd eaten a quick supper and tried to decide where an early retiree with no relatives or friends—except Evie—could spend an evening. When the phone rang and an operator announced a collect call from Derek Washington, Stan thought back as far as he could. Maybe he'd heard the name before, maybe back when he worked for Eugene McCarthy or when he was in school. An old fart like him, too cheap to get a cell phone and use it to call long distance. Maybe someone from school. And so, thinking about the possibility of a class reunion, he accepted the call.

"Mr. Johnson?" said the almost feminine voice, smooth and fast.

"Yes?"

"This is Derek Washington in New York. Thank you for taking my call. The reason for the call is to ask if you'd like to support the President in his campaign for re-election. Our committee has received your name as a possible contributor to this worthy cause. As one who values family, tradition, moral values, and Homeland Security, we're hoping that, at this critical juncture in America's War on Terror, you might see fit to contribute . . ."

He slammed the phone down, cheated, taken for a long distance call by a politicking bastard. He wondered if he was being mistaken for another Stanley Johnson. New York? Last time Derek Washington called it had been from Los Angeles. The operator had definitely said Los Angeles last time. Instead of Internet access, maybe he should fork over a few bucks for caller ID.

He left his apartment at dusk and drove south of town. When he saw the marquee of the Route 43 Drive-In flashing yellow and orange, he pulled in. He thought the only thing the drive-in was used for was a Sunday flea market. He thought he'd read in the paper that the place had been sold to developers. A sign just ahead of the ticket booth explained. It said the theater would be open until the end of October. It said that during that time everyone was invited to join in the nostalgia. They'd be showing movies from the seventies and eighties. Pretty clever. The movie royalties were probably next to nothing, the projector was still there, so what the hell, make a few bucks until the place is leveled. One other thing it announced was that tonight was adults-only night.

The first movie was full of cowgirls riding bareback on their bare asses. The next was about a girl who supposedly wanted to make love to anyone or anything that was handy. Because these were old, and cheap, adult films, the sex was mostly implied. He fell asleep during the second movie and was awakened by drive-in commercials, which were also vintage.

As the animated clock ticked off the minutes until show time, as an animated family consumed peanuts and popcorn and pizza and candy and soft drinks, it started to drizzle. "Getting It on the Range," the bare-assed cowgirl movie, started again and he watched the distorted credits through beads of water on his windshield. The rain increased steadily and he decided he'd better use the restroom before the deluge. He got out, locked the Toyota and walked to the concession building. He patted his pocket several times to make sure he had his keys, imagining the embarrassment of locking himself out of his pickup on adults-only night.

While he was in the toilet stall, he heard the door to the men's room open, heard the echoed sounds from the movie come in. "You from Texas, ma'am?" "Why shore 'nuff I am." He heard strong streams of piss clattering in the galvanized tin urinal. He listened to the two at the urinal.

"What you think of the movies?" said a teenaged boy, his larynx straining to keep from cracking.

"I can see why we didn't have any trouble getting in," said another boy in a deeper voice. "I've seen more skin on the free previews on the Web."

"My folks got Net Nanny."

"I'll show you how to disable it."

The door opened and the two boys were gone.

Adults-only night. What a joke. The two boys had sounded like they were about fourteen. Still at that age when they think they're indestructible. Not yet aware that everything they do now has an effect on their future. Or maybe these days, with terrorist attacks looming and the environment going to hell, they've figured out ways to make themselves oblivious to consequences. He wished there had been a fisheye lens on the toilet stall door so he could have seen the boys, seen if they looked like him and his buddies when he was a kid. By then Uncle Jack had him delivering newspapers so he could afford to buy his own damn bed, and was probably already lining up the job hauling parts at the Zenith plant. No time to be a kid. Had to hurry and grow up, get a job, get married, have a kid, only to lose it all.

The door opened and closed again. No sounds. Probably a kid combing his hair. If the door had a fisheye he'd be able to see. Just like the fisheye on his apartment door. Never used to use it until the last few days, until he found the head inside the bag of tricks. Looking out through the fisheye was like looking out from inside a bubble. During a History Channel special on the Secret Service a while back, they said that the President—or candidates, or family members—were, "inside the bubble." They said that people protected by the Secret Service were called "protectees." They said that the limo that carried the President was called, "the beast." Limos and sport utes, that was what the Secret Service used to maintain their bubble . . .

Sure was a long time to comb hair. He finished, stood up and looked over the top of the stall just in time to hear the door open and see a tall man in an overcoat step out quickly.

Stan went around the building to the concession entrance. There was no man in an overcoat. He got a drink from the drinking fountain and, running back to his pickup in the rain, cursed himself. A man wearing an overcoat because its pouring out has to take a leak, maybe can't because the old bladder's wearing out, and he gets paranoid. Maybe he should take his .45 with him when he leaves the apartment. Maybe his paranoia would drive him crazy. Maybe if he was smart he'd try to forget the whole thing. Yeah, be a kid and forget everything.

Back in his pickup, he wiped the rain from his face with the lower part of his sleeve that hadn't gotten wet. It was really coming down now, pummeling the hollow bed of the pickup like the drum of nervous fingers. The drops hit and spread on the windshield making millions of melting lenses. A sex scene, that he had watched four hours earlier, was taking place on the screen. Betty Lou in the bunkhouse with Big Hoss, the ranch foreman. He watched Betty Lou strip off her leathers, climb the ladder and mount Big Hoss on the upper bunk. The raindrops hitting the windshield seemed to strip away pieces of flesh. He watched Betty Lou and Big Hoss go to it as the rain distorted their bodies.

The image of writhing bodies seen through raindrops seemed sexier than it had been the first time around. As though Betty Lou and Big Hoss did not know they were being watched. Or, better yet, like being Big Hoss, seeing it the way Big Hoss would see it. For some reason, seeing the scene through the raindrops was also beautiful. More like nature, like creatures in the forest doing what comes natural. Doing what needs to be done.

As if heated up by the sex on the big screen, the drops of rain on his hand felt warm as he re-hung the speaker on the post. His windows had steamed up and it was after one-thirty. Even though it was a warm night, the pickup's heater felt good, dried out his damp clothes.

As he left the drive-in, he noticed a pair of orange parking lights following him. Out on the highway, headlights came on and followed him at some distance. He slowed to forty, ten miles under the limit, and the headlights kept a steady distance, illuminating the water spray of his pickup. The headlights were mounted fairly high up and he could not help thinking about the sport ute that had parked by the dumpsters, the men who had deposited the bag then retrieved it the following night, last night.

Normally he would have taken Route 43 all the way to Elmwood Drive where it curved east at the intersection. Instead, he turned west on a well-lit side road and watched as the vehicle, an old full-size pickup, kept going north on 43. He laughed at himself for being such a fool. Only two directions to go from the drive-in, north or south, and since all of Chicago's suburbs were to the north, and it was farmland to the south, most cars would naturally head north. He turned around and drove home. It was already after two. If the limo and sport ute had come again at one o'clock, he hadn't been there to see them. He would mind his own business from now on and forget the whole thing.

The rain had diminished to a fine drizzle. As he walked toward the entrance of his apartment building he could hear frogs and bugs from the marsh. He could hear water gurgling and draining from downspouts. When he opened the door to the vestibule, lights reflected off the glass, blinding lights. He turned and saw the two vehicles moving slowly toward the dumpsters in the parking lot, the headlights of the limo and the spotlight on the sport ute aimed directly at him.

Stairs two at a time, unlocking and re-locking his door, key lock and chain lock. As he ran into the hall a bright light through the front window lit up the living room. He fell to his knees and crawled to the bedroom. He gasped for breath as he lay on the floor between his dresser and bed in the dark, his hands covering his face. After a while his breathing eased some and he listened intently, waiting to hear his door crash in, the chain lock flying off, its screws ripped out and clattering across the floor. But there was no sound except the in and out of his breathing.

CHAPTER 12

THE PRESIDENT'S NEMESIS

EVIE POURED HIM a cup of tea from a pot resembling a pumpkin. "You should have called the police, Stan. I certainly would have if someone parked in front of my place late at night."

He was at Evie's house. They'd eaten out, and during their conversation over dinner he'd casually mentioned seeing a limo and sport ute out front of the apartment building. He didn't tell Evie they were waiting for him after his return from the drive-in. He didn't mention the head of the child. He was treating that part of the story, even in his own mind, as if it hadn't happened.

Evie wanted details—What make were the vehicles? How many men were there? Did they appear at the same time each night? He had answered truthfully about the vehicles, both black, the limo probably a Lincoln. But about the men, he said he thought there were two in each vehicle but he couldn't be sure. He didn't want to mention the man in the back seat of the limo because he figured Evie would want to know what that man did that made him noticeable, like getting out of the limo. As far as Evie knew, the vehicles simply parked out by the garbage dumpsters at one in the morning, for a few minutes, four nights in a row.

"What about last night?" asked Evie.

"I don't know," he said. "I went to bed early last night."

"Really? I wouldn't have been able to stand it. I would have stayed up."

He really had gone to bed early last night, Friday night. After calling Evie to confirm their date, he'd gone to bed and fallen asleep around nine, knocked out cold until nine the next morning as if he'd taken sleeping pills or something. After what happened Thursday night, the vehicles showing up in the parking lot when he got back from the drive-in, he'd been afraid to go out. If the vehicles came last night he was locked in his apartment, key lock and chain, safe in bed. The reason he slept twelve hours without interruption was probably because of all the stress he'd been under.

As he sat on the sofa next to Evie, faces stared at him from a lamp table. Framed photographs of Evie's two daughters and one son at various ages, their families, at least five children between them, and her ex, probably when he was a lot younger, dressed in a business suit. They all smiled, except her ex, which was understandable considering the current situation.

The carpet in Evie's living room was beige, the sofa was beige, the walls were beige. The only thing not funeral-parlorish about the room was a built-in shelving unit that contained a portable television on a middle shelf and piles of murder mystery magazines on the upper and lower shelves.

A pendulum wall clock near the vestibule ticked loudly, reminding him of his Aunt Lillian. Aunt Lillian alone in the old house after Uncle Jack died, alone with a pendulum wall clock that chipped away relentlessly at what remained of her life. He and Marge used to visit Aunt Lillian, his only relative. The house felt like this, silent except for the incessant ticking that made not talking seem dangerously odd, as if something terrible would happen if they did not fill the silences between ticks. He continued visiting Aunt Lillian until she died. Her house and her money were left to her two real children who lived far away and never visited. In all the times he had visited the old house he never went into the attic, never went up to see the corner of the attic at the front of the house that was his room as a boy. As far as he knew the bed he had bought with his paper route money, the bed on which he was deflowered by Tammy, the junior-high cheerleader, was still there awaiting his return. As a boy he had wished for the future. Now he would gladly start over again. Back before climate change and terrorist attacks. Back before his son's murder and his wife's suicide. Back before time rushed ahead, disallowing his wish to do things differently. A day off from work the day his son played in the backyard, an offer of hope for the future, perhaps a trip somewhere. Anything that might have altered the chain of events on that day, and on the day he went to work and his wife lifted the container of liquid drain cleaner to her lips and . . .

As the pendulum clock on the wall ticked, Evie sorted through the piles of mystery magazines on the shelves. She piled a dozen or so on the glass-topped coffee table in front of him. He wondered why she was doing this, then remembered he had asked to read some. She sat down next to him on the sofa.

"I picked out a few relics. You can take them home if you like, but don't feel obligated to read them. Just because I get carried away with my hobby doesn't mean you should."

"It's all right. I don't mind."

Evie wore a black outfit, slacks and a bulky sweater. She had on bracelets and ring-shaped earrings. Her hair, usually boyish, was airy, framing her thin face and making her look younger. The wine with dinner had made her cheeks rosy. He could smell her perfume. A fresh smell, like Marge after a bubble bath. A momentary image from the past slipped through, then faded as the seconds ticked forward. Marge dead on the bathroom floor, bubbles of foam on her lips.

"I really like your hair that way."

Evie blushed, took a sip of tea. "Thanks, Stan. Went to the salon yesterday morning. At work everyone liked it. Even Glen, if you can believe that."

Glen was the butcher at Bud's IGA. He recalled the time Glen—close-cropped blond hair, round face pink like the front of his apron tinted from meat juices—stood at the entrance to the meat cooler holding a two-foot long salami between his legs and saying in a mock-immigrant voice, "If mine was like dis, I'd go to Hollywood, be big movie star."

"Is Glen still managing the meat department?" he asked Evie.

"Sure, he's still there. The guys in the back room still call him Porky. They say he bears a definite resemblance to the pig face on the wall above the meat counter."

Stan pictured the meat counter across the back of the store, the row of pink lights in the ceiling to give the meat a pleasing color, the stainless steel swinging doors to the butcher room, the plaster faces centered on the wall behind the meat cases. A steer and a pig both painted with shiny enamel, the steer brown and white, the pig pink, both faces plump and smiling, ready for the kill. The faces were vivid in his mind even though he never remembered having paid much attention to them while he worked there.

"Yes," he said. "I remember that pig on the wall." He pictured human bodies, men wearing suits, but with the pig's and the steer's heads on them. A dream he'd had. Not the dream of hanging on a rising drawbridge with Marge and Timmy. Another dream.

After they were quiet a moment, Evie said, "Stimulating conversation, huh?" and they both laughed.

"It's funny you should mention that pig," he said. "I had a dream a few nights ago, and again last night, about the pig and steer on the wall above the meat counter. I was in my kitchen, sitting at the table in my pajamas, and the steer and pig . . . Wait. There was an eagle, too, with a huge beak. Yes, all three animals standing around my kitchen table and me sitting there in my pajamas. All three with animal heads but human bodies dressed in gray business suits. And one of them . . . the steer, I think . . . keeps handing me cards to fill out. I write my name and address on card after card and hand the cards back to the steer. The pig's standing across from me at the table and, in a deep voice, keeps repeating my name and address over and over as I write it down. After I fill out the last card, the pig gives me a soldering gun just like the ones I'd used at the lab, except this one has a miniature gun sight on top with cross hairs. The pig unravels an extension cord and gets the soldering gun plugged in. Then the pig hands me a printed circuit board."

"What's a printed circuit board?" asked Evie.

"Those boards full of electronic components like you see in computers. Anyway, these boards are usually rectangular or square and they have a plug on the end. But the board in the dream was round and all the components— resistors, capacitors, integrated circuits—formed kind of an eagle with spread wings. I insert components into the holes, turn the board over and solder the components in, just like I used to when I worked at the Joliet Lab. While I'm soldering there's this siren . . ."

"Siren?"

"Yes. At first I thought I had the soldering gun too hot. Sometimes when it's too hot the solder on the board gives off a squeak. But this sound was louder. Definitely some kind of siren . . ."

"That's one hell of a dream, Stan. I've had some strange ones, but I can never recall that kind of complexity."

"The siren was painful, like getting your teeth drilled, or like the melted lead of the solder is really a pool of blood and someone sticks a red hot wire into it."

"That sounds terrible. And these faces, the steer and pig, looked just like the ones in the store?"

"Big smiles and all."

"So where did the eagle come from?"

"I don't know."

"Dreams are fascinating," said Evie. "Don't you just love analyzing them?"

"There's one more thing about the dream. You know how you sometimes have the feeling someone else is there even though you don't see them. Well, I had the strangest feeling Jimmy Carter was there watching the whole thing."

"That's not so strange. You said in the seventies you worked for Carter's campaign. It's all there from your past, Stan. Even the red-hot wire in the blood. That cellophane-wrapping machine in the meat department works on heat, and then there's the blood from the meat department . . ."

"When I was a boy my aunt said I dreamed too much. I guess I used to walk in my sleep. I might walk in my sleep now for all I know."

"Have you ever gone outside while you were sleepwalking?"

"Not that I know of."

"I hope not," said Evie. "That could be dangerous. You mentioned your aunt. Did your aunt and uncle bring you up?"

"Yes. Guess I never told you I was an orphan."

Evie moved closer, held his arm. "Poor little orphan."

Enough. He didn't want to tell Evie about his corner of the attic, about sleeping on a moldy mattress until he was able to buy his own bed, about how he was more or less an unwelcome boarder in the house. "Yes," he said. "I guess I was pretty glad to get out of the orphanage."

"Poor baby." She let go of his arm and stood. "I'll be right back."

She came back with a bottle of crème de menthe and two tiny stemmed glasses. They talked and drank glass after glass of the smooth green syrup. "These glasses are so small," said Evie, as she filled them again.

They talked about people at the store—Bud always walking so fast nobody could keep up with him, Bertie who always got into arguments with customers, Glen who looked like the pig on the wall, the part-time boys with their pierced body parts.

He put his glass on the coffee table, had to put the glass down carefully because he could feel the effects of the crème de menthe in his arms. Evie also put her glass down, but it tipped over and crème de menthe flowed out in slow motion, spreading across the coffee table like green blood from a wounded beetle.

Evie put her arms around his neck. Her hands were hot on the back of his head.

"I would feel sorry for little Stanley," she said in a baby voice as a tear ran down her cheek. "I would give him a place to live any old time."

It had been a while since he and Evie had made love and there'd been no other women in his life. To control his passion he tried a unique version of thinking of baseball. He thought about the limo and sport ute outside his apartment. He thought about the head in the plastic bag on his kitchen table. This not only delayed his climax, but made it seem painful. He had tears in his eyes as he held Evie.

Now, as Evie slept beside him in bed, snoring gently, he wondered if the limo and sport ute were outside his apartment again tonight, perhaps shining a spotlight at his window. He wondered what Evie's reaction would be in the morning when he asked to stay with her for a few days. Poor little orphan Stanley. He reached out and touched Evie. He lay his head on her shoulder. When she did not react, when he was certain she was asleep, he wept quietly, holding his body as steady as he could while tears ran down his cheeks.

Across town at the apartment complex, the receiver in the back of the van had been silent for some time. The only sound being picked up now was the ticking of the living room clock. The man took off the earphones and put them down near the dull light of the sound meter on the recorder. He spoke softly toward the front of the van.

"If you think he's a sex maniac now, he'll be an even bigger one when he gets back home and has his Wheaties."

"I don't think he's a sex maniac," answered the driver from the darkness in the front seat.

"Sounded like a steam engine to me."

"She didn't do enough moaning for me."

"Guess he'll be there all night."

"Yep, but bring the portable in with us in case he wakes up and changes his mind."

"I still think we'd make him a little crazier if we left some trace we'd been there. You know how these paranoid guys are. Give'em a bone to chew on and they dream things up."

"You were at the meeting today," whispered the driver somewhat harshly. "You heard the plan. Don't let him know anyone's been there until the time is right. And it may never be the right time. So, don't try outguessing the man who doles out bonuses."

"All right. I was just talking. Shall we go in now, Mr. Conservative?"

"Yep. And bring those masks. We can store them in the cubbyhole so we don't have to carry them in every time."

"That didn't come up at the meeting."

Silence.

"All right. Anything else you think we should store in his apartment?"

"No."

When the two men got out of the van they could barely be seen in the darkness as they moved over the lawn, past garbage dumpsters, and between apartment buildings carrying their satchels.

CHAPTER 13
THE PRESIDENT'S NEMESIS

STAN HAD LEFT his Toyota at his apartment so it would not be seen in front of Evie's house. On Monday morning Evie dropped him off on her way to work.

"I'd love to have you stay, but I'm at work during the day anyhow. It's just . . . well, if you wouldn't mind I'd prefer it this way. Sometimes Ruth next door comes over in the evening. But we could plan for next weekend."

While most people were leaving for work, he was arriving home. On the way up the stairs he actually hoped his apartment had been broken into while he was gone so he could call the police and report it. But everything was just as he'd left it, dirty dishes in the sink, garbage not taken out. The apartment smelled like Aunt Lillian's house shortly before her death, windows closed tightly against drafts, against intruders, against death.

He placed the stack of murder magazines Evie had given him on the kitchen table and went through the apartment opening windows. He had some cold cereal, smelling the milk before he poured it to make sure it hadn't gone sour. He washed the dishes while a breeze from the window above the sink brought in the smell of the woods to the north. Soon it would be fall and when the leaves fell he'd be able to see the fence surrounding the lab. Not the buildings, they were too far away. But sometimes, in winter, he could see one of the lab guards walking a path inside the fence. Retirement from the lab was permanent, couldn't even get in to visit without a pass. Sometimes he imagined the section of fence behind the apartment complex was actually the perimeter of a fence holding him here in this apartment, in this town, in this life of retirement. But he'd sure as hell broken out of his bubble this weekend.

He wondered if the mental activity associated with the men and the dumpster and the child's head had something to do with the awakening he felt, his middle-aged bones forced from their middle ground, his body rejoicing in something new and different. And then last night and Saturday night with Evie. At first he'd been nervous, fearful he'd be unable to perform. Then he'd been confident, a confidence he felt now. He wanted to be with Evie again, yet he felt strangely extroverted. Ancient hormones had surfaced, the thrill of the hunt having left its mark.

In an attempt to relish these feelings, he lay down in bed and closed his eyes. The breeze from the window washed over him, generating visions of tall grass blowing in the wind, of trees and flowers in full bloom. Even though he knew it was almost autumn, he focused his thoughts on spring, on rebirth. Time unfolding like layers of petals on a tight rose in a garden of roses. Evie with him in the garden, a coy smile, a downward glance.

But when Stan fell asleep, the dream he tried to promote did not continue. Instead, he dreamed of the child's head and the menagerie in his kitchen. The child's head was there in the bag of tricks on the kitchen table, then it was swept aside and he was at it again. Writing his name and address on cards, using a soldering gun with gun sight and cross hairs to spell out

E PLURIBUS UNUM on a circuit board, soldering like crazy because if he stopped the siren went off in his head. It was the same dream he'd told Evie about. And within the dream he thought, "I spoke of the dream and now I'm dreaming it again. The more I dream it, the more I'll speak of it, and the more I speak of it . . ."

When the soldering was finished, the kitchen was all smoke and haze from burnt solder rosin and he lay his head down on the kitchen table and tried to sleep so he could leave that world and come awake back where he belonged. His head on the kitchen table, cold, while the rest of his body glowed warmly, the warmth spreading like soup gulped, only he hadn't gulped anything. And besides, his head was there on the table, in a bag, while he was . . .

He awoke thinking he heard a sound in the kitchen, the rattling of a paper bag. But when he ran dizzily into the kitchen he saw only the flutter of curtains in the breeze and the washed dishes he had left next to the sink. The dishes were dry. The clock on the stove said almost one and he realized he had slept through the morning. Perhaps it was simply the change in shadows, the slant of sun having moved west, the shadows shifted from one corner to another. Perhaps that is what made him feel that someone had been here. He'd slept, someone had come into the apartment, and now he was here in the kitchen again. He felt the warmth of having run from bedroom to kitchen, the pounding of blood at the sides of his neck.

The chain lock was not in place on the door, but he could not remember having locked the door when he returned home from Evie's. When he went into the living room he saw that the curtains were closed. He tried to imagine he'd left them open, but recalled having closed them before he'd left for Evie's. Back in the bedroom he noticed the tiny green light on his computer, meaning it was turned on. Then he laughed at himself. He always left his computer on, ever since the time the clock battery ran down and he had to take it in to the computer store to have its system rebooted or whatever-the-hell they called it.

He sat down at the computer and turned on the monitor, which he did shut off to conserve electricity. When the monitor warmed up, the top half of a woman appeared. She was perhaps in her forties, but excellently preserved. That's what the banner lettering above the photograph of the woman said. "Excellently Preserved."

The woman smiled at him. She had dark hair and light skin. She sat leaning back in a chair, her arms outstretched on the arms of the chair. She was not as thin as Evie, and her breasts were significantly larger. Though the word was not printed on the screen, he thought the word *voluptuous*. The computer mouse, that little rascal, had escaped its pad and hid between computer and printer. He retrieved the mouse and fumbled nervously with it, his hand shaking as he found the browser's navigation down arrow and scrolled down so he could see the entire photograph. The woman's legs, instead of being crossed, were outstretched and spread wide. She was naked.

He tried to recall the last time he had gone on the Web. He thought it was the day last week when he'd taken Evie to lunch. He'd come home and gone on the Web then. He remembered one site after another opening until he'd finally had to shut down the computer. At least he thought he shut it down. Not the power off, but a restart because the keyboard had locked up.

He studied the woman on the screen. Voluptuous. He glanced down at the browser's status bar, saw that only one browser screen was open, the one he was looking at, not screen after screen like he thought he remembered. He looked at the Web address. Instead of a Web address, the browser address field showed the address of a file in the Internet temporary file cache directory.

He moved the cursor to the back arrow on the browser and clicked on it. Another woman appeared on the screen. Another "Excellently Preserved" woman in her forties or fifties. Another voluptuous woman seated in a chair. As he clicked on the back arrow, voluptuous woman after voluptuous woman appeared, all of them under the "Excellently Preserved" banner, all of them seated in a chair staring at him. All of them naked.

A sound in the kitchen. He turned slowly from the computer screen and stared at the door to the hallway. He stood and walked into the hallway. Another sound like before, paper rattling. Not loud but definitely there. He stopped in the hallway. From where he stood he could see the entry door and noticed again that the chain was unhooked. He still could not remember if he had hooked it after Evie dropped him off that morning.

He inched forward, seeing first the kitchen table with the stack of murder magazines from Evie, then the refrigerator, stove, kitchen sink.

The rattling of paper again. He leapt forward, one hand out front to defend himself.

But there was nothing to defend himself against. Nothing but a tall brown bag standing on the cupboard next to the kitchen sink, on the opposite side of the kitchen sink from the stack of dishes left out to dry. As he watched, the breeze from the window over the sink billowed the curtains inward, one edge of one curtain catching the top edge of the bag and rattling it. Instead of toppling over as the curtain edge dragged across it, the bag remained upright. Obviously something was inside the bag weighing it down.

He went to the cupboard, leaned slowly forward and looked into the bag. Inside was a can of corn and a can of green beans. The cans were upright and clearly printed on the price labels was, "Bud's IGA." As he stared at the cans he recalled the checker saying, "Paper or plastic?" and he remembered thinking, back in the store, that perhaps paper would be better. Paper, like the paper inside the garbage bag that he'd opened on his kitchen table.

After moving the bag away from the window so the curtain would not reach it, he stared at the kitchen floor. Something there. He reached down and poked at tiny bits of something that looked like green lint. He wiped his finger across the floor and some of the green bits stuck to his finger. He stood and rubbed his fingers together over the kitchen counter so that some of the green fragments fell onto the counter. He went into the bedroom and got his magnifying glass from the drawer in which he kept newspaper clippings of missing children. Back in the kitchen he examined the green fragments. They looked fibrous, skinny, and flexible.

He walked slowly back into the bedroom, put away the magnifying glass, and sat down at the computer. He paged back and forth through the images of naked women stored in the browser's cache file. He knew that images from Web browsing were stored in the cache file, but he could not recall ever having retrieved them like this before. Normally he would simply dial in and go on the Internet and browse the Web. Perhaps someone had sent him a virus. But he'd erased all the e-mail he'd gotten. None of it was ever worth reading. Or maybe it had to do with the way the computer was last shut down.

He accessed the computer's file explorer, created a directory called "\ beautiful" and moved the files to that directory so they would not be lost from the temporary cache directory. The files were in numerical order, named snatch001, snatch002, snatch003, and so forth. He began looking at all the files again, double-clicking on one file after another.

As he paged through image after image of women his age or somewhat younger, he wondered if sexual arousal had caused him to forget what the hell he'd done last time he was on the computer. The women *were* quite sexy after all. And there was something else about them. Something so personal about the look in their eyes as they stared at the camera, as they stared at him. It was as if he and the woman on the screen were inside the same bubble.

Crazy bastard, he thought. Dirty Old Man Stan so horny he doesn't even remember what he's doing. For all he knew maybe he came back from the drive-in the other night and, instead of falling asleep, turned on the old computer and went searching for an older version of Betty Lou who screwed Big Hoss in the bunkhouse. Yeah, to try to forget that the limo and sport ute had been waiting for him when he returned from the drive-in, he'd turned on the old computer and now here they were, dozens of Betty Lous.

He turned off the computer monitor and went back into the kitchen. He put away the dishes, all except one small dish. He palmed the green fibers he'd taken from the floor into the dish. He went to the hall closet, got out the vacuum cleaner and vacuumed the living room carpet. He cleaned the bathroom and gathered dirty clothes for the laundry. He changed out of the clothes he'd worn at Evie's all weekend. He showered and shaved and put on a pair of blue jeans and a red shirt he found at the back of his closet. While he did this, the outside air flowed through the apartment making it fresh. For a moment he thought he smelled perfume in the air, the perfume of women standing outside his windows. Naked women in the woods, last chance for an exhibitionist outing before the cold weather sets in. Maybe the green fibers were from the woods. Maybe the fibers had fallen from the naked women as they'd walked through the kitchen on their way to his computer.

Yes, he was going nuts all right. Maybe it was the old sexual reawakening that was driving him crazy. Dirty Old Man Stan's pecker sitting up in its coffin like Dracula on a moonlit night. Damn, he had to get out of this apartment!

The afternoon sun was hot as he headed toward the garbage dumpster. He held his breath, lifted the lid, threw in his bag of garbage, and hurried off toward the office at the far end of the complex to pay his rent. Even though the sun was out and he'd just spent the weekend with Evie, nothing could make him forget about the head, about the men in the limo and sport ute.

He usually paid his rent just before lunch so he would not have to listen to Marion's gossip for more than fifteen minutes. But today he was anxious to hear what Marion had to say. Maybe someone else had seen strange vehicles in the middle of the night.

For the price of her rent plus a small salary, Marion manned the complex office, collecting rents, answering complaints, checking pool passes for the pool next to the office, hiring plumbers and electricians and painters, making sure the scavenger service emptied the dumpsters twice a week. Marion was a widow, a little younger than him, perhaps Evie's age, and sometimes made it pretty obvious she was hunting for a man. "Do you realize how many single men and women live here?" she'd say. "We should start a singles club, Stan. Friends Over Forty."

Every month when Marion mentioned the singles club idea, Stan simply said he would think about it. The only thing resembling a club he'd ever been active in was politics. Volunteer work back in sixty-eight for Eugene McCarthy had resulted in a beating and a trip downtown to be arrested as a protester. Should have learned a lesson from that. But he ended up working for Carter and voted for Carter's second run the day Timmy disappeared. Carter lost, Timmy disappeared. So much for volunteering.

When Stan entered the office, Marion was speaking with a young man in coveralls who he'd seen doing outside painting all summer. He could tell by the way the young man slouched and leaned to one side on Marion's desk that the guy had been stuck with Marion for quite some time. Stan decided to wait until the young man left, so he walked along the perimeter of the office. Wood-paneled walls, a stone fireplace, plush carpeting—as if any of the apartments looked like this. He sunk down into the leather sofa that faced the glass sliding door with a view of the pool while he waited for the painter to leave.

A young woman was swimming. She climbed the pool ladder and walked to the diving board. She wore a blue bikini and matching blue swim cap. The sun glistened on her tanned skin. As she tested the diving board, Stan wished he had a view of the pool from his apartment. All he could see from his window were the apartments across the way, and those damn dumpsters. The woman dove with very little splash, sliding in like an eel. Instead of swimming to the ladder at the side of the pool, she swam underwater toward the shallow end. When she climbed out this time she did not use the ladder and the bottom of her bikini stretched taut as she lifted one leg up to the edge ahead of the other. She took off her cap and shook out her long brown hair. Thin muscular legs, firm buttocks, small breasts, but small breasts do look good in a bikini.

The woman was probably in her twenties, married, a baby in bed taking a nap while mom takes a dip. A nameless woman, a woman who might have been Timmy's age, if Timmy had lived. Girls, then young women, now young mothers. Any one of them could have ended up his daughter-in-law. So many lives altered because Timmy, his and Marge's only son, was not there to pull pigtails and go to the movies, to date and court, to make love.

The young woman wiped the tips of her hair with a large striped towel, then spread the towel on the cement and lay down on her stomach. Her buttocks had seemed small when she was standing. But now, lying on her stomach, her buttocks curved up sharply from her waist and tapered smoothly to her muscular thighs. Then the young woman reached behind, undid the top of her bikini and let the straps rest on the towel.

It was one of those animal moments when a guy says to himself, "Forget everything else. We should have sex right now." He wished for a distraction violent enough to make her jump up. A siren, an explosion, a plane crash, a wild animal, anything. But the door to the office closed quietly and Marion called out to him.

"Hi, Stan. Come on over and sit where we can talk."

He pushed himself up out of the depth of the leather sofa, taking his time. He glanced out at the young woman by the pool once more on his way to Marion's desk. But the woman had not budged.

Although Marion was about Evie's age, she had the relaxed movements of an adolescent girl bored with school. She had curly black hair and large breasts. A little on the heavy side—heavier than the women stored on his computer—but well proportioned. Marion had a shape much like the young woman by the pool, except everything was doubled. Even though Marion probably weighed close to one-eighty, she was pretty good-looking. Small nose and mouth, brown eyes set far apart, large-framed glasses, pink lipstick.

Usually he avoided getting into long conversations with Marion, but maybe he could get some information. "What's new, Marion?"

"Just a minute. I have to keep track of the painter. I write down what he says he's going to paint each day. Today it's window trim on building five."

Marion tore the pink slip of paper that said "from the desk of Marion" from the pad, put it in a slot in her orange plastic desk caddie, put her pen in a hole in the caddie, and folded her hands on her desk, a girl on her first day of school.

"There. All nice and neat. Neatness is a virtue people who live here should follow. Not you, Stan. You're neat as a pin. But some people . . . well, I shouldn't name names. But this new couple from the South . . . not that being from the South means anything, I'm from the South myself . . . but this couple named Hurley, Libby and Bob, have been leaving their charcoal grill out in the middle of the lawn all night. Do you know what Libby Hurley said when I called the other morning and asked quite politely if she could please put it away?"

Marion had started. He would find out about the limo and sport ute. All he had to do was vaguely bring it up at some point. "No," he said. "What did she say?"

"She says, 'Just what is my husband supposed to do with the hot coals, dig a hole in the lawn and bury 'em?' Complain about one thing and she suggests doing something worse. We just had that company come in last month to seed the lawn for winter. I don't know what this world's coming to. It's not at all like when we were younger. Like that Chuck who was just in here. The other day I had to open up the maintenance shed out by the pool for him and he practically propositioned me. Just like that he asks if I'm busy that night and says maybe we can get together."

Stan thought for a moment about the naked women on his computer, each of them sitting in a chair, leaning back, arms outstretched on the arms of the chair. Except for her legs being crossed rather than spread, and except for the fact that she wore clothes, exactly the way Marion was posed. "You should be flattered, Marion. You're an attractive woman."

Marion pulled at the curls around her ears. "Um, did I hear what I heard, Stan? Or did I hear what I heard?"

"I guess you heard right."

"Thank you, Stan. You're much more the gentleman than a lot of people I know. I have to deal with all kinds in my job and most of them can be spelled on one hand, t-r-a-s-h. By the way, how are your new neighbors?"

"Did somebody move in across the hall from me?"

"This past weekend. Didn't you hear the racket? All that furniture going up the stairs? I thought you were home because I saw your pickup there."

"Some friends picked me up Saturday and I was gone all weekend."

"That's nice. I wish I could pick up and leave like that. Can't seem to get away from this place for a minute. If I'm not dropping off past due notices I'm calling up tenants to tell them they can't put out political lawn signs because it's not their lawn. So, Stan, did you have a good time on the weekend?"

"Nothing special. Played cards." Cards indeed.

Marion looked past him out the front window. "There goes Mrs. Jenkins. I guess her afternoon exhibition is complete. Either that or her husband, who works nights, might have signaled that it's time to change the baby."

Stan turned slowly, though he had wanted to leap up and check the bikini top. The young woman was walking away, whipping her towel at the air, her buttocks twitching. As she entered her building he could see that the top of her suit was firmly in place. "Does she swim every day?"

"Yep. Distracts the hell out of my painter. A little sun, then back inside for a mid-afternoon nap. I suppose you noticed she doesn't like strap marks on her back. Pretty effective thing to do in front of a young man who's on the prowl. Except the result for me is probably a lot of paint where it doesn't belong."

"Say, Marion?"

"Yes?"

"Speaking of someone being on the prowl, has anyone reported any prowlers around here at night?"

"Prowlers? Why? Did you see someone? If you did you should tell me and I'll report it."

"Not really. I just saw a couple of strange vehicles one night. I stayed up late and saw this light flash in my living room. When I looked out, a car and what looked like a sport utility vehicle were pulling away. Probably nothing."

Marion looked at him seriously. "If you see anything you should call the police. This is our community, and even if we can't always control who moves in, we can at least keep it safe."

Marion pulled out a file drawer in her desk, peeked inside a file folder. "Your new neighbors are Mr. and Mrs. Delaney, by the way. John and Sue. Just thought you'd like to know."

Since Marion had nothing to report about strange vehicles, he thought about the young woman in the bikini. If he lived nearer the pool he'd put his binoculars to good use.

"Mr. and Mrs. Jenkins," he said. "I'll have to pop over and introduce myself."

"Not Jenkins," said Marion. "Delaney. John and Sue Delaney. Mrs. Jenkins is the woman who just left the pool. Still thinking about her and her bikini, huh?"

Marion pulled at her curls and smiled coyly. "I don't blame you, Stan. Being single and all. Speaking of young women, Sue Delaney's no slouch. When she and her husband first came in, she asked about aerobics classes. Man, all these young bodies around this place. Yet another reason for a singles club."

"What?"

"I told you about my idea, Stan. We should start a singles club. We haven't got forever. We should live it up a little, do our own thing while we've still got life in these old bones. We're the boomers, Stan. Instead of complaining about Social Security we should do our thing."

Marion pushed back from her desk, stretched her arms upward, yawned, uncrossed her legs, crossed them the other way. Her skirt was quite short, it was quiet in the office, and he could hear the sound of her nylons, hosiery against hosiery. She leaned forward toward him, lifted her elevated leg up and down, the short-heeled shoe on her foot lifting away, dangling. She stared at him above her glasses. He imagined Marion staring out at him from his computer monitor.

"Well, Marion," he said. "I'm here. You're here. Our things are here. Let's talk about it."

He had never seen Marion blush before. She fiddled with the collar of her blouse. She cleared her throat and opened a side desk drawer, looked inside, then closed it. "I'd love to talk now, but with all these rent checks to log in and everything . . . I'll tell you what, Stan. If you'd like, how about coming over to my place tonight and we'll . . . we'll talk then."

A chance to be away from his apartment one more night. Yeah, right. Who was he fooling? Maybe all those women on his computer had the answer. "Stan the Man on the move," they'd say. Doesn't even know what he's doing. Or does he? Maybe the old saw palmetto taken to protect against prostate problems had another effect. Maybe his dreams had kicked out some hormones he didn't even know existed. Maybe this was all part of going crazy.

"Okay, Marion. Sure. I'll be over about eight." He stood, feeling like someone shot full of Spanish Fly.

"That's a little late," said Marion. "But . . . all right, eight o'clock at my place. I guess that'll give me time to freshen up after dinner."

He left the office and trotted in the sun back to his apartment, feeling like a dreadful little boy running away from a nasty prank. This morning Evie drops him off after their weekend together and, like a sex-starved deviate, he's already plotted his next encounter.

The running and the heat of the sun made his skin tingle, made his head feel light as if he were drugged, as if he would float aloft and be exploded like a clay pigeon. Then he slowed down, walked and panted and wondered, for the first time in a long time, if perhaps he should call Dr. Todd and find out if he was going through a change of life, or if he really was going insane.

CHAPTER 14

THE PRESIDENT'S NEMESIS

STANLEY JOHNSON

JAKE ARRIVED FROM the airport in time for dinner. They ate at the Italian restaurant in the building, then went to the health club to burn off the carbs, watching one another sweat in the wall of mirrors. The other guys watched, too. A personal trainer and three regulars who pumped iron, young apes with ripply abs and bulges straining their briefs as she did spread-legged toe touches. Jake obviously becoming aroused as he watched the apes drool. They could look all they wanted, but no touching. Jake had made that clear from the beginning.

When Jake first started taking her to the health club he suggested she wear a leotard and tights from Frederick's of Hollywood instead of a sweat-suit. Little stretchy jobs that could be balled up in one hand. Tonight she wore the flesh-colored see-through job. One of the apes, a chunky Mex, practically had an orgasm. She was on the Nautilus lifting weights with her legs, up on her elbows, legs spread, the leotard riding up her crack, while behind her the Mex pulled the cables on his machine like a madman.

Compatible, that's what she and Jake were. An exhibitionist and a guy who gets off watching her and watching the watchers. And then later, back up in the penthouse, making love to her better than the apes from the health club could manage even if they tried a team effort. Maybe age gave a guy staying power, slow to go up, slow to come down. They'd made love for at least an hour, then she fell asleep, dreaming dreams of how good it was to be off the street.

When she awoke, Lena reached out and flicked the switch on the nightstand that operated the drapes. Morning light, bright as the purest smack, stretched its loving arms across the ceiling. What a life. A girl could get used to this. She would have kissed Jake, snuggled up to him, but he was gone, the covers thrown back on his side, way over on his side of the bed that was as big as some of the rooms she once used for tricks.

She put on her robe, went into her bathroom and took care of business, business-business and the other business. Smaller dose this morning. Give it a try. Like a stiff drink on an empty stomach. A slow motion avalanche that couldn't hurt a flea. God, she felt good. Some day. Some day soon. She'd show Jake. Share the news with him. Some day no more needle. She'd told Anita about not mainlining anymore. But she knew Jake wouldn't consider that an accomplishment. She had to get completely off the stuff.

She looked out the floor-to-ceiling windows as she walked through the apartment. The smog hovered below, only a few buildings poking above making the landscape barren. Barren like a stage waiting for someone to give a speech. Barren like farm fields, here and there a tree poking up from the fog. Barren like a front lawn with a couple trees showing their bare branches. Like a day a long time ago when the tractor drove up on the front lawn and her father jumped off and ran in the front door. No. Don't think about that. The morning was much better than that. The world, no matter how much senseless terror took place, no matter how many fake speeches and phony promises were made, was much better than that.

Jake wasn't in the living room or kitchen or game room or library. She would have knocked on the door to his study but she heard him talking. The door was ajar just enough for her to see that he was on the phone. He wasn't shouting, but she could tell by the tone of his voice, a forced smoothness, that he was angry with whoever was on the line.

"I left you in charge at that end because I can't be there all the time. Don't give me that let-George-do-it crap!"

She paused out of sight and listened. Maybe she'd get a clue about Jake's business.

"That doesn't mean a damn thing," said Jake. "Old guys get horny once in a while . . ."

"Yeah, I know. That's how we all got here . . ."

"Look, those days are over. Pay attention to your job and proceed as planned!"

Jake's chair squeaked, rocking back and forth, obviously he was pissed at whoever was on the other end, maybe anxious to get back to the bedroom for breakfast in bed.

"Impossible," said Jake. "It wears off in twenty-four hours."

More chair squeaking.

"Listen, we'll discuss this again when I'm out there. Don't call me unless it's for something a little more out of the ordinary!"

The phone clattered on the cradle and she hurried down the hall.

Jake joined her in bed a few minutes later and seemed perfectly calm. She touched him, a deflated balloon.

"Where were you?"

"On the phone answering messages."

"Business?"

"Yes."

The little balloon began inflating inside Jake's pajama bottoms.

"I could take calls for you, use a sexy voice. You could say I'm your secretary."

"I don't think so."

"You have a chauffeur. Anyone with a chauffeur should have a secretary."

"Walter's more than a chauffeur. He's been with me for a long time and isn't involved in my business."

She let go of Jake. "I wasn't trying to pry."

Jake stared at her. His dark brown eyes so unnerving when he stared. "Yes you were."

"Okay, so I was. You can't blame me for being interested. I thought maybe some day I could help out. I'm smarter than I look." She laughed, then became serious again. "And I'm good at keeping things to myself. Lord knows I've had to do that all my life. My family, whatever's left of them, doesn't even know where I am."

"Or what you've been?"

"No. They don't know that either."

"I'll make you a bargain, Lena."

"Sure. What?"

"Do what you're told, which, for the most part is doing just about anything you want. But don't pry into my business. Be patient, stick around, and some day, if I need your help, I'll ask."

"Like Walter?"

"No. Walter is just . . . Walter."

She motioned toward the rest of the room. "Is this like a test to see if I'm a good girl?"

"You can put it that way if you like."

"You have to be able to trust me first, is that it?"

"Trust, Lena, is a strange thing. It slips in and out of focus." Jake lay back on the pillow and stared at the ceiling. "Sometimes when you think trust is at its height, something happens to indicate there may be another motive, another reason for people acting the way they do."

"You mean you don't trust me?"

Jake laughed, a kind of old-man's cackle that revealed his age, or his experiences, a laugh that said things. I've seen this before. I know things you don't know.

"Very funny, huh?"

"No, Lena. I'm not laughing at you. It's this whole business of trust. I'm in the business I'm in because people I thought could be trusted through the years proved me wrong. You mentioned your family earlier. Mine was a single parent family. Only a father. He was a busy man and hired people to take care of me. Then, when I'd grown older, I found out he really wasn't my father at all. My real father was someone totally different. My real father thought he was the ultimate mover and shaker. I never knew him, but in a way I've taken the legacy from him. There are values to be upheld, values I support. So you see, Lena, you're not the only one without a family. In a way, perhaps the work . . . my work . . . can become a legacy for us both. Perhaps the work can become family for us."

"What is the work?"

Jake continued staring at the ceiling. "That takes us back to values. Personal values. Long-held values. Call them family values if you like. Except in my case family means something much larger in scope. The main objective is to gather people around who can be trusted. And if one is fortunate and accumulates sufficient funds, as I did in the seventies and eighties, then I feel one must use a portion of those funds to promote personal values, to have an effect on a world gone to hell."

"Conservative values."

Jake laughed. "I love your candor, Lena. Yes, conservative values. If you like, I'll even admit to being a bit of a neo-conservative. In our world, all convictions and doctrines are cyclical in popularity. Where man over nature was once all the rage, now it's concern for global warming. In the end, though, it all comes down to who controls the purse strings. Business. Sure, it's been made fun of in the arts. The young man in *The Graduate* being told the key word 'plastic' by the savvy businessman. But business really is where it's at. Businessmen are the ones who go out from the cave and bring back the goods for men who stay behind out of fear or laziness."

"Sounds pretty chauvinistic."

"Welcome to the real world."

"Are you in the real estate business?"

"Real estate is one of many methods for manipulating funds."

"Then there's something else you do. Something you'd rather not talk about yet."

Jake turned and stared at her. "It's something you'd have to experience to understand. Or learn. And that will take time."

She leaned her head against his chest. "Listen, after the life I've led so far I'm all set for learning."

"Then stick around, Lena. Be patient and it will all come to you."

"What will come to me?"

"Trust. Simple trust. And by the way, in case it crossed your mind, I have nothing to do with terrorists, or with those whose job it is to defend us from terrorists."

She pressed her ear to Jake's chest, listened to his heartbeat while she looked at the teardrop-shaped nostrils in his hawk nose, his nose even more prominent from this angle because of his small chin. Men seen from this angle looked so comical, their chins and mouths like the snouts of porpoises at Sea World, their noses like black-eyed cartoon characters peeking over a horizon. So many johns seen this way, their eyes hidden by their cheeks as they look to the ceiling, sometimes howling. Jake's eyes were hidden now and this seemed to make him weaker, to make her more powerful.

She walked her lips, as if they were feet, down Jake's belly. Then she engulfed him.

Old guys get horny, too. Wears off in twenty-four hours.

What wears off? What did it mean?

CHAPTER 15

THE PRESIDENT'S NEMESIS

Mid-fifties AND on the make. "Hot to trot," as they said back when he was a young man. This past weekend Evie had welcomed him to her home, and to her bed. But was it him or the alcohol? And now Marion, another woman a few years younger than him, seemed willing. Dirty Old Man Stan with his porn mail and his on-line harem and his reawakened sex drive. Dirty Old Man Stan with plenty of free time to think about how he'd gotten the nickname.

He had been in his thirties, a widower mourning the loss of his son, the death of his wife. The nights burdened with visions of Marge dead on the bathroom floor. Then, two years after Marge's death, a girl fifteen years younger than him came into his life to comfort him, to help him forget, to help him gain the reputation as a dirty old man.

Her name was Terri, a receptionist at the lab's Physics Division. Poor Stan standing at the bulletin board on another Friday afternoon before another weekend alone in the empty house. The ad said, "Ride wanted from south side of Joliet, will pay." He'd thought it might be good therapy to have someone to talk to on his way to and from work. So he called Terri and she rode with him every day for several months.

Terri was twenty at the time, short blond hair cut up around her ears, and big blue eyes, of course, and a small nose. Her upper lip was thin but her lower lip was full, shadowing an area above her chin. She was petite, like a little girl sitting next to him in the car, her legs short so that her knees bent exactly at the edge of the car seat. She had five different outfits, skirts and blouses, one for each workday. The reason he knew she had five outfits was because, after a few weeks, he had memorized how far each skirt would inch up as they rode in to work. The powder blue skirt was best, sometimes revealing the start of her thighs. He and Terri did not talk much during those first weeks.

"Morning, Stan," she would say. "How are you today?"

"Fine. And you?"

"Oh, I'm fine."

And after work, "Hi, Stan. How was your day?"

"Busy."

"Mine, too."

After about a month of "Nice day," and "Busy," Terri started talking about her job at the lab, her family, her boyfriends. She asked about his family, and when he finished his story she said, "I didn't know. I'm so sorry." What else could she say? After that they talked a lot, every morning and every evening. The more they talked, the more Terri turned toward him in the seat until finally her usual position, especially after work, was to sit sideways with one leg tucked up beneath her on the seat after she had slipped off her shoes.

Back in high school Terri had written an extensive paper on the Kennedy assassination and had become an assassination buff, so she sometimes talked about that. Stan could have told her a thing or two about later assassination attempts. About how the attempts on Ford and Reagan seemed to figure so prominently in his life. But he stayed away from that and, instead, rifled through his memories of the Kennedy assassination.

Terri said that she hadn't yet been born when Kennedy was assassinated, and wanted to know if he recalled what he was doing when he found out that Kennedy had been shot. He told her he was in junior high at the time and that they'd called a special student assembly in the auditorium. He told her he didn't recall too much except that kids were crying and that the girl who sat next to him even held his hand she was so upset. Actually, Tammy held his hand before they found out what the assembly was for, but he didn't go into that. The only person he ever went into that with was Dr. Todd.

Discussions about things like the single-bullet theory and Ruby's eventual cancer and the relationships between Giancana and Kennedy Senior and J. Edgar Hoover and other prominent figures seemed to draw Terri closer to him, closer than he'd been to anyone since Marge died. For several weeks he became obsessed, going to the library in the evenings and photocopying articles that he'd discuss with Terri the next day. At the time he wondered how much of the obsession was a real interest in the assassination, and how much was because he had wanted Terri to respect him, perhaps even love him, even though she was so much younger than him. But as the weeks passed, the conversations about the Kennedy assassination began to die out, and so did the possibility of Terri and him becoming lovers. Eventually, the conversations before and after work each day centered around Terri's future, obviously a future without him. It was the closest he had ever come to giving fatherly advice.

"You know, it's funny, Stan. The guys at work, the technicians, seem to find about ten reasons a day to come up front to my desk and shoot the bull. How much sick leave do they have, have they used their floating holiday yet, they lost a quarter in the Coke machine . . . you know, all that kind of stuff."

"They obviously find you attractive, Terri."

He was busy driving so he couldn't tell if she had blushed. But she did lower her head, she did look down at her lap and say, "Oh, come on, Stan."

"Well, you are."

"So why don't any of them ask for a date? They hang around the desk with their hands in their pockets and their feet shuffling and all they end up saying is that it's a nice day or something."

"What do you say?"

"I agree with them and get back to work. The division director gives me all his data entry to do besides my regular work, so I'm always behind."

"Haven't any of the guys asked you to lunch?"

"They brown-bag it and sit in their offices playing computer games."

"What if I ask you to lunch tomorrow?"

"That's nice of you, Stan, but . . ."

"Just to make them take notice. It's like one of their analytical games, the scientific method, step by step." He recalled, as he said this, holding out the remote possibility that Terri would actually want to go to lunch with him.

He recalled her giggling at first, then putting her arm along the back of the seat, almost touching his shoulder and laughing. "Probably just the way their brains work, like life is a big game."

It didn't exactly work out as planned. The guys still stood around shuffling their feet, and he and Terri met for lunch every day in the cafeteria. He treated her several times until she insisted on buying her own lunch. Then to pay him back for the lunches, she brought a picnic lunch one day and they ate at the pavilion in the lab park.

Some of the guys from his division spent their lunch hour playing basketball in the park, and after they saw him with Terri the trouble began. First it consisted of locker room teasing. Then one day in the coffee room a machinist nicknamed Turk, who was sitting at a table behind him, said, "Some guys just look, others like to chase." He told Turk to go to hell, heard the chairs at Turk's table scrape across the floor, and suddenly Turk stood over him. "Watch yourself, you cradle-robbing bastard! You watch your own ass instead of somebody's daughter's!"

He wanted to throw his coffee in Turk's face, but of course he didn't. His anger concerning what life had dealt him had been pretty well spent. He simply said, "Mind your own damn business," and watched as other machinists convinced Turk to get back to work. As Turk left the coffee room with the others, Stan knew by the way Turk turned to look back at him that one of the machinists had spilled the whole story about Timmy and Marge, had told Turk to leave a poor bastard alone.

But he wasn't left alone. For several weeks following the incident in the coffee room, he found notes that had been slipped through the vent holes into his locker. "Do you take the rattles out of the crib, or does the sound excite you?" "Did you ever get stuck with a diaper pin?" Eventually the notes became threatening. "Stay off the playground or you'll end up in Sag Canal!"

He kept telling himself that whoever wrote the notes—probably Turk—needed help. He didn't tell anyone about the notes, not Terri, not Dr. Steinberg, not even his buddies. Then one afternoon there was a brown paper bag in his locker. The steel door had been pried out from the top and was bent out of shape. There was a hollowed-out apple in the bag. The note with the apple said, "Try this, it's sweet and only a couple weeks old." He put the note back in the bag and went to Dr. Steinberg's office.

Dr. Steinberg threw the note and the apple into his wastebasket and scratched his beard, scratched and scratched at his beard.

"Maybe I should tell you what it means."

"I know what it means, Stan. You've been having lunch with one of the administrative assistants and somebody doesn't like it. It doesn't matter what you do in your free time. That's your business. I hate this part of the job, but I'll see what I can do."

What Dr. Steinberg did was publish a memo about the locker being damaged. After that everyone found out about the notes, including Terri, who stopped having lunch with him and stopped riding with him and got a boyfriend.

So much for reawakening his sex drive. After that his mid-life crisis came on in high gear and he wasn't even forty. Sedgwick, the guard who later sold him the guns, said people should mind their own business, said he'd watch out for him. Nothing else happened, except the name Dirty Old Man Stan caught on and lasted all the years he worked at the lab. Terri left to get married, friends retired or quit, but the name hung on even though few knew how it had started.

Sometimes he wondered why all these things happened to him. Sometimes he wondered if he should pray for an answer. He and Marge had stopped going to church after Timmy's body was found because they both agreed there was nothing left to pray for. And after Marge died he didn't go back. If he went to church what would he say? What would he pray?

Dear all-powerful and all-merciful God. This is Stanley Johnson, one of your lesser humble servants. That's right, Dirty Old Man Stan, the guy whose son was murdered and the one whose wife you allowed to commit suicide when you were busy watching someone else . . .

Dr. Todd's answer to all this had been to not blame himself.

"I'm not blaming myself. How could I blame myself for what happened to Marge and Timmy?"

"In the past you said you did blame yourself. You said you thought you should have known what Marge would do? If you really feel that way, if you do blame yourself in any way, just admit it, let it out."

"Okay, sure, I blame myself. But then I blame a lot of people."

"Like who?"

"Like the police for not doing their job. The courts for letting murderers run loose. The government, not giving a damn about a little boy and his mother. Presidents get shot at or cop a feel with an intern or start a war and everyone's in an uproar, thousands of investigators on the job. Who gives a damn about a little boy? Who gave a damn about Marge? Why can't the government or the President do something about that? No. Ever since they pissed Carter out the back door of the White House everyone in government has been too damn busy hustling votes. Marge isn't a vote anymore so who gives a shit about her?"

He had wept then, Dr. Todd consoling him, standing and holding his shoulders, telling him it was good to let it out. Weeping the way he had at Evie's apartment over the weekend. And why had he wept? Because the men in the limo and sport ute, who'd tricked him into looking at the severed head of a child, had brought back all the fear and anger from his past.

He stood before the mirror in his bathroom. He had just splashed on aftershave, a musky smell for Marion, a woman of ample flesh, musky odors residing in folds of skin. A way to escape, to forget.

He combed his hair, a little forward to cover scalp. Years earlier he had prepared for Marge this way. A young man running a comb through thick black hair, probably smiling, not knowing the future, not knowing death, not yet being called Dirty Old Man Stan. Preparing himself, as he was now, for the unknown.

Something would happen. He knew something would happen. The head of the child had, like the rotten apple in his locker, been meant for him. He couldn't tell the police because they'd blame him, Dirty Old Man Stan, for the murder, or at least for dreaming the whole thing up. Women appearing out of nowhere on his computer screen. Crazy dreams crawling into his skull as soon as his head hits the pillow. Green shit on his kitchen floor. Conversations with Dr. Todd coming back to haunt him, reminding him how vivid the memories of Timmy and Marge could be when a shrink forces him to open up his head so he can step right inside!

He tried to smile in the mirror, tried to look younger by cocking his head to one side. But it did not work. His face was that of a man who has experienced some of the best, but mostly the worst in life, a man who, though he goes on living, is inhabited by many men.

Dr. Todd would have loved these thoughts. Dr. Todd would have analyzed the hell out of them, weighed them like raw meat on a scale, acknowledged the seriousness of it all. But in the end, Dr. Todd would have told him to live, would have congratulated him on the past weekend with Evie, would have encouraged him to go to Marion's apartment tonight, screw her brains out, and stay until morning.

CHAPTER 16

THE PRESIDENT'S NEMESIS

STANLEY JOHNSON

O CTOBER, A SOMBER month with rainy days and windy nights that rattled the loose storm windows in Stan's apartment. He hadn't gone out at night since his journey home from Marion's at three in the morning. But he had looked out, peeked between drawn curtains. No limo or sport ute since the night he'd come home from the drive-in, the night they shined the spotlight at his window. No limo or sport ute in almost a month.

He hadn't seen Marion since the night at her apartment when she sent him home to sleep it off. Gin and tonics, Marion's favorite drink. He'd gulped four or five like sport drinks until the smell of alcohol permeated his nasal passages, just like the smell of laboratory-grade ethyl alcohol at the lab.

While he drank, Marion had talked about starting a singles club. She wore pink slacks and a blouse with a frilly collar. A blouse opened three buttons wide so he could introduce himself to her breasts. He and Marion sat across from one another on plastic-covered chairs. He felt like he was in a set for a television commercial for a room full of furniture at a discount price. The gaudiest furniture in the world, its price sliced to the bone. Marion rested her elbows on her legs in a kind of at-the-starting-block position. He tried to calm himself, but the booze took over so fast he didn't know what hit him.

"What do you think, Stan? Should we send out announcements? I can get names from the files. I don't know if we should ask for money right away. First we'll see if there's enough interest for an initial get-together. I can get the clubhouse for nothing so all we have to pay for is food and entertainment, maybe a DJ. Seems like a good idea, don't you think so, Stan?"

The idea sent signals to his noggin for more booze. He imagined himself wearing a Hawaiian shirt, moving from guest to guest. While Marion went through her sales pitch, he got drunk. At one point he tried to change the subject.

"This is a little off the topic, Marion. But I've been wondering if there were any vacant apartments, you know, one-bedroom units like mine. Maybe near the pool."

Marion went into the kitchen and refilled his drink. When she came back she walked with exaggerated hip-swings.

"Stanley, you devil," she said. "I know why you want to live near the pool. You want to watch Mrs. Jenkins when she has her coming out party in that bikini she almost comes out of." She giggled. "But you're too late 'cause the pool's closed for the season. Even if you did move, you'd have to wait 'til next summer before you'd have a chance to warm up the old binos."

"I wasn't thinkin' about that, Marion. I jus' like this end of the complex, tha's all. I thought it'd be nice to live closer to you."

That had done it. Marion pointed to the sofa, said something about it being more comfortable. He moved dizzily to the sofa while she made herself another. The gin took over then, his hand resting on the sofa and he didn't even know it was there, palm up, until Marion came back from the kitchen and sat on his hand and screeched as he pulled it out. She grabbed his drink away, put both their drinks on the coffee table and was all over him.

"Oh, Stan. Oh, my God, Stan."

He passed out.

He must have mumbled a bunch of personal stuff while he was out because when Marion sent him home that night to sleep it off, she mentioned something to the effect that rumors about perverts alone in their apartments with their computers were true. He vomited near the pool, held onto the cyclone fence, worked his way along the fence. Then, with no more fence to hold on to, launched himself and headed home. As he passed the dumpsters he wished the men in the limo and sport ute would come and haul him away, maybe kill him and return *his* head to the dumpster. Oh, his head!

During the days following the disastrous visit to Marion's, Stan left his apartment only to visit Evie. Evie so thin and manageable compared to Marion. Evie whose kindness toward him doubled the guilt he felt. He asked to spend another weekend at Evie's house, but she was somewhat standoffish as if she knew, as if she'd seen him stumbling along the fence that night.

Each night he watched for the limo and sport ute. And each night after the limo and sport ute failed to appear, he went to bed in a state of fear he could not comprehend. As the continuing nightmares became more and more confused with reality, he wondered if he could trust his own memory.

The rut again, the rut reinforcing his loss of youth. And now the trees doing their thing, the trees outside his windows throwing their leaves to the ground one after another in rapid succession. Time consumed by tedium except on weekends when he dated Evie. The only time he felt like he wasn't losing his mind was when he was away from his apartment with Evie.

If only he could start fresh, get an apartment facing a different direction. Maybe if the sun came into his bedroom window in the morning he'd get up more quickly instead of sleeping late. Sometimes, in the morning, he felt as though he hadn't slept at all. He had, in the last several weeks, even considered going to a doctor. Not Dr. Todd, not a shrink so he could talk his head off. A GP who could pep him up, tell him why he felt tired and dizzy every morning, even mornings after he hadn't had anything to drink.

New apartment, sure. The apartment wasn't the problem. It was him. New neighbors moved in weeks ago and he hadn't even met them. Once, when he heard a noise on the landing, he peeked through the fisheye lens instead of opening the door and introducing himself. All he saw was the back of a man going down the stairs. Another time he heard his neighbors talking and giggling before they entered their apartment. Voices happy as clams. Newly married clams. Just like him and Marge during their first years of marriage.

Screw the new apartment. What would he do there all day except sleep late, watch television, read the paper, surf the Web, and open all the damn junk mail?

The amount of pornographic mail had increased. Beside photographs, he'd received sample rolls of black-and-white movie film he couldn't view because he didn't have a projector. He didn't even know if eight millimeter film projectors were made anymore and wondered who the hell would be sending this stuff. Was there a warehouse so full of this shit it was worth trying to sell it? Was it some kind of nostalgia thing? Would he be watching the auction show on PBS some day and there'd be people outbidding one another for vintage porn? For the hell of it he sent in nine-ninety-five for a portable viewer with a crank handle that was pictured in one of the ads. He figured the crank viewer would be better than unrolling strips of film and squinting at the frames against the overhead light in his kitchen. He even tried his magnifying glass on the frames. Snatches of time in the lives of tiny naked figures from the past whose eyes were so small he could not see them even with the magnifying glass. Like peeking into a faraway window back when he was a kid.

After sending for the viewer, he looked at the ad again to make sure he hadn't dreamed he'd done it. But there it was in his stack of porn, an ad that had come with sample film strips, an ad showing a cartoon guy whose eyes bugged out as he cranked the handle. All he had to do was go down to the video store and visit its back room and he could rent all the action he wanted, and here he was saving sample film strips that looked like they'd come from the fifties. But the box number for the viewer in Las Vegas, Nevada, had a zip code, so he knew the ad wasn't that old.

The chain letters had become more ridiculous. One letter told about a sea captain who lost his ship because he didn't "keep the chain going." Another seemed to threaten him personally. It said, "Many people who failed to keep the chain going have experienced ill luck in their personal lives. Many have lost jobs and been unable to find work or been put in situations of extreme danger because they failed to keep the chain going!!!"

The day after he received that letter he figured, what the hell, and went to the Joliet Research Lab to apply for a job. He had to fill out a form to get a guard escort to the employment office. He recalled the thousands of times he'd driven into the lab in the past, waved through by the guard because of a measly sticker on his windshield. Once upon a time he'd been somebody at the lab. Now he was a sea captain who'd lost his ship.

The young man in the personnel office said there were no openings on the technical staff. So he asked for any kind of work. Like, a job on the groundskeeping crew, even part time. The young man said those jobs required experience in the field. Finally, he asked if there were any openings for sea captains. The young man didn't see the humor in this and called the guard to escort him and his beat-up Toyota pickup back outside the fence.

If he'd had a job last month he would not have been up late and seen the limo and sport ute in the first place. For several nights in a row he tried going to bed early, his plan to awaken refreshed and call for job interviews. At least this part of his routine he could change. But in the mornings, no matter how early he went to bed, he felt exhausted, a strange antiseptic taste in his mouth as if he'd gotten drunk the night before. His recurring dreams had increased, sometimes waking him before his alarm went off.

The dream in which he and Marge and Timmy hang by their hands from a rising drawbridge was a repeat. Black water below, Johnny Tate, his boyhood nemesis, above smiling down at him, Timmy and Marge gone, apparently fallen, him trying to hold on, falling, then awakening in a sweaty tangle of sheets.

The dream with the pig and steer and eagle in men's bodies had distinct variations. Sometimes he's filling out his name and address on card after card being handed him. Sometimes he's drinking milk out of a miniature glass milk bottle, the kind milkmen used to deliver back in the Middle Ages. Sometimes he's soldering the printed circuit board with components arranged in the shape of an eagle. This was the most frightening variation of the dream because of the pain he'd feel in his head, a pain like a sound too loud, so loud he thought his head would explode. Part of the reason the sound was painful was because it had a squeak to it like a branding iron on flesh. Yes, that was it! His soldering iron a branding iron on flesh. The folded-back flesh of the child's head!

Once, in the dream, he thought his head had exploded and that it was in a garbage bag inside one of the dumpsters. Except the dumpster's not in the parking lot outside his apartment. The dumpster's been bumped out of its wooden enclosure and rolls on its dolly wheels down the highway pursuing the limo and sport ute with oversized wheels in a Keystone Cops chase. The dream ends with him back in his kitchen, sitting at the kitchen table. Sometimes he has the feeling Jimmy Carter is there watching him. Sometimes not. But he always ends up putting his head down because he's tired, and the kitchen table slides away so that he's falling, sometimes falling from the bridge.

On mornings when he awoke from the nightmares, when he pieced together his life—Timmy's kidnapping and death, Marge's suicide, the head of the child, the men in the limo and sport ute—when he realized he had nowhere to go, nothing to do, he sometimes wished he were dead. And he wished he could take someone with him, kill someone to make up for his fucked up life.

CHAPTER 17

THE PRESIDENT'S NEMESIS

Except for muted sounds of traffic filtering in through closed windows and drapes, it was quiet in the room. It was also dark. No lights at all. The way she liked it. Especially after arriving home from the bright lights of yet another Washington fund-raiser.

She reached over and touched his chest. "What's the matter, George? Didn't you like the e-mail?"

"I loved it, honey."

"So, what's the problem?"

"Who says there's a problem?"

"I can always tell. You know that." Domenico's wife snuggled closer, put her head on his chest, her hair like a gentle evening breeze from somewhere far away. "It started earlier this evening, before dinner. Something happened today and you need to talk about it."

"You know there are some things it's better not to talk about."

"We're in our bedroom, George. You said from the beginning it was important that you talk to me about things that happen during the day. You said it did you good to get things off your chest." She kissed his chest. "Does it have to do with Montgomery's Chicago visit? You said something about the Chicago visit the other night."

He held her head with one hand and felt the curve of her lower back with his other hand.

She kissed his chest again. "You know me. Mum's the word."

"I know. It's not that. It's just that I'm beginning to wonder if I'm the puppet."

"What do you mean?"

"It's Thorsen from Protective Operations. He tells me things it seems I should do something about, and I'm beginning to wonder if he's trying to get me to do or say something that will affect the election."

"For or against Montgomery?"

"I'm not sure. He's been giving me this line about some poor sap being set up in Chicago. Then he tells me about the FBI checking into it. And of course there's always the dark figure in the background. I get the feeling this kind of thing has always gone on, and in this administration I'm the only one not in on it. Thorsen's got all these contacts and I've got squat."

"You think he's spoon-feeding you."

"Yes."

"And you think his reason might be to make you do something, or to make you *not* do something."

"That's it in a nutshell."

"Didn't my e-mail help you forget?"

"Of course, honey. It always does for a little while. But then reality comes back like it always does."

She slid her hand beneath the top sheet and fondled him. "Speaking of things being hidden under the covers . . ."

"Yeah," he said. "Deflated things."

She left her hand where it was and touched his lips with the fingers of her other hand. "My take on the matter is to leave it alone."

"Why do you say that?"

"Because if you do something about it, you're out in the open. You can't turn back later and say you had no knowledge. But if you do nothing, you can claim you were unaware of the situation and it's Thorsen's word against yours."

"Pretty good advice for not knowing the details."

"I'm a woman. I know these things. Did you see the new bumper sticker for the Haney campaign?"

"Which one is that?"

"Rose knows."

"Clever. They used the term on her Web site a while back. We tried to counter it on our site with, 'Rose knows what?' "

"George?"

"Yes?"

"Do we still hightail out of this town after the election?"

"You're damn right."

"No matter what Montgomery offers?"

"Yes."

They kissed, and outside the traffic on the Capital Beltway moaned.

CHAPTER 18

THE PRESIDENT'S NEMESIS

INSIDE IT FELT like something gnawing, hundreds of pairs of teeth nibbling on vital organs. Not chewing hard, not yet.

Lena sat on the window seat and leaned against the window, leaned the way her play baby used to lean, not moving a muscle. Perhaps the window would give way and she'd take a great fall. *All the king's horses and all the king's men couldn't put her back together again.* As she leaned against the window she could see the glass flex, bowing out like the skin of a bubble. Maybe the smog would slow her fall. Maybe the smog would change into smack.

Jake was gone, out of town two weeks already. He had not called since last week when he said he might be delayed for "some time." She had no idea then that "some time" could be weeks. She thought Jake would be gone a couple extra days until Walter popped in the other day and asked if she needed anything. What she needed Walter could not get her.

She needed cash for smack. Raphael had doubled the price and she was running on empty, using codeine to dull the ache, holding herself together with arms wrapped about her in strait jacket pose.

Living in an ivory tower and she couldn't change the ivory into cash. Credit at shops and restaurants in the building, all the best food, maybe even a dress or two. But Jake, her Jake, had taken the advance off the cards and put a ceiling on the credit so she couldn't buy jewels or a fur coat and hit the pawn shop. In order to get enough to satisfy Raphael, who had already given her a couple thousand in credit, she'd have to sell a truck load of clothes, and a waste of money like that wouldn't sit well with Jake. A mistake like that could put her back on the street. She even looked on the Internet for a connection but couldn't find shit. Yeah, real shit because one of the Web sites she'd sold photos to a couple years back was still using shots of her on their sample page and she wasn't getting a dime for it. She e-mailed the webmaster about it, saying she should be getting royalties. The two-word reply was, "Yeah, right."

So there she sat, staring out the window of her tower, staring northwest toward Hollywood where strangers, rich dudes, were wondering right now if Raphael, that slimy pusher, would get this chick he'd been bragging about to come to the private party for which they were willing to pay dearly.

When she turned to the south she could see the landing lights of planes out over the bay lined up for L.A. International. Any one of those planes could be bringing Jake to her rescue. She had spent two days like this, two days alternately looking out the window, losing herself on the Web, or knocking herself out with sleeping pills.

Raphael had cut her off, had squelched other connections. She'd even called Anita to see if she knew any hookers on the stuff who might be willing to advance her a couple day's worth. But Anita couldn't help except to fix her up with a few tricks. And if she hit the street again, Jake might find out. Put her back on the street permanently. One trick she could cover. Raphael's so-called party for which he had promised her enough smack to

133

hold her until Jake's return. Part of the reason she'd looked up the old Web site with her photos on it was because Raphael said he told the party boys to look there for some shots of her, Raphael's party boys saying they liked what they saw, Raphael saying the guys were young and loaded and willing to pay for an experienced gal who's not on the street. "It's a user-friendly setup," said Raphael. "They seen you on the Web, they're thinkin' mature professional lady with a secret life takin' care of business, which means you'll be in control, Miss Lena. And this way they each chip in a chunk of change and you walk away with the bundle."

She told Raphael she'd think about it.

She considered selling her car, but this would be a sign of weakness Jake would certainly notice. If she sold the car or borrowed money from a shark or did anything to show weakness, to show Jake how much the big H had her . . .

The planes lined up over the bay represented hundreds of people coming home, business travelers back for the weekend, Friday afternoon rush. Agents and movie stars and producers and maybe a man whose business she did not know, maybe Jake.

Before he left on this trip she had overheard another phone call. This one had been in the middle of the night, Jake apparently thinking she was asleep so that he left his study door open. Jake had spoken about votes, telling whoever was on the phone that there were many ways to get votes. They could "change the collective mind of the voting public," he had said. "One incident capitalizing on the media vultures." Later in the conversation she heard bits and pieces in which Jake referred to a man, an unnamed "he" who was to play a role in something. But she couldn't figure out what that something was.

Jake said, "What do you think? A spin here, a nudge there. We can't act brazenly. That's a female trait. I learned not to do that long ago."

Silence, then Jake responded. "Look, you know my past and I know yours. You know this comes from our fathers, and definitely *not* from our mothers, whoever they were. That's all you need to know. Just enough so you'll do your part and I do my part and we all keep our mouths shut."

A pause, then, "Enough said."

Just before she gave up on the one-sided phone call and crept back to bed, Jake said something about "dreams becoming reality." Maybe Jake and whoever was on the phone were dealing in mind benders, LSD, some other test tube stuff, or coke.

She laughed, laughed at the city floating below in its sea of smog, laughed at the planes disappearing down into the smog. Wouldn't it be funny if Jake was a main importer? Bringing everything, including smack, into the country by the ton while his girlfriend in the glass tower is willing to do almost anything for a hit.

Of course there wouldn't be any here. Main supplier never touches or is touched by the stuff. Even if she did suspect there might be some stuff right here under her nose, Jake's study was locked tight when he wasn't in it. The one time Jake had let her in all she saw were books, most of them political, and framed photographs of Republican Presidents. Jake definitely on the neo-conservative side like he said, because during recent campaign coverage she heard him mumble "liberal dick-licker" when a gay congressman was making a speech in support of Rose Adams Haney. Jake had had a few drinks that night and it was the only direct political statement she had heard him make about the campaign. When it came to politics, she had been afraid to butt in, get on his bad side, get her free ride cut off before it got started. Only now the free ride, the months living with Jake in the ivory tower, had cut off all her connections.

The sun eyed her through the smog, made her sneeze when she stared at it. She stood up from the window seat and pushed a button on the wall. The breeze from the closing drapes chilled her. She took three sleeping pills and got into bed. Maybe when she awoke Jake would be there.

But when she woke up that night she was still alone, and even beneath the blankets she shivered, her skin tightened by goose flesh, her insides squeezed empty.

She picked up the phone and called Raphael.

The deal was that she would receive a couple fixes before the party and two grams after. A two-month supply, maybe three months if she stretched it. Yeah, that's always the doper's plan. I'll be good this time and stretch it. Maybe she would this time. Maybe she'd just have to!

Raphael gave her the two initial fixes and the instructions in the park. Raphael would follow in his car to wherever she decided to fix herself. Then she would follow him to the party.

Raphael was hyped up, probably anxious to join the party or simply watch her and the five customers. "Don't forget, my little pretty, big bag of stuff after the party."

Bastard. He knew he was her only supplier. Back in her car, in the dark, she kept one of the capsules out and put the other into the passenger side sun visor, the place she always transported her smack, a razor cut along the inside seam. How long ago had it been? Two years? Should have used the razor on her wrists. No! She'd feel better soon. She'd feel just fine.

When she drove out of the park and saw the gas station on Sunset Boulevard all lit up like an oasis, she could already feel the rush. And, once inside the ladies' room, its floor strewn with toilet paper that had been used to cover the seat, she knew she was home. She knew she would never kick the god-damn habit unless she were locked up. She wept as she sat on the edge of the lidless toilet fixing herself.

The new Lena, the fixed Lena, followed Raphael's Riviera down the Santa Anna Freeway all the way to Anaheim where he drove up and down a few side streets near Disneyland and finally parked in a tourist motel lot. Then Raphael got into her car.

"Drive around a little."

"Why?"

"I thought someone was followin'."

"Yeah, I was following you."

"Do yourself a favor and try not to be smart-assed, Lena baby. The paying customers want experience, but I don't think they want their mom bitchin' at 'em."

Raphael watched out the back window as she drove, but with all the Disneyland traffic—moms and pops and kids going back to motels—there would be no way to tell if they were being followed.

"These clients of yours afraid of media exposure, Raphael?"

"Why you ask?"

"Because it seems like you're going out of your way to protect their iden-tities."

"Yeah. Turn in at that next motel on the right. It's not far from here. We can hoof it."

They waited in the car a few minutes, Raphael watching the cars out on the street. The rush of the fix had passed and she felt normal again, normal enough to wonder, to be careful, to protect herself.

"Before we go you're going to tell me exactly what's planned at this party."

Raphael put his hand on her knee. "Why, Lena baby, you don't got to worry 'bout nothin'. I'll be there. And besides, these dudes're high class, just like you was sayin'."

"If they're so high class, why couldn't they get their own chicks?"

"You know, babe. It's the mystery of it all, an experienced lady who's been off the street for some time. A chick who maybe one day gets it in her head she'd like to try the group thing. Girls they hang out with too stuck up for the group thing."

"Just so they keep their belts in their pants. One of them tries any rough stuff, I skip."

"Relax, babe. I said I'd be there. And don't forget you're supposed to be lookin' forward to this. I got to see horniness oozin'."

"Yeah."

As she walked next to Raphael through the motel parking lots, she could hear kids squealing in the outdoor swimming pools, could smell chlorine and pizza. A day at Disneyland followed by an evening of pizza and a frolic in the pool, dear old dad flipping you into the air, you holding your nose so as not to take in too much water. The childhood that passed her by in Kansas where her parents probably clicked their heels when she ran away because it cut down on expenses so her brothers could go to fuckin' trade school and learn to rebuild fuckin' diesel engines.

She took long steps, the seam of her short skirt riding her thighs, the silk underwear sliding like soft fingers on her flesh. Black panties and bra, garter belt and black stockings, red dress, not too much makeup, hair curled loosely, a mature woman looking for adventure. She would put on the nympho mask, act surprised at her enjoyment, beg for it from the others while one gives it to her. Young men wanting so much to be fooled.

The room was on the second floor. As they walked along the outside balcony with its rows of yellow lights above red doors, cars pulled in and out of the lot below, dads looking up through windshields at her and Raphael, dads wishing themselves out of their cars, their lives, their jobs, their wives and kids.

The door to the room said "Bridal Suite" and she had to laugh.

"Shut up," said Raphael. "You're supposed to be hot."

She got hot, which simply meant putting an expression on her face as though she had a million-dollar diamond hidden beneath her tongue and nobody was supposed to know. She took a deep breath. Soon she'd be the hell out of here with her bags of stuff driving back downtown.

But her act, no matter how she played it, didn't impress the dudes. The room was dark. The faces were dark. Middle Eastern. She thought of terrorists. Before she got her dress off, one of the guys slugged her, her teeth smashing her tongue. She tried acting scared. She tried acting like she enjoyed it. Nothing made any difference. They said nothing. They hit her hard enough to hurt but not hard enough to break bones. They took turns sodomizing her. When they held her to the floor and two of them pissed on her, she dropped the act. "You goddamn queer cock-sucking sand niggers!"

In the corner, in a fog of smoke from cigarette after cigarette, Raphael sat silhouetted against the yellow lighted window. As the bastards went at her, she thought, Raphael must be nervous because he was chain-smoking and she'd never seen him smoke before.

Later—a few minutes or an hour later, she couldn't tell—there was someone else in the room. One of the men screamed. Raphael chattered like an old woman. Someone fell to the floor so hard she could feel the floor lift her backbone. She closed her eyes, rolled into a corner. Someone fell on her and she couldn't breathe. She dreamed of the beach, the endless sand, the cleansing surf. She was being carried by the surf.

She awoke in bed, in *her* bed, in *Jake's* bed. The lamp was on, the drapes closed, no light leaking at the sides. Night. Not a dream. Aches all over, mouth puffy, taste of blood and salt . . . urine.

She got up, saw she was wearing her robe, held the wall as she stumbled to the bathroom where the light was on. She could smell soap, her hair wet and cool at her neck.

Walter stood before the sink looking into the mirror. He opened and closed his mouth, then saw her in the mirror.

"One of your customers connected."

"You followed me. You've been following me all along."

Walter turned. There was blood speckled on his shirt. "It's my job. I do what I'm told."

Her underwear and the torn red dress were on the floor with several towels. The top edge of the mirror was steamed from the shower.

Walter walked past her out of the bathroom. "I'm glad to see you're up and about. I was afraid I'd have to call a doctor." He stopped in the hallway, turned toward her. "Are you all right?"

"Yes. Thank you. I . . ."

Walter waved his hand. "Don't thank me. It's part of my job. To watch over you. And to report back to Mr. Serrantino."

"Must you?"

"Yes."

"He'll be angry."

"Of course. But he would be even angrier if I were not able to tell him how you were bruised." He turned and walked down the hallway. "Your car is in the garage."

She was going to ask about Raphael and the five Middle Eastern men, what condition he had left them in. But then she remembered what they'd done to her and ran to the toilet. As she vomited she heard the door to the apartment click closed.

CHAPTER 19

THE PRESIDENT'S NEMESIS

STANLEY JOHNSON

WEDNESDAY. ALONE. ELECTION news on television. But elections reminded him of the past and he'd turned the sound down. He'd finished his daily stack of mail, thrown most of it away, but added a few of the juicier samples to the stash in his bedroom dresser. At this rate, he'd have to get a larger dresser. While he was at it he should get a computer with a bigger hard drive to store all the babes from the Web browser's cache file. Hard-drive Stan, Stan the Man. Right. The only reason he hadn't thrown away all the sex mail or deleted the files containing images of nude mature women from his computer—so he told himself—was because voyeurism gave him something to do on long weekday afternoons.

He still dated Evie on weekends. Every Saturday night a dinner out, Dutch, then back to her apartment for a slug of crème de menthe and a "quickie," then back home to wait for the next weekend. He had returned Evie's murder magazines without reading them. At first she wanted to know how he liked them. But all he did, all he had to do, was tell her he didn't care for the stories because they reminded him of the past. After that, Evie avoided talking about murders or police cases.

He liked Evie, he really did. But with the dreams he'd been having and the way he'd been feeling lately, he was starting to wonder if he was too much of a dirt bag for her. Too scared to tell anyone about the head in the garbage. So scared he drives himself nuts with nightmares and gawking at pictures of women. Maybe if Evie had a computer he could send her e-mails during the day, long drawn-out e-mails full of passion that she could answer after she got home from work. For a moment he imagined writing to Evie about the beauty of nature, its plants and animals. But this made him think of the phrase *au naturel* and of the photographs of naked women stored on his computer. Sometimes he called Evie on the phone in the evening, but it seemed she was always busy—making dinner, doing dishes, cleaning house, getting ready for the next day at work.

He glanced at the television and saw President Montgomery standing at a lectern, pointing his finger at whoever was in the audience, smiling with that familiar smirk on his face. It was especially noticeable with the sound off. The President leaning forward, lecturing to the imbeciles. Lecturing like he knows better than anyone else and you'd better just go shoot yourself in the head if you can't get with the program. Especially if you're close to collecting Social Security. Better for everyone else if you just shot yourself in the head.

Stan turned and glanced at his gun cabinet against the wall opposite the television. From this angle the television reflected in the glass of the cabinet. President Montgomery leaning forward, jabbing his finger toward some poor bastard who'd probably asked an insane question like, where was the extra money for Social Security supposed to come from?

Stan looked toward the window. The sky was blue, not a cloud in sight. For a moment he considered standing up and looking down into the parking lot at the dumpster enclosure. Instead, he turned back to the television. The President was gone and now two attractive women were on. He picked up the remote and turned up the sound. The two female commentators were discussing the upcoming presidential election between President Montgomery and Senator Rose Adams Haney. He sat forward in his chair, waiting. Soon the women would notice him, quit talking politics and put their mouths where they'd do some good. He leaned back, closed his eyes.

The doorbell rang. At first he thought the doorbell was part of a commercial break, but the two women were still talking. He turned off the television and went to the door.

A tall young man wearing a tan sport coat, creased jeans, suede shoes. A young man with blond hair covering his ears, reminding Stan of "well hung dudes" in outdated sex photos he'd gotten in the mail. The man held a clipboard and pen. His eyes seemed doll-like as he glanced down at the sheet on the clipboard. The man did not blink his eyes, did not shuffle his feet or put his hands in his pockets, and when he finally spoke his voice was self-assured.

"Good afternoon. You're Mr. Johnson, Mr. Stanley Johnson?"

"Yes, what . . .?"

"This won't take long, Mr. Johnson. I'm not selling anything. Just a few questions."

"About what?"

"The upcoming election, Mr. Johnson. I'm canvassing the area for voter turnout. Are you registered to vote?"

He vaguely recalled the last time he'd voted, his wife and son both safe at home when he'd left for work that morning. But when he was called home early from work that afternoon . . . "I don't know if I'm registered or not."

"I can give you the location where you can register."

As the young man pulled a card from his pocket and wrote on it, Stan was reminded of young men who kept their jobs at the lab when he got his early retirement notice. In an instant he recalled the anger he had expressed during coffee breaks back then. He recalled Dr. Steinberg overhearing him in the coffee break room, calling him to his office, saying, "There's nothing I can do, Stan, until we get a President in the White House who knows the value of basic research."

The man handed him the card. "You can register here, Mr. Johnson."

"Why should I?"

The man did not seem nervous, did not try to leave. "We should all vote, Mr. Johnson. In a democracy we all need to take part in the future of the nation, especially in a Presidential election that has the magnitude of this one."

"No President ever did me any good." As soon as he said this he felt stupid, an ordinary jerk with nothing better to say.

"How's that, Mr. Johnson?"

Normally he would have shrugged this off, told the guy he'd rather not discuss it. But there was something about the guy's eyes. Something about the way the guy looked at him. Like he knew him. He felt a rush of adrenaline as he began speaking, and as he spoke wondered why the hell he was bothering with this.

"I was forced to retire early because of a President, pushed out when I was in my fifties. They called it an opt out. As if I had a choice. You should try getting a job when you're over fifty and you tell the interviewer you've been opted out. Sure, I get a retirement check, enough to survive. So why the hell should I complain? I've got a retirement check coming in. And in a few more years . . . If I live that long . . . I'll be able to collect Social Security. Of course, if guys like you wipe out your private accounts investing in oil stocks . . . It all comes down to this. I can't even keep a lousy job in a grocery store because high school kids with pierced body parts need jobs so they can keep their Hondas and Mustangs running!"

The man had the clipboard down at his side and was staring at him. The man's eyes were gray and unblinking like . . . like the eyes of the head in the bag. Eyes that seem to know so much. Eyes he'd seen before.

"Hey, I'm sorry to hear about your bad luck. But that's the point, isn't it? Voting is the only voice you have. The only voice we all have. Our freedom and liberty are depending on us."

Stan felt like he was on a roll now, only he still didn't know why the hell he was bothering. Maybe because he'd just seen Montgomery lecturing someone in the audience. Or maybe it was this young man's smile. Not quite supercilious, but there was something there. Or maybe it was simply the eyes. Those gray eyes.

"What about all the criminals running around loose?" he said. "We send troops into battle where we're not wanted . . . What about the god-damned murderers who get set free? I had a son once. He would've been your age if some bastard hadn't killed him! What about that? What the hell good is voting when something like that can happen? Half the goddamn politicians are crooks!"

The man continued staring at him, the smile fading. "I'm sorry to hear about your son, Mr. Johnson. I can understand your bitterness."

"Who says I'm bitter? I just don't want to vote!"

"I don't mean to argue with you, but I still think you lose something if you don't vote."

"What! My manhood?"

The man simply stared now, no trace of a smile.

He didn't have to prove anything to this man. But the man just stood there. After a moment he motioned around him, at his kitchen, the rest of his small apartment. "Look, this is all I have in the world and it takes most of my retirement check. I can't afford to eat out. I can't even afford a decent car. I have to nurse along an old rattletrap and I don't know how long that will last. But then I suppose you'd say pretty soon I won't be driving anyhow."

"Don't you have any money saved? Nothing of value you can sell?"

The man looked beyond him into the apartment, pointed. "What about those?"

It was the first time the man had taken his eyes off him and this took him aback. "What?"

"In the cabinet. Those guns look valuable."

Stan glanced behind him, realizing that the gun cabinet in the living room was visible through the kitchen doorway. He looked back at the man, was tempted to tell him to mind his own business and slam the door in his face. But the man was looking down now, averting his eyes like an embarrassed kid.

"I'm sorry," said the man. "I should learn to mind my own business. I didn't mean to imply you should sell anything. It's just that I'm kind of a gun collector and the first thing that came to mind was a bargain. I apologize."

"Oh . . . Well . . . It's okay. Actually I've been thinking of selling the guns." All except the .45. He'd keep that for protection.

The man looked up, smiled again. A real smile this time. A damned kid at Christmas. Just like Timmy on his last Christmas morning. "Do you mind if I look at them?"

Stan held his breath as the young man stared at him. He felt a sudden surge of pain at the loss of all those Christmas mornings. Him and Marge up first, anxious to see Timmy's reaction when he comes out and sees the surprises beneath the tree. Surprises like the blue tractor that makes a clicking sound when he pushes it. The tractor he was playing with in the backyard when . . .

"No," he found himself saying. "I guess I don't mind if you look at my guns."

One minute they were talking about voting, the next minute the guy was like a kid in a candy store. Stan took a few deep breaths and tried to forget about past Christmases. What the hell, maybe the guy would offer to buy a gun or two.

The man left his clipboard on the kitchen table and followed him into the living room. After Stan unlocked the gun cabinet, he stood back and watched the man inspect the guns. He hadn't noticed before, probably because the man had been facing him, but now he could see that the man was wide-shouldered and muscular. Even though the man's blond hair was long in back, he could see a thick straight neck like that of an athlete.

"None of these are loaded, are they?"

"Of course not."

The man pulled the shotgun from the rack. "Still, it doesn't hurt to check." He opened the shotgun, looked down the barrel. "This one hasn't been fired or cleaned in quite some time."

"I clean them sometimes, but it's been a while. I'm not really a gun fancier." Maybe his professed ignorance would tempt the man to make an offer. "I bought them quite some time ago from a friend."

"You must have gotten a bargain."

Now the bickering over price and who was being taken advantage of would commence. "No, actually I felt sorry for him. He needed money after *his* retirement. Forced out before I was by another of our fine Presidents."

The man took a white handkerchief from his pocket and wiped at the shotgun's barrel. "If you want these guns to hold their value, you've got to clean them. Some gun oil would help."

The man returned the shotgun to its slot in the cabinet and picked up the .30/06 as if it were a delicate piece of china. He checked the chamber, fingered the stock and barrel. Then he walked close to the front window and took aim at something in the parking lot below, his shoulders rising as he aimed so that the edge of his jacket lifted to his slender waist.

Stan went to the window and looked out, was glad to see that nobody was in the parking lot.

"Nice rifle," said the man. "Well-made. Is the scope adjusted?"

"I think so. The fellow who sold me the guns adjusted it and I haven't changed it since, so I guess it's still adjusted."

"How long ago was that?"

"A long time, maybe twenty years."

"And it hasn't been fired in all that time?"

"Well, just after that I used it a little when I went on this outing with . . . with this shooting club, but not since then."

The man was still aiming out the window. "From up here you could hit pretty much anything down there. Don't worry, I'm just recalling a simpler time, back when I was a kid with a toy rifle, me at the front window of my folk's apartment defending the neighborhood from a third world invasion. Our apartment was up a floor, too. I remember thinking of the place as a kind of fortress. Nobody could get to me as long as I had ammo."

"Yeah. Sure. We all like to remember when we were kids. Hey, look, could you maybe move away from the window? The neighbors, you know . . ."

The man moved back from the window. "Sure, sorry. The kid in me got carried away. I needed a break from the tedium of getting out the vote."

The man continued messing with the rifle and Stan wished he would finish. Pretty soon the guy would pull out a pocket multi-tool and break the

.30/06 down to its components right here on the living room carpet. Stan didn't want to talk about guns. All he wanted was for the guy to make his offer. Anything over fifty bucks and he'd probably go with it.

"Would you like to buy that gun?" Stan finally asked.

The man held the rifle over his shoulder like a hunter walking through tall weeds. "No, Mr. Johnson, no thanks. I just wanted to look at it. And anyway, I've got to get going."

Before gently placing the .30/06 back in the cabinet, the man wiped it thoroughly with his handkerchief. "You really need to keep your guns clean. They'll be more valuable. It's true what they say on those antique shows on television. A simple cleaning. No chemicals, except maybe a little gun oil."

The man walked to the kitchen, picked up his clipboard from the table, and stood by the door. "And you really should vote. It's like hunting. You'll never bag anything if you don't pull the trigger. Pick the moment in history, make your decision, and pull the trigger."

"Uh, yeah . . . Sure."

The man turned, his clipboard held up in both hands just like he had started. "Don't you approve of my analogy?" The man frowned, almost menacing, the muscles in his neck tensed.

"I didn't say that."

"Voting is a form of action. It may seem useless at times, but every vote is like a shot fired in a particular direction. Sometimes the bullet hits the target, sometimes not. The critical thing is that the shot is fired. I use the analogy because of your interest in guns."

"I just happen to have a collection that I got from this guy."

Stan wanted to reach around the man, open the door, but the man blocked the door. He wondered if he was having another early retirement paranoia attack. Another young man outsmarting him, taking advantage of him.

"I assume, Mr. Johnson, you believe in the constitutional right to bear arms?"

Stan thought of a bumper sticker he'd seen. "Support the Right to Arm Bears." He thought of the bullet ripping through his son's body, the gun that did it having more constitutional rights than his son.

"Sure, why not, I guess."

"You guess?"

"Yeah. I'm not an activist or anything, that's all."

The man smiled. It was the smile from earlier. Something there, behind the smile.

"If you do support gun rights, Mr. Johnson . . . If you support those rights and all the other rights we have in this great nation of ours, then you'd do well to cast your vote in the upcoming election. The incumbent has strong views on citizens' rights, *all* citizens' rights. And he'll do what it takes to protect us in this dangerous world. How about if I give you that information on registering?"

"Sure. I'll register."

"I'm glad you're willing to demonstrate pride in your country."

After the man was out the door, Stan threw the registration address into the garbage. He heard voices outside his door in the hall. The young man and a woman. He crept to the door and spied through the peephole's fisheye lens.

The man's back was to him, his shoulders, made even wider by the lens, blocking Stan's view of the woman. The new neighbors across the hall who he'd still not met. The Delaneys, Marion had said, John and Sue. Sue Delaney at home today. Wednesday off, maybe works weekends. He watched as the man stood talking with Sue Delaney, their voices coming through to him as syllables hummed. Could be talking about anything, maybe him. More likely about where the voter registration office is.

Finally the man stepped away and he could see Sue Delaney. She was wearing blue jeans and a red T-shirt. Late thirties or early forties at the most, blond hair, built like a brick shithouse. She stood in the doorway looking straight ahead at his door as the young man pounded down the stairs to the lobby. If Stan's door was open she would be staring at him. The distortion of the fisheye lens accentuated her nose and her breasts. Firm breasts, no bra, nipple bumps. A healthy body. Marion had mentioned aerobics. Sue Delaney stared at his door for perhaps five seconds, then withdrew into her apartment and closed the door. During those seconds Stan memorized her image and imagined Sue Delaney entering a time warp to be with him for the afternoon. Later she'd be back home none the worse for wear with no memory of the few hours she'd spent in Stan's apartment.

He bolted the door and walked to his bedroom. Each step took a year from his age so that by the time he reached the bedroom doorway he was only forty. A man in his prime staring down at Sue Delaney stretched deliciously across the bed. A younger man with gray eyes staring down at Sue Delaney.

Timmy had gray eyes! The child's head had gray eyes! And now he was a young man with gray eyes!

Crazy bastard, he thought. "Crazy fucking bastard," he said out loud.

CHAPTER 20

THE PRESIDENT'S NEMESIS

Aɴ URGENT PLEA to detach himself from the sticky wall of sleep. Arms
and legs disconnected and askew. Pillow squashed beneath him where the
imagined Sue Delaney had been. Phone ringing. He groped his way down the
hallway in the dark, turned on the kitchen light, looked at the kitchen clock.
Almost nine. The afternoon and most of the evening sacrificed to sleep.

"Hello."

"Mr. Johnson?" A deep male voice, not the self-assured voice of the
young man from that afternoon, not the smooth-talking Derek Washington
who had called him collect.

"Who's this?"

"My name is Raymond Youngblood, Mr. Johnson. I've got your name
on this list of retired men. Our organization is called Men in the Middle.
It's not a name I would have chosen. But I have to live with it. Anyway, we're
made up of early retirees looking for work."

Retired. Looking for work. Half-asleep. Stan sat down at the kitchen
table. The man continued.

"I know it's a little late to be calling, but what I've got to say could be very important to you. Many members of our organization have been placed in jobs and we're seeking new members because each of us contributes information about possible leads. We keep extensive files on employers who have track records of hiring men over fifty. We're non-profit, supported by grants and gifts. Women have their groups. This is a group for out-of-work men."

Normally Stan would have hung up on a telemarketer, especially at this hour. But the possibility of a job . . .

"Well, Mr. . . . Mr. . . ." He'd already forgotten the man's name.

"Youngblood. Raymond Youngblood. I realize it's an unusual name at my age, but I've had it for sixty-three years and I don't think I'll change it to Oldblood." Mr. Youngblood laughed and coughed. "So that's it. If you're interested in our organization there's no obligation. All you have to do is fill out a form that tells us what kind of work you're interested in. And by answering questions about former employers and the like, we may get some leads. We've found that employers tend not to rehire their previous employees, but do often hire men who've worked elsewhere. That's where you come in, and that's what Men in the Middle is about. We're a non-profit employment agency and action group for men like you who've been forced into early retirement. We don't have a Web site because that would ruin the way we work. Our goal is to find jobs for men who want to come out of retirement, not younger men who, for the most part, are more computer savvy than us."

"So I don't have to sign anything or pay anything?"

"No indeed. Like I said, we're non-profit. We solicit new members to make our files as extensive as possible. The goal is to find jobs. What was your last job, Mr. Johnson?"

"At a grocery store."

"And before that?"

"At the Joliet Research Lab."

"Yes, I believe we have a couple of other members who once worked at the Joliet Research Lab. It's always a different story with a government job. As with other government labs, the contract for the Joliet Lab has recently been rewritten and that means management has shifted. Because of that we may even be able to get you a job there."

"How can you do that? I already re-applied."

"And what did they say?"

"Something about too much experience for some jobs and not enough for others, the old Catch 22."

"The Men in the Middle organization applies pressure . . . legal pressure . . . in just the right places. If, in fact, we can show an organization, especially a government-funded organization like the Joliet Lab, that they've discriminated . . ."

"You really think there's a possibility you can get me a job back at the lab?"

"We can try. Shall I send you a form to fill out?"

"Well, sure, send me a form. I'd like to read it."

"Of course. You'll see there's absolutely no obligation. We old guys have to stick together. It's the only way we'll get anything done. And now, with the election around the corner, we may get some of our rights back if we get rid of the man in office. I know a lot of people say he's helped us and he's strong on national defense. But that's simply an indication of how good a job the spin doctors are doing. They've even got people believing Social Security benefits have gone up in the last few years, and we both know better than that. All they have to do is give it a name. They call it 'The Stronger Retirement Initiative' and we all think we're getting more, when actually we're getting less. It's just like that 'Clear Skies Initiative.' In that case the only skies that remained clear were the skies over the resorts frequented by the executives who cashed in. I've started collecting my Social Security, Mr. Johnson, and in not so many years you'll get yours. It may look fine now, but wait until inflation and private accounts for younger workers take hold. Benefits will sink faster than a guy with cement shoes because the current administration has knuckled under to big business. Why do you think our nation is so divided? Energy companies and credit card companies run the show. I hold President Montgomery personally responsible."

"You do?"

"Of course I do. I have my sources. Do you realize there is even a movement in the works to abolish the twenty-second amendment?"

"The twenty-second . . .?"

"Yes. Enacted in 1951. The amendment that limits the President to two terms. If the twenty-second amendment were abolished, and if Montgomery won his second term, who knows where it would end?"

Youngblood spoke more quietly. "I know people in Washington. Folks who work as lobbyists know exactly what's going on, but they can't say anything because if they do . . . Believe me, Mr. Johnson, this administration doesn't give a damn about our age group. We're being sacrificed. Montgomery cares only about the men in his generation who've made it, oil men among them. We've got to fight the system. Putting pressure on business is what Men in the Middle is about. Next year, if we get this President out of office, things will be different. But we can't assume that will happen. Money talks, and Montgomery has the backing of oil money and Wall Street. Don't rock the boat no matter whose head gets lopped off. I'll send you a Men in the Middle application form. If you'll just give me your mailing address . . ."

Although Stan felt a little uncomfortable about the last part of Youngblood's speech, he gave his address. He did not want to become involved in politics, but he did want a job. Before Youngblood hung up he said something very strange.

"One more thing, Mr. Johnson. In our society, people fall through the cracks all the time. Some disappear without a trace. You've seen photographs of missing children. They put photographs of missing children on tollbooths and the backs of trucks. We hear about children all the time because they have parents who want to find them. But what about others? What about me or you? If you disappeared do you think there'd be a massive search? I'm sorry. Don't answer that. Sometimes I get carried away because of things my friends in Washington tell me. Things so bizarre I don't dare repeat them. Some day I wouldn't be surprised if they chop off our heads when we hit fifty-five and use us for fertilizer."

Although what Youngblood had said startled him, Stan laughed when Youngblood laughed, waited for him to finish coughing, then said good-bye and hung up.

Stan sat staring at the phone. Crazy. The world was full of crazy old bastards. Maybe everyone had gotten paranoid after Nine-Eleven, and as all these paranoid bastards aged . . .

The comment about missing children and chopping off heads had really been odd. Or was it? He couldn't help picturing his own head in a plastic garbage bag. Worms crawling in and out of his skull in the trapped heat of a dumpster. He wondered if there was a connection between the government and the men who'd put the head of the child in the dumpster. Black unmarked limos and sport utes with oversized wheels and spotlights. But more than likely the mob also drove vehicles like that. Huge sport utes so hit men simply ran people down instead of bothering with assault weapons. But why would anyone throw the head of a child into the garbage, then stick around and show up at the same spot night after night?

If he had called the police, would Inspector Jacobson have been put on the case? Inspector Jacobson who questioned him and Marge concerning their whereabouts during every minute of the day Timmy disappeared. Maybe he'd never stopped being a suspect. Maybe that's why Inspector Jacobson had spent so much time with him. If Inspector Jacobson were to question him now, what kinds of questions would he ask?

"Why did you go out and retrieve a bag of garbage, Stan? That's what puzzles me."

"Because of the way those men put the bag into the dumpster, and the fact that they wore suits and had large vehicles."

"Men who drive large vehicles and wear suits have garbage, Stan."

"I know that. I thought maybe it was money or something."

"Most people don't make a habit of throwing money away."

"I thought maybe it was counterfeit or something."

"Then why didn't you call the police? Why didn't you let us see what was in the bag? Would you have tried to spend counterfeit money? Is that what you want me to believe?"

"Yes, I guess so."

"Not a very good alibi, is it, Stan?"

The police would have researched his entire life. They would have gotten his personnel file from the lab. And what would they have seen? "Good worker, but had trouble adjusting after the death of his wife and son." Or maybe there was something in his file about Terri, the girl who had befriended him, the girl who had no idea why anyone would call him a cradle robber. Maybe his personnel file contained a note, "Stanley Johnson was known as Dirty Old Man Stan during his last several years at the lab."

Was someone trying to frame him? Maybe someone from his past had gotten into a position of power. Someone sitting behind a desk in an agency office under the broad banner of Homeland Security. If that were true, there wasn't much he could do about it except mind his own business and not get involved. If he could get a job, maybe through this Men in the Middle organization, things would be different. He'd been much better off when he had a job. Sitting around the apartment all the time was nothing but trouble. Even all this thinking was crazy. A sane person would have convinced himself by now that the head wasn't real. He had to get busy. Do something, anything, instead of sitting in front of his television or gawking at naked women on his computer. Maybe he should use the Web for something constructive, act his age instead of rotting away in his apartment like someone in his eighties or nineties. Find a job using his computer instead of saving images of women over forty, so many images he couldn't remember having saved them, even though he probably had. How else could they have gotten there?

Or maybe he *could* be interested in guns. The young man this afternoon had said his guns were worth something. All they needed was a good cleaning. He decided to go to the all-night convenience store down the road and get a gun magazine, find one that had something about cleaning guns. He put on a jacket, and just as he walked through the kitchen the doorbell rang.

Marion stood in the doorway wearing a tight pair of black slacks and a red sleeveless blouse with a deep vee neck. She held a jacket and a bottle of gin in one hand, and a bottle of tonic water and a lime in the other hand.

"Hi, Stan. I know it's a little late, but I just thought I'd drop by. I had to ring your doorbell with my nose."

Marion walked past him toward the kitchen sink.

"Uh, sorry I got sick at your place the other night, Marion. I guess that was a couple or a few weeks ago."

"It's okay, Stan. I didn't feel so good either the next day, probably the twenty-four hour flu that's been going around. Anyway, I've been busy, busy, busy lately. But I'm free tonight and I don't have to go into the office until tomorrow afternoon. I thought if we sipped our drinks instead of gulping them like a couple of winos . . ."

As she put her armload down on the cupboard, the lime rolled to the sink and splashed into the dirty dishwater.

"Oops! You little bugger. Get the ice and glasses, Stan. I'll wash off the lime."

Marion held the lime under running water, stared out the window over the sink. "It's getting dark earlier these days, isn't it?

"Yes, it is," he said.

Marion rubbed the lime vigorously with a dishtowel, at the same time squinting out into the darkness as if she were a pitcher watching for a sign from the catcher at home plate. When she finished drying the lime, she turned, put the lime to her pink lips, and kissed it.

"There, good as new."

He made love to Marion that night. Or, more precisely, she made love to him. They did it on the living room floor, boozed up with several gin and tonics.

Afterward, they got back into their clothes, turned the lights back on, lounged on the sofa, giggled for a while, then took turns counting their heartbeats by fingering their carotid arteries. Stan brought out some crackers and cheese spread with a recent expiration date he'd managed to salvage from the back of the refrigerator. After munching these for a while, the effects of the gin and tonics began wearing off.

Marion talked about different tenants, about how some apartments are kept clean and some are filthy, about how some people stick their garbage out in the hallway as if they expect someone else to carry it out to the dumpsters, about one tenant who lined up a row of Haney-Ingersoll signs along Elmwood Drive near the entrance to the apartment complex making it look like the entire complex supported the Democratic ticket. Marion saying that, although she didn't like to discuss politics, she would be voting for the Montgomery-Nelson ticket because she and her husband—"God rest his soul."—had always been staunch Republicans.

While Marion spoke, Stan sobered up and began thinking about Evie. If Evie were here he could tell her about Mr. Youngblood and his Men in the Middle, about the young man who looked at his guns, about his strange day. He could not tell Marion about his day. And now he wondered, as Marion continued, what Evie would do if she knew about Marion.

Evie had never revealed who she would be voting for in the upcoming election. Evie would never say, "I usually don't like to discuss politics, but . . ." During all the time he knew her, Evie had been a good listener. He'd never be able to talk to Marion about the death of his wife and son. He'd never be able to tell Marion about the things that had happened to him because he was certain she would make all kinds of suggestions about him becoming more active and joining clubs. And what that really meant, what she would really be thinking, is that perhaps the death of his wife and son was his fault, or at least partially his fault because he'd let it happen.

It was the story of his life. Things happening to him instead of him doing something. Falls asleep dreaming about his next door neighbor who he's never met, and Marion shows up and kisses a lime. So what does he do? He proves he's too weak to say no. Can't simply have a drink, say thanks, say goodnight. He wondered what Marge would have been like at middle age had her husband cared enough to console her, to ask how she felt, to do something that would change everything. By doing nothing he had committed the greatest sin of omission. By doing nothing he was sinking into a vast cesspool of guilt. By doing nothing, he really might be better off dead. So, there it was, a purpose for the guns, a reason to clean them.

When Marion stopped talking he nodded, even though he had not been listening. He smiled, even though he knew it was a fake smile. He even reached out and touched her shoulder. Through her blouse he could feel heat and moisture. Life. At least she was alive. At least she thought enough to come visit him. He, on the other hand, deserved everything that had ever happened to him. Instead of being honest, instead of telling Marion that he was already dating Evie, he had felt sorry for himself and let Marion seduce him. And now, as he stared at Marion, he wished he could apologize, but knew this would only hurt her.

Hurting people. It was the one thing he was really good at.

CHAPTER 21

THE PRESIDENT'S NEMESIS

"DID YOU HAVE to kill him?"

"I didn't kill him."

"You *had* him killed. It's the same thing."

"You would have been killed if Walter hadn't intervened."

She sat on the bed, looked at herself in the vanity mirror. A forlorn little girl wearing a ruffled white nightdress, hands folded on her knees, hair still mussed from sleep. But the black eye and fat lip and sore rectum resulting from the gang rape did not at all fit the picture she wanted to see in the mirror.

Jake had not touched her since his return home. He simply came home the night after she'd been beaten, got into bed beside her, said, "Walter told me what happened," and went to sleep. She had been too frightened to say anything. The next day Jake went out and came back later in the evening, again crawling into bed and sleeping. And this morning, when she saw the news of Raphael's death on television . . .

Jake spoke to her from his bathroom, his voice muted by the clothes hanging in his walk-through closet. "Have you composed yourself yet?"

When she didn't answer, he came back into the room buttoning a dress shirt. "Did you hear me, Lena?"

"I heard you."

"And?"

She remained silent, assuming Jake wanted her to beg forgiveness. But then he did something that made her weep. He sat beside her on the edge of the bed, touched her knee, and said, "They were pretty rough on you."

They hugged and he held her for a long time as she sobbed like a baby.

Later, when she admitted addiction was the reason she'd gotten in trouble, Jake made her talk about it.

"So you went through a withdrawal episode?"

"I don't know if I went all the way through. But it was pretty close."

"And you really want to kick it?"

"Yes."

"I'll help you."

"You could have a younger girl if you wanted. A girl without a habit."

"I want you."

"I won't be able to go cold turkey."

"I've arranged for a supplier." He stared at her in the mirror. "But you must be totally honest with me. When you need it, when anyone needs it that bad, you can't trust yourself."

"What should I do?"

"I'll do it. I've assigned Walter to get the supply and ration it out. A physician I know has given me a program. Eventually, he'll switch you over to methadone."

The diamond necklace felt cool on her skin. Three new outfits and a new bathing suit were back in the apartment unwrapped, hung up in her closet.

After shopping, Jake dismissed Walter and they went out alone in her car. They drove down the coast and ate in a restaurant near San Clemente where they could watch the sun set beyond Catalina Island. Just like in the movies, the haze and fog had cleared and the sun shimmered on waves stretching to the horizon. She felt a mild rush even though her last fix had been hours earlier. For the first time in years she thought she might live to be an old lady. Back on the street she had never had such a dream, had never even wished it.

Jake, normally stern and businesslike, seemed relaxed at dinner. After dinner it grew dark and Jake lit the glass-enclosed candle in the center of the table. The restaurant was nearly empty, most of the guests having moved to the lounge where a flamenco guitarist played. Jake ordered brandy, candlelight danced on the white tablecloth as they spoke.

"I haven't felt this relaxed in a long time, Lena. There always seems to be something to take care of. Perhaps my age is beginning to show."

"You're not old, Jake."

He waved his hand, smiled. "No, let me talk. I've not done much of that. I've not told you who I am, what I'm about. I feel I should.

"You see, Lena, I'm a fighter. Not the way you've had to be a fighter. I'm referring to causes, beliefs. Everyone has them, but few devote their existence to them. Clergymen think they do, but most of that is nonsense. True causes are far-reaching with worldwide significance."

The orange of the sunset glowed on Jake's face as he smiled at her.

"Don't worry, Lena. As I've said in the past, I'm not a terrorist. If you need a label, I guess you could say I'm a conservative. But there are conservatives, and then there are conservatives. The question is, what deserves being conserved?"

Jake took a sip of brandy, then continued

"You've heard the term 'powers that be.' Most people think of the current resident in the White House, or leaders in congress, or members of the cabinet, especially the Secretary of State. But it's an illusion . . . the power, that is. True power is in the background, has always been in the background. Man or woman, Republican or Democrat, the power is in the background. It's always easier to see this in retrospect. Take John F. Kennedy, for example. While in office he appeared to be his own man, no strings attached except those of his family, and perhaps his religion. But now that we know so much about him, now that we know about some of the hundreds, or perhaps thousands, who associated with him behind the scenes, an entirely different image emerges.

"There's always another layer deep within the workings of a nation that cannot be penetrated, but has tremendous power. Not the so-called power we're spoon-fed on the evening news. Not the handpicked advisors or heads of security agencies. True power operates within an entirely different time scale. Its time scale is in decades rather than twenty-four-hour sound bites."

Jake took another sip of brandy, looked out the window where the last light of dusk hung above the sea.

"I've never been in the armed forces. I wanted to. Oh, how I wanted to join up. My father got me out of it. I'm not sure exactly how he did it, my status never made it up to 1-A even though others coming out of graduate school with me were drafted. Ironic that I never went to Vietnam, even though I was perfectly willing.

"I never knew my mother. I did some checking a few years back and found out she was a showgirl. I guess there were a lot of showgirls sleeping around with my father's associates. My parents weren't married. The man everyone thought to be my father when I was a kid was actually a stepfather. Or, rather, I considered him a stepfather. Not really a stepfather because he was not married to my mother. No one married my mother."

Jake continued staring out the window, took another sip of brandy before continuing.

"When I was in school I was looked down upon because my stepfather was rich. My father died when I was in my twenties. My stepfather died shortly thereafter. Many men have come and gone. Today the modern media sees to it that those in the limelight are written off when they are accused of something, anything. That's why I've chosen to work underground."

Jake turned from the window and laughed. "I'm babbling. You must think I'm foolish."

"How can you say that, Jake? After what I've done, after what I've put myself, and you, through, how could *you* be foolish? If anyone's a fool, I am."

Jake reached across the table, put his hand on hers. "The only one you've ever hurt is yourself. You've sacrificed your body to a society ready to eat you up. And they nearly did. You're too trusting for this society, Lena. We both are."

"I've never heard you talk like this, Jake. You must have been burned pretty badly when you were young."

Jake smiled. "You're very observant. I started out a normal boy. An all-American kid." He stared out the window again. "Once upon a time, when I was a vulnerable young boy in junior high, I became infatuated with a girl in my class. She said she loved me and no one else. I trusted her. I trusted everyone. Then one day my best friend took her away. But that wasn't all.

I was humiliated in front of the entire student body. One of the reasons I've carried that memory with me all these years is because it happened the day President Kennedy was shot." Jake paused, stared at her. "I've gone on much too long. It must be the brandy."

"We all remember the day Kennedy was shot," said Lena. "At least that's what they say."

Jake reached out, put his hand on hers. "I know. Tell me again what you remember, Lena. Only this time be more specific, as I've been."

Lena looked out the window as she spoke, unable to look Jake in the eye. "It was on the farm. I was only three years old. My father came in from the fields on his tractor to tell the news to my mother. He had a radio on the tractor. I remember the radio on the tractor turned up full blast. At the time I didn't realize what was happening. It was only later, when I was maybe six or seven, that I was able to grasp what the memory meant. It was one of the only pleasant memories I have of my father. Imagine that, the day J.F.K. is shot one of my most pleasant childhood memories."

"Your father abused you?" asked Jake in a whisper.

She turned from the window, surprised to see that her eyes were clouded with tears when she looked at Jake. "Yes."

"Is your father still alive?"

"No."

"When he died, did you feel relief?"

Any other time in her life she would have said no. Even to Anita she had said that her father's death had provided no relief. Perhaps she had given this answer again and again through the years to herself. A lie.

"Yes," she said finally. "I felt relief when my father died."

When they left the restaurant, Jake said that rather than staying the night at his San Clemente cottage, he needed to return to L.A. so he would be fresh for a morning appointment. As Lena drove them back to L.A., the sea breeze whipped about in the Miata. Once on the freeway she put the Miata in fifth gear and put her arm around Jake. He fell asleep on her shoulder and probably dreamed he was a boy again, out on a date with the girl who said she would be true to him.

Jake was not in bed. A light shown from the hall. She rolled to his side and breathed from his pillow, smelling his aftershave and the sharp scent of their lovemaking. At first she thought Jake's last words to her had been part of a dream. But as she breathed deeply from Jake's pillow she knew he had said it. He had said, "I love you," just before going to sleep.

She put on her nightgown and went into the hallway. The light was coming from Jake's study and she could hear his voice. Rather than listen in she stood in the doorway.

Jake sat at his desk in his robe. He put his hand over the phone's mouthpiece. "Get me a cup of coffee, would you, Lena?"

When she came back with his coffee she expected Jake to motion her to leave. Instead, he took the coffee from her and motioned her to sit. She sat in the leather sofa, the cushions exhaling a sweet aroma that reminded her of saddles and the fact that as a girl she, like all girls at one time or another, loved horses. But the smell also reminded her of something else. A dark barn, the night her father forced her against a saddle draped over one of the stalls and told her she was no longer a little girl and proved it by raping her. She remembered running back to the house, lying in bed with her play-baby, wishing she could be little again and that her father would come and ask if she wanted a ride on the tractor.

Jake swiveled in his chair, facing the side wall as he spoke on the phone, facing the portrait of Ronald Reagan that hung there.

"Yes, I know. Are you sure he'll be there? You take care of your end and we'll have our man ready. He's pretty well set but we'll give him a final treatment."

Jake turned in his chair, smiled at her while he continued talking on the phone. "No inkling at all. We've monitored everything and he's made no unusual contacts." He sat forward, pulled the telephone base closer. "Yes, when it's over everything that's happened will be erased. All the i's have been dotted." Then he hung up.

The chair squeaked as Jake leaned far back, staring at her from behind his desk, sipping the coffee she had brought. He put the cup down.

"Did you understand anything I said?"

"Not really. Just that some guy is being set up for something."

"Very observant, Lena. Not just any guy. A very special person. Years ago it became obvious he could be used someday. That time has finally come. Even though he's being used, you cannot feel sorry for him because what happens to him now is for the greater good. He'll do something for all of us and won't even know the full ramifications. Sounds like a plan, don't you think?"

"Sure, I guess."

"Of course it is. Two birds with one stone, as they say."

"You mean like getting rid of Raphael?"

"Close. His being gone I'm sure won't do any harm to society. But this man is more of a pawn, has been one all his life. The trick is to find strength in weakness and to cover all the bases."

Jake looked toward the window, which was covered by thick drapes. "Stay in the background and pull the right strings. Anyway, what I wanted to say was that whatever happens to this man, it's something that was bound to happen one way or another."

"I'm not sure I understand, but it sounds okay."

Jake laughed, came and sat next to her on the sofa. "I'm sorry, Lena. This isn't fair, I know. But it's complicated and I think it best not to fill you in on all the details. You mentioned recently, though, that you wanted to help me."

"Of course I do."

"I may not need your help right now, but I have to be certain you're ready just in case. I'll know more next week."

Jake put his arm around her and stared into her eyes. "I was touched deeply last night when you spoke of being abused by your father, Lena. In a way I, too, was abused by my father. Not physically. Psychologically. My abuse was never having been allowed to know him. I found out he was my father after his death. He was killed by someone he knew in his own home, someone he'd invited in for dinner. But forget about my father. You've shared your past with me, and now I realize that the abuse you suffered was a thousand times greater than mine. But at least in one way you've healed quickly."

"How is that?"

"The black eye." Jake kissed her eye. "It's almost gone."

They made love on the leather sofa, the smell and the feel of leather against her skin heightening her pleasure so that for the second time that night she had an orgasm, a real orgasm, not an orgasm faked like she'd done so many times before she met Jake.

She felt, for the first time, like a mature woman instead of a lovemaking machine. She felt needed. And as she lay next to Jake that night, she vowed to kick the damn habit and make of herself a woman Jake could trust and love forever.

Emilio was on his own behind the bar at the Three-Peat Club. It was past four in the morning and the club was quiet, only a few patrons scattered at the tables. When Mr. Serrantino came into the club Emilio immediately recognized him and nodded toward the alcove where Walter waited at their private table.

During the past couple of weeks, Mr. Serrantino and his chauffeur had been meeting quite often early in the morning at the club. Emilio wondered about this, wondered why the boss wouldn't just have his chauffeur come up to his pad or call him if he wanted to tell him something. But Emilio learned a long time ago that, when it came to Mr. Serrantino, it was best that he mind his own business and keep his mouth shut. He hadn't even told Sheila, the head bartender, about Mr. Serrantino and Walter meeting down here early in the morning. After all, Sheila was the one who'd taught him the ropes, and part of the ropes in this place was keeping your nose out of what the big boss did or didn't do at the Three-Peat Club.

The alcove was dark, the candle on the table out. Walter sipped his beer and Jake nursed a glass of ice water with lime Emilio had brought without asking. They had stopped talking when Emilio came into the alcove, but now that Emilio was gone they resumed.

"You did the right thing," said Jake. "If not for her sake, then for my sake."

"I know you're fond of her," said Walter.

"Yes, that's true. But also, I've begun to formulate ways she may be able to help. She's becoming part of my backup plan should things turn sour in Chicago."

"I thought the men in Chicago could be counted on."

"They can be counted on, Walter. But things don't always turn out as planned. We live in an imperfect world."

"Especially when your plan includes one man's reaction to outside stimuli . . . Is that it?"

"That's part of it."

"And you're positive you can trust her to help if things turn sour?"

"I'm not *positive* about anybody. Not her, not you, not even myself. We're all human."

Walter smiled. "Something you picked up from your father?"

Jake smiled back. "As I've said in the past, it's best we avoid discussing my father. But if you like, yes, it might very well be something I picked up from him."

"I didn't mean to discuss your father, I simply wanted to allude to his situation. Was he killed by a friend he trusted, or was he killed by his failure to evaluate his own judgment?"

"Very good, Walter. But let's get back to the situation at hand. I'm fond of her, I admit it. She's fond of me, and wants to do what she can to help. What's wrong with that?"

"What's wrong with it, Mr. Serrantino, is that she's still a product of the street."

"Once from the street, always from the street. Is that it?"

"Right."

They sipped their drinks in silence for a moment. Then Jake continued.

"Walter, I want you to take care of her habit exactly the way we discussed except for one detail."

"What's that?"

"Rather than reducing the doses, keep them the same for a while."

"Should I tell her they're the same?"

"No. Tell her the doses are being gradually reduced."

"And the purpose of this?"

Jake smiled. "The purpose is to allow her to be in peak form should we need her for the backup plan."

"And after that?"

"After that we'll see." Jake reached out and clasped Walter's shoulder. "*Coppish?*"

Walter smiled broadly. "*Coppish*, Mr. Serrantino."

CHAPTER 22

THE PRESIDENT'S NEMESIS

"I'M SORRY BUT Dr. Todd's not available."

"Not available?"

"The doctor's had an automobile accident. Not that serious, but he'll be in the hospital for a few days. His colleague, Dr. Erickson, can see you."

"But I've never seen him."

"Her, Mr. Johnson. Dr. Erika Erickson. According to my records you haven't been to see us for quite some time. Dr. Erickson is quite capable."

"I wanted to see Dr. Todd."

"Like I said, Mr. Johnson, I'm afraid that's impossible for a few days at least. I can call you when he's available, or I can set up an appointment with Dr. Erickson."

"No. I'll wait."

Something was wrong. Everything was wrong. He was sleepwalking again. This morning he had awakened in the living room, the chair in which he slept pulled up to the front window. But he knew he had fallen asleep in bed. And he was dressed, his slacks and a shirt put on over his pajamas.

His feet were dirty. The bottoms of his feet looking like he might have gone outside. When he went into the hallway, he could see that the safety chain on the entry door in the kitchen was dangling free and tried to recall if he had put the chain lock in place the night before.

He walked through the kitchen to the door. The floor was gritty even though he was sure he had swept it yesterday. He reached out to check the doorknob, then reminded himself that it was always locked to the outside. Yes, at least he could be assured that the doorknob was locked. He lifted the chain lock and slid it home, imagining as he did so that he was making it even harder to escape quickly should someone be in the apartment with him. He turned slowly and stared at the hallway, listening. He heard something, a whining, then concluded it was the whine of the plumbing, someone in another apartment running water.

He went into the bedroom and lay down. He closed his eyes and tried to remember, tried to imagine himself getting out of bed, getting dressed.

The closet door had banged his toe. He did recall that. No, the door didn't bang his toe, he banged his toe on the door. He had gotten up in the middle of the night and kicked the closet door. The hallway light had been on though he knew he'd shut it off. He followed a man down the hallway. Not a man. A pig. Man's body, pig's face.

The dream again. All of them assembled in his kitchen. The pig, the steer, the eagle. More filling out his name on cards, more soldering circuit boards, more pain in his head.

He opened his eyes, saw the day-lit ceiling of his room. Not a dream now. He was remembering, thinking back, analyzing like Dr. Todd would have him do. Poor Dr. Todd. Poor Jimmy Carter. He closed his eyes.

He is standing before a mirror. His reflection rather vague. No, it's a window. His front window. Night. Vehicle lights below. A limo and a sport ute. Something in his hands. Something long connecting his hands together. When one hand moves the other moves. He looks down. A rifle, one of his guns, the .30/06 with its scope. The gun the young man pointed outside where men now stand next to the limo. One man is holding up his arm and in his hand is something. Something.

A light flashes on. He is looking through the gun scope. The head. The child's head is there. The man is holding the child's head up by the hair and people are cheering somewhere and blood is dripping. The man is smiling, a perpetual leering smile. A disdainful, mocking smile. The man's face is a mask. A mask of a man. Ears and nose too large, lips too thin, chin too long. Eyes—real eyes—stare from cutout holes. The crosshairs jump and the pain that had been there is gone.

He opened his eyes. It was dark. Or was he dreaming he was opening his eyes?

He opened his eyes again and saw the ceiling. He got out of bed. Dizzy. Sick. He ran to the bathroom holding the walls.

Hot tea and toast. His kitchen silent. So silent that someone could be behind him. And if he turned they would simply stay out of his line of sight by scurrying about the kitchen. After taking several sips of tea and a couple bites of toast he took the cup and plate to the sink. He held onto the counter with one hand and inspected the bottom of one foot. He poked at what looked like tiny fibers. One stuck to his finger and he inspected it in the light from the window. He opened one of the cupboards, pulled a small dish from the top shelf. The dish contained green fibers he had gathered from his kitchen floor. It was the dish he'd put on the top shelf what seemed like ages ago, but it really wasn't that long ago. He deposited the piece of fiber with its brothers in the small dish and put the dish back on the top shelf.

The dreams last night had been too complicated. At one point Uncle Jack had been there giving him a Dutch rub, making his scalp burn. And then in another part of the dream, or in another of many dreams, he and the young man wearing a tan sport coat, creased jeans, suede shoes—the young man with gray eyes—sat on his living room floor cleaning all his guns.

In the bathroom he washed his face several times. In the mirror he looked the same as always.

Dreams. His brain dumping its contents into a vat to be stirred. His brain an enormous cache file that has saved the debris of his miserable life.

If only he could talk with someone. Dr. Todd, a priest, anyone. He'd tell about the dreams, the vehicles, the child's head. He'd tell about Marge and Timmy. He'd tell how Marge's eyes had looked when he found her dead on the bathroom floor. Marge's eyes greenish-gray, not gray like Timmy's had become after he'd outgrown his infant eyes, not gray like the young man who'd admired his guns, not gray like the head in the bag. He'd tell about how he got his Dirty Old Man Stan nickname. He'd tell about Johnny Tate and Tammy. He'd tell about his lousy attic room in Uncle Jack's house where Tammy deflowered him. He'd tell about how Tammy let it slip at school and how word got around about him and Tammy and how Johnny Tate swore he'd get even. He'd tell about his suspicions that the thugs who hauled him downtown in 1968 so he'd be arrested as a protester were put up to it by Johnny. Put up to it by Johnny years after junior high, years after he'd sworn he'd get even. If only he could talk with Dr. Todd again. Those good old days when they'd talk about good old days when he was a kid, the two of them finding things to pin the guilt on. Just like Pin the Tail on the Donkey. Dr. Todd, who seemed to want to pin lots of things on Johnny Tate. Dr. Todd, who said this would ease his guilt. Except if his past could make him feel guilty now, then everything he did now was just another past that would make him feel even guiltier in the future. So guilty he'd probably explode.

As he stared at his face in the bathroom mirror he imagined his eyeballs exploding from their sockets, smashing into the mirror like tomatoes thrown at passing trains when he was a kid. An old man riding in one of the coaches looking out the window and seeing the flash of red, the wind-driven pulp and seeds oozing down and back as the train sped onward, relentless as time. An old man scared shitless, maybe even getting a heart attack later that night because some kid in a field along the tracks doesn't realize he'll be old someday. Unless, that is, someone puts a bullet through his heart before he can ever meet that girl he was supposed to have met if the universe had gone the way it was supposed to have gone. Maybe a girl who'd grow up to be President someday so that he'd be First Man and invite his tottering parents to Rose Garden parties. "A Rose in the Rose Garden," a bumper sticker he'd recently seen.

He blinked his eyes. Too much thinking.

"Sometimes too much thinking isn't good," Dr. Todd had once told him. "Sometimes you've just got to get out of the house and do something."

Bud's IGA seemed crowded for a Thursday afternoon, almost as crowded as the days before the meat scare. The electronic registers beeped as checkers pulled bar-coded items across the laser windows, fingers flashed on keys when un-bar-coded items arrived, printers churned out receipts, baggers with pierced body parts asked if customers wanted paper or plastic. The plastic bags had a barely perceptible airy sound, the stiff brown paper bags crackled as packers stuffed them with rattling cans. Shopping carts clanged against one another like muffled bells.

Bud was in the produce aisle supervising a part-time boy stocking bananas. The kid had no body piercing that Stan could see and he wondered if this was why the kid was back here in the store instead of bagging up front with the rest. Bud an old-fashioned guy, giving the kid precedence simply because he has no body piercing visible. If Timmy had lived, perhaps he would have worked here, saved money for college, gotten a good job, a wife, grandchildren by now, babies bounced on his knee. He wouldn't have cared if Timmy's kids pierced their ears, noses, lips, tongues.

Bud finished with the kid and walked up the aisle toward him, his round blemish-free face smiling, his hands straightening his tie, the sleeves rolled up on his white shirt.

"How's it goin', Stan? Haven't seen you in a while."

"I'm okay, Bud." A lie. A way into a conversation in which he would plead for a job. But he had to act fast before Bud ran off.

"On the other hand, there's one thing I really need. I suppose you can guess what that is." The words, as he said them, sounded foolish, his voice somewhat shrill.

"I can't hire anyone now, Stan. In a few weeks maybe, but not now. I'm still keeping you in mind, though."

They were standing next to the potato bins. He had to wait while Bud helped an old woman put a ten-pound bag into her cart.

He cleared his throat, lowered his voice. "Well, since you're thinking of hiring again, how about signing me up today? Just a couple days a week would be fine. I've got experience and I'm willing to work limited hours. When things pick up I can work more hours. You could use someone like me on a busy day like this."

Bud had a straight-lipped look on his face now, stepped sideways around the potato bins, headed toward the swinging doors to the back room, said hello to another customer, smiled again, then led the way through the doors into a section of the back room stacked high with canned goods. In the back room Bud's smile was gone. He never smiled in the back room, no customers there.

"Listen, Stan. I said I'd keep you in mind. That's the best I can do."

"But I'd like a yes or no, Bud. I've been waiting a long time."

Bud couldn't keep still. He stooped to the floor and picked up a torn-off cardboard box flap.

"So, you've been waiting a long time, have you, Stan? Well, I've been waiting a long time for business to pick up. Sure, it looks busy today. But we still haven't recovered from that damned meat scare. And now there's that new Wal-Mart. I can't hire anybody right now and that's that."

"Then the answer is no?"

Bud refused to look him in the eye and instead folded and unfolded the cardboard flap he'd retrieved from the floor. "For now it is. I can't guarantee anything, Stan. My advice is that you look around somewhere else. Now if you don't mind, I've got work to do."

Instead of leaving the back room, Stan stood his ground.

Bud turned, tucked the cardboard flap he'd been folding and unfolding between two tall stacks of canned goods cases that swayed dangerously. Then Bud turned back to him. "Goddamnit, Stan! I said . . ."

One of the stacks began falling. The top cases breaking away from the stack like a squadron of fighter planes breaking off in slow motion. Stan had been busy thinking of a response, and before he could say watch out, the cases hit the floor behind Bud. A couple of the cases exploded open and cans flew across the floor and into the far wall. Bud almost knocked him down getting out of the way.

"Jesus Christ! Why didn't you tell me they were falling? I could've been killed!"

Bud kicked a spinning can of peas across the floor and it skidded beneath the swinging doors and out into the store.

"But, Bud. I didn't see . . ."

"You didn't see! You didn't know! Get the hell out of here, Stan! Leave me alone!"

Bud paused at the swinging doors a second. The anger disappeared from his face and he smiled as he pushed through.

After Bud was gone a tall black-haired kid named Danny came through the swinging doors carrying the can that had been kicked out. Danny smiled, stretch marks around his acne scars. "Had a little accident in here, huh?"

"Yeah, a little accident. Bud couldn't leave well enough alone while he was talking to me. Had to mess around with the stacks and one fell."

Stan left the back room and walked toward the customer service counter. He saw Bud round the corner and head toward the far end of the store, smiling like hell.

Evie was just leaving the counter. She carried a cash drawer to one of the registers. "I'll be right back, Stan."

It was over. He would never work at Bud's IGA again. In a way he was glad. Now he could work harder at getting another job. Maybe he'd be a Wal-Mart greeter, crack jokes as he rolls carts toward customers. Bang a cart into some guy's shin and wait for the next victim.

That's the way it was lately, always waiting. Like now. Standing near the customer service counter waiting for Evie to come back. Then if he asked her out again on Saturday night he'd have to wait for her to make up her mind. He stood back from the counter because two women were awaiting Evie's return, two women wearing shorts and blouses, taking advantage of the October warm spell, one woman quite heavy, the other woman slender with a tight little ass like Mrs. Jenkins at the pool. He looked at the slender woman's ass, imagined himself reaching out to trace the outline of bikini panties beneath her white shorts with his finger.

The fat woman glanced back at him and he turned, looked toward the back of the store. Bud passed between two aisles, boys stocked shelves in blurred movements, grocery carts squeaked. And beyond it all on the wall above the meat counter, the pig face and the steer face leered at him. Bodiless faces as if the heads poked through holes in the wall, the bodies on platforms in the meat department being butchered. The pig and steer trying to smile though their flanks are being cut away so the fat-assed woman at the so-called customer service counter could add yet more girth to *her* flanks.

In the produce aisle an old woman, the same one who'd needed help with her bag of potatoes, rifled through heads of lettuce. A head of lettuce hit the floor, rolled a lop-sided course toward him, stopped in the middle of the floor and stared at him. No, not really a head minus a body, simply a lettuce head. The old woman looked down at the head of lettuce, seemed quite angry with it, pushed her cart around it and walked away. Suddenly he was sad. The head of lettuce on the floor reminded him of a school lunch he'd once seen thrown from a school bus window. A lunch slaved over by a mother for a child only to be strewn on the street like garbage. To treat food like that. To treat a head like that. To treat a child raised five years by loving parents like that . . .

For a moment he thought he was dreaming again. He recalled having heard that stroke victims sometimes break into tears for the simplest reasons. Then he heard his name called. Evie's voice behind him. If he turned would she be there? If he closed his eyes would he be in bed? What a hell of a time to go crazy!

The fat woman and the thin woman walked past him into the clatter and bustle of the store. The thin woman bent to retrieve the head of lettuce and returned it to its place among its brothers and sisters. As she bent she spread her legs slightly, the panty lines raised in her shorts flexed their muscles and dared him to see inside. She was in her forties. Perhaps she was one of the women saved in his cache file.

"Well, Stan, how are you today?"

He turned. Evie was there at the counter, her eyes blinking, her thin hands adjusting her hair.

"Oh, fine." The lie. Terrible, Evie. I think I've gone nuts.

"I see you're" . . . She cleared her throat . . . "still healthy enough to admire a lady in shorts."

"It doesn't hurt to look, does it? It is quite a long wait between Saturday nights."

Evie folded her hands on the counter and looked down.

"I'm sorry, Evie. I didn't mean to say that."

"That's all right. The problem is I have to work this Saturday night. I just found out that it's my turn on the graveyard shift."

"And you still have to work Friday night?"

"Everyone does, you know that."

"Well, then you don't work during the day tomorrow, and you don't work tonight, do you?"

"No."

"Want to go out tonight?"

"The final Presidential debate is tonight. But that doesn't matter. The pundits can fill me in later. Anyway, during the last debate I couldn't stand the way Montgomery lectured Haney. Sure, let's go out. Do you have any place special in mind?"

He didn't want to eat out again, then back to her house. Something different, anything to get out of his apartment, out of his rut. Something to help him forget the dreams, forget about Marion and the past and guilt.

"How about a movie? We could go to a drive-in."

"A drive-in?"

"Yeah, the one on Route 43. They're tearing it down in a few months for a development, but in the meantime they've opened it back up for a while and they're showing old movies from the sixties and seventies. I read about it in the paper. Kind of a nostalgia thing."

"Do you know what's playing?"

"No, I guess they show different films every night. Cheap B films that were originally shown at drive-ins." He lowered his voice conspiratorially. "I read that one night a week they show old adult flicks. Maybe we'll luck out and see some skin."

"Aren't you in a mood."

He touched his face as if he could feel his mood. But all he felt was the bristle of his beard.

"I didn't shave."

"I can see that."

"I came to ask Bud for my job back and I didn't shave."

"It doesn't matter, Stan. You look fine."

"He turned me down. It could have been that." He looked around the store for Bud but didn't see him. "Maybe I should see him again."

Evie touched his hand, held his hand on the counter. Pulled at his hand. "Wait!"

He turned, saw Evie looking so sad, looking like a mother, the way

Aunt Lillian sometimes looked when Uncle Jack punished him. Uncle Jack grabbing him in the kitchen. Uncle Jack holding him in a headlock and giving him the old Dutch rub and laughing as if that would keep it from hurting. Aunt Lillian turning slowly from the kitchen sink and looking at him so sadly.

He wanted to hug Evie but the counter was in the way. He held both her hands and squeezed them. Something was different about Evie. Something about the way she looked at him that made him want to hold her, to tell her something . . . something. She became teary-eyed, not weeping, nothing vocal, not bawling, just tears in her baby-blues and her lips all crumpled like a little girl about to cry.

"Stan, what's wrong?"

"I don't know."

"You used to crack jokes. We used to have a good time."

"I know."

"Do you want to talk about it tonight?"

"Tonight? Sure. We'll talk tonight."

She was looking down at her hands again. He let go.

"Do you still want to go to the drive-in or do you want to come to my house?" asked Evie. "I could cook something. We could talk."

"No. Let's go to the drive-in. Let's . . . let's do something different. We'll pick up a pizza on the way."

"Well, okay, Stan. Maybe it would be fun."

"I'll pick you up at seven."

"Okay."

During the drive back to his apartment he imagined Evie pulling him down on the front seat. He looked at the front seat of his Toyota pickup and wondered how they would do it, if they would have room.

He drove fast the rest of the way, the old Toyota pickup responding with bursts of speed as he pressed on the accelerator. The old pickup and him reliving the energy and strength of youth as he sped through the curve just ahead of the entrance to the apartment complex. The pickup leaned into the curve, its tires squealing. Feeling the sideways pull of centrifugal force and gripping the wheel as if it were a living thing, he felt a sluggishness leave him and, for a few seconds, he was young and in love.

At the entrance to the complex, someone had put up a dozen or so Montgomery-Nelson signs where Haney-Ingersoll signs had been a couple days earlier. But a set of tire tracks leading up onto the entrance lawn looped through the row of signs where someone had obviously gone off the road to flatten several of the signs to the ground.

After Stan parked in front of his apartment he could see the dumpsters in the rearview mirror. He laughed out loud at the dumpsters and their bag of tricks. Then he leaned to the right, looked at himself in the rearview mirror and saw that his face was red and he was smiling like a maniac.

CHAPTER 23

THE LANDSCAPE WAS barren, gravel and weeds battling it out on man-made mounds encircling the screen, rusting speaker posts lined up like soldiers at attention. Soon the place would be plowed under for development, its droppings blended into the soil so that someday archeologists would speculate about their findings. Artifacts in a certain layer of soil would consist of aluminum can tabs, plastic spoons, used condoms, shards of beer bottles worn smooth by time. The weathered wooden fence surrounding the place was like the vague perimeter in a dream. But he was not asleep.

As he drove up an aisle, rows of speaker posts merged and parted, lined up and separated like sights on hundreds of rifles aimed at a spot below the screen where wild bushes had taken over. Some weeds that had fought their way through the gravel between rows of speaker posts scraped the rusty bottom of his pickup like hands from the grave.

Once, when he was a boy, Uncle Jack and Aunt Lillian had taken him, along with their two real children, to the drive-in. He was older than their real children and didn't associate with them. He recalled that he sat alone in the car while Uncle Jack and Aunt Lillian and their two kids went to the playground at the foot of the screen. Then, when the movie started, instead of sitting in the back seat where there wasn't much room, he had sat alone on one of the slope-backed wooden chairs in front of the projection building.

There was no playground below the screen here. But there was something, something that could not be seen in the bushes, something that might make its appearance now or wait until dark. A man perhaps. A man holding a child's head aloft. Or the man who'd killed Timmy. The man being aimed at by row upon row of speaker posts as gravel crunched beneath the tires of the pickup. The gravel sounding the way the distant popping of guns had sounded at Sedgwick's survivalist weekend.

He shouldn't have napped because the dreams had returned with a vengeance. When he awoke his bed had become the bed of his childhood, a raft floating in shark-infested waters, a floating platform above sharpshooters, a place beneath which someone might hide and grab his ankle when he stepped out. This afternoon when he awakened from his nap the fears of childhood had descended upon him. Now, as he drove the pickup into the decrepit drive-in, he wondered if, after a certain age, everyone went a little crazier each day until the day they died.

Although he was not alone in his pickup, he felt alone. The afternoon dreams had isolated him. Thoughts about men with guns had started long before he pulled into the drive-in. In a farm field along Route 43 he had seen a bright hunter orange sign that said, "Sportsmen for Monty." He'd seen a sign like this before. But on this sign, down low in the corner, someone had written, "Rose," and over the name had drawn a bull's-eye.

He had agreed with Evie that the sign was in bad taste and that should have been the end of it. But for some reason he was having trouble getting his mind off guns and what they can do to a human being. Maybe it was the sixties feel of the drive-in. Maybe that was what made him think of the Zapruder film. John F. Kennedy's brains blown out onto the trunk of the limo. The Secret Service man leaping up onto the back of the limo and Jackie reaching out. The countless television specials over the years showing a view of Dealey Plaza through a gun sight. A gun sight like the one on his .30/06. A gun sight like the one in the nightmare. Crazy. A gun sight on a soldering gun. Imagine him shooting anyone when everything that was important in his life ended when a man with a gun aimed at his son's chest. His life taking a turn toward hell when a trigger on a gun was pulled so long ago. A simple thing. Like reaching out to turn off the ignition. A simple thing like shutting off the engine of his pickup and feeling the vibration as the engine dies.

Pizza cheese stretching thin like fine hair looping around fingertips. Lower lips drooping to catch the cheese before it slides off into their laps. Open cans of beer on the floor of the pickup.

"This is fun, Stan. I'm glad we got here early enough to eat before the show starts."

Evie catching another string of cheese with her mouth. Evie turning to smile at him.

"Stan, I said this is fun. Don't you think so? You can talk with your mouth full. It's allowed with pizza."

"Oh, sure. You want another beer? I've got a six pack behind the seat."

Evie bent to reach her beer. "No thanks. I've got plenty left. I see what you meant about this place being run-down."

"I'm surprised they don't even bother cutting the weeds," he said.

"That's fine with me. If there weren't weeds here I'd wonder about car-cinogens left over from weed killer. It looks like they've been letting the place run down for some time. I noticed some of the speaker posts don't have speakers on them. I hope ours works."

"We'll find out when the show starts."

"This is really pretty funny when you think about it, Stan."

"What's that?"

"We don't even know what's playing."

When he picked Evie up he had been surprised to see that she was wear-ing shorts. Even though the days had been warm, the October evenings were cool. He imagined how good she would look with a tan. Evie's legs like Mrs. Jenkins' legs as she lounges in her bikini at the pool.

After they finished the pizza, he watched Evie walk to the ladies' room at the side of the concession building. In the cool dusk, with a slight breeze blowing her hair, Evie became a teenaged girl walking between the pregnant mounds of the ancient drive-in.

He recalled how Evie had gone teary-eyed at the store earlier in the day when she said, "Stan, what's wrong?" He had been unable to answer. Per-haps this was all a dream, Evie looking younger because she cared for him as no one had cared since Marge. Or since Terri at the lab had dismissed his attentions so gently. So gently.

He went to the men's room, stood at the rain gutter trough for at least a minute because of the two beers he'd had. On his way back to the pick-up, country music began playing, coming from hundreds of ancient tinny speakers. There weren't many others at the drive-in, a few cars, a few small sport-utes, a few small pickups like his. Back in the pickup he lowered his window, hung the speaker on the window and rolled it back up. He turned the speaker up to make sure it worked, then turned it back down again.

When Evie came back and opened the passenger door, Willie Nelson sang "On the Road Again" as Stan watched Evie slide in beside him.

"I'm glad you've got this old thing. No center console to keep us apart."

"Except there's not that much room."

"Does it have a name?"

"What?"

"Your pickup. Sometimes people name their cars or trucks. My car's called Sue. I have no idea why. It just popped up one day."

"I've never named my truck. Rusty would be good, I guess."

After they were silent a moment, Evie leaned into him a little. "Stan?"

"Yes?"

"After what happened today at the store, you don't still think Bud will consider giving you a job, do you?"

"I doubt it. He was pretty upset even though it wasn't my fault."

"I know it wasn't your fault. I think Bud was laying for you."

"What do you mean?"

"Maybe I shouldn't tell you this, but since Bud is so two-faced I think you should know. He said something the other day when he was adding up receipts. He said some men had been in the store asking questions about you."

"Men?"

"Yes. Bud wanted to know if I knew anything about it. He mentioned badges. I'm sure he knew what kind of badges, but of course he wouldn't tell me that. He tried to be cute, saying they had, 'Stinking badges.' "

"What did the men want?"

"The usual information, if you were a good worker and all that."

If he was being considered for a job at the lab the FBI would do a security check. But he wasn't being considered for a job. He looked out the windshield toward the clump of bushes below the screen. The thickness of the bushes reminded him again of things hidden. He thought of the men in the limo and sport ute. Though he hadn't seen the vehicles in over a month, he'd dreamed of the men. Last night one of the men held the child's head aloft as if it were a trophy. He felt a chill as he stared at the bushes and knew he was staring there because it was a place men could hide and watch him if they wanted. For some reason he knew the men would come back eventually.

"Who could they be, Stan?"

"Huh?"

"The men questioning Bud. Who could they be?"

"I guess maybe the FBI. Sometimes they check up on people who used to have a security clearance."

"Oh, that's it. You worked on secret projects at the lab."

He didn't want to explain to Evie that his clearance had been limited. He didn't want to tell her he simply worked on electronic instruments and really didn't know anything about what was being measured.

"That's probably it, Evie. They have to run a check on top secret workers every few years to protect themselves."

"I have to admit I was a little concerned."

"Nothing to be concerned about."

"Maybe this is good news, like there's a job opening and that's why they're checking on you."

"Could be."

An announcer's voice echoed through the drive-in.

"Turn it up, Stan."

"What?"

"The speaker. It's finally dark enough and the show's starting."

"Yes, it is getting dark."

As he turned up the speaker its dirty volume control sent out a blast of static and the announcer said it was "adult nostalgia night."

"Stan, you devil. You knew it was adult night. You planned it."

"I didn't know. Honest."

"Sure you didn't. Do they show everything?"

"I don't know."

"Don't be surprised if I cover my eyes at certain . . . ahem . . . key scenes."

"You can do whatever you like, Evie."

"Stan?"

"Yes?"

"Is something wrong?"

"Wrong? No, I'm just nervous about bringing you here. I'm worried you really think I knew it was adult night."

Evie put her arm around his neck, propped her feet up on the transmission hump, kissed his cheek. "Don't be worried. I'm an adult, too."

After a few seconds of silence, she said, "Hey, this is supposed to be fun."

He turned to her, tried to smile, kissed her. Then he looked back out the window and realized the clump of bushes below the screen was about the same distance away as the vehicles had been from his apartment window. He hung on to Evie as darkness fell.

A few more cars and pickups and sport utes came into the drive-in with parking lights lit. They moved slowly just like the limo and sport ute had in the parking lot below his window. First was the sport ute by itself, then the sport ute following the limo, then the men next to the dumpster, then the head of a child, then men asking about him. If they were that interested in him, they'd be watching all the time. They'd know where he went, what he did.

He looked around at the other vehicles. Two cars ahead were moving to different spots because a tall Jeep and a van had parked in front of them. None of the sport utes he could see were large enough to be the one he'd seen in the parking lot. But he could see only those in front. Behind it was dark except for the glare of the projector poking its steaming head out the projection booth in the concession building. A car to the left had its inside lights on and he could see two young couples dividing up the contents of a cardboard food tray.

If it was police who questioned Bud, what did they think he'd done? Dirty Old Man Stan. His only son killed, no suspects. His wife commits suicide. A child's head found and he's connected to its discovery because he's a greedy fool thinking he'll find jewels or money or drugs. No wonder he was going crazy.

On the screen was a commercial for the drive-in's foot-long hot dogs.

Evie squeezed him. "I wonder when they'll get this show on the road."

"I don't know."

"All right. What's wrong?"

"Huh?"

"With you. Something's wrong."

"Sometimes I just feel tired."

"How have you been sleeping lately?"

"Not so good."

"Have you been having those nightmares?"

"Yes."

"The steer and pig and eagle dressed up in suits?"

"Yes. And a new one."

"Tell me about it, Stan. Tell me before you forget. Just let it out."

"Last night I dreamed I was a kid again. I was kneeling by my bed saying prayers but I was hurrying because I was afraid someone would grab me from under the bed. Then my Uncle Jack came up to my room and gave me a Dutch rub."

"What's a Dutch rub?"

He made a fist and rubbed Evie's scalp a little with his knuckles. "Like that, except harder."

"Oh, so it hurts."

"Yes, it hurts if it's done right. Anyway, he gets me in a headlock and rubs and rubs my head until I can't stand it. I try to move away but I can't. I look up at him, trying to get him to stop, but he just keeps rubbing. He's got this weird smiling face. And although I thought it was Uncle Jack, it's not him at all. It's a man with a very long chin that hangs down so low it covers the top of his tie. His eyes are narrow slits but I can't see any eyeballs, only holes. His forehead is wide, I mean really wide like this." He held his hands a foot apart to demonstrate for Evie the size of the head. "His head is too big for his body, his eyes are close together, and he's got big ears. You know, like a caricature."

"Like in political cartoons?"

"That's right. In fact, now that I think about it, he looked like President Montgomery. President Montgomery staring at me with that smile of his."

"There's always a reason for these things," said Evie. "You were probably reading the newspaper before you went to bed."

He hadn't been reading the paper. What he had been doing was looking at the photographs of nude women saved on his computer, hoping he would dream about women, about sex. Because if he dreamed about sex, if he thought about sex, he might not have the nightmares. But he couldn't tell Evie that. So he said, "Yeah, maybe from reading the paper."

"You really do have crazy dreams, don't you?"

"I guess so. And I'm pretty sure I've been sleepwalking lately. I probably knelt by the bed during the dream, saying my prayers like a damn kid. Then out to the kitchen for a glass of milk, then I might have gone outside because the next morning I found the chain on the door unhooked again. And there's been this green stuff on my kitchen floor."

"Green stuff?"

"Some kind of fiber. Not stringy, little bits of something. I saved some of it."

"You saved fibers you found on your kitchen floor?"

"Yes. I figured I could find out where I'd gone to. That is, if I really had gone out sleepwalking, which I'm not all that sure of."

"Don't throw those fibers away."

"Huh?"

"Save the fibers from the kitchen floor. My lawyer knows this detective who helped out when I was divorcing my ex. He could take the fibers to a lab and have them analyzed . . . Oh, look, Stan. The show's starting."

He fumbled with the speaker, knocked it into his lap where it smacked one of his testicles, hung the speaker back on the window, turned up the volume. Rock and roll guitars circa 1960 or 70. Red letters on the screen with flamed edges said, "Hot Rod Honey."

"Not a very sexy title," said Evie.

Guitar music played and hot rod engines roared as credits rolled by too quickly to read. Then everything was silent except for the gentle sound of wind. On the screen was a gray highway in what looked like a desert of brown weeds and sand. The camera was positioned in the middle of the road, down low capturing the perspective, the white center line and both edges of the road merging into a silvery mirage. There was the faint sound of an engine, then a car breaking out of the mirage, coming closer and closer, louder and louder until it exploded past the camera to the left. A red '57 Chevy with fat black tires. The camera reversed its position and watched the car move away toward the mirage on the other horizon. Then the camera was in the back seat of the Chevy looking forward. Two teenaged boys, or young men acting like teenaged boys, sat in the front seat. The Chevy's windows were open. Both boys had long black hair that blew in the wind.

"How fast now?" shouted the passenger above the roar of the engine.

"One-twenty."

"Is it red-lined yet?"

"I'm savin' it for the race Sunday."

The camera zoomed ahead to a figure standing at the side of the road. A girl in a blue dress, hitchhiking. The car smoked its tires skidding to a stop past the girl. Through the rear window, after capturing the grins on both boys' faces, the camera watched the girl walk to the car swinging her hips in the too-large blue dress. The passenger got out to let the girl sit in the middle, got back in, and the Chevy roared off.

"Where to, honey?"

"Goin' up to Sweetwater for the day. Where you boys headed?"

"Why, we're goin' to Sweetwater, too, ain't we, Buster?"

"Yeah, that's right."

The camera stared at the backs of their heads for a while. The girl had long red hair. Then the camera had a mind of its own, a dirty-old-man mind. It went forward over the girl's shoulder and looked down the front of her low-cut dress. It paused on her breasts, the nipples barely hidden by the fabric. Then the camera examined her legs. And, as if the girl knew what the dirty old camera wanted, she inched the hem of her dress ever so slightly up above her knees and rubbed her legs together as if they were palms rubbing in warmth on a cold day.

"She's really asking for it," said Evie.

"I just love fast cars," said the girl.

The camera stayed with the girl's legs for a while, then it studied the faces. The two boys looking almost the same—rough wide-eyed faces smiling down at the girl's legs. The girl's face was not that young. But, in the movie, she was supposed to look young—no makeup, long straight hair, an innocent smile faked—as she looked ahead at the road.

The car pulled into a grove of trees that miraculously appeared in the desert. The girl rubbed the boys' legs near their denim-covered crotches. The boys rubbed the girl's legs, spread them, one apiece like making a wish. The girl's white underwear made its debut on the screen as the Chevy's engine roared and was finally shut down.

Then the scene switched to a blanket on a fake lawn with fake trees behind. The girl sat naked atop one boy while sucking on the penis of the other boy who was standing.

Evie said, "Whoa, great segue. I like it better when they at least take time to undress. Did you know there are really young girls here, Stan? I saw them in the restroom. They were dressed in long skirts and Angora sweaters like they were from the sixties. But they couldn't have been more than fifteen."

"We're the sheltered ones," he mumbled. "They've seen it all."

The girl on the screen moaned, a deep repetitious moan to go with close-ups of genitals. But despite what was on the screen, Stan conjured up an image of young girls in their sixties skirts and sweaters doing a striptease while he sits in a slope-backed wooden chair in front of the projection building. All this, yet he did not feel aroused. For some reason, tonight, sex was unfriendly, like a whirlpool dragging him down. Crazy bastard.

He conjured up another image, this one of prehistoric men and women having sex because it was the only way to forget, for a few moments, the trials of life. The only way to forget that night would come again as it always does and bring with it all its monsters.

But despite the sex on the screen and the images he conjured up in his head, he couldn't stop thinking of guns and gun sights and targets. The dreams he'd had, the man who'd come to his apartment and looked at his guns, the bull's-eye drawn over Haney's name, the Zapruder film over and over—all of it led him to the conclusion that violence was the only thing understood in the world. What had been done to him had changed him. Therefore, the only way to change the world was to do something to someone else. Even the cheap movie on the ancient drive-in screen had the answer. Do it to someone before they do it to you.

As the movie became clinical and repetitious, Evie became indifferent to it, wanted to talk.

"I haven't been out to a movie in a long time. In fact, not since before the divorce. Did I ever tell you about the divorce?"

"You said your husband was running around in the city, something like that."

"He still is. But why complain? I've got the house and it's paid for."

"Have you ever thought of selling it?" When he said this, the phrase "selling it" took on another meaning and he glanced at Evie who looked back at him strangely, the rhythmic movement from the screen flashing in her eyes.

"Sure, I've thought about selling it. In fact, I've looked at apartments. But there's something about the house I can't seem to let go of. It's like a person. Someone you can count on. Always there, never changing. Probably has to do with the memories of the kids when they were younger. The bad part is that it makes me feel old sometimes. All the years in that house add up to more and more molasses piled on until I can't move. Can't even take a trip without a big turmoil about who'll watch the house and bring in the mail. I guess what I've been thinking about is that if I got an apartment I'd have more freedom. How do you like your apartment, Stan?"

His apartment with its two-dimensional women in his dresser drawer and on his hard disk. His apartment with its cabinet full of guns. His apartment full of nightmares. "It's okay."

"Maybe I should look there. We'd be neighbors."

He imagined Evie and Marion meeting, discussing their relationships with him, his life laid bare like the characters on the screen. A movie called *Dirty Old Man Stan* in which his porn collection comes alive, surrounds him, degrades him. If he were young he'd simply be sowing wild oats. But a guy his age would be considered a crazy bastard capable of anything, even murdering children if they could pin that on him. Blaming him when the real killers have an unlimited budget so they can sneak around in expensive limos and sport utes. Blaming him when they should be blaming . . . Who? The government? Pretty vague, Dirty Old Man Stan, pretty damn vague.

There was an oral sex scene on the screen now, two women taking turns on one guy. Evie had stopped talking. He forced himself to look away from the screen and studied Evie's face. She stared at the screen with apparent interest, her mouth slightly open like a mother spoon-feeding a baby. She stared like this until the scene was over.

"I don't know whether I should be disgusted or not," she said.

"Disgusted with me?"

She turned and smiled, her face lit up in flashes of light. "Hey, you're the one who brought me here."

"Do you want to leave?"

She moved closer. "Don't be silly. I'm not totally backward."

She pushed her hand beneath his shirt collar and rubbed his neck. Then she poked him in the ribs and his knee hit the steering column.

"Ouch!"

"What's the matter?"

"I banged my knee. I'm ticklish."

She spoke in a mock juvenile voice. "Oh, my poor little orphan. Him so fragile. Him don't like to be tickled."

She poked his ribs again, but when he tried to tickle her it didn't seem to have any effect. He tickled her low on her belly, rubbed her belly lower and lower until his hand pressed into her crotch.

"Hey! Watch it, Stanley Steamer. I'll rub your head."

She giggled while she said it. Just kidding. But rub his head? Something wrong with that, something emerging. An image, as if on the screen, of a little boy relegated to an attic room, a little boy who never wanted any trouble. His head began burning as Evie rubbed. Rubbing hard, his scalp on fire. The nightmare, trying to stop the pain by doing something, by soldering the eagle, by shooting the man with the child's head. Do something! Anything! Before his head explodes!

Screaming. Someone screaming, yet two people talking as if nothing's happening. But those people were on the screen.

Evie screaming and him holding her wrist, twisting it. A maniac. He let go and Evie pulled away, moved to the other side of the seat, rubbed her wrist.

"You hurt me!" she shouted. "You really hurt me! What the hell's wrong with you?"

"I . . . I don't know. I guess I don't like my head rubbed."

"Oh, you can do anything you want but I can't rub your damn head without getting my arm busted! Just like a man! Do anything you want . . . Let's get the hell out of here!"

Evie sat against the door with her arms folded, her legs crossed. He had never heard her swear before. On the screen the girl was hitchhiking again. Only now she wore sexy clothes, white boots and a miniskirt. The girl on the screen stared at him and for a moment he thought he and Evie were the movie.

"I said let's get the hell out of here, Stanley! That means take me home in case you can't understand God's English!"

"Wait! I can explain!"

"There's nothing to explain! Just drive!"

"All right! All right! Son of a bitch! I'll take you home!"

He threw the speaker out on the ground and drove off spinning his tires on gravel. In other vehicles he saw annoyed faces lit up by his headlights. On the screen he saw the girl slide in next to a middle-aged red-faced man. Next to him, in the glare from the screen coming through the window, he saw a gap of empty seat, then Evie, legs crossed, rubbing her wrist and looking out the side window. She had already retrieved her purse from the floor. It rested in her lap.

He drove fast and steady, both hands on the wheel. The pickup misfired and rattled. The lights bordering the road ahead kept going in and out of focus as if he were drunk. He followed the white line, turned so sharply down Evie's street, she shrieked. When he skidded to a stop in front of her house, a figure came out of the darkness toward them. Evie turned abruptly as the passenger door opened from the outside.

A man in an overcoat standing beside the pickup. The man's head hidden by the roof of the pickup. Stan gripped the steering wheel as tightly as he could. The steering wheel of his pickup was real, while everything else . . .

"Jason!" said Evie, almost shrieking again. "What are you doing here?"

Jason bent lower, looked at him. Evie's ex-husband, the one he'd seen in the photograph in her house. A puzzled face. "Maybe you can tell me, Evie. I tried calling your cell phone but . . ."

"What? Oh, my phone. I don't have it on."

"I tried calling you because someone phoned me a while ago. A man. He said I should meet you here. He said it was urgent."

Evie got out of the pickup, the two of them standing, both their heads cut off by the roof. Stan wanted to drive away but the door was still open.

"A man called you?" Evie spoke in an exaggerated whisper as if Stan would be unable to hear.

"Yes," said Jason. "He said I should be here, but refused to give his name, or any other details for that matter." Jason bent and peeked in at Stan. "Is something wrong?"

"No," said Evie. "Nothing's wrong. Stanley was dropping me off. He'll be leaving now."

The door slammed. Evie and Jason walked away, gesturing to one another. He could no longer hear what they said. He wanted to spin his tires and squeal away like an angry hot rodder, but the pickup sputtered and died. By the time he got it restarted, Evie and Jason had already disappeared into the darkness of her house.

He was going too fast when he turned into his apartment complex. He lost control, and as he skidded to a stop his front wheel slammed into the curb near the campaign signs. The Montgomery-Nelson signs had been replaced by Haney-Ingersoll signs, except for one remaining Montgomery-Nelson sign, which was upside down. The pickup's engine had died and when he restarted it he drove more slowly into the complex. After he shut off the engine in front of his apartment he heard a tire hissing. He sat and waited as the right front of his pickup sunk down. Down and down as if it would not stop, as if it would keep on sinking and drag him and the pickup into a hole in the Earth.

His apartment building loomed above, lights on in all the apartments except his. The dark front window of his apartment a gaping hole, a tomb excavated into the side of the building.

A man calling Evie's husband, men asking about him at the store, men calling him. Maybe they were waiting for him, sitting in the dark waiting the way he had waited night after night for the black sport ute and the black limo.

He felt cold all over. His mind tricking him. Why should he be frightened? He should be angry. He should get even, do something.

He walked across the parking lot, past the dumpsters, past the fence around the pool to Marion's apartment. He talked out loud as he walked. "There's other fish in the sea. I don't have to take this crap. Son of a bitch. Bitch!"

Marion came to the door in a pink robe. Her hair was in curlers making her head look small.

"Stanley. Uh, what is it?"

"Just thought I'd stop by, Marion. Thought maybe you and I could have a little fun."

She looked businesslike despite the curlers, no smile, no cute remark. She held her robe tightly around her with one hand and held the edge of the door with the other as if at any moment she would slam it in his face.

"Isn't it a bit late? You should have called first. Perhaps we can get together on the weekend. Call me tomorrow."

Marion probably assumed he was drunk. Who wouldn't? As he made his way back to his apartment he stumbled several times as though he really was drunk and decided that might be best, getting drunk, feeling warm inside if only for a little while. He'd drink alone because he was better off being a loner. Dirty Old Man Stan trying to use sex to help him forget his fears instead of leveling with Evie because she'll think he's crazy. So crazy his nightmares, waiting for him in his apartment, might come alive.

He began sobbing as he climbed the stairs to the apartment and hurried inside so his new neighbors would not hear him, peek through their fisheye lens, and see him rushing into his hole like a rat.

Because they had been called by the surveillance team at the drive-in, the two men were out of the apartment and back in their van at the far end of the parking lot before Stanley Johnson dropped Evie Schneider at her house. Using the transponder at the house, they listened to Evie and her ex argue for a while, then switched to the apartment transponder just as Johnson came speeding into the complex. They saw Johnson walk across the complex to another apartment building, then watched as he stumbled back in the dark to his own apartment.

"Man, he's ripe for it tonight," said the man in the passenger seat.

"All in the timing," said the man in the driver's seat.

"Remind me again. Why the hell did we go with Carter instead of another Prez?"

"Doc said Johnson admired the guy, identified with him somehow. He figured we could use Carter to get into some deep recess, something like that."

"He's the same doc who said the pig and steer would send Johnson off the deep end. I wish someone would explain all this to me someday."

"If you researched the guy's life like the doc and got hold of his shrink's files, the whole thing would probably be crystal clear."

"When we finish this job we should get some kind of report. You know, like what the goal was, and whether we succeeded or not."

"I'd rather be in the dark. Better to take the bonus and run back south for a few months until the next assignment than to get all tied up in the details of these things."

"Yeah, it is nice down there. Much better than in the Contra days."

"All right, enough. Sounds like he's going to sleep in his clothes so you might as well release the stuff in his room and we'll get on up there."

"Think he chained the door this time?"

"If not, we'll figure something else to leave behind."

"It'll be interesting watching the news coverage tomorrow night."

"Yep. Better than the debates."

CHAPTER 24

THE PRESIDENT'S NEMESIS

DESPITE THE REDUCED dose, Lena slept through the night and now felt relaxed, pleasantly flushed as she lay in bed in the dawn light seeping in at the sides of the drapes. Last night, Walter had casually announced this would be the first reduction of many in order to break her habit. According to Jake's instructions, in order for the program to work, it was important to keep from her the exact amount that the dose was being reduced.

The routine was always the same. Walter would arrive promptly at ten, remove his cap, and chat with Jake a while. She would join them, fidgety like a little girl who had waited patiently for the ice cream man, then she and Jake and Walter would go into the living room. Jake would take out a box of South American cigars he'd begun smoking lately, offer one to Walter who always took one and pocketed it. Then Jake would turn away, lighting his cigar while Walter handed her the packet. After more brief chatter about the weather and the next day's agenda, Walter would leave and she would go into her bathroom to fix herself. When she came out of the bathroom, the living room would be layered with cigar smoke on which she imagined she was floating as she joined Jake on the sofa.

Last night Jake had made love to her on the sofa. The bittersweet taste of smoke still lingering on her breath as if she had smoked the cigar, the long brown cigar that reminded her of Raphael's dick.

She sometimes wondered if, at the moment before death, Raphael knew why he was being killed. Although most of the time she felt Raphael deserved what he got, sometimes, like now when she was so content and relaxed, she knew that in a way she was sorry for Raphael. He represented the life she knew, the people of the street, everyone part of some deal, merchandise. And if your worth got too low or too high, you'd be discarded, trashed, killed. Stupid. Stupid to think about that. She had escaped, survived. No looking back.

She heard voices, continuous chatter of men and women. She knew Jake had gotten up earlier and now, as she listened, she realized it was not Jake talking to someone. It was the television in the living room. She'd slept all night and now wondered if Jake had been unable to sleep.

Last evening, before Walter arrived, Jake had seemed angry, had made several phone calls in his study. As she walked down the hallway she heard Jake shout, "Fuck George!" to someone on the phone. Between calls, Jake paced the apartment and she knew that if he wanted to talk about it he would tell her. So she kept to herself, busied herself straightening the apartment even though the housekeeper had been there all afternoon. Mostly she simply rearranged things, kept moving about, not sure whether she was jumpy because of the usual need for her fix, or whether she was nervous about the first try at a reduced dose.

Although pretty much consumed by her own need, she was quite aware of a change in Jake's mood just before Walter's arrival. When the phone calls ended Jake came into the living room and kissed her. He had smiled then, said something about everything being "back on track." And later, when they made love on the sofa, Jake had voiced his love for her and the pleasure she gave him.

She rolled to Jake's side of the bed. The sheet and his pillow were cool. She looked at the clock. Only seven. She walked down the hall, saw Jake sitting in his robe in front of the television watching the news. She went to the kitchen and started coffee.

Jake called from the living room. "Up already?"

"I'm making coffee. Couldn't you sleep?"

"I slept fine, Lena. I planned on getting up early. Today's a special day."

When she brought the coffee into the living room, Jake held his finger to his lips. The television remote was in his other hand. He stared at the television, at the newswoman talking there.

"During his campaign stopover in Chicago today, President Montgomery is expected to visit a Joliet, Illinois, research lab that has been instrumental in creating portable radiation and explosive detection equipment for the War on Terror. The President's reason for the visit is to highlight the fact that another division at the lab recently won several contracts to investigate and consolidate breakthroughs in solar power. George Domenico, the President's campaign manager, said the President will also visit several neighborhoods to seek grass roots support for his new environmental policies. Although Domenico did not comment further on the visit, we're certain the President will shake lots of hands and kiss lots of babies before the day is over. On the other side of the ticket, Rose Adams Haney today visited a children's hospital in Los Angeles. When asked about her performance last night in the final debate, Ms. Haney said . . ."

Jake muted the volume and took his coffee. "How nice of you, Lena. Sit with me."

He kissed her cheek, put his arm around her, sipped his coffee. He was smiling. Not that he never smiled, but in the morning he usually seemed preoccupied. She didn't want to pry, but the way Jake was acting . . .

She put her cup on the coffee table and lay her head on his shoulder. "What's special about today?"

He was silent. She wondered if he would become serious, tell her it was none of her business. The television screen had shifted to a male commentator.

"See that newsman, Lena? Notice how rapidly his lips move. I mean with the sound off, doesn't he look strange?"

"I guess."

"No. Look. His lips are moving, his eyes are moving, following the prompter, but watch his head. Not moving at all except for those eyebrows. His head perfectly still like a puppet. I suppose that's why they call them talking heads. He's not even aware of what he's reading. Simply words to be transformed into lively enunciated sound waves that will become electrical impulses so we can hear what he's saying and be tricked, by the raising and lowering of eyebrows, into thinking he's actually interested in what he's saying. He's definitely a puppet, groomed to perform a specific task."

Jake turned, making her lift her head from his shoulder. He smiled broadly. "No, Lena. It's not the first stages of senility. I'm simply trying to make a point."

She laughed, poked him in the ribs.

"Careful, you'll make me spill my coffee."

"You can spill it on me and lick it off."

"Not a bad thought. But it's too hot."

"The coffee or me?"

He put the cup down and kissed her, a very long kiss as if he were trying to prove how truly happy or content or satisfied he was.

After the kiss he stared at her. "I wanted to tell you, Lena, how much I enjoyed our drive to San Clemente, and the drive back."

"I'm glad you enjoyed yourself."

"Not only the drive and the meal. What I'm trying to say is that I greatly enjoyed our conversation. I feel I know you much better than I had in the past."

"I also feel I know you better," said Lena.

"And that's something I'd like to bring up. I said things about my stepfather and my real father. Do you remember?"

"Yes, I do."

"Don't feel hurt in the least, Lena, but I need to say this."

"What is it?"

"I want you to keep that kind of personal information about me to yourself. If certain people found out who my real father was . . ."

"No problem," she said. "I'm good at keeping things to myself."

The doorbell rang.

"Sorry to be abrupt, Lena. But I wanted to make that clear. Also, I forgot to tell you I called for Walter."

"Are we . . . are you going somewhere?"

"I'm not sure." Jake glanced at the television where people dressed like fruit were apparently singing a product jingle. "Something might come up and I wanted Walter here in case I needed to leave in a hurry. I'll put him next door in the guest apartment." He smiled again. "Be right back."

While Jake spoke with Walter in the entrance hall, she sat and stared at the television. The commercial with singing fruit ended and suddenly there was an eagle on the screen, an eagle on a blue background. The picture was somewhat jittery until the camera zoomed back and she saw it was Air Force One with the Presidential seal on it. A stairway was already rolled up to the doorway, a caption on the lower screen said, "O'Hare International Airport, Chicago."

The camera zoomed back again to reveal a small crowd, then a podium, also with the Presidential seal on it, then some limousines and sport utility vehicles, then a larger crowd. No sound, and that empty doorway as if no one was on the plane, reminded her of pictures she'd seen of Kennedy's assassination. Reminded her of the day her father drove the tractor up on the lawn and ran inside to tell her mother the news.

As she watched the scene, where now a wind-blown commentator down on the field was obviously waiting for the President to emerge from the plane, Lena recalled an anniversary documentary revisiting the implications that there had been a conspiracy to kill Kennedy, perhaps involving underworld figures.

She could hear Jake and Walter mumbling in the hall. And, as she listened and watched, she remembered Jake's words last week when he'd spoken to someone on the phone in his study. "Yes," he'd said, "when it's over, everything that's happened will be erased."

She wondered what had happened and what would happen today. And she wondered if her dreams, just being realized, would come to an end because of some very different dreams of her lover.

Who could Jake's real father be? The only reason she could come up with for the father-son relationship being kept secret was that Jake was illegitimate. And if that were true, the father—the real father—must have been someone quite important.

After White House scandals of the recent past, she tried to imagine a President making an attempt to keep an illegitimate child secret. Pretty hard these days. But what about the distant past? Jake said his real father died in 1975. Off hand, she couldn't think of anyone, let alone a President, who'd died in 1975. The only year for a President's death she could recall was J.F.K. in 1963.

As Lena mulled this over, the television zoomed in on the doorway to Air Force One. President Montgomery and the First Lady emerged from the plane, began waving, and descended the stairway. Watching the President and First Lady wave to the crowd caused Lena to dream fantastic dreams of the future, a future in which she and Jake are together, traveling the world on their honeymoon.

CHAPTER 25

THE PRESIDENT'S NEMESIS

THE BACK OF his head throbbed with pain every time he bent over—when he bent to pick up the half-empty scotch bottle from beside his bed, when he bent in the kitchen to pick up the torn edge of an envelope from beneath the kitchen table, when he bent at the bathroom sink and splashed cold water on his face. It was worse at the base of his skull, feeling like his spine had grown up into his brain during the night. Perhaps the pain in his head was a symptom of the real problem. A brain tumor caused by his dismal state of mind. The tumor eating away at his past and at the same time making him act the way he acts. Perhaps everything—the headache, his behavior with Evie at the drive-in, the men in the limo and sport ute—had emerged from tumorous brain cells. And if not a tumor, then the only conclusion would be that he was insane. And if a guy was insane, why shouldn't he go nuts when someone gives him a Dutch rub?

But it was all too real. Everything that had happened during the last few weeks had really happened, and there seemed nothing he could do about any of it except wait for something else to happen.

His face in the bathroom mirror looked swollen, his eyes shadowed. There was a metallic taste in his mouth. He brushed his teeth and gargled. The toothpaste and mouthwash tasted sickeningly syrupy and he vowed to never get drunk again. When he combed his hair the plastic comb tips felt like needles on his scalp. Why was his scalp so sensitive? Why had he attacked Evie when she rubbed his head? Perhaps an aneurysm would take him at night in his sleep. That would be the way to go. His body would rot for days before someone discovered it, and when they pulled the blanket off . . .

While the water was heating for tea and he was getting out a cup, he noticed the small dish on the high shelf. He took the dish out of the cupboard and held it in the light from the kitchen window, studying the green fibers in the bottom of the dish. He put the dish on the cupboard and glanced down at the floor. He got down on his hands and knees and gathered yet more fibers with his fingertips. When he put these into the dish next to the others and held the dish in the light from the window, he saw that all the fibers were the same greenish color. He looked up at the ceiling, wondering if something was falling from there onto the kitchen floor. He thought of a television ad he'd seen recently for an asbestos claims attorney, an 800 number to call and get what's coming to you. But the ceiling was painted white, drywalled. He went to the heating register on the other side of the kitchen next to the door. He stooped down and examined the register and the floor directly in front of it. But here he saw no green fibers. The fibers seemed to be around the table and in front of the door.

The door! He stared at the door, at its chain lock. The slide on the end of the chain was not in place, but dangled free. He went to the door and tried the knob. When it turned, he felt a momentary chill until he once again had to remind himself that it always opened from the inside but was always locked to the outside. But why was the chain not in place? He was certain he'd put the slide into its slot the night before. Yes, he'd had the scotch bottle in his hand. He'd taken a swig of scotch, noticed the chain undone, and put it in place.

After he put the chain lock in place now he inspected the doorjamb and the door near the lock. There were small scratches along the edge of the door and the jamb, but he wasn't sure whether they'd been there all along. He pictured himself coming in with groceries, holding the door open with one elbow, pushing through, the metal buttons on his jean jacket or a bag of canned goods rubbing across the doorjamb, and also rubbing against the outside of the door as he turned and allowed the spring-loaded door to swing closed. He recalled that sometimes, when he had to make more than one trip, he'd prop the door open so he wouldn't have to push through that way.

Right, a bottle of scotch in one hand, a bottle of scotch from which he'd gulped after getting home last night, he's hungover like a damn wino, and *he* thinks he remembers locking his damn door. Idiot. Asshole!

As he sat at the kitchen table sipping hot tea, the tea he hoped would cleanse his system and clear his mind, he heard the dumpsters rattling outside. He knew it couldn't be the garbage men. They had picked up the garbage Thursday morning and this was Friday. Besides, he would have heard the whine of the diesel engine.

When he opened the curtains in the living room he saw Chuck the painter in his white coveralls shoving one of the dumpsters out of its wooden enclosure on the other side of the parking lot. Although it had dolly wheels, the dumpster was awkward and Chuck struggled with it. Chuck pushed it off to the side, against the curb, then lifted one side up over the curb, pushed it forward onto the sidewalk, then lifted the other side over the curb. Chuck pushed the dumpster over the sidewalk and off into the grass where he really had to struggle with it across the lawn until he finally disappeared around the side of the building on the other side of the parking lot.

As Stan continued watching, Chuck returned and muscled the other dumpster away and hid it the same way. After this, Chuck picked up a cardboard box from the corner of the dumpster enclosure, threw a few stray cans and scraps of paper from inside the dumpster enclosure into the box. Then Chuck took the box and walked across the parking lot toward the office, pulling up an edge of his coveralls with his free hand to wipe sweat from his forehead.

What the hell was this about? Surely the dumpsters had nothing to do with painting. Maybe Chuck was going to paint lines in the parking lot. But why move the dumpsters all the way in back of the buildings? Crazy. The view out his front window turning into a mystery sideshow. Just like those damn green fibers deposited on his kitchen floor. Exactly what he didn't need right now, to sit around all day trying to figure out what putting dumpsters out of sight had to do with anything. All this while the tumor at the back of his head grows to the size of . . .

Maybe there was a truck on the other side of the building across from his, here to pick up the dumpsters and take them to the crime lab. The noose tightening around Dirty Old Man Stan's neck. He knew he wouldn't be able to take it, not for the entire day. He'd go nuts. So, rather than wait around, he called the office.

"Hello, Marion. It's Stan."

"Good morning, Stan. How are you today?"

"Okay, I guess."

"That's good. I wondered because you looked a little green around the gills last night. I wanted to ask you in, but I was pretty tired and I had my hair in curlers and everything. I'm free tonight if you'd like. Is that why you called?"

He'd forgotten about going over to Marion's last night and making a fool of himself. So what else was new?

"Well, yeah, that, and I wondered why Chuck moved the dumpsters." He didn't want to sound overly concerned about the dumpsters even though he was. "I mean, I was just about to head outside with my garbage, and there was Chuck pushing the dumpsters behind one of the buildings."

"Oh, the garbage dumpsters. You want to know about the garbage dumpsters. Don't worry. He'll put them back later this afternoon."

"He'll put them back this afternoon?"

"That's right, this afternoon, Stan."

"Any special reason?"

"For putting them back?"

"No, for moving them. I wondered why he went through all the trouble. He had a hell of a time hauling those things over the lawn. They're heavy, you know."

"Yes, they are heavy. But they have wheels."

"What's the big secret, Marion?"

"Secret?"

"Yeah, why don't you want to tell me why Chuck moved the dumpsters?"

"Well, I'm just not supposed to tell, that's all. Anyway, it's just a couple of crummy garbage dumpsters. You used to have a classified job at the lab, didn't you?"

"What's that got to do with this? My job at the lab was important."

Marion's voice went up in pitch. "Well, *my* job is also important, Stanley. I know it may not seem important to you, but sometimes it's a very important job."

He was glad he was talking on the phone and Marion could not see him.

He realized he had clenched his fist and that he was shaking. His head felt as if it would explode. Or maybe his heart would give out. He tried to control his voice.

"Sorry, Marion. I didn't mean that your job wasn't important. I was simply curious. Besides, I thought maybe you'd tell me about it since I really called to ask if I could come over tonight anyhow."

"Well, that's all right. Maybe I misunderstood. Sure, I'd love to have you over tonight. You know what, Stan?"

"What?"

"I really would like to tell you why I had the dumpsters moved."

"*You* had them moved?"

"Yes, I did. All I can say right now is that the reason is very important. You're going to be home today, aren't you?"

"Yes. Why?"

"Well, keep close to your window. We're in for a surprise. But that's it. I can't say any more. I promised I wouldn't tell. You'll see for yourself, Stan. Just keep an eye on the parking lot today and you'll see. You just wait and see."

So he did wait. He sat in the living room the rest of the morning with the curtains wide open. At first, when he saw Chuck moving the dumpsters, it was natural for him to think about the child's head. But he knew it wasn't there anymore. The men had taken it. Besides, that was a month ago. What had always worried him, in fact the reason he'd given himself for never having called the police, was the possibility of an investigation. Before he called Marion he thought maybe the head or other parts of the body had been found. And he thought somehow the dumpsters had been linked to the crime. The police would have their technicians use their "fine-toothed combs" on the insides of the dumpsters. They'd find a piece of hair or a fragment of skin or a spot of blood. They'd know a body or part of a body had been disposed of in one of the dumpsters. But how could they? The head had been wrapped in paper, then sealed in plastic. Maybe someone else saw the men in the limo and sport ute and reported them. Maybe the police would look for fingerprints. If they did, they'd have to print everyone in the complex for comparisons, and they hadn't done that. Of course his prints were on file from when he worked at the lab, probably in the FBI database. This is what he thought about before he called Marion. Thank God he had called Marion. There was no investigation. From the hints Marion had given, it sounded more like a parade.

Thinking too much and imagining too much served no purpose but to feed his newly found tumor. His imagination had become a cesspool into which anything and everything is thrown.

He ate lunch. Tuna on toast to settle his stomach, more tea to flush out the scotch. He ate in the living room. He got his mail and spread it out on the coffee table. He tried watching the news for a while but gave up on that when they began reporting on the latest proposal to save Social Security. The administration's so-called "Stronger Retirement Initiative" that Raymond Youngblood had told him about. He watched some daytime soaps and game shows figuring there was more truth there than on the news. Just like any other day, imprisoned in his own apartment because there wasn't anything else to do. Except today he was told to stay here. Couldn't go anywhere with a flat tire anyhow. Below his window the pickup looked sad the way it listed to one corner, looked like a discarded heap waiting to be towed away. Its sadness reminded him of Evie, of the way he'd treated her last night. He touched his head, wondered if he'd go crazy if he gave himself a Dutch rub. Maybe he should call Dr. Todd again, see if he's out of the hospital yet.

Dr. Todd would make him say all of this out loud instead of thinking it.

Maybe that was the trick. Maybe he should start talking to himself. Yeah, walk down the street talking to himself. Then they'd put him away for sure. But he had to tell it to someone, someone who wouldn't laugh or say this was all his imagination, all in his mind. If he couldn't talk to Dr. Todd, maybe he could talk to Evie. First he'd have to apologize for being an asshole. God, he really liked Evie. Or was it love? Could he love someone again?

The phone rang. A man's deep voice, a man talking softly but very close to the mouthpiece so that he could hear breath and lips rubbing against the mouthpiece.

"Mr. Johnson?"

"Yes."

"I'm calling on behalf of Mr. Youngblood."

"Youngblood?"

"That's correct. I believe he called you the other day saying he represented an organization called Men in the Middle?"

Men in the Middle. Youngblood. The man he'd just been thinking about a while ago. The man who said he might help get him a job, the man who blamed President Montgomery for all kinds of crap. "What do you want?"

"I don't *want* anything, Mr. Johnson. I've been asked to inform you that you won't be receiving the application form Mr. Youngblood promised to send."

"How come?"

"Because the organization has been disbanded and Mr. Youngblood is in jail."

"Oh, so that's it. The whole thing was a scam."

"Not exactly, Mr. Johnson. The organization known as Men in the Middle was found to run counter to American society. In fact, it was against the principles of any ethical society. Evidence has come out that the organization may have been involved in child pornography. So you never received the application?"

"Child pornography? Jesus."

"Nothing specific yet, Mr. Johnson, but that seems to be the case. Again, you never received an application from Men in the Middle?"

"Right, I didn't. Anyway, you just got through telling me I wouldn't be getting the application. I was only interested because Youngblood said they'd help me get a job. That's all I was told, that they helped guys like me get jobs. Jesus, child pornography. I wouldn't have signed any kind of application without checking it over anyway. I just said it was okay to send me an application to get rid of the guy."

"I'm glad to hear that because this is the worse kind of child pornography you can imagine. I simply wanted to make sure you weren't involved. I'm calling everyone on their mailing list."

"Are you from the police?"

"Let's just say I'm an interested party."

"What . . . what do you mean by the worst kind?"

"Children have died."

"Jesus!"

"I can't say anything more. I simply wanted you to know how important this is."

"Well, I didn't do anything except answer the phone and let Youngblood have his say."

"Very good, Mr. Johnson. The best thing for you to do is forget that the Men in the Middle organization or Mr. Youngblood ever existed. Our lives and the lives of our families are too valuable to allow these kinds of organizations to get started."

"What do you mean, these kinds of organizations? All Mr. Youngblood said was that he would try to get me a job."

"That's not all there was to it, Mr. Johnson. He wanted commitment."

"What kind of commitment?"

"He wanted people he could use to do his dirty work."

Warnings about child pornography—the worst kind of child pornography—but no answers. Men checking up on him at the store, men calling him, but no one telling him why. Or had Youngblood tried to tell him? The President. Old men and young children disappearing. Youngblood had hinted at that. And he had hinted that President Montgomery was in on it.

"Say, listen, Mr. . . . whatever your name is . . . I haven't done anything. And I'm busy, so I'm going to hang up now."

"I know you're not busy, Mr. Johnson. You're exactly the type of person Mr. Youngblood preyed upon. And his real name isn't Youngblood."

"So, what is his name?"

The man laughed caustically. "I can't tell you that. I shouldn't even be calling you. I simply want to make sure you don't know anything before I destroy this list of names. I simply want you to know the Men in the Middle organization had quite a bit more in mind than finding jobs for you men. That's all I can say, Mr. Johnson. Forget you ever got that phone call and forget you ever got this one."

He remembered the last thing Youngblood had said before laughing and coughing and hanging up. He decided to try to shock this man into telling him more. "I suppose Mr. Youngblood wanted to chop off our heads and use us for fertilizer."

Silence.

"Hey. You still there?"

"Yes." The voice was even lower now, a slight change in pitch as if what he'd said meant something.

"Who are you?"

"I can't say."

"Do you work for the government?"

"I can't say."

"Is all that stuff Youngblood said true? Or is what you said about child pornography true?"

"Good-bye, Mr. Johnson."

"Wait!" But it was too late. The man had hung up.

Stan tried to recall exactly what Youngblood had said. Besides saying he could help get him a job, Youngblood had criticized the President, had said he held the President personally responsible for screwing up the lives of retirees. But there was more, screwing up other lives, maybe even the lives of children, maybe even implying that lives had been sacrificed. He definitely said children. He said something about retirees and children disappearing all the time. And then that joke about cutting old guys' heads off and using them for fertilizer . . .

Stan sat back in his chair, wiped his forehead and realized he was sweating. He closed his eyes for a moment. The image of the head of the child in the garbage bag was as vivid in his mind as the night he'd seen it. The blond hair wet, the slice in the neck laid back like boiled meat. The gray eyes.

Stan opened his eyes, stood up too quickly so that the living room tilted to one side. After his dizziness subsided, he went to the window, looked down at the enclosure in the parking lot where the garbage dumpsters had been. He felt decades older than his age, ancient, retired too soon, waiting. What could men forced into retirement do? What would Youngblood have had them do?

The man who just called, if he was a government agent of some kind, would have access to all kinds of records. Records at the lab that said Dirty

Old Man Stan was a troublemaker who once befriended a girl young enough to have been his daughter. Police records about his son's unsolved murder. Maybe even some Patriot Act records about pornographic Web sites he'd accessed, the ones that implied they might have child pornography on them appearing on his screen when he least expected them, appearing on his screen after he'd tried to close another site. The pornographic Web sites opening one after another relentlessly, coming at him and at him the way everything was coming at him.

He sat back in the lounge chair and took deep breaths. He stared out the window and wondered if all of this was connected with the men in the limo and sport ute. The garbage dumpsters were gone and something was going to happen. That's what Marion had said. Something good because there had been excitement in her voice. Had to be something good.

He waited this way for a long time. When he finally lost patience, when he could piece none of the strange incidents together, no matter how hard he tried, he went into the kitchen. He saw the broom leaning against the wall in the corner. Did he dream he put the broom there? Or did he really put it there? The broom . . . something about the broom.

He went to the broom, grasped it firmly in both hands and, unable to think of anything else to do, began sweeping the floor. He tried to imagine Evie and Marion as part of some plan for him. Two women pretending to have the hots for a crazy-assed loner, or at least he *had* been a loner until all these insane things started happening to him. No. Marion was just Marion who ran the complex office. And Evie? God, he wished he'd leveled with Evie about all this. Especially about the head. And now, since it all seemed to have started with the night he saw the child's head in the bag, he was afraid he would see something terrible in the parking lot below his window, something that would be the end of him.

He heard a short siren blast nearby, cut off at its highest pitch. The siren blast frightened him and he held his broom more tightly, squeezed the handle as hard as he could, and went to the living room window. A line of black limos with two motorcycles in the lead was entering the complex from the far end. Behind the last limo in the line were three large black sport utility vehicles.

At the base of his skull a pain began, mild at first, but growing steadily as if it would not stop until he was dead.

CHAPTER 26

THE PRESIDENT'S NEMESIS

STANLEY JOHNSON

THE AFTERNOON WAS cloudy, not individual clouds hiding the sun occasionally, but one huge cloud over the Earth. The world outside his window looked weary and tired as if, after a long struggle, it was time to rest, to lie down, to give in. But the general grayness, gray like his face had been in the mirror, gray like the eyes of the dead child, was disturbed by the flashing strobe lights of several Joliet police cars and by the blue lights of several Chicago police cars.

Police cars parked at the Elmwood Drive entrance. Several others followed the procession being led by two motorcycle policemen. More police cars came into the parking lot from the other entrance. The motorcycle policemen wore white helmets and black leather jackets and trousers with gold stripes up the legs. The limos following the motorcycles had their headlights on. The sport utility vehicles had their headlights on.

When the procession rounded the corner and headed toward him, he could see that the last two limos in the procession were longer than the others. They rounded the corner taking up more room than the other limos.

Like long boards floating in a stream, the cars swung sideways around the bend pivoting on their tails. The motorcycle policemen kept looking back like mother cats waiting for their young. Another electronic siren blast, this time cut off at its lowest pitch, startled him, made him grip his broom more tightly, made the pain in his head increase.

The two largest limos had miniature flags mounted on their front fenders and emblems on their sides. Gold-rimmed emblems with a white-headed eagle in the center. The President of the United States. Two Presidents of the United States.

A vague recollection of a news spot. Two limos used sometimes to thwart assassination attempts. Two limos used extensively now because of a recent embassy bombing somewhere. Two limos used because of terrorist threats. The limo carrying the President called The Beast by the Secret Service. Maybe there were even more than two limos used now because . . . because the bastard needs to hide from his constituency.

Limos and sport utes in the parking lot. Men asking questions about him. Men calling him. The man saying it—What?—had to do with child pornography. The young man with gray eyes examining his guns, pointing the .30/06 out the window. And now here was Marion's surprise. Marion's giddy parade. A visit by the President. The President with his great big smile and his great big friendly wave. The President who was . . . who was personally responsible. Yes, personally responsible. "I take full responsibility," past Presidents had said. "Full responsibility." Which really meant what? That he could do anything he wanted. That he could get away with things that put others behind bars. That he could have things done and therefore did not really take full responsibility at all. The President with his contemptuous smile and his condescending wave could do any fucking thing to anyone he wanted. Even children. Even their mothers.

Stan glanced back at his gun cabinet, and as he did the kitchen dreams came back to him as a kaleidoscope of things he'd done, and of things he must do now. It was the only way to stop the pain. It was the only way to stop the dreams. It was the only way to stop the killing of children.

He looked back out the window, saw women and small children streaming out of apartment buildings, spreading across the lawn like multi-colored marbles. One of the women was Mrs. Jenkins from the swimming pool. Mrs. Jenkins carrying a child that couldn't have been more than a year old. Mrs. Jenkins wearing shorts and a fur jacket. Shorts in October! Her legs still tanned from basking at the pool in September. He wondered if President Montgomery, whichever limo he was in, had noticed Mrs. Jenkins. He wondered if President Montgomery would notice the flat tire on his Toyota pickup, if he would think it was an abandoned vehicle, first sign of a neighborhood going bad.

He could not see the President in either of the limos. From this angle all he could see was the reflections of parked cars and apartment buildings on the tinted glass. Maybe he'd be able to see the President in the back seat as the limos passed by. But when the limos approached the garbage dumpster enclosure on the far side of the parking lot, the procession slowed and stopped.

The two motorcycle policemen and several police cars U-turned in the lot, forming a half-circle around the limos. The procession sat still for a moment—three lead limos, the two big limos with Presidential seals on them, three unmarked sport utes, at least a dozen police cars, a brown station wagon, a white sport ute, a white van that said NBC on the side. Oversized wheels. Yes, two of the three black sport utes had oversized wheels.

More people came out of apartments so that both sides of the parking lot were lined. Some were men, a few in sweats, most were women and children. Women and children with jackets thrown on over sweats and jeans and pajamas. Only Mrs. Jenkins wore shorts. One woman ran back into an apartment building across the way and reappeared a few seconds later with a camera. Three more women and an old man came out with her. People were arriving from the far end of the complex. He saw Chuck the painter and Marion running together. Marion was dressed to the hilt, wearing a short skirt and jacket and white blouse and high heels. Of course she was dressed to the hilt. She knew who would be visiting. Chuck the painter wore khaki slacks and a jacket instead of the coveralls he'd worn earlier when he moved the dumpsters. When Chuck passed Mrs. Jenkins he slowed a little and gawked at her, but caught up again when Marion apparently shouted something to him.

The crowd moved closer and closer to the Presidential limos so that now some women lifted children into the air so they could see. Most of the people were on the lawn on the other side, some of them gathered around the garbage dumpster enclosure. A couple of boys climbed up on the enclosure and stood above everyone else. But the two motorcycle policemen and some policemen from squad cars shooed the boys down from the enclosure and moved everyone to a spot on the lawn to the right of the enclosure, keeping them away from the front of the limos and away from this side of the limos. Soon the policemen had everyone herded, like cattle, onto the lawn. Now only policemen were in the parking lot, and more policemen surrounded the dumpster enclosure.

The doors on two sport utes at the far end of the line opened and Secret Service men got out and moved forward. Stan watched in fascination as they ran forward and formed a perimeter around the limos. He watched as each of them took up a position, facing away from the limos, scanning the area. He wondered if there were Secret Service men in apartments, but saw no one in windows in the building across the way. Although weapons were not readily apparent, he saw that some of the Secret Service men carried what looked like briefcases and knew there must be automatic weapons in the briefcases. Several of the Secret Service men were on this side, facing his building, but several also faced the crowd on the other side.

One Secret Service man addressed the crowd, shouting something Stan could not hear. When the man raised his hands into the air, the people in the crowd did the same. The crowd cooperating in a show of hands to demonstrate to the Secret Service man that there were no weapons in their hands. But now there were weapons visible. Secret Service men with automatic weapons stood behind and to the side of the man who had asked for the show of hands. Men with automatic weapons at the ready facing children. All those children with their arms in the air. Some, too small to hold their arms in the air, being held up so they can see. All those children held up by loving mothers who want their children to have an experience they'll remember for the rest of their lives.

However long that is.

All of this had happened before. Standing in front of his window, limos and sport utes in the lot, something in his hands. A rifle. His rifle held ready across his chest. Someone behind, encouraging him, pushing him closer to the window. The monster from beneath his bed. Lights flashing, the lights on the circuit board in his dream. Him soldering the board, pulling the trigger to stop the pain, a pain that would last forever if he did not stop it. Overheated solder squealing, screaming like burning flesh.

He turned, saw his apartment tip dizzily. No one else here. No one! When he looked out the window again, the doors of the two sport utes directly behind the limos swung open.

Oversized wheels. Spotlights.

More Secret Service men got out, these dressed more formally in dark suits. Two of them wore overcoats. Four of the men converged on the lead limo and two stood next to the second limo looking up at the apartment buildings. One man scanned the buildings on the other side of the parking lot. The other man scanned his building, might have even seen him, though he could not tell because the man wore sunglasses and kept moving his head slowly from side to side. The four men at the lead limo split up so that one stood on the parking lot side and three stood on the other side.

A few people had gathered below Stan's window and began moving out into the parking lot. Another squad car drove into the complex past the procession and parked in the middle of the lot. Three policemen got out and made these people move away from the limos. The larger crowd on the lawn on the far side closed in but were held back by a line of police forming a half-circle, the half-circle starting at the corner of the dumpster enclosure and ending at the rear of the second limo. It soon became obvious this is where the President would emerge. Two men with cameras who had come from the NBC van aimed at the spot. Everyone waited. Everyone watched the cleared area except the Secret Service men. And the Secret Service man standing on the parking-lot side of the sport utes, the man wearing sunglasses, the man with short hair and large shoulders, seemed now to be staring at Stan's window. Staring at his window just like the man from the sport ute had stared that night a month ago.

Alone. He was so alone. Floating above the crowd as if he were dead. No one down there caring whether he lived or died. Most of them smiling and cheering, pushing their children forward, unaware that he even lives here. So why not float away? Alone in a room with one window and a bed, him just a kid then, a kid all alone with no one to laugh when he laughs, or to cheer when he cheers. No one holding him up to see. Marge could be there, holding Timmy up to see. But it wouldn't work now. Timmy a man by now. Too big to hold up. And Marge? Marge would be his age but well-preserved, much better looking than the cache-file women.

A voice. His own voice calling, "Marge! Help me!"

No. Marge was in the bathroom, her eyes staring away, past him, her neck twisted uncomfortably—so uncomfortably—against the tile. And down there no one cared. No one gave a damn that they . . . He! He had killed his wife and son! But what about the other man? The man who killed children, the man powerful enough to ruin lives without consequence because he's isolated, protected behind his mask that smiles and nods perpetually like a grotesque caricature, a target on a firing range.

He was calling again, had to listen to hear who he was calling. Not shouting. A whisper. "Evie. Evie, I'm sorry. I should have told you everything. I love you, Evie."

Not too late. He could call Evie, tell her about the nights he saw the limo and sport ute, the night he brought the child's head into his kitchen.

He felt even dizzier. His hands gripping the broom were shaking. He leaned on the broom, wanted to sit down, but was afraid to move. The Secret Service man was still watching him. He wished he wasn't standing so close to the window. He wanted to lie down. The sour taste of his lunch gagged him and he coughed. He remembered running from the kitchen and vomiting in the bathtub that night. The head gray, folds of flesh gray, staring eyes gray.

The gun. The gun could fix it. A brain bullet burrowing through and taking memories with it. Memories exploding out a hole like seeds sown. Jackie Kennedy, so fastidious, gathering bits and pieces of memories in her white-gloved hand, not knowing that outside Chicago, in just a few minutes, after the news from Dallas spreads, a smart-assed kid will sit with his cronies in a junior high auditorium, a smart-assed kid holding the hand of a girl he's stolen away from another smart-assed kid. Tammy's hand so soft and warm as he dreams of having her in the sack up in his attic room. Then, much later, when Reagan takes it in the gut and the brain bullet hits Brady, he and Marge will be driving home, trying to find a home again after being told that Timmy is nothing but a decomposed corpse with a bullet hole through it.

One of the Secret Service men opened the back door of the lead limo and the President got out. Stan heard muffled applause and cheering. He heard a whistle and saw Chuck's hand to his mouth. He saw Marion with her hands clapping above her head. The President wore a gray suit and his hair seemed darker than in his pictures or on television. The President raised his hand, waved slowly, his hand level with his head. The President turned a full circle, raised his hand higher. Then the President, a tall man seeming even taller among all the women and children, walked to the edge of the cleared area and began shaking hands two at a time. The President nodded and sometimes his head or his whole body would shake with laughter. The President reached down to a little boy near him, a little boy with blond hair who had his finger in his mouth. The President rubbed the little boy's head, rubbed and rubbed and rubbed the little boy's head.

Stan felt the rubbing on his own head. He wanted the President to stop. He wanted his brain to stop because he knew what was happening. He recalled the nightmare. The nightmare that had made him twist Evie's arm. The nightmare that made his scalp burn. He took one hand off the broom and touched his scalp, expecting his fingers to burn, expecting to feel raw flesh where his hair had been. But when he touched his head he felt only the soft greasiness of his hair and the pain on his scalp lessened.

"Evie, I'm so sorry."

The Secret Service man on the parking-lot side of the sport utes was moving. The man moved to the front fender, stooped a little, looked toward Stan's window and spoke, lips moving rapidly. Whatever the man said affected other Secret Service men. Two of them ran to the half-circle, crowded the President, pressed their bodies against the President. Now the rest of the Secret Service men and some of the policemen looked up toward Stan's window. The briefcases carried by the Secret Service men in the parking lot were down on the pavement, open, and the Secret Service men aimed guns at him.

Something poked his right shoulder and he thought how gentle to be shot. He looked toward his shoulder, expected to see blood there, but instead saw stitching and bristles there, bristles poking his shoulder. He was holding the broom like a rifle, the head of the broom against his shoulder, the handle a barrel aimed toward the parking lot.

He reacted to this by gently laying the broom down as if it really were a rifle, and by lying on the floor himself. Just before the scene disappeared over the windowsill, he saw the President being pushed into the lead limo.

As he lay on the floor Stan heard screams. He heard car doors slammed. A siren blasted again and again. The motorcycle engines roared. And then it was silent except for the heavy sounds of footsteps coming up the stairs to his apartment. Footsteps and laughter, laughter coming from deep within his chest. When he looked at the locked gun cabinet on the other side of the room he laughed even harder.

CHAPTER 27

THE PRESIDENT'S NEMESIS

WHEN THE PLANE climbed out over the bay, Lena imagined it would keep going west, perhaps to Hawaii or the Orient. She imagined that instead of going east, she and Jake were heading west over the Pacific on the extended vacation he had promised. But the sun through the window slid warm across her lap as the plane banked toward the mountains that trapped the smog in the valley. Trapped the way she had been trapped until she met Jake.

She had never flown first class before, had never felt comfortable being waited on until she met Jake. On the street back there somewhere beneath the gray-white smog, she had always suspected that waitresses and clerks and even busboys had known she was once a hooker. Things were different now. She was flying out on a business trip with Jake. The two of them together on their way to Chicago. As she leaned back in the wide leather seat, she hoped that after Chicago they would again fly first class, her and Jake flying to destinations last seen in her high school geography book.

Even though she, Jake, and Walter had driven together to the airport in L.A., Walter had taken a slightly earlier flight and was probably in Chicago already. She had not questioned why Walter took a different flight. Had not even asked for details of why Jake was taking her along. And Jake seemed pleased by this, by her willingness to cooperate without pumping him with questions. The one thing she had asked Jake about, as they waited to board their flight, was Walter's ability to travel with her supply of stuff. The only reason she asked about that was because she feared that in the rush to leave for Chicago her supply might have been left behind by accident. But Jake assured her that Walter would take care of it. The things they needed in Chicago did not necessarily need to be taken with them.

Back in the terminal waiting for their flight, Jake had also revealed more about his past, saying that he grew up in Chicago, that both his powerful father and his wealthy stepfather called Chicago their home. He said that he'd spent his earlier years running his stepfather's computer business. He'd been a hands-on manager, gaining experience and friends from the bottom to the top of the organization. He said that in subsequent years, after his stepfather's death, he found out more about his real father and became involved with powerful men outside the computer business. Because of all these associations through the years he had many friends in Chicago and she had nothing to worry about.

They had begun packing for the trip right after the special news report on television this morning. A man in Joliet, Illinois, a suburb of Chicago, had been suspected of trying to assassinate President Montgomery. There were wobbly camera shots of a window with no one in it, of policemen and Secret Service men running into an apartment building, of the President's motorcade speeding down the road. There was an out-of-breath commentator saying that several people had seen a man with a gun in the window. And, finally, after only a few minutes of confusion and speculation, a uniformed policeman told the gathered crowd of newsmen that the man had only been holding a broom. As soon as the uniformed policeman said this, he was escorted away from the newsmen by two angry looking Secret Service men.

She and Jake had been sitting together on the sofa when the news report came on. She had known something would happen because Jake never sat and watched television during the day, especially game shows. The special news report had interrupted a game show. Jake had taken his arm from around her and turned up the volume, had held his hand up so she would not interrupt. As she watched the report she knew Jake had something to do with it, something to do with this man who was mistakenly thought to be an assassin. All of the phone calls and trips out of town must have been in preparation for this. At first she thought everything was going as planned. But she knew this was not true when Jake shut off the television and threw the television remote control across the room.

So here they were, heading for Chicago. The only explanation from Jake had been that he needed her help, that others would meet them in Chicago and she was not to talk about it until they arrived.

Behind them she could hear a man and woman talking about the incident.

"The guy's lucky they didn't shoot him," said the man.

"Maybe they did," said the woman. "Who's to say the guy they rushed out of the building was really the one in the window?"

"Yeah," said the man. "You never know. Could be another Watergate or Travelgate or some terrorist thing they don't want us to know about. They'll call it Broomgate, a crazy-assed conspiracy to give Montgomery a clean sweep, keep him in office another four years." The man laughed. "Broomgate would be appropriate. Keep the lady out of the White House and she'll fly back home on *her* broom."

"Very funny," said the woman, speaking somewhat harshly. "Besides being the most sexist thing I've heard come out of you, I think your theory is full of shit. If anything, the way the Secret Service jumped the gun would only hurt Montgomery. I think the Secret Service overreacted."

"Maybe you're right," said the man. "But these days I can't help thinking anything that happens is planned way ahead of time. Tricky bastards all of them. Anything for a vote. A damn circus side show." He spoke more softly. "And, by the way, sorry for the sexist remark."

"One thing bothers me," said the woman.

"What's that?"

"Why didn't the Secret Service search through apartments overlooking the place they stopped? I mean if they plan everything, why wouldn't they have at least done that? I thought they always sent out advance teams."

"Montgomery likes to make these impromptu stops," said the man. "Or better yet, he likes to make it appear like he's making impromptu stops. Who the hell knows? None of these photo ops are for the people on hand anyhow. It's all for the media. And that's what makes me think the guy with the broom was a plant."

As the man and woman spoke, Jake stared straight ahead and Lena noticed his fists were clenched on his lap. She remembered that his fists had also been clenched during the ride to the airport. At one point he'd even pounded his thigh repeatedly. Because of this she knew that the plan, whatever it was, had to be more than just trying to embarrass the President or the Secret Service. She'd never seen Jake so close to losing control, so close to becoming violent. Maybe Jake had acted this way when he found out what Raphael had done to her. Maybe she hadn't seen his anger then because she'd been so busy licking her wounds. One thing she knew for sure, no matter what happened. Somehow Jake would have vengeance upon his enemy, or enemies. And she knew she would play a part in this vengeance.

What the hell. She'd wanted in on Jake's business, wanted to be trusted, needed, indispensable. And now it seemed Jake's business was a lot more far-reaching than computers and stocks and real estate.

When the male flight attendant asked about drinks, Jake waved him away angrily.

CHAPTER 28

THE PRESIDENT'S NEMESIS

STANLEY JOHNSON

SECOND FLOOR OF Joliet Police Headquarters. The same building Stan had visited so many times more than two decades earlier, the millennium come and gone. The cement and steel and plaster of the building outliving the humans who inhabit it—the policemen, criminals, and victims who file through its hallways and offices. The air in the building smelling faintly of perspiration, bathroom disinfectant, copy machines, gun oil. A different set of smells than the last time he was here. Then, the air in the building had been permeated with cigarette smoke. Now the smokers were outside somewhere. He recalled catching a whiff of cigarette smoke while he was being led in from the garage.

He sat in a chair with his eyes closed because he was tired and the fluorescent lights made his eyes burn. He recalled how it had been back in 1980, imagined the wooden chair on which he sat able to carry him back in time, the tree-ring pattern on the seat setting up a field in which he could travel. What the hell. He could do it. A crazy man could do anything.

He and Marge had been in a cubicle office on this same floor, an office with frosted glass not quite to the ceiling, probably dozens of offices just like it. Inspector Jacobson had been across the table from them asking questions. He remembered the questions and Marge's answers in detail.

"Did Timmy have older playmates he might have followed?"

"No."

"Did he like animals?"

"As much as any other child."

"Could he have followed a dog?"

"No. I told you, we have a fenced yard so he never followed animals."

"Do you have relatives in town he might have gone to?"

"No. I told you, Stan's relatives are all gone and my sister lives in Arizona."

"Do any of the neighbors ever watch Timmy?"

"No. The times we had a sitter she came to the house."

"This sitter, does Timmy know where she lives?"

"She lives several blocks away and Stan always drove her. Anyway, you've already gone to her house, haven't you?"

"Yes, Mrs. Johnson, we have. But we'd check between your house and her house more closely if we had reason to believe Timmy knew where she lived."

Questions and answers. Sometimes Marge answering, sometimes him answering. The two of them like one person except for a fraction of a second pause to see whose turn it was.

The words were still here, perhaps floating about in the building somewhere. But the details, except for that frosted glass office and the questions and answers, had faded somewhat. The one other detail he recalled, besides the smell of cigarette smoke in the place, was Marge's wrinkled handkerchief sticking out from between the fingers of her tightened fist as she sat beside him.

Now, here he was in the same building, on the same floor. But he was not in a frosted glass cubicle office. He was in an interrogation room. A room with a thick wooden door, dark from coat after coat of varnish, the door with a small rectangular window in it. He'd studied the door before closing his eyes. The glass in the window had wire mesh imbedded in it like a checkerboard turned on edge. The door was locked from the outside. Every time someone came in he heard the key pushing through the tumblers, a warning. He recalled that when they led him down the hall to this room he'd seen other closed doors with electronic keyless entry locks and wondered why the room they chose for him had an old style key lock. Perhaps it was all part of the interrogation plan. Even the old wooden chair. Perhaps the next interrogation would be accompanied by cigarette smoke. Perhaps they'd transport him back in time so he could confess killing his son by not being there when he was needed, and killing his wife by not realizing how depressed she'd become.

He readjusted himself in the uncomfortable chair, opened his eyes and looked at his hands, at the lines on his palms, rivers on a landscape of sparkling dew. The lights in the room were very bright, not a single overhead light, not the interrogation floodlight he'd imagined, but fluorescent lights that made everything in the room give off a light of its own. No windows. No shadows.

The four off-white walls shined. The varnished door shined. The dark brown floor tiles and matching kick plates shined. Varnish and wax and enameled walls. Above the fluorescent fixtures were acoustic ceiling tiles that looked like slices of white bread with the crusts cut off. Everything with sharp, well-defined edges. Everything square inside this cube, except the brass doorknob, except the slightly rounded edges of the table, except the prisoner's D-ring bolted to the center of the table, except him.

It was a very old table. His hands, when he lifted them from the worn dark green vinyl top of the table, left clouds of perspiration behind on the surface, clouds that slowly evaporated. When Chief Jacobson of the Joliet Police asked him if he needed an attorney he wondered if the Chief had noticed the clouds of perspiration his hands had left behind. The vinyl on the table was set into the wood, seemed to have sunken into the wood from the weight of criminal hands over the years. Hands that rubbed the vinyl, fingered the rounded blond wood along the edges. Varnish streaked with wear like church pews. Pleading hands, lying hands, murdering hands, innocent hands, all sweating in exactly the same way through the same human pores.

So Inspector Jacobson was Chief of the Joliet Police Department now. And he had to be near retirement age because the skin on his face had moved down away from his eyes, had slipped into folds on his cheeks and chin. Decades of robberies and rapes and murders and gang-bangers had pulled his face into a serious thin-lipped frown and had taken most of his hair.

He had not recognized Chief Jacobson until he sat across from him at the table, until he saw the same dark brown eyes. Chief Jacobson's voice was also the same as in the past. Deep, slow, serious, a space of time between each word for thought or consideration.

A Secret Service agent, the oldest, the one with brown skin and shaved head who had flashed his credentials back at the apartment, stood behind Chief Jacobson during the first few questions. He noticed that the agent's skin was slightly darker than Chief Jacobson's and that the agent was younger than Chief Jacobson. He wondered who had authority, the Secret Service or the local police, but these thoughts were fleeting and vanished when the questions began.

"You've been given your rights, Mr. Johnson?"

"Yes."

"Did you call your attorney?"

"I don't have one."

"Shall we appoint one for you?"

He had wanted to shake Chief Jacobson's hand, remind him who he was, stir his memory. But he was afraid to do anything. On television the criminals always said they had nothing to hide. Not enough time—expensive television time—to bother with an attorney. On television the "beans" are often spilled at the scene of the crime, at the end of the program right before the final barrage of commercials. He was not on television. He was in hell.

"Yes, an attorney."

So now he was alone in the room waiting for the attorney. Chief Jacobson and the Secret Service agent had left without saying another word. His pockets were empty. A police sergeant with one arm had put his wallet and keys and change and comb and wrist watch into a plastic bag after the young policeman—the policeman who had sat next to him in the back seat of the squad car on the way in—took off the handcuffs.

He felt as though he had been sitting in the room for at least an hour. But the time it took to get to the station seemed like seconds. He remembered lying on the floor in front of his window. He remembered his cackling laughter. He remembered footsteps and voices, one voice in particular saying, "I've got him! Search the place! Where the hell's the gun? All I see here is a goddamn broom!" The same voice gave him his rights, told him he had the right to remain silent. So he did. He hadn't said a word until he was in this room. There wasn't time for words, just mumbling, hands helping him up, cuffs being put on, the rush down the stairs, someone pushing his head down so he wouldn't bump his head as he got into the police car, the shrieks and screams of women, a baby crying, the drive into downtown Joliet. He had opened his eyes only when he had to. He had opened them on the way down the stairs. The dark-skinned Secret Service agent with shaved head, the one who stood behind Chief Jacobson during the first few questions in this room, had led the way. The agent wore a dark brown suit and the back of his head was thick with rippled layers of fat and muscle.

The same agent sat in the front seat of the squad car next to the driver. He was aware that the driver and the policeman who sat next to him in the back seat were very young. The two policemen and the agent did not speak as they drove him here. He really hadn't seen their faces during the drive. In the car he'd stared at his hands, his hands locked in shiny cuffs, a chain locked to the cuffs dangling in his crotch, the other end of the chain fastened to a D-ring bolted to the floor of the squad car. He'd stared at his hands until the rocking of the car made him sick. He'd closed his eyes for the rest of the trip and only opened them again when the daylight, purple through his lids, went black as if he'd come out of a dream about falling. The squad car had descended a steep ramp into the dark low-ceilinged garage beneath the police station, the garage in which he'd smelled cigarette smoke.

He had followed the same dark thick rippled head up two flights of stairs. A hand from behind held the belt of his trousers, jerked his stomach tight with each step. His mouth had been dry and his clothes, except for the tight belt, felt like they touched only the hairs on his body. His belt was gone now, but he did not remember anyone taking it off. It had probably been pulled from him like a dead snake while his pockets were being emptied.

His story. He would have to explain. Explain what? That he was going crazy? No. Not that. He had been standing at the window with his broom when he saw a man look up toward him and duck. He had gotten scared, scared that he might be shot, and he, too, had ducked. That was the story, that was the truth. But what about his guns? They were locked in the cabinet, unloaded, and they hadn't been fired in years. The guns were registered. Sedgwick had seen to that. "Everything on the up and up," he had said. And what about the pornography in his bedroom and the load of un-opened mail—some of it probably pornography—on his coffee table? And what about the images of women stored on his computer? Okay, so he was a voyeur. So what? A guy's got a right, like it says on the inner envelopes, or like it says on the warning pages of Web sites, to view what he wants in the privacy of his own home. And what about Evie and Marion? "What about them?" he would say. "They're my girlfriends." He would sound like a juvenile delinquent. And what about the limo and sport ute? What about them? He saw a couple vehicles one night, thought they might have been prowlers, told Evie and Marion about them. There was no head of a child. Not ever. There was no call from Youngblood, or that other man who said Youngblood was in jail, or even Derek Washington. Nothing. Just a dirty old man without a job barely making ends meet who thought he might be interested in guns but really wasn't.

What about the dreams? How could he tell anyone about the dreams? Dreams that made him want to shoot the President. Except the President was alive. This did not bother him so he must not have really wanted to shoot the President. He could have shot anyone who'd rub a kid's head like that if he'd really wanted to, if he'd taken time to pull the rifle from his gun cabinet, load it, and, like the young man who'd visited him, aimed the gun out the window. A gun instead of a broom.

Could he have really aimed a gun instead of a broom? If he hadn't felt so guilty about letting Marge die and about the way he treated Evie and even the way he treated Marion—if he hadn't felt guilty about all these things, would he have taken out his anger on the President because that's what he was supposed to do?

Or was it all coincidence? His paranoia making the appearance of the limo and sport ute into something significant. The Secret Service sends an advance team to a place the President is going to visit and he goes nuts. Or maybe it was a training exercise. Place a bogus package at the site to be visited and then have some agent trainees come back and search for it. Maybe it was his paranoia that made him think he saw a child's head in a garbage bag. His paranoia turning everything into a plot against him. His paranoia dredging up his subconscious stew, turning his guilt and fears against him in nightmares that come to life. If he had been able to see Dr. Todd he would have been fine. When this was over he would see Dr. Todd and they'd have a long, long talk.

There was laughter somewhere. Him again, laughing like an old witch. Add some nightmares to the pot, stir it up, and what do you get? Maybe this was a nightmare. In a moment he would awaken at home, or in Evie's apartment. Evie reassuring him, comforting him, forgiving him, kissing him.

He lifted his hands from the table and watched the clouds of sweat evaporate like storm clouds filmed at high-speed. Time racing ahead so fast that any moment the end could come, all whiteness, then black. He wondered if death was like that. He wished that years could go by in seconds—all forgotten, all forgiven—even though it would bring him closer to death.

The D-ring in the center of the table was just like the one he had been chained to in the squad car and he wondered why they had not left the cuffs on and chained him to this D-ring. He pushed at the table edge and when it did not move he concluded that it must be bolted to the floor. He returned his hands to the top of the table and stared at them, first the backs with their veins, then the palms with their rivers.

All the while a tiny closed-circuit camera in one corner of the ceiling watched him.

CHAPTER 29

THE PRESIDENT'S NEMESIS

Having arrived in Chicago before them, Walter rented a car and picked them up at the terminal. When Jake said he needed to meet alone with the "others" in a restaurant on a street called Rush, Walter dropped him off. Meanwhile, Walter drove downtown to the Marriott where Jake had told her to register.

It was a gray cloudy day. On a side street off Rush Street Lena saw a hooker bending to peer into the open window of a late model sedan. The hooker wore a jean skirt and a rabbit jacket and spike heel boots. The hooker rested her hand on the door edge as if gently touching a child, then looked about quickly as if she were the child and was about to steal candy, perky mouth partly open. The millennium had come and gone and hookers still dressed the same. Maybe they'd always dress this way. Maybe in the so-called afterlife they'd dress this way. The john in the sedan turned the hooker down and the next vehicle was a Ford Explorer. Now, the only difference in the hooker's body language was that she did not have to bend down to peer into the open window. The hooker got into the Explorer and drove away with the john into the cold rain that had just begun.

Lena registered under the name Mr. and Mrs. Bertrand R. Feinstein, using the American Express card Jake had given her. The room faced east and she could see Lake Michigan. The lake was gray, blending into the gray sky. A river that led to the lake, the part of the river she could see between two corncob-shaped buildings, was green like something rotten.

Though nowhere near the size of the penthouse apartment in L.A., the hotel suite was elegant, with fully stocked bar and entertainment center behind sliding panels. Lena made a bloody Mary, changed into a comfortable caftan Jake had bought her. A woman of leisure, her only concern where to have dinner.

Tonight Jake would probably drop a few hundred at dinner while the hooker she saw this afternoon gave about her fifteenth blow job of the day. And while she was in bed with Jake tonight, the hooker would be gargling like mad to get the disinfectant taste out of her mouth, that is if the hooker cleaned the dicks off before she sucked them.

The world was upside down and for a change Lena was on top. She recalled, back in L.A., telling Anita that at first she thought Jake was a little quirky and laughed at herself.

"Lena."

Lena the doll girl in her bed, someone tucking pillows at her sides, beneath her head. The doll girl whose mouth makes a tongue-click sound when Mommy Lena pulls out the pacifier.

"Lena. Wake up."

The sofa. The conversation pit. Unfinished bloody Mary on the coffee table. Jake at the entertainment center, messing with a video player. The click of Baby Lena's tongue had been the clicking of the video player as is sucked in the recording Jake had fed it. The large window through which she had viewed the lake and the corncob buildings and the green river was dark.

"What time is it?"

Jake turned, his face serious. "It's late, but I need your help."

She stood, felt a little dizzy, knew she must have slept several hours. She went to the entertainment center where Jake was now tuning in the large-screen television. "What can I do?"

Jake faced her, his eyes looked tired but serious. She could smell cooking oil on him.

"Have you been to a fish fry or something?"

"I met some people at a restaurant. I thought I had all the friends I needed in this town. You'd think when I mentioned my father, but these fuckers today . . ."

Jake touched her arm. "Are you ready to help, Lena?"

"Of course. I said I would. I always said I would."

"You'll know things, Lena. You'll know things that could hurt us."

"You and me?"

"Yes. And others."

"I'll do whatever you tell me. You don't even have to say it. I'll keep everything to myself. I mean it, Jake. You don't have to give me the details. Just tell me my part and I'll do the best I can."

"Good. That's what I need to hear."

Jake kissed her. She thought it would be a quick kiss, but he hung on, squeezed her, trembled slightly with the force of the squeeze as if he were a child clinging to her.

They sat on the sofa in the conversation pit and watched a video recording on the huge television screen again and again. There was no sound. The recording was only a few minutes long.

The recording showed a woman running errands. First the woman was walking in a parking lot, disappearing into a store. Then the woman was coming out of the store with packages. This was repeated at different stores, at a post office, at a bank. The final scene showed the woman getting out of her car and going into an apartment building. The camera stayed on the building after the woman went inside and Lena could see drapes open. Then the camera backed up to show the whole building, a three-story apartment building in a complex of buildings that all looked the same. She could tell the recording was made through a strong telephoto lens by the way the picture jiggled when the scene changed.

As she watched the recording again and again, Lena noticed that the woman wasn't bad looking, probably about her age. In the various scenes the woman wore blue jeans and bright blouses or T-shirts. The woman's hair was blond like hers. After seeing the recording only a couple of times, she knew that her job would be to impersonate this woman. And, though she was curious, she kept her mouth shut and studied the woman's movements.

When they finished with the recording, Jake turned on a news channel. The top story was about the man who had panicked President Montgomery's entourage, and the resulting media deluge about a possible assassination attempt. She saw the same coverage she had seen before they left L.A., the police rushing into an apartment building, wobbly cameras pointing at a window, the President's motorcade speeding away, a policeman saying the guy was only holding a broom. Then there was a newsman standing in front of the apartment building and she realized that the building on the news and the building in the video recording were the same. The woman she was to impersonate lived in the building where the man had supposedly stood in the window aiming a broom at the President.

The newsman in front of the apartment building was asking open-ended questions. Why did the man aim a broom? Why didn't the Secret Service and the police react more violently if they really thought it was a gun? Why did the motorcade make an unscheduled stop at an apartment complex where, apparently, according to reliable sources, the Secret Service did not perform their usual advance probe of the area?

The newsman told about the man with the broom. Stanley Johnson, an early retiree living alone. "Perhaps it's ironic," said the newsman, "that a man, apparently forced into early retirement before he's eligible for Social Security because of federal cutbacks, should come back to haunt the current administration? Some may say Mr. Johnson would have made the same gesture with his broom regardless of the past, regardless of his apparent below-the-poverty-line financial situation. But I can't help thinking that without realizing it, Mr. Johnson has made a statement about our society, about its violent nature, and about its domestic priorities."

Jake shut off the television and continued staring at the blank screen. Lena knew she had promised not to ask unnecessary questions, but it was obvious the woman in the video recording lived where Stanley Johnson lived.

"Jake?"

"Yes."

"It has to do with this, doesn't it?"

"Yes, Lena."

"Maybe I should have brought my computer along."

"Why?"

"I could have gotten on the Internet and seen what's being said on newsgroups or in blogs. Get a feel for public opinion."

"It doesn't matter what the public thinks at the moment, Lena. All that matters now is that we finish this the way it needs to be finished. It's ironic we'll be finishing it here in Chicago where so many of these things have started over the years."

Lena could tell Jake had said as much as he was going to say for now. She asked no more questions, but that didn't stop her from speculating.

When he said "these things" was he referring to assassination attempts? And when he said things had started in Chicago, was he referring to the mob? The mob, the Kennedys, Sam Giancana, Castro, J. Edgar Hoover . . . all ancient history. Or was it?

Jake went to the window and stood looking out at the darkened skyline. His hands were folded behind his back. It was a stance she'd never seen him take before, standing there with his hands folded behind his back like . . . like an old man. Like he had suddenly aged many years.

CHAPTER 30

THE PRESIDENT'S NEMESIS

T HE ATTORNEY LOOKED a little like Glen, the meat department
manager at Bud's IGA. His face was round and red, his eyes were blue, but
his hair wasn't as short as Glen's. His hair was reddish blond and curly. His
name was Bob McLean—"Call me Bob," he said—and he kept pulling a pen
from beneath his pin-striped jacket and putting the pen back after jotting
something down in a notepad he'd put on the table near the D-ring. On his
way in the door, the sergeant with one arm had handed Bob a Styrofoam cup
of coffee. Stan watched Bob drink the coffee, watched Bob pull his pen out
and write a note, watched Bob put the pen back again and again instead of
leaving it out on the table. To Stan, Bob seemed somewhat fatigued as he
told his story.

Stan told the story to Bob just as he had planned, nothing more, nothing less. Bob pulled his pen out, jotted something down, put his pen back,
sipped coffee, yawned a few times. Stan tried looking into Bob's blue eyes
when he got the chance so that Bob would know he was telling the truth.
And, except for the things he left out, he did tell the truth, especially when

he told Bob that he was frightened.

Bob put away his pen. "I don't think you have anything to worry about, Stan. I've spoken with Chief Jacobson and Agent Philips and their stories match yours. They've made a mistake and they know it. Normally I'd try to speed things up, demand your immediate release, but they need time to let things cool down. They need time to explain the mistake to the media. I'd say the best thing to do at this point is to answer their questions. But don't go overboard. If you volunteer too much it tends to stretch things out and only lengthens the amount of time they can hold you. Actually, the only reason you're being held now is for your own protection."

"Is someone after me?"

Bob took out his pen, made a scribble on the notepad. "Nobody we know of. But you've got to understand the public reaction to such a thing. The only people who went into your apartment were the police and the Secret Service. The public has got to be told the whole story so there won't be any problems when they do release you."

Bob put his pen away. "If they were to send you home now, you'd be mobbed by reporters. And I think you'll agree you wouldn't want that."

"I guess not."

"All right then, Stan, there's one more formality. I know you've been questioned quite a bit already by the others and me. But they want to question you one more time tonight. Will that be all right?"

"What time is it?"

Bob reached for his pen, seemed confused for a moment, realizing his watch wasn't inside his jacket. He withdrew his hand and held it up so he could look at his watch. "Almost two in the morning."

"Can I sleep soon?"

"Yes, they're going to put you up in a hotel tonight and maybe a couple more nights depending how things cool down. Shall I ask them in now?"

"I guess so."

Chief Jacobson and the Secret Service agent, Philips, carried their own chairs into the small room. Modern vinyl chairs, not old wooden ones like he and Bob sat in. Bob put his notepad away in his pocket and pulled his chair around to Stan's side of the table. After sitting down next to him Bob nodded for him to go ahead and answer questions. Chief Jacobson asked the questions and, again, did not acknowledge their having met in the past. But by now everyone was calling Stan by his first name.

"Sorry we have to do this again, Stan."

"That's okay."

"What were you doing at the window?"

"I was watching the President. I heard the sirens."

"Were you holding anything in your hands?"

"Yes, I was holding my broom."

"And that's all you were holding?"

"Maybe I was holding my dick, too."

They all glanced at one another, a mixture of exhaustion and amusement on their faces.

"All right," he said. "Sorry. I'm pretty tired is all."

Chief Jacobson continued. "So the only thing you held in your hands was the broom."

"Yes."

"Why were you holding the broom?"

"I was sweeping the kitchen when I heard the sirens."

"Did you have any reason to be angry with the President?"

"Nothing special."

"By 'nothing special' do you mean you had been angry with the President at one time?"

"Well, I didn't vote for him. I didn't care for him one way or another."

"Were you angry because you were laid off from your job?"

"You mean my job at the Joliet Lab?"

"Yes."

"Sure, I was kind of angry at the system at the time for forcing me into early retirement, but I got over it."

"Were you angry because of recent cuts in Social Security benefits?"

"It doesn't affect me yet. I'm not old enough to collect."

"But when you are old enough you'll probably be getting less. Does that make you angry?"

"It doesn't make me happy, but there's nothing I can do about it."

"Were you angry because of the deaths of your wife and son?"

Earlier, when they asked about Marge and Timmy, he had become quite upset. Even though he knew they would ask again, he was surprised at how much this bothered him. Maybe it shouldn't have bothered him this much. The old time-heals-all-wounds argument. But asking if he was angry because of the deaths of Marge and Timmy . . .

He could hear the anger in his voice as he spoke. "Again, I was angry at the system for not catching the murderer. Since they didn't find the murderer I had to be angry at someone. But, like I said before, that was years ago!"

"I know, Stan. Be patient with us. We'd like to go through it one more time, then you can get some rest."

Chief Jacobson's hands were folded on the table while he asked his questions. The Secret Service agent didn't say a word, just sat with his hands hidden beneath the table and his head down. His brown bald head shined beneath the fluorescent lights. Beads of sweat were visible in the folds of skin at the sides of his neck. Probably thinking about all the trouble back at headquarters for

259

him. Wondering if the other agent—the one wearing sunglasses, the one who spotted Stan in the window—should be reprimanded. Wondering what the hell the President was going to think about his agents hauling in a bystander with a broom. Wondering what the voters were going to think.

Stan told them about his job at the lab again, about his job at Bud's IGA, about the trouble he was having finding another job. He told them about his guns, how they hadn't been fired since the gun-nut outing after he bought them from Sedgwick as an investment. He said he simply cleaned them once in a while after that. He told them about the pornography he'd been getting in the mail, said he sent in for a couple things and must have gotten on a bunch of mailing lists, said he was afraid to throw the stuff away for fear some kids would get hold of it.

Suddenly, Agent Philips spoke up. "What about Rose Adams Haney?"

"Who?"

"The President's challenger. Do you have any reason to be angry with her?"

"No. Why the hell would I be angry with her?"

Philips paused a few seconds, collecting his thoughts, then asked, "What about your computer?"

"My computer?"

"Yes. Since we spoke last we had someone look at the files that are stored on it. What about that?"

"I've surfed the Web just like anyone else. I haven't had Internet access that long and I was curious."

"Curious?"

"Any guy who gets on the Web the first time takes a look at the sex sites. Haven't you looked at them?"

Agent Philips did not smile. "Maybe I have, Stan. But I'm asking about the files you've saved."

Stan glanced toward Jacobson, then looked back at Philips. "Look, I'm tired as hell. Sure, I might have saved some pictures of women. For Christ sake, I live alone. What the hell's wrong with saving a few pictures of women to look at?"

"What about the pictures of children?"

"Children?"

"What if we found pictures of naked children on your cache files? What about that?"

"I don't know anything about that. Jesus! Children?"

"Yeah," said Philips. "And what about the mail you've gotten. Where did you send for it?"

"I don't remember. All I know is I must have sent for some pictures a long time ago and gotten on a bunch of mailing lists."

Bob McLean, his attorney, broke in. "This is all irrelevant. There was nothing illegal about what you found on the computer, was there? If so, I sure as hell would like to see it."

Philips rubbed his eyes. "I don't know if anything on the computer is illegal yet. We're having someone look at it."

Bob asked, "So why did you say you found pictures of children?"

Instead of answering, Philips took out a handkerchief and wiped his forehead. Then he changed the subject. Philips wanted him to tell again about the deaths of his wife and son. And so he went through it one more time, even detailing the visits to Dr. Todd.

When they were finally finished, Chief Jacobson took Stan to his office. "A more comfortable place to wait," Jacobson said, after Bob McLean and Agent Philips were gone. In the hallway, on the way to Jacobson's office, even though Bob McLean had told him not to volunteer anything, Stan wondered if he had done the right thing. Because the dreams were unreal, he had not told about them, not even when asked if anything unusual had happened to him recently. And because the phone calls from Derek Washington and Raymond Youngblood and the man saying Youngblood was in jail were unreal, he had not told about them. Somehow it was easier to convince himself the phone calls were imagined than to consider the other possibility. The possibility that he had been set up and that whoever did the setup was still out there, either outside the system or inside the system. Someone powerful. Someone who could get to him if he did not simply let what had happened slide on through like a good crap. Someone like the young man who had admired his guns, the young man with gray eyes.

Jacobson's office was dark after the bright lights in the small interrogation room, the bright lights in the hallway, the bright lights in the men's room. There was no light from the office window. He took his watch out of the plastic bag that had been handed back to him by the one-armed sergeant who said something about having to work a double shift. Four o'clock. He had been in the police station over twelve hours. Jacobson led him to a sofa against the wall and he wondered if he could sleep now.

"Excuse me a moment, Stan. I'll make one quick call, then we'll get something to eat. You must be starving. After that you can rest."

Jacobson looked at him sadly as he spoke on the phone.

"I'll be home in a couple hours, dear."

"Yes, that's it."

"Yes, yes, that's what happened, all a mistake. He's here now. I'm going to take him to a hotel myself."

"I know."

"Yes, unfortunate."

"An over-anxious agent, I guess."

"All right, see you later."

Jacobson took off his suit jacket and hung it on the back of his chair. He sat down at his desk, propped up his elbows and rubbed his eyes with his palms.

After a few moments of silence, Stan said, "So you're the Chief now."

"Yes, Stan, I'm the Chief now. I guess this is the kind of thing a police chief has to deal with. Mistakes, the big ones. I remembered who you were as soon as I saw your name. I'm sorry we didn't meet again under more pleasant circumstances."

"I have to admit I was confused as hell when they grabbed me. All I did was shut my eyes and hang on. It was like riding a roller coaster."

"I know this doesn't mean much after all that's happened, but I'm sorry, I really am."

"What about my computer? What about those pictures of naked children he said were on it? I never . . ."

Jacobson waved his hand. "Philips was fishing. I had a look at the files with him. The sites saved on your computer were the usual ones saying they had pictures of barely legal teenaged girls, but what they really showed were models in their twenties and thirties dressed in cheerleading outfits and sneakers. There was nothing to it."

"But I don't even remember accessing stuff like that."

"It happens, Stan. These sites open up other sites and the next thing you know you've got all kinds of crap on your cache files. We had a case in court recently where they tried to use this stuff. Judge threw it out. As far as I'm concerned you've suffered an invasion of privacy and I apologize on behalf of my department."

He wanted to say, "That's okay," almost automatically, but didn't. He accepted the apology, even felt somewhat honored by it, although he knew he shouldn't. Filing a lawsuit crossed his mind, but he thought, the hell with it. All he wanted at this point was to be left alone.

Jacobson called out for sandwiches and coffee. They sat across from one another at the desk and ate, two men carefully chewing their food in the yellow lamplight. Jacobson older than him, his face wrinkled and thin, his brown skin seeming to have lightened with age.

"You know, Stan, I've seen a lot of people in trouble. That's the problem with this job. You spend your life trying to help people, and usually the most you can manage is to deal out a little revenge, try to make things balance. But what a balance. Innocent people get hurt, they always get hurt. I'll be retiring soon. I've always told people I liked my job. Ever since the terrorist attacks in oh-one I've not been so sure. It's like people have lost importance in the world compared to other living things. Maybe the plants and animals are taking revenge. We humans are an uncivilized bunch as far as the plants and animals are concerned. Like my lawn. I never worried about my lawn before, except to cut it. But this past summer I spent my weekends making sure there wasn't one damn weed in that lawn. And for what? So I'd make sure I'd have something to do after this?" Jacobson waved his hand in front of him, acknowledging the size of his office with the long sweep of his hand. "Besides a pretty good pension, what can they give me? What value have I been?"

Twelve hours earlier Stan thought he was going crazy, thought the top of his head would blow off and he'd end up in a straight jacket. Now, here he was listening to Chief Jacobson and thinking about everything that had happened to him, trying to make sense of it. Chief Jacobson was about his age and, in a way, sounded a little crazy himself. Plants and animals taking revenge. That really made sense. But who said life was supposed to make sense? Maybe it was all a dream, even this. Maybe someone threw away a rotten melon in the garbage. Maybe some other hunks of garbage stuck to it, made eyes and a nose and mouth on it. Maybe the limo and sport ute were never there, or if they had been there, the men who came in the limo and sport ute somehow knew that the President would make an unscheduled visit later and had considered planting a bomb in one of the dumpsters. Maybe they did plant a bomb but were foiled by Marion's need to create a good image, having her handyman move the dumpsters. Anything. Absolutely anything could be true. And some of it could simply be in people's minds and that could make it true.

Jacobson was staring at him. Jacobson's mind creating his own personal hell, wondering what it's all for when all you do in the end is rot away like garbage. Jacobson looking toward retirement, facing the life Stan knew so well, a life where things that once seemed insignificant are enlarged and become symbols to hang onto during that fall toward the grave.

After a moment, Stan said, "Your job is important."

Jacobson seemed surprised by this, waved his hand. "Sorry. Didn't mean to go on so. Guess I'm tired."

"Yeah, me, too. Tired in the head. It's easy to get into that trap, thinking you're not worth anything. My psychiatrist used to say our value lies in concern for future generations. Guess that's true for you. Taking criminals out of circulation so they won't be able to hurt anyone down the road."

Jacobson sighed. "That may be true, Stan. But a long time ago I didn't come through for you and your wife. We never caught your son's murderer."

"Maybe he wasn't really a murderer."

"What do you mean?"

"Maybe he committed one crime and changed. Maybe that's why you couldn't catch him, because he was no longer the same person. What if I had done it?" He surprised himself when he said this. But by saying it he felt he was gaining respect from Jacobson.

"You didn't do it, Stan."

"Of course not. But you looked into it. You questioned the hell out of me."

"We had to."

"Of course you had to. Just like that Secret Service agent had to duck and holler. If he thought there was the remotest possibility I had a gun and didn't act, he wouldn't have been doing his job."

Jacobson stood and walked to the window. In the darkened office without his jacket he looked even older, shoulders low and narrow, his upper back arched outward slightly as if weights were dragging him down.

Then Jacobson turned and stared at him. "There's something that bothers me, Stan."

"What's that?"

"The way you've gotten so philosophical all of a sudden."

"What's wrong with that?"

Jacobson waved his hand and sighed again. "I don't know. You're right. Nothing's wrong with philosophy at a time like this."

But there was something different. He was talking to someone. He was letting things out. Why now? Except for being tired, he felt better now than he had in weeks. Was it the guilt? Had his mistaken arrest taken away some of his guilt? Had he welcomed the humiliation with open arms? Is that why he felt a great sense of relief? Had he aimed the broom at the mocking smile of the President to humiliate himself?

Jacobson looked out the window again. "I'm surprised there's so few members of the media out front. Guess we outlasted most of them. We'll go out the back. My staff keeps that clear."

Jacobson turned from the window, his face in the shadows. "Shall we go to the hotel now?"

"Whatever you say, Chief."

Jacobson took his jacket from the back of his chair and put it on. "There's still one thing in all this that doesn't add up, Stan."

"What's that?"

"With all the stress that's put on security these days, why the hell didn't they check the place out before they let the President stop there? As far as we knew he was simply doing a drive-through. Any other time he made an extended stop like this they've sent in an advance team. In a perfect world they should have visited you, maybe confiscated your guns for the day."

"Can they do that?"

"Sure, if they get you to agree. Wouldn't you have agreed?"

"Of course."

"That's what I mean. In some ways it almost seems as though someone was waiting for something to happen. The President stops to give a little speech. An impromptu stop, they say, but I can't believe they'd be so careless. Be patient with us over the next few days, Stan."

"More questions?"

"Yes. I can't help thinking there's more to this."

"Well, I suppose anything's possible."

"And one more thing."

"What's that?"

"The media vultures have already descended. They've been trying to contact you."

As soon as they exited the underground garage in Jacobson's car, several reporters, who had apparently hidden behind the concrete wall bordering the ramp, leapt from the wall and ran alongside. One reporter tried to ask questions through the closed window. Jacobson said, "Goddamn leeches!" and sped away leaving the reporters looking hungry like the crowd of agents and policemen who had rushed into his apartment the previous afternoon with guns drawn.

CHAPTER 31

THE PRESIDENT'S NEMESIS

GEORGE DOMENICO, PRESIDENT Montgomery's campaign
manager, and Charlie Thorsen, the Secret Service Director of Protective
Operations, sat in Domenico's office staring at Domenico's notebook
computer, which was opened up between them on the desk. They both sat
at the same side of the desk, very close to one another so they could both
reach the keyboard. Domenico had called Thorsen from another meeting
and Thorsen had not brought his own computer with him.

Both men were red-faced. The last part of their typed conversation was
still displayed in the Notepad window on the screen. This is what it said:

"You must have known S was planning something for Joliet."

"I say again, we had no idea it was anything like this."

"But he's always up to something. It's your job to find out what the
hell it is? You spoon feed hints without detail, letting me know something's
bound to happen, then when it does . . ."

"I did the best I could keeping you informed."

"You wanted me to go to Monty without details?"

"Yes."

"Great. My head in the fucking noose!"

Although their faces were red with anger, both Domenico and Thorsen looked tired. Their jackets were off, ties loosened, shirts wrinkled. The computer was facing more toward Domenico because he had typed last. Thorsen turned the computer his way and typed.

"George, I'm the one in the security business. I'll take the rap if this goes public."

Domenico turned the computer back his way.

"What about the psychologist S had working for him? What about the drugs they used?"

Thorsen: "They'll find a trace. But they won't make it public."

Domenico: "Yet another botched investigation swept under the rug."

Thorsen reached anxiously toward the keyboard, thought for a moment, then withdrew.

Domenico: "Is that why you don't want me to go to Monty with it now? Because of the fuckup?"

Thorsen: "There's more to this. We know enough now to convince us the best thing is let it die a slow death."

Domenico: "What if S has something else in mind?"

Thorsen: "He's covered. It's over. That's why going to Monty now is a mistake."

Domenico: "A few days ago you wanted me to go to him. Now you don't want me to tell anyone."

Thorsen: "We didn't have all the facts then. You haven't told anyone?"

Domenico: "Not my wife nor my confessor nor my guardian angel."

Thorsen: "That's the way I've handled it. The only ones who know are those who need to know."

Domenico: "Maybe someone should figure out a way to give S a retirement package he can't refuse."

Thorsen: "Maybe we will."

Domenico: "Keep me out of it."

Thorsen: "I will."

After a pause, Domenico turned the computer toward him, erased the text, exited the Notepad program, and ran the program that erased extraneous temporary storage. While he did this, Thorsen picked up the *Washington Post* from the desk and rattled its pages before throwing it back down on the desk.

"Yeah," said Thorsen, aloud. "That's some article. Especially the reference to the posterior of a horse."

"Well," said Domenico, "now that we've sat here like two horses' asses for the last twenty minutes, and now that you've had a chance to read about yourself in the *Post*, I think we can conclude neither of us knows any more than we did earlier."

"Right," said Thorsen. "The most we can hope for is that this thing blows over and doesn't affect Monty's chances too much."

After Thorsen left the office, Domenico picked up his phone. He wanted to hear his wife's reassuring voice. He wanted to talk about plans for the future once this damn campaign was over. But his wife's voice mail came on after one ring, which meant she was on the phone, and he hung up.

He stood, turned from his desk and went to the window. Instead of opening the drapes, he stood staring at the drapes. He spoke to the drapes.

"I want it on the record that tomorrow I'm going to tell the President I'm concerned that incidents surrounding the Joliet visit were orchestrated, and continue to be orchestrated. I'm going to tell him I don't like it one bit. I'm going to tell him we need to do something about it. I hope to God he agrees. If the President hedges, well, then I'll know where I stand."

Domenico folded his arms about him and looked down.

"I also want it on the record that I've not communicated any of this to anyone other than Thorsen. I especially want to make it clear that I never spoke of it to my wife."

Domenico turned back to his desk, picked up the phone and hit the redial button. This time his wife answered.

"Hi, honey."

"Hi, George. Sounds like you're not having such a great day."

"What makes you say that?"

"I can always tell by your voice. I'll e-mail you tonight. Will that make you feel better."

"Of course," said Domenico. "Maybe we can also plan the vacation we're going to take once the election is over."

"With or without the kids?"

"Both," said Domenico. "We'll take one by ourselves, then a longer one with the kids."

"Sounds like a plan" said Domenico's wife.

CHAPTER 32

THE PRESIDENT'S NEMESIS

STANLEY JOHNSON

W HEN STAN FINALLY awoke, he saw, on the noon news, a glimpse of his close-mouthed stare through the window of Chief Jacobson's car as they drove up the ramp from the Joliet Police Headquarters garage during the dark hours of the morning. The coverage of a press conference recorded later in the morning showed a tired Agent Philips responding to questions about the now-famous Stanley Johnson of Joliet, Illinois. According to the commentator, Philips had been given the task of offering a public apology to Stanley Johnson, the man mistakenly arrested when he stood at his window holding a broom while the President of the United States greeted well-wishers below.

The questions made Philips sweat. He looked like a linebacker who had rushed from the showers and thrown on a business suit after a losing game.

"So there is absolutely no reason to suspect Mr. Johnson?"

"Correct. Mr. Johnson was an innocent bystander."

"Will the agent who aimed his weapon at Mr. Johnson's window be reprimanded?"

"We haven't decided that yet."

"Agent Philips, do you think this will have an effect on the election and, if so, will it be for or against the President?"

"I can't answer that."

"Won't you at least admit a mistake like this, made while protecting President Montgomery, increases Rose Adams Haney's chances to win the election?"

"I can't answer that."

"Why not, Agent Philips?"

"Because I don't know the answer."

"Will this incident alter the Secret Service's tactics in the future?"

"We've always tried to learn from our mistakes. But I want to remind you that the Secret Service will continue to follow up on all leads. When an agent sees someone in a window holding what may or may not be a weapon, he or she has a duty to act."

"You said Mr. Johnson owned guns. Could any of those guns have been used to shoot the President?"

"Any gun can be used. As I said before . . . and I want to make this unmistakably clear . . . Mr. Johnson's guns were locked in a cabinet. There was very little ammunition in the cabinet, and the guns were properly registered. This was a collection of guns Mr. Johnson owned for many years. The fact that he owned guns had absolutely nothing to do with the incident. This was, quite simply, an unfortunate misunderstanding, the kind of thing that can happen when guarding the President. No potential danger to the President can be overlooked or we wouldn't be doing our jobs. The best thing to do at this point is leave Mr. Johnson alone. He's been through enough. We apologize for any inconvenience we may have put him through."

"But Agent Philips, isn't it true that none of this would have happened if Mr. Johnson had not held the broom as if he were aiming a rifle?"

"No comment."

"Why haven't you allowed Mr. Johnson to have outside contacts? Several networks would like to interview him. Is Johnson under some kind of gag order?"

"Nothing of the kind. He and his attorney simply want to maintain some semblance of privacy for the time being. Thank you. That's all I have for now."

"Is the Secret Service aware that Mr. Johnson's son was kidnapped in 1980 on the day President Reagan was elected, and that his son's body was found in 1981 the day Reagan was shot?"

Philips had already backed away from the podium. He had his handkerchief out and was wiping his neck. He glanced at the questioner, but another agent had him by the arm and the entourage of agents and police left the podium.

Stan lay on his back in the center of a king-size bed. He wore a pair of boxer shorts and a T-shirt. It was enough to make him laugh. Stanley Johnson sequestered in a hotel to protect him from a horde of reporters and photographers and talk show reps and celebrity agents.

Without him to talk to, the horde had latched onto Agent Philips. And now that the rerun of the press conference was over, the commentator, a good-looking blond in her forties, put in a teaser for an upcoming interview in which Presidential challenger Rose Adams Haney would give her views on the incident. Then the commentator went into a rerun about the previous afternoon when the President made an unscheduled stop at an apartment complex in Joliet, Illinois, forty miles southwest of Chicago.

Stan got out of bed and turned off the television. He walked to the window, parted the curtain and looked down several stories to the partially drained outdoor swimming pool, the parking lot, and, beyond that, the flow of traffic on Interstate 80. It was raining out, the cars and trucks on the interstate followed by plumes of mist. Yesterday at this time he had been at his apartment window wondering why Chuck was moving the dumpsters. Yesterday at this time he would never have dreamed he'd be in a hotel suite in Joliet. A hotel suite! Separate sitting room and bedroom, fancier than anything he and Marge had ever stayed in, even on their honeymoon.

He went into the ornate bathroom complete with whirlpool tub. He washed up, brushed his teeth, and shaved using the bath kit that had been provided. Instead of putting his own dirty clothes back on, he put on the gray slacks and blue shirt draped on a chair. The clothes were a bit loose and he wondered if this was how prison clothing fit, elastic waistband just tight enough to keep the slacks up. Perhaps he had lost weight. Bad eating habits and all the worry and excitement lately.

He heard voices in the sitting room. He sat on the edge of the bed and waited, wondering if Chief Jacobson were here. Or Agent Philips here in body while his artificial self drones on and on in reruns of the pre-recorded press conference. But when the door opened it was the same policeman who'd been on guard outside when he was brought here early this morning.

The policeman introduced him to another policeman, said he'd see him again tomorrow. The changing of the guard. And lunch. A tray had been brought in. He sat at the table, lifted the stainless steel lid and saw a steaming Cornish hen. The new guard said, "Mmm, smells good."

Stan wondered if he could live this way forever. Last night, for the first time in weeks, he could not remember having dreamed. He felt completely at rest. Even his breath tasted better, no antiseptic taste in his mouth like he used to have, even after he brushed his teeth.

But the tranquility did not last long. Shortly after lunch the table was cleared and the questioning began. A microphone was put in the center of the table. The police guard was asked to wait in the lobby. Two FBI agents sat across from him. Both were dressed casually. Agent Douglas was a young white man in khaki slacks and shirt with black hair cut short. Agent Ross was a young black woman in jeans and sweater, also with black hair cut short. They both showed badges and identified themselves to him and to the recorder that sat in the center of the table. Ross explained that she and Douglas were inquiry specialists and that he should not be offended by any questions. Then Douglas began the questioning and the two alternated.

Douglas: "I'm wondering about your guns, Stan."

"What about them?"

"How do you clean them?"

"How?"

"Yes."

"With a rag and some of that oil."

"If I give you my gun . . . unloaded of course . . . and a handkerchief, can you show me?"

"Sure, I guess so."

Ross: "Stan, we've been looking at some chain letters you received."

"So?"

"Did you ever answer them?"

"No."

"Why not?"

"Because they're asinine. Trying to get money from gullible people."

"Why did you save them?"

"I didn't save all of them. Some I threw away."

"Any idea who might be sending them to you?"

"No."

Douglas: "Believe me, Stan. I'm a normal guy myself. I like to indulge in a skin flick now and then. And magazines, a *Playboy* or *Penthouse* once in a while that my wife tosses out when she finds it. What puzzles me is why you have so much of this sexually-oriented material at home."

"It's not against the law."

"Oh, I know, I know. It's just that you've gotten so much of it."

"I said I sent in for a few."

"You said a couple."

"Well, maybe it was more than a couple. I don't know how many. But once they get you on their mailing list, the junk keeps coming."

Douglas looked at Ross, smiled. "Yeah, that's the way junk mail is. A lot of it's the same." Douglas looked back at him. "However, you've got duplicates. Why didn't you throw some of it out?"

"I didn't want kids rummaging in the garbage and getting hold of it."

"Do kids rummage in the garbage where you live?"

"I don't know. I just thought they might."

"So why didn't you burn it?"

"There's no place to burn anything. Outside fires are against the law."

"Oh."

Ross: "About those photographs of women you've got stored on your computer."

"What about them?"

"I noticed they're all stored in a directory named 'beautiful' on your hard drive."

"I figured it was a logical name."

"Did you name the files?"

"What do you mean?"

Ross referred to a notepad she'd been holding. "They're named 'snatch001, snatch002, snatch003' and so on. I wondered if you thought up those names."

"No. I just found them on the cache file and made a directory and copied them to the directory."

"Why didn't you copy them as you viewed them?"

"I don't know. I guess I didn't think of it until afterward."

"Do you recall the Web site you got them from?"

"No."

"Do you make a practice of erasing the browser's history file?"

"No."

"I noticed all the photographs in the directory are apparently of women in their forties or so. Perhaps it was a Web site devoted to women in their forties?"

"I guess it could have been."

"And you still don't recall the name of the Web site? Maybe something like women-over-forty-dot-com, or a variation of that?"

"I can't remember. In fact, when I found those files on the cache file, I couldn't even remember the last time I'd been on the Web."

"According to the service provider, you accessed the Web only a few hours before the images were saved."

"That could be. I remember I left the computer on and fell asleep once. Maybe they timed me out and when I woke up the photographs were there and I just saved them without thinking about it."

"Have you ever changed the date and time on your computer since you purchased it?"

"Once, maybe a year ago when the battery went dead, the place I took it to reset it."

Douglas: "Back to your guns. You say this ex-guard at the lab sold them to you."

"That's right."

"And you say you didn't even want them?"

"Right. I was helping him out because he needed the money."

"Why didn't you simply give him a loan?"

"I don't know. It was a long time ago. Maybe I thought I wanted the guns at first. I really don't remember."

"What about that survival group you joined?"

"I told you, I didn't join. I just went with Sedgwick on one of their outings. That's the last time I shot a gun. How many times do we have to go over this?'"

"Does it bother you to discuss these things?"

"No. I just wondered how much longer."

Ross: "In your kitchen cupboard we found a small dish with bits of something green in it. Can you tell us about that?"

"Sure. I've been finding the stuff on the kitchen floor when I sweep. I wondered what it was. Some kind of green fibers or something."

"Right, green fibers. So why would you collect them?"

"I guess I wondered what they were and how they got there."

"Do you have any ideas?"

"I don't know what the fibers are, but the reason I collected them was because I was worried I'd been sleepwalking."

"Sleepwalking?"

"Yeah, I thought I already told you, or someone. I used to sleepwalk when I was a kid and I had the feeling I might have done it again recently. Since I found the green stuff on the kitchen floor, near the door to the apartment, I thought I might have tracked it in while I was sleepwalking."

"Why couldn't you have tracked it in at another time, like when you weren't sleepwalking?"

"Yeah, I thought of that. But one time I thought I noticed more of the stuff in the morning when I'd just swept the floor the night before. Hell, it was something to do. And my friend Evie is into mysteries and maybe I was just messing around. It's probably nothing."

"Would you like to know what the fibers are from?"

"Sure. What the hell."

"They're wood fibers dyed green. It's used in hydro-seeding."

"You mean for putting in lawns?"

"That's right, Stan."

"Did they use it at the apartment complex?"

"Yes, they did. A contractor put some down in late August and in early September. Mostly around the office and swimming pool, but also around your apartment and around the enclosure for the garbage dumpsters."

"Oh, so I could have tracked it in when I took out the garbage."

"Yes, that's possible."

Later that afternoon an FBI psychologist named Dr. Wimer joined them. Dr. Wimer had half glasses, looked down at notes through his glasses, then up at Stan above the glasses without moving his head. The bald spot on top of Dr. Wimer's head glowed greasily beneath the overhead light. The questions about Timmy's disappearance and Marge's suicide reminded him of questions Dr. Todd had asked years earlier.

"Would you say you loved your wife and son?"

"Yes, very much."

"There seemed to be no reason for the tragedy?"

"None that I know of."

"No one who would have wanted to get even with you?"

"I can't think of anyone."

"Do you blame yourself?"

"For Timmy's death? Not really. But for Marge, I've always blamed myself. I should have known she was going to . . . I should have been there when she needed me. I . . ."

"It's all right, Stan. Take your time."

"These clippings of missing or murdered children they found in your apartment . . . what about those?"

"Like I already said, I thought I could help. I thought if the murderer was still out there killing little kids . . . I guess because I had first hand experience. You understand."

"No, I don't understand."

"Well, damn it! Neither do I! You're the damn doctor!"

"Are you aware of the many Web sites concerning missing children?"

"I've heard of them."

"Have you ever accessed these sites?"

"Not that I recall."

"Wouldn't this have been a good way to help out?"

"What do you mean?"

"I mean instead of writing a letter to the Barrington Police offering to help capture the killer of a six-year-old girl, you might have gotten on the Web and gone to the missing children sites. They also have support groups and you could have . . ."

"Jesus Christ, that letter to the Barrington Police was years ago! What the hell was I supposed to do? Invent the Web so I could use it? Or is this just some psycho bullshit to get me to blow up? If it is, it's sure as hell working!"

Sunday was a day of rest. Chief Jacobson visited in the morning, assured him there would be no more questions until Monday, told him he'd be able to go home Tuesday or Wednesday.

"Why are they asking all these questions?"

"They have to be sure, Stan."

"Of what?"

"That this wasn't part of something larger."

"A conspiracy?"

"Yes."

When he laughed, Jacobson laughed with him. "I know, I know. Why would anyone want to conspire to have you in your window with a broom? But with the election so close, it could have an effect. That's why everyone's so touchy about this. And the media's going nuts. One organization of women insists it's a setup to pull votes away from Rose Adams Haney."

"I know. I've been watching it on television."

"How's everything been here? Food okay?"

"Sure. There's just one thing that's been bothering me."

"What's that?"

"There's someone I'd like to call."

"A relative?"

"No. A friend."

"The woman you were dating?"

"Yes."

"I'm sorry, Stan. They asked if you could hold off until maybe Tuesday."

"Why Tuesday? I thought I was getting out of here Monday or Tuesday."

"It'll probably be Tuesday, Stan. Please go through with this. It's the best way to put the whole thing to rest. Best for you, too, because you're out of the limelight for a few days. And you . . ."

"I know, I agreed. So why can't I call Evie until Tuesday?"

"I'll be honest with you, Stan. They aren't only questioning you."

"Evie, too?"

"Yes."

After Chief Jacobson left, Stan turned on the television and watched *Meet the Press.* President Montgomery's campaign manager, George Domenico, speculated about the positive and negative effects of the incident on the campaign. Domenico said it could hurt the President, that if it did he would blame the media for making so much of it.

"Mr. Domenico, as an ex-CIA agent and a former official for the National Security Council, I would think you'd see a plot here."

Domenico laughed at the question. "Believe it or not, even people trained in security see nothing of the kind here. I can't believe the way the media keeps searching for conspiracy at every bend in the road. It was a fluke, pure and simple. Of course, if we had it to do over again, we never would have let the President talk us into yet another impromptu stop."

"Have you given any thought, Mr. Domenico, to the prevalent rumors that, if the President is re-elected, he will seek your appointment as Director of Central Intelligence?"

"No, I haven't."

Monday morning, news about the Joliet incident had lessened significantly. The fatalities caused by serious late season wildfires in the Northwest had taken the top news spot. There were no more pictures of Stan in Chief Jacobson's car, no more pictures of his apartment house, the scene of which was now a big joke on the news, no more sickening interviews with Marion saying he was a "nice man."

At ten o'clock sharp Monday morning Ross and Douglas and Dr. Wimer were back.

Today, Agent Ross wore a skirt and blouse, and he found out her first name was Myra. "That collect call you took from New York last month . . . are you certain you don't remember who called?"

"Like I said, I vaguely remember someone trying to sell something. I'm not sure what. Maybe magazines. I hung up on them."

"Was it a man or a woman?"

"A man."

"Name?"

"I don't remember."

Douglas wore his khaki slacks and shirt again, making him look like an underling of Agent Myra Ross. "Tell us about your involvement with the Eugene McCarthy campaign in 1968, and about your arrest in Grant Park."

"I told you. There was a big crowd that night when the whole world was watching. Someone had to be there. I was young. I don't think I was even twenty yet. There was a draft, in case you don't remember your history. A lot of us were against the war. Somehow I ended up there."

"But you'd had no record of being a protester before that."

"Jesus Christ! It was the Vietnam War!"

"No need to be sensitive about it, Stan. We're just doing our jobs."

"I know. But that was so long ago, I don't really remember much."

"Well, do your best."

Dr. Wimer wore the same old suit he'd worn Saturday. "Your son was born on September 22, 1975, the day President Gerald Ford was shot at. On election day, November 4, 1980, your son was kidnapped. On March 30, the day President Ronald Reagan was shot, your son's body was found and identified because of an anonymous tip. Doesn't this seem unusual to you? Major tragedies in your life tied so closely to events involving Presidents?"

"Sure it's unusual. I can't even think about Presidents or voting without remembering Timmy and Marge. Why do you think I never went back to work at the damn polls after that? I can't keep reliving those memories. It's just . . . it's just too . . ."

"Relax, Stan. Take a little break. We'll be done soon."

"So, after your involvement with this young woman . . . what was her name?"

"Terri."

"Yes. After that you received a bad reputation at the lab. Coworkers made fun of you, and so on."

"Yeah, and so on. I wondered at the time if that garbage got put into my personnel file. I guess it did. Did they have a record of what everyone called me?"

"What was that?"

"Why, Dirty Old Man Stan, of course."

"Yes, that was in your file."

"Wonderful. The government in action."

"What do you mean by that?"

"What?"

"Does it anger you?"

"Why not? And don't try to tie my lousy twenty-year-old personnel file in with this . . . this broom thing. Wouldn't you be angry if they stuck a personal thing like that in your file?"

"They do, Stan. Anyone who works in a secure area or agency has to expect it. It's just the way it is these days."

"Why do you think you became upset with Evie at the drive-in?"

"I don't know. We were just goofing around. She kind of rubbed me the wrong way."

"Rubbed you?"

"Yeah."

"She mentioned your uncle? Something your uncle used to do?"

"Yeah. She rubbed my head really hard. You know, like this. A Dutch rub, they call it. Only you had to be there. She did it fast and hard."

"She actually hurt you?"

"No, not that. She did it . . . see, she did it right after I said I always hated it when my uncle did it. He actually did hurt me. When he gave me a Dutch rub my scalp burned for days. It was just one of those things. Evie caught me at a bad time, being depressed and all. I don't know what the big deal is. It was my fault. I admit it. If I ever get the hell out of here, the first thing I'm going to do is apologize to Evie. She didn't deserve the way I treated her. She's . . . she's my only friend."

"And the phone call that night. What about that?"

"You mean the one to her ex-husband?"

"Yes."

"I don't know who could have called him. I thought she did when she went to the ladies' room or something."

"But her ex-husband insists it was a man who called."

"I know. I know. It wasn't me. Maybe he had a private eye following us or something."

"Why would he do that?"

"I don't know."

Ross and Douglas and Dr. Wimer stared at him like vultures.

"Look. I can't account for everything. I don't know why someone would call her husband and tell him to be at her house. I just don't know the answer to that."

"So, Stan. Why did you call Dr. Todd's office prior to the incident?"

"I told you. I was feeling depressed. In fact I'm pretty depressed right now. After this is over I'll probably have to see Dr. Todd for a couple years to straighten my head out."

"You said you'd begun drinking quite heavily?"

"Yeah, and that depressed me even more."

"Is that why you aimed the broom?"

"I don't know. Maybe. Maybe I was . . . or am . . . generally pissed off at the world. I don't know."

"Have you ever felt angry enough to kill?"

"Yes."

"When?"

"When they found Timmy. When I found Marge. If Timmy's killer had been there at those times, and if I had a gun . . . or I guess just my bare hands . . . I would have killed him."

"And now? If that killer were here now?"

"I . . . I don't know. I just want to be left alone. I just want to go home."

★ ★  ★ ★

Monday night it was over. Chief Jacobson called, said he could go home any time, but he might as well rest up and go home Tuesday. Stan agreed, had two twelve-year-old scotches and a room service prime rib on the taxpayers. During the halftime of the Chicago-Green Bay Monday night game, the newsbreak commentators made no mention at all of him or the incident. True, most of the news was focused on the election and on the wildfires in the Northwest. But since that first day when one paper's headline read **"PRESIDENT'S GUARDS SWEEP QUIET NEIGHBORHOOD,"** the media seemed to have purposely been trying to put the incident aside. Maybe it was being swept under the rug because news organizations were uncomfortable with the thought that Rose Adams Haney, the woman challenging the incumbent, appeared to have gained several points in the polls. Maybe the idea that something like this could cause such a shift in the electorate made even the media uncomfortable. Maybe they were afraid they'd generate copycat incidents if they talked about it too much.

He took the phone into the bedroom, plugged in there while the policeman on duty stayed in the other room watching the football game. He wondered what he would say to Evie. Then he remembered his promise to himself not to think so much, not to make something out of nothing, just let things happen. What the hell, if he could talk to Ross and Douglas and Dr. Wimer for two days he could certainly strike up a conversation with Evie.

"Hello?"

"Hello."

"Is that you, Stan?"

"Yeah."

"Are you all right?"

"Yeah."

"Where are you?"

"At a hotel."

"In town?"

"Yeah. In Joliet. Evie?"

"Yes, I'm here."

"God, it's good to hear your voice."

"It's good to hear yours, too, Stan."

"I . . . I've missed you."

"I've missed you. And I . . . "

"And I'm sorry, Evie. I really am."

"You don't have to be. I understand."

"They questioned you, too."

"Yes. But it's over, Stan. The men who questioned me said it's all routine. That they simply have to follow through on these things involving the President. And they said they really felt sorry for you, the way you were dragged into it."

"Yeah. What a way to become famous. Maybe I should write the book myself. Someone's been talking about book deals. Did you hear about that?"

"You *could* write it yourself, Stan. I could help. I mean since I read quite a lot I could give you some ideas."

"Yeah, sounds great."

"Stan?"

"Yeah."

"When can I see you?"

"I'm supposed to go home tomorrow. But let me get settled in. I really do want to see you, Evie. And I meant what I said about missing you. It's just . . ."

"Just what?"

"I'm sure the investigation will go on for a while. They haven't said so, but I know I'll be under guard, not really house arrest, but the result is the same. I guess I'd like to be sure they've come to some conclusions before . . ."

"The investigation could go on for months, or even years, Stan. You know how these things are."

"I know. But at least, for the first couple of days, I'd like to make sure I'm not swamped with reporters. If I am they'll probably get tired of me after a day or two. I just don't want the two of us dragged into any more of this. Can you understand that?"

"Yes. I understand."

"I'll call, though. I'll call tomorrow night."

After he hung up with Evie he wondered if he really was worried about reporters or if it was something else. The phone call to Evie's ex-husband. The dreams he'd had in the apartment and not here. Not here! The phone calls from Youngblood and Derek Washington. The young man who messed with his guns. The head. The head of the child.

Thinking again. Always thinking. But he had to. He wouldn't want Evie hurt if something happened when he went home. But what could happen? And when? How long would Chief Jacobson keep a guard outside his apartment?

In the next room he heard a football crowd cheer. The policeman hooted, his piercing yell sounding like a reaction to pain. When Stan opened the door he saw the policeman standing near the television.

The policeman turned, grinned. "The Bears just tied it!"

CHAPTER 33

"YOU'LL NEED TO be convincing, Lena. You'll need to use all the skills you can muster in order to further the cause, and in order to save Stanley Johnson's life. The others are out of it now, so it's just you and me, and Walter. You, dear Lena, have become a critical player."

Lena sat next to Jake on the marble ledge of a gushing fountain. Behind Jake's head was a monster made of bones, a skeleton perched on its hind legs, short forearms extended forward as if about to attack, huge grinning jaw lined with hundreds of pointed teeth. The sound of the fountain along with the shouts of children echoed in the hall's vast sky-lit ceiling so that Jake could speak quite loudly without a chance of being overheard.

They were in a museum along the Chicago lakefront. Walter had driven them to the museum in the rental car and was now standing some distance away staring up at a pair of woolly mammoths frozen in time. Walter was probably wishing he had tusks like those mammoths, or a dick as long as their trunks. Or maybe Walter was wondering what her part of the plan was, Jake choosing to give each of them their instructions separately.

"We don't have much time," Jake had said to them both. "We have to act tomorrow night. We'll go to a public place to avoid being overheard and I'll give you each your instructions."

So, here they were, amidst dinosaurs and mammoths and school tours, finding out about a guy named Stanley Johnson who they were going to save. Stanley Johnson, the guy who threw the country for a loop by pointing a broom out his window.

Everything was different now. Instead of telling her to simply do what she was told and keep her mouth shut, Jake was inviting questions.

"I want you to understand the situation we're in, Lena. I want you to know what's at stake and exactly how dangerous the situation is."

Jake looked around at the museum hall, then turned back to her. He reached out and touched her hand.

"Meeting here at The Museum of Natural History is appropriate because it reinforces the cyclical nature of our planet. Everything comes full circle. Ice ages come and go. Creatures suffer extinction. But in the midst of it all, something we humans cannot give up is our dominance over nature. If we allow nature to dominate us, *we* will become extinct. And in order to maintain this dominance we must remain powerful in our values and in our politics. I don't use the term, 'You're either for us or against us,' the way some have mistakenly done. The way I look at it is more global. What I mean is that we need to make certain our children and our childrens' children can find their way forward."

Jake smiled, squeezed her hand. "Are you with me on this, Lena?"

"Of course, Jake. But I . . . I've never had anyone talk to me like this."

Jake leaned forward and kissed her on the cheek. He held both her hands, stared at her seriously. "I had a feeling no one had ever spoken to you this way. That's why I needed to do it now. I want you to know how important you've become to me. I want you to know that your importance to me goes beyond the job ahead of us."

"You're making me blush."

"Good. And now that I've gotten that off my chest, let's get back to business. We have friends who are counting on us. If we succeed, the rewards will be substantial. If we fail, Mr. Johnson will lose his life."

Jake let go of her hands and paused, seemed to be waiting for a response from her. So she asked, "Why is Mr. Johnson so important to us?"

"Because he was set up to do what he did in order to hurt President Montgomery's re-election chances. Operatives in the Rose Adams Haney campaign arranged the entire episode. And now they're trying to capitalize even further by killing Mr. Johnson."

"How can they capitalize by killing Johnson?"

Jake reached behind his back, tested the water in the fountain with one finger. "A suicide note. But not an ordinary suicide note. A suicide note in which Mr. Johnson blames the President personally for his bad luck throughout life. A suicide note designed specifically to drag the President down in public opinion polls days before the election."

"I knew the world of politics was rotten, but this . . . How do you know all this?"

"As I said before, friends in high places. Some of them playing both sides."

"Double agents?"

"If you like. Except in this case both sides are American. The groundwork for today's politics . . . rotten politics, as you call it . . . was laid after Nine-Eleven. So much attention was paid to security, the two sides tried to outfox one another."

"The two sides?"

"The right versus the left, Lena. Those who want to retain what our country is about versus those who want change at any cost." Jake stared at her, his eyes unblinking. "I once said I was not a politician. That's not entirely true. We're all politicians just as senators are politicians. We have an opportunity here. It's not entirely for financial gain, although there is plenty of that to go around. It's more a set of beliefs and ideals. It's a war, a war behind the scenes that's gotten quite dirty. Their side has used Mr. Johnson as a pawn."

"And, in this war, we're on the side that matters?"

"Yes. Trust me, Lena. There's too much behind all of it to fill you in completely right now. There isn't time. But there are things you must know in order to convince Mr. Johnson we're on his side. You see, quite recently the other side mounted a campaign to drive Mr. Johnson insane, to ruin his credibility. Listen carefully. It's complicated.

"Years ago, Mr. Johnson's son, a young child, was killed. Shortly thereafter his wife committed suicide. Recently, in order to rekindle his anger at the system, the other side planted the newly-severed head of a child where Mr. Johnson would find it."

"My God! They killed a kid to upset this guy?"

"As I said, the stakes are high. You need to know about the head of the child in order to convince Mr. Johnson to go with you. He saw the head but was too frightened to tell anyone. Perhaps he thought he imagined it, or perhaps he thought he would be blamed. As I said, Mr. Johnson's past is complicated."

"So I tell him we know about the head of a kid he saw?"

"Yes. There are three things I want you to say. First, Chief Jacobson sent you to get him out because of a plot against his life. Second, we know about the child's head he found in the garbage."

"In the garbage?"

"Yes, Lena. Don't interrupt. Just listen."

"Okay. Chief Jacobson sent me, and then the kid's . . . child's . . . head in the garbage."

"Correct. Next, tell him we also know about Mr. Youngblood and Mr. Derek Washington."

"Who are they?"

"It doesn't matter. They're simply men who phoned him recently. Their purpose was to provoke him. After you tell him all this, you explain that he must disguise himself as his neighbor, John Delaney. You'll be impersonating Sue Delaney."

"The woman on the video you had me watch."

"That's right. You're doing well, Lena. I have great confidence in you. There's one more thing."

"What?"

"If you have difficulty convincing Mr. Johnson to go with you, if you've told him what I just said and he's still hesitant, then tell him we know who killed his son Timmy."

"Do you?"

"It doesn't matter. The main thing is to get him out of there and telling him that will do it. He's been obsessed by the murder for over twenty years and recent events have rekindled his obsession."

"God. This guy Johnson's sure had a rough time."

"They've fucked up his life, Lena. But we'll put an end to all that soon."

Jake had her repeat what she was to say to Stanley Johnson several times. Then he explained that Mrs. Delaney attended an exercise class on Wednesday night. Lena was to dress as she had seen Mrs. Delaney dress in one of the video segments. Pink tights, violet gym shoes. She would shop for these and fix her hair to match Mrs. Delaney's. The disguise for Stanley Johnson was to consist of a toupee, sweatshirt, sweatpants, and gym shoes. This would be to make Johnson resemble Sue Delaney's husband. Walter had observed John Delaney and would supply the clothing and the toupee.

Jake stared at her, serious. "All right, Lena. Now repeat the entire plan to me."

She wanted to get it right the first time, impress the hell out of Jake, let him know she would be good to have around for this or any other job. Much better than anything she'd done with her piss-assed life. She thought about telling Jake how easy it all sounded but decided she'd better not.

"First, Walter grabs Sue Delaney's car at her exercise class without her knowing. Then I take the car and go convince Stanley Johnson to dress like John Delaney and come out of the apartment building with me. Then we meet at the place you'll show me."

"Very good, Lena. How does it sound? Any holes in it?"

"Well, okay. Where's Sue Delaney's husband all this time?"

"He works nights. He'll be asleep next door. It's across the hall so you'll have to be fairly quiet."

"Okay. What about later when they question Sue Delaney. She'll deny going home and they'll know it wasn't her."

"Doesn't matter. We'll be finished by then. Our job is to get Stanley Johnson out alive. After that someone else takes over."

She almost asked if George would be taking over, but caught herself. She didn't want Jake to know she'd overheard him on the phone talking about someone named George. Jesus, Lena, get with it. This is your chance. Don't blow it!

"Any other questions?" asked Jake.

"No," she said. "Sounds like a plan."

Jake held her shoulder and stared at her. "There's one more thing, Lena."

"What's that?"

"I want you to know that as far as I know, Rose Adams Haney personally has nothing to do with this. It all has to do with old enemies of President Montgomery. Some say he's too old and refer to questionable past indiscretions. Like anyone else, he's not perfect. The problem is, a group of radical partisans who have been working for years to oust Montgomery have wormed their way into Rose Adams Haney's campaign and the only way to weed them out is to thwart their plan to kill Johnson. It really wouldn't matter that much to me who won the Presidency if it weren't for the fact that, as we speak, there are some very bad apples in Haney's campaign."

Jake paused, but continued staring at her. He reached out and held both her hands again. "In the past I may have seemed somewhat old fashioned and chauvinistic to you, Lena. But I want you to know right now that I'm not doing this to hurt Rose Adams Haney. What's at stake here is the Presidency itself. If the Presidency is damaged it could mean the extinction of our political system. I want to be certain you understand where I'm coming from before we continue."

"I understand."

Hunters, naked except for strategically placed animal skins, carried a bleeding wild boar hung by its feet from the center of a long pole. Bare-breasted women squatted near a fire pit. Naked boys mimicked the hunters, played with miniature spears and carried a dead rabbit tied by its feet to a pole. Naked girls squatted with the women near the fire pit using stones to squash beans or grain or something. Maybe drugs, something to chew on and forget pain and fear and the long hunger between feasts of meat.

Struggle, survival, dog eat dog. Or maybe it was dog wag dog. Not much different from her life before Jake. A few tricks a day at first, then a few more to make ends meet and support the heroin habit that came around the corner like a whisper and had her on her knees before she knew what hit her. Then a couple years in the real world before the sex business hit cyberspace and she made her debut on the Web. That was about the same time the heroin came back and smacked her forty-year-old ass to the ground.

No place for greed in this survival shit. The tribe shares and shares alike. Someone tries to take more, and he, or she, is dead meat like Raphael. Have to learn to make do. Don't bite the hand that feeds you. You scratch my back, I'll scratch yours. Let the tail wag the dog if that's what it takes.

As she walked amongst the exhibits in the hall called "Man in his Environment," she remembered the night she and Jake drove down the coast. That was right after the bad scene at the motel where she'd gotten stomped on and pissed on before Walter got her out. She remembered the dinner at sunset, Jake getting a little drunk, telling her about his life, about his stepfather and his real father. One rich, one powerful. Both leaving Jake behind as their legacy. Jake involved with getting the President re-elected. Now that was power. It sure as hell was. She remembered the drive back that night, Jake's head on her shoulder. Her at the wheel and this man's head on her shoulder. She'd walked into hell that night at the motel and come out in sunshine. Jake loved her and she loved him, would do anything for him. Squat in front of a fire pit all day and grind grain between rocks if she had to. Or, better yet, kick the damn heroin.

When Walter gave her the last dose he said he hadn't decreased it too much yet. And tomorrow's dose he'd hold off until later when their job was finished. Keep her on her toes, something to look forward to. She agreed. Better to have a little craving than to be high. She'd be bouncy like a jazz dancer in her pink leotard. She'd get Stanley Johnson out and then get her fix, get her back scratched, make Jake happy. After that they'd probably fly out of the country for a while. Maybe somewhere warm where she and Jake would soak up the sun and get skin as dark as prehistoric hunters.

When she came out of the "Man in his Environment" hall, she saw that Jake was still giving Walter instructions at the fountain next to Tyrannosaurus Rex. Walter's instructions were taking longer than hers. Maybe because Walter wasn't exactly a whiz kid, or maybe because stealing a car was more complicated than her job.

She kept her distance, circled Tyrannosaurus Rex and waited. At one point Walter glanced up at her, looked at her with that dumb look. She laughed then, had to laugh because she had stopped on the far side of Tyrannosaurus Rex and Rex was in profile, the base of his bony tail appearing to be directly above Walter. If Rex were still alive and took a healthy shit, it would land right on Walter's head.

Jake and Walter saw Lena laughing, then they saw a little boy, not three years old, giggling while he ran tottering from his mother who was desperately trying to catch him. Jake and Walter also laughed when the little boy was caught, screaming, by his jacket at the entrance to the "Man in his Environment" hall.

When Lena turned to walk slowly back down the "Man in his Environment" hall, Jake and Walter resumed their conversation.

"I'm concerned about something you said, Mr. Serrantino."

"What's that, Walter?"

"You mentioned coming back here to Chicago where it all started. You mentioned your father and how he met his fate. It seemed to me you were questioning the merits of having come here."

"I was simply being realistic, Walter. You and I both know that plans change, and that nothing is forever."

"You mentioned the men who have been involved with this over the years. I sensed a concern for their future should something happen to you, to us."

"I told you, Walter. I took care of that weeks ago. A chain of command exists and we don't have to think about it."

"Yes, Mr. Serrantino, that's what bothers me."

"What?"

"We shouldn't be concerning ourselves about the possibility of a bad outcome, yet I sense you are concerned."

Jake smiled, looked toward where Lena had been standing, saw she was gone and put his hand on Walter's shoulder. "Yes, Walter, there is one thing that concerns me."

"What is it?"

"I failed to tell you who is directly below me in the chain of command."

"You said Menendez was."

"I said Menendez was responsible for the men, Walter."

"What do you mean?"

"I mean if something happens to me, if I fail to survive this episode, I want you to go south with the others. Stay there until Nelson's people contact you."

"The Vice President?"

"Yes, Walter. If something happens to me you'll be working directly with his people."

Walter glanced down. "I'm not sure if I'd be ready for that role."

"Don't be modest, Walter. If something happens to me, you'll be ready. Between you and Menendez, I'm certain the baton can be passed. I don't mean to imply I've weakened in my resolve, Walter. But none of us is immortal. *Coppish?*"

Walter touched Jake's arm, which was still extended to his shoulder. "Does Menendez know this?"

"Yes."

"I don't know what to say, Mr. Serrantino. Except that I'll do my best to see that we both get through this unscathed."

"Very good," said Jake, glancing up and seeing Lena exiting the "Man in his Environment" hall once again.

Jake let go of Walter's shoulder and Walter let go of Jake's arm. They both looked toward Lena who walked their way when Jake motioned for her to join them.

CHAPTER 34

THE PRESIDENT'S NEMESIS

STANLEY JOHNSON

THE TWO MEN watching Stan's apartment were parked below his window next to his old brown Toyota pickup with its lousy flat tire that he'd gotten when he plowed into the curb years ago. Not really years ago. Only a few days. But the nostalgia night at the drive-in with Evie seemed like something that really had happened back in the seventies. And the next afternoon when he aimed his broom at the President seemed like something that had happened in the sixties. Hustled out of his apartment the way Oswald had been hustled by cops, one on each arm. Maybe it would have been better if he'd been shot the way Oswald was shot by Ruby. Stanley Johnson, shot to death outside his apartment for aiming a broom. At the funeral, the poor sap recruited to come up with a eulogy can't keep from laughing.

Chief Jacobson said the two men out front were FBI and that two more FBI agents just off the main road were watching the back of his apartment building. Jacobson's own men were patrolling the perimeter to keep the curious and the media out of the complex. A prisoner in his own apartment. But he didn't mind, not for a while at least. So far, from what he could see, there hadn't been many curiosity seekers or media. Either the FBI agents and the cops were doing a bang-up job, or there simply wasn't that much interest in him, his fifteen minutes of fame long gone.

The only person the FBI agents out front had let into the apartment besides Jacobson had been his attorney, Bob McLean. Bob said that keeping him sequestered was best for all concerned and for now he should go along. Bob also said he'd gotten calls about future television interviews and appearances and even the infamous book deal. Bob seemed quite excited by all the possibilities. As Stan stood looking out his window, he could picture Bob.

In the interrogation room at Joliet Police Headquarters, Bob had looked older. Perhaps everything looked older that long day and night, everything worn out and gone to hell. Actually Bob was a young man. Here at the apartment, when Stan told Bob he looked like he was twenty, Bob laughed and said he was almost thirty. Bob's eyes were blue like Evie's eyes, or the way Timmy's eyes were blue at birth. Timmy would have been Bob's age. Timmy could have become Bob if his eyes hadn't gone gray and he hadn't been killed. Bob's excitement about television appearances and book deals could have been Timmy's excitement.

Marion had tried to visit. The FBI had put her on a cellular phone.

"I wanted to see how you were, Stan. We've all been concerned for you and wondered if you needed anything."

"I appreciate your concern, Marion, but right now I don't need anything. I just need to rest. Maybe in a couple days."

"Do you have food and toiletries and everything?"

"Yes. They went shopping for me. So, you see, everything's just fine."

"Well, if there's anything you need . . ."

"Thanks, Marion. I'm fine."

After hanging up he had gone to the window to watch Marion go. She waved and he waved back. A television van that had parked briefly on the main road had been shooed away by then so he would not see himself waving on the evening news.

The police, Chief Jacobson, the FBI . . . they'd taken care of everything. His freezer stocked with Healthy Choice dinners. His cupboards full of canned soups and vegetables, cereal, chips. They'd changed his phone number and the phone was tapped so that all he'd have to do is pick it up and the FBI guys would hear him.

The guns were gone. The gun cabinet with its felt-lined brackets empty. Chief Jacobson said he'd get them back soon, that they'd been taken to be tested, just in case, everything documented.

His computer was gone. An FBI computer nerd probably combing files for hidden information, for more images of women over forty, or for hidden images of children that might have somehow made their way onto his hard drive.

The Chevy Tahoe in which the two FBI men sat was silver-blue. Another Tahoe, burgundy, had dropped off fast food and he watched as the two FBI men sipped drinks and devoured fries and sandwiches. When the FBI men finished eating, one of them left the Tahoe and threw their garbage into one of the dumpsters. Both dumpsters were back in place and everything was calm outside. He closed the curtains and went into the kitchen.

On the ten o'clock news that evening there was speculation about how the Joliet incident would affect the election. Clips showed Vice President Allan Nelson and Senator Bill Ingersoll, the two running mates, voicing their outrage about how the incident would hurt their candidate. Apparently, according to the commentator, both parties had decided to keep their Presidential candidate out of the fray and let the running mates go at it.

There was also speculation about whether the President had called Stanley Johnson to apologize, and if not, why not. A representative from Rose Adams Haney's campaign speculated that President Montgomery might be waiting to call Johnson in order to time the call in such a way as to provide a better spin for election day. A representative from Montgomery's campaign responded that the President felt it was appropriate to allow the investigation to be completed before contacting Mr. Johnson, and that the President would certainly not want to bring politics into the matter. During the debate between the two campaign representatives that followed, a video inset of the outside of Stan's apartment was shown. Because of the slant of the sun and the fact that the silver-blue Tahoe was parked next to his pickup, Stan judged the video was shot just before the television crew was shooed away earlier that day out on the main road.

After the news, Stan picked up the phone and told the FBI man he wanted to make a personal call. The FBI man said they would not listen in and told him to call their cellular number when he was finished. Then he called Evie.

"Did you just get home, Stan?"

"This afternoon."

"Are there reporters outside? I didn't see anything on the news except a picture of your apartment."

"They hung around out on the road for a while, but eventually gave up. The only ones outside are the FBI agents guarding me."

"Good. It makes me feel better knowing you're safe."

"Yeah. They have a bug on the phone but they said they'd shut it off while I called you."

"Do you think they did?"

"It doesn't matter because there's nothing to hide from them."

"Well, I guess it's for your own protection, until things settle down."

"Right."

"Stan?"

"Yeah."

"Can I ask about that night at the drive-in?"

"Sure. I'm used to answering questions. That's all I've done the last couple of days."

"If you rather I wouldn't . . ."

"No. Go ahead."

"Well, I guess I'm really puzzled about that call to my husband, my ex."

"Aren't we all."

"It wasn't you?"

"No."

"I'm glad, Stan. I believe you. But I have to be honest and tell you I was really angry with you that night. The way you acted after that Dutch-rub thing, I was prepared to think anything."

"I understand."

"They questioned my ex about the call. Played a recording of your voice for him."

"What did he say?"

"That it didn't sound like you. He said it was a younger man."

"What did the man say?"

"Something to the effect that he should go to my house and meet me there because I might need help."

"It must have had something to do with the fact that we were out together."

"I know. Maybe a nosy neighbor saw us. When we first started dating I heard second hand gossip about you staying over. There's a widow down the block who thinks I should be sitting in a rocker knitting. Maybe she had a grandson make the call or something."

"I guess anything's possible. Did you tell all this to the investigators?"

"Yes, but who knows if we'll ever find out who called. I get the feeling the FBI and whoever else is investigating might keep the details under wraps. If it was one of my neighbors who called my ex, maybe they just figure why get more people involved."

"You're probably right. Hey, Evie?"

"Yes."

"I'm really sorry about how I acted. I don't know what got into me. Things have been going lousy for me the last few weeks. I can't exactly put my finger on it, but it almost seems that what happened when the President's motorcade pulled in here was inevitable. That it was bound to happen and that the way I was feeling beforehand was in anticipation of it. Does that make any sense?"

"Of course it does, Stan. Especially with you seeing those vehicles out front of your apartment those nights. Did the FBI ask you about that?"

"Yes. But I could only tell them what I told you. They seemed interested at first, but I think they eventually dismissed it. Just someone throwing away their garbage and my imagination running with it. They even questioned why I used the term 'sport ute' instead of sport utility vehicle or SUV. I told them I liked the term better because it pokes fun at sport utility vehicles. Sport ute sounds like sport utensil, kind of like a utensil to be sporty. Listen to this, Evie. At one point during the interview the FBI even wondered if I didn't like the idea that they drove sport utes. They wondered if I was angry at them for adding to atmospheric pollution and global warming."

"They were trying to get you into an argument."

"Yeah, maybe so."

"Did you tell them about those green fibers you found on your kitchen floor?"

"I didn't have to tell them. They found the ones I'd saved."

"Did they tell you what the fibers were?"

"Yes. They were wood fibers. They use it in hydro-seeding. The fibers keep the seeds from blowing away or washing away. They said hydro-seeding was used around the complex at the end of summer and that the wood fibers were left over. They said I'd picked it up on my shoes and tracked it inside. Or maybe I even went out sleepwalking and picked it up then."

"You'll have to be more careful about sleepwalking from now on, Stan."

"Not with the FBI outside."

"I mean after that." Evie's voice softened. "When the FBI no longer needs to guard your apartment, and when life gets back to normal, you'll need some other way to keep you from sleepwalking. Maybe you'll need someone to watch you while you're asleep. Someone to make sure you don't sleepwalk."

After a pause, Evie said, "I don't believe I just said that."

For the first time in years Stan felt a boyish yearning in his gut. "After all that's happened, Evie, I think life's too short to worry about saying what we think. It's been a long time since someone's looked out for me. Maybe I had to go through all this to get beyond what's happened in my past. Not that I'll ever forget Marge and Timmy. Not that I'll ever stop wondering who killed Timmy. But right now I feel like doing something with the rest of my life despite what's happened. And when I try to imagine my future, I see you in it."

After a pause, Evie said, "And I see you in my future, Stan."

He awoke Wednesday from a good night's sleep, a sleep without dreams. Although as soon as he thought this, as soon as the concept of dreams descended upon him, he recalled the dreams. The steer and pig and eagle in the kitchen making him fill out name and address cards and making him solder circuit boards. The dream of seeing a man in a mask holding a child's head aloft. A dream of cleaning and aiming guns. Cleaning guns? Did he dream that or was it simply part of the interviews? No. Must have been real. All the guns had been cleaned, they said. Made him show how he'd done it. Had he really cleaned his guns or had that been a dream, too? Or maybe someone else had cleaned the guns to make it appear he really had been preparing to assassinate the President.

He pulled the covers to his nose, tried to regain the warmth that was slipping away. Warm fluid changing to cold water, icy water, dark water reflecting night lights. The fall from the bridge, Timmy and Marge gone in already and him following, seeing Johnny Tate leering at him from above.

Maybe it hadn't been such a good night's sleep. Maybe he *had* dreamed. Maybe if he weren't so alone. But tonight he would have company. Evie would be here tonight to hold him, to smooth the jagged edges of his screwed-up life.

He got up, showered and shaved. Too late for breakfast so he had lunch instead. Then he cleaned the apartment, made his bed, vacuumed. He vacuumed the tiled kitchen floor, too, because his broom—exhibit number one—was gone and no one had thought to buy him another. What a laugh. Stanley Johnson stuck at home without a broom to defend himself.

Later that afternoon Chief Jacobson called, asked how he was. He admitted he still had a lot on his mind, that it might take a few days to settle down. Jacobson advised him to call Dr. Todd, so he did.

"I'm sorry I wasn't available when you called the other day, Stan."

"Oh. Yeah. They said you'd had an accident."

"Yes. Quite frightening really. A truck ran me off the road then left without stopping."

"Were you badly hurt?"

"No. A few cuts and bruises. I saw you on television, Stan. I assume we'll have a lot to talk about."

"What's happened has brought back a lot of old fears, but I was in bad shape before it happened. I think my state of mind fueled the fire. A lot of the old thoughts and strange dreams had come back recently. So when I was just standing there at the window I probably looked . . . you know . . . crazy."

"I see. Of course I don't really see, Stan, because we're not face to face. When would you like to come in? I think we should talk it out. Chief Jacobson said you might be calling."

"He called you?"

"Yes. At first regarding the investigation. The Secret Service and the FBI grilled me, too. But don't worry. It's over. Chief Jacobson assured me of that. This morning he said he'd encourage you to call. I'm glad you did. Maybe I'm not the first person in the world you want to speak with, but at least I'm a willing listener. Don't worry about the insurance. We'll make these visits on the house. After all, I feel I know you more as a friend than a patient."

He made an appointment to see Dr. Todd on Friday. By then he'd have the flat fixed on the pickup. By then he'd be ready to venture outside. By then he'd be better because tonight, and perhaps tomorrow night, Evie will have soothed him, hugged him, mothered him, jumped his bones. Thinking of Evie had become extremely comforting. His anticipation of tonight's visit made him feel younger. Made him forget momentarily who he was.

The knock on the door was soft, Evie a little earlier than she'd said. Because the visit was planned, the FBI guys had not bothered to call up to tell him Evie had arrived. Imagining the FBI guys imagining him and Evie together made him feel giddy. He paused a moment to light the candles on the kitchen table, to observe the table set for two, the wine glasses sparkling the way Evie's eyes would sparkle across from him. He did not look through the fisheye lens because he did not want to see Evie's face distorted by the lens. He wanted to see her as she really was. He wanted to hold her. But when he opened the door, a younger woman stood there smiling at him.

The woman wore a black nylon jacket, unzipped. Beneath the jacket was a pink second skin, and her legs were pink. An exercise outfit, tight tights. The woman held a paper bag in one arm, a loaf of bread sticking out the top. She wore black gloves. As soon as he opened the door she stepped forward out of the hall light and into the candlelight.

"May I come in a moment? I have to speak with you."

He reached to the side of the door, turned on the overhead light. Her hair was blond.

She looked to the kitchen table, then back to him. "You're expecting someone?"

"Yes. A friend. Are you with the FBI?"

She closed the door, spoke softly, no longer smiling. "I have something very important to tell you."

Blond hair, in her early forties, bag of groceries. His new neighbors? The woman he saw through the fisheye lens? "Are you Mrs. Delaney?"

"No. Chief Jacobson sent me because I look like her."

"Chief Jacobson?"

She put her finger to her lips and continued softly. "Yes, Chief Jacobson. Please listen carefully because there's not much time."

As the woman spoke she placed the bag she was carrying on the counter and emptied out the bread and some potato chips and some clothes and white sneakers. The things she said made the walls of the kitchen close in about him. He backed into one of the kitchen chairs almost knocking it over. He looked to the table setting, studied the flickering candles. All this was still there. He held onto the chair, then sat down. This woman, who looked like a well-preserved nymph in her pink tights and purple sneakers, was speaking quickly, calmly, softly.

Chief Jacobson had sent her. Stan's life in danger. A plot to kill him, a plot that has been going on for some time. The head of the child. She said something about the head in the garbage. Something about it having been put there to drive him crazy. And because he hadn't gone crazy, because he hadn't shot the President, they were coming to kill him.

A dream. A dream had come while he was awake, making him dizzy. He was standing. Did not remember standing up from the chair. He sat down again, held his knees, felt the bones inside shudder, felt his hands squeezing his knees as if someone else were doing it.

The woman held up a pair of sweatpants. "Are you listening, Mr. Johnson?"

"Yes. I'm listening. How . . . how did you get in?"

"I'm dressed to look like your neighbor, Sue Delaney. She's at an exercise class. It was the only way to get you out. Chief Jacobson is waiting for us. The men guarding you may or may not be part of the plot. But whoever gives them their orders is part of the plot."

"A plot? The FBI?"

"Yes. It's a wide-ranging conspiracy. I'm not privy to all the details. All I know is I've been told to get you out and to tell you what I need to convince you."

"Chief Jacobson told you what to say?"

"Yes."

"What else did he say?"

"He said they found out about two guys named Youngblood and Washington who've been harassing you."

Youngblood trying to get him to join Men in the Middle, then the call about Youngblood being a crook, or maybe a child pornographer. And Washington, Derek Washington weeks ago trying to call him collect.

"What else?"

The woman came closer, stared at him. "I'm really sorry, Mr. Johnson."

The way she stared at him he knew something terrible would happen, or had already happened. Evie. Had something happened to Evie?

"Please," he said. "Get it over with. Tell me everything or I won't go."

"All right," she said. "It's about your son Timmy. They've found out who killed him."

Although the hairpiece the woman gave him covered his thinning gray hair, the image staring back at him from his dresser mirror was not that of a young man. His face looked pale, frightened. He backed away from the mirror, sucked in his gut. The sweatpants and sweatshirt hung loosely, hid the out-of-shape body. It would be dark outside, the woman said. As long as he acted the part, the FBI agents would think he was his neighbor across the hall, John Delaney. He took a deep breath, raised his shoulders, held back the scream he felt in his gut.

They had killed a child and arranged that he see it so that he might go crazy and shoot the President. They had done other things—the phone calls, the mail, maybe even the dreams. And Timmy. Had someone killed Timmy over two decades earlier just to make him crazy now? No. The woman hadn't said that. She'd simply said Chief Jacobson knew who killed Timmy. But why, after all those years, would he know now?

Stan went back into the kitchen to go with the woman. In a few minutes he would see Chief Jacobson, and Evie. The woman had assured him that Evie was safe with Chief Jacobson. Or maybe it was all a lie and this woman coming to him, telling him these things, was the real plot to kill him. If only he could call Chief Jacobson without being overheard. He could ask if Chief Jacobson really knew who killed Timmy. So what? Nothing would bring Timmy and Marge back. He could tell the woman that. He could refuse to go with her. But he had to go. By going with her everything would be made clear to him. Even if he died he would at least know why.

Back in the kitchen the woman looked him over, nodded. "Pretty good. I think we'll pull it off. Only remember, you've got to act younger."

"How?"

"Jog in place." She pointed to his feet. "Go ahead. Try it."

The cowboy movie city slicker dancing to the outlaw's pistol. A fool performing for this woman who smiled again the way she had when he opened his door.

"Good," she said. "We'll run out to the car. I'll hold your hand and pull you along." She held his hand. "I'll stop and kiss you." She kissed him quickly on the cheek. "I'm driving the Delaney's car, a black Firebird. When we get to the front of it, you run around and get in the passenger side. Door's unlocked. And when I get in put your arm around me. We're newlyweds.

Act like it. Don't stop or slow down, just keep moving." She held his hand, pulled him toward the door. "You ready?"

He felt rigid, imagined the woman pulling a zombie down the sidewalk. "What if the FBI men . . .?"

"Oh shit," she said. Then she grabbed his shoulders and shook him. "Look. Too many people have spent too much time setting this up for you to screw it up now! They're waiting. They're counting on you. You've got to act like you're married to me."

Then she kissed him. Pulled him to her and really kissed him. A savior. An angel come down from heaven to save Dirty Old Man Stan. He felt warm. He felt younger. He was in another world.

"All right," he said. "Let's go."

CHAPTER 35
THE PRESIDENT'S NEMESIS

ON THE WAY to the woods west of town Lena drove past the school where she and Walter had lifted Mrs. Delaney's Firebird. She imagined Mrs. Delaney, having discovered that her car keys had been taken from her purse, running out of the exercise class in her pink tights screaming, "Hey! That's my car!" Less than an hour earlier crazy Walter had simply entered the side entrance of the school gym and walked out a few minutes later handing her the keys and telling her to take off. She had left Walter at the school in the rental car. But now the parking lot was empty. No cops, no Mrs. Delaney in pink tights. Probably reported the Firebird stolen already and she'd be pulled over. The cop holding the gun would say, "Who's that guy with you?"

Lena the loser. Lena the pincushion left holding the bag. Lena being a little paranoid, antsy for her fix. No problem. She'd be to the meeting place soon and be rid of the Firebird. Jake and Walter waiting for her there. She and Jake would probably drive together in the rental car and Walter would take the old man in the rented van. Take the old man somewhere to be hidden away or shipped out of the country. None of her business. Of course the guy wasn't that old, only about ten years older than her, but for some reason she thought of him as an old man. Maybe because he was in trouble and she was on her way to a new life. Everything would be fine from now on.

But then she noticed that the Firebird's gas gauge was almost on empty and said, "Shit!"

"What's wrong?" asked Stan.

"Nothing. Just thought of something. Nothing to do with you."

Nothing indeed. Try to explain to Jake that she'd run out of gas. Should have checked before she picked up the guy. But gauges on these older cars were always wrong. Probably a few gallons left.

She eased off the gas. Not too far now. Easy does it. Hardly any traffic. Full moon glistening on the Firebird's throbbing ebony hood. Harvest moon. Two lit-up combines in the farm fields as she leaves town. Farmers gathering feed corn to last the winter. Once rode in a combine at night when she was a kid. Rich Uncle Bill's combine. Goddamn Uncle Bill copping a feel in the heated interior of the combine under the harvest moon, a chip off Dad's block. No wonder she ran away to the coast. No wonder she became a hooker and jammed junk harvested halfway 'round the world into her veins.

"Where are we going?"

"It won't be far now," she said. "We're going to meet the others. They'll take care of you."

"Will Chief Jacobson be there?"

"He'll be there."

"And Evie?"

"Yeah. Her, too."

Poor bastard. She felt sorry for the guy. Talk about minding your own business and getting sucked into the political cesspool.

She looked in the rearview mirror to be certain she was not being followed. The gas gauge had not moved any lower and she drove faster. She was not sure if she was driving faster because she wanted to get the job over with, or because she needed her fix. Cinderella racing the moon down the highway because she needed a fix so bad. Cinderella's gauge almost on empty.

"Are you a friend of Chief Jacobson?" asked Stan.

"Yeah. I know him."

"Good guy."

"Yeah. He's a real sugar daddy."

About ten miles west of town the woman turned onto a gravel road between farm fields. Stan knew it was ten miles because they were near the place Timmy's body had been found. A gravel road, or maybe it had been dirt then. Chief Jacobson driving, except he was not Chief then. Inspector Jacobson. Inspector Jacobson driving him to the spot where they'd found Timmy's body. Marge had not wanted to go, had already descended into the period of silence and withdrawal preceding her death.

It had been a cold day in March. On the radio they were giving news of President Reagan's condition, saying the wound was serious but not life threatening. The day was so gloomy and somber Stan remembered recalling sacred music playing on all the radio and television stations after Kennedy was shot and thinking that was how it should be throughout the country now that Timmy's body had been found. Families sheltering themselves in their homes awaiting coverage of Timmy's funeral.

Inspector Jacobson had driven down the farm road to a small woods. And in a clearing within the horseshoe-shaped woods had stood with him staring down at Timmy's recently excavated grave. A shallow grave resembling a fire pit, the surrounding growth trampled by the unsuccessful search for clues. He remembered seeing a branch as thick as his arm near the gravesite and wondering, at the time, if Timmy could have used the branch to defend himself. He remembered becoming sick, Inspector Jacobson waiting nearby while he bent over at the edge of the clearing weeping and vomiting.

The woman drove somewhat fast for the condition of the road, the Firebird bottoming out when it hit washed-out sections. Stan could see the woods ahead in the moonlight. He was certain this was the woods where Timmy's body had been found.

Why would Jacobson want to meet him here? Was the solution to Timmy's murder here? Had it been here all along? And what did Timmy's murder years earlier have to do with his being in danger now? The reason he'd gone with this woman was his need to know the truth. If Timmy's murder had been solved, he needed to know who did it.

What about Evie? The woman had said Evie would be there. Too easy, too simple, the woman saying things to shut him up. Her job simply to get him to this meeting place in the horseshoe-shaped woods that loomed ahead.

Perhaps the Secret Service agent, Philips, would be there. Perhaps other agents he had never seen would be there. Perhaps Agent Myra Ross would be there to question him again, the location meant to trigger something in his memory.

Evie would not be there. He was sure of that now. And he doubted Jacobson would be there.

He imagined Evie knocking repeatedly at his apartment door. Poor Evie, face so sad and worried. And then where would she go? To the FBI agents—if they were FBI agents—watching his apartment? To the police?

To Chief Jacobson who would calm her, have her sit in his office. A strange time to feel breathless infatuation, imagining his lover sobbing over his disappearance. Or perhaps his death in the woods where Timmy had died.

Ahead he saw the glint of moonlight on two vehicles. And as they drove closer he could see that the vehicles were a car and a van. Beyond the car and van he saw two figures standing in the moonlight. Men, shoulders squared by coats. One of the men was substantially taller and stockier than the other.

As the woman turned the car into the clearing the larger man walked toward them. The headlights lit up the man from the waist down. And in the distance the smaller man walked away into the darkness toward the center of the clearing where Timmy had been found.

The smaller man walked differently than the larger man. His legs, lit by the headlights, somewhat apart, bowed, an older man. When the headlights went out, Stan could barely see the older man in the distance. But he could see that the man had stopped in the center of the clearing. And he knew the man was waiting for him, felt somehow—something in his walk—that this man had great patience and had been waiting for a long, long time.

Lena sat in the back seat of the rental car while Walter sat in front. Walter had handed her the syringe and she'd chosen the back seat because she didn't like anyone near her when she fed it to her insides. Crazy. Sticks herself with the needle but frightened to do it around anyone because they might bump her and make her stick herself with the needle. Walter had measured out the dose, preparing the stuff as Jake had arranged. "Like spoon-feeding a baby," Walter had first joked back in L.A., causing Jake to turn and glare at him. After that Walter was much more serious with her dose.

The rush was just beginning, like being in an auditorium when applause starts from somewhere way back and begins to spread. The applause she always dreamed of when she was in high school at student assembly and imagined singing or dancing or doing something so fantastic on stage that the kids and even the teachers would go crazy clapping their hands off. She recalled Jake having said something similar to that once. A fantasy in which you are suddenly a school kid again and you know what you know now, or you have this great talent or this great power, and there you are in the school auditorium and you impress the hell out of everyone.

The beginning of the rush was always best, had really become the only pleasant part of the habit. So little for so much pain.

"All better now?" said Walter.

"Sure," she said. "All better."

As she leaned against the seat waiting for the full effect to come on, she imagined she was a baby leaning against her mother's breast, listening to her mother's heartbeat. And there *was* a thumping there, a thumping in the seatback as if it had a heart. Or something behind the seat.

"I hear something, Walter."

"What do you hear, Lena dear?"

Lena dear? Only Jake called her that. "Like behind the seat. In the trunk."

A rotten taste in her mouth. Heroin-taste, heavy and thick, her saliva like oil.

"What's going on? Walter, what's going on?"

"How are you now, Lena my dearest?"

More thumping behind the seat, louder.

"Shut up! Listen! In the trunk!"

"Oh. The trunk. That's Mrs. Delaney back there."

"But you said . . . Jake said no one would get hurt."

"No one who matters," said Walter.

"And who matters?"

"Just us," said Walter.

"Johnson, too? You'll kill him, too?"

"Have to. Mr. Serrantino's orders."

Something in Walter's voice. Something dangerous like a john who talks too much, acts too calm. Like the john's got plans for you besides . . .

The taste in her mouth became heroin-taste multiplied a thousand times. She felt disembodied as if she no longer had arms or legs. In the distance the shadowy figures of Jake and the guy named Johnson seemed to be speaking calmly, so calmly at a time like this.

She sat forward but Walter pushed her back.

"Relax, Lena. Let it happen. It's got to feel real good by now."

A hand touched her face. Her own hand swiping at her face. Inhaling. Inhaling without exhaling so that it was impossible to speak. The moon out the window was huge. Just the moon and nothing else. Not me, God! Not me!

No sound came out of her. No sound came in. Just the moon. Just an arm around her on a moonlit night. Or many arms. Too many arms. Arms squeezing because they all love her. All those arms squeezing and hugging poor Lena. Arms squeezing and rocking her to sleep.

Just the moon watching. The moon far off and safe and away, away from here, away from all this, away from Jake and goddamn Walter and the horse. The horse inside prancing now, hoofs kicking out at her insides.

Away, baby Lena. Away into the darkness beneath the covers where it's warm, and safe, and dark.

"No, Daddy! No!"

Alone.

CHAPTER 36

THE PRESIDENT'S NEMESIS

IN THE CLEARING in the woods where Timmy had been found, the only sound was the faint rumbling of traffic on highways several miles distant. Interstate 80 and 55, old Route 66 where someone got their kicks. Not him. He just stuck around through it all, let it all happen, let it all lead to this. Standing in a clearing in the woods. One of the few remaining strongholds of nature surrounded by farm fields that would eventually be swallowed up by subdivisions. A townhouse or condo built on the site where Timmy died. No cross with candles and flowers and stuffed animals. Nothing to mark the spot.

The man facing him did not speak, did not identify himself. Because the moon was behind the man, Stan could not see a face. The man wore an overcoat that made him sharp-shouldered, a knit cap that hid his head. Stan knew the man was about his age because he'd seen the man's slightly bow-legged walk from the car. The younger man, a large man with a deep voice, had sent Stan into the clearing, had gone with the young woman into the waiting car. The last sound of any significance had been the slamming of car doors. At first he had thought, had even prayed, that the old man was Chief Jacobson. But Chief Jacobson was taller, heavier, dark-skinned. This man had pale skin, the light of the moon shining at the sides of his neck.

As Stan stood before the man a chill ran through him. His head was cold and he wished he had kept the hairpiece on instead of leaving it in the car. He could understand the man wearing a knit cap if the plan was to stand outside like this on such a chilly evening. The earth beneath his feet was soft, the undergrowth and weeds making his footing unsteady. The sweatpants he wore had elastic at the ankles and he felt tied down and sinking into the very earth in which Timmy had been buried.

When Stan stepped forward seeking firmer ground where his heels would not sink in, the man took one hand from his coat pocket. In the man's hand was the unmistakable shine of a pistol in the moonlight.

"What do you want from me?"

No answer. The pistol pointed at him.

"Are you going to kill me?"

"Simply a precaution, Mr. Johnson. I've been hired to do a job. If I sense danger I never hesitate to protect myself."

The man's voice was somewhat high-pitched. Had he heard the voice before? On the phone? One of the men who had called him? The gun was steady, aimed at his chest.

"There's no need for a gun," said Stan, surprised at the steadiness of his own voice. "I'm not going to do anything if that's what you're worried about."

"I'm not worried, Mr. Johnson. Or perhaps I should call you Stanley. I feel I know you well enough. Of course, who doesn't know you? You're a celebrity. Everyone wants to be a celebrity, so you have what everyone wants."

"I don't think so."

"Why not?"

"I don't think anyone wants to become famous the way I did."

"Then it hasn't been quite as enjoyable as you'd like, Stanley?"

"Not at all."

"Shall I tell you all about it, Stanley?"

Something was strange about the way the man repeated his name, pronouncing it distinctly in a high-pitched voice that reminded him of . . . of what? A little boy. Little Stanley with a name too big for his britches. Kids in school saying, "Stan-ley," in an exaggerated way like Oliver Hardy sometimes did in the movies.

"Yes, I want you to tell me about it. But first I want you to know that no one I know is involved in any of this."

"No one you know is involved in any of what, Stanley?"

"This. Me being here. No one that I know has anything to do with what happened back at my apartment. That *is* the reason I'm here, isn't it?"

The man paused before answering. Then the pistol he held wagged slightly in the moonlight and he said, "Not to worry, Stanley my friend. Your latest lover . . . Evie, I believe . . . is safe. And your amorous landlady is quite well. Are there others?"

"No."

"Too bad. I prefer younger women myself. They always seem to be in better condition, if you know what I mean."

Stan could tell by the slight motion of the man's pistol back toward the vehicles that he was referring to the woman who brought him here, the woman who kissed him so he could better impersonate her husband and escape the FBI agents outside the apartment, if they were FBI agents. The woman who told him he would find out who murdered Timmy. Timmy's shallow grave somewhere here in the clearing, perhaps directly beneath his feet, the hole filled in years ago. He realized suddenly that his fists were clenched at his sides, that too much had happened too fast, and rather than being frightened he was angry, ready to either find out what would happen next, or simply end it all. He wondered, as he looked at the pistol glowing in the moonlight, what the bullet would feel like as it burrowed into him.

He took a step forward. "Are you going to tell me what this is all about or not?"

"Yes," said the man, holding his ground. "I'll tell you. But if you move again you'll be dead, so you'll never know. I don't want to kill you, Stanley. I'm here to help. You see, nothing is as it seems."

"No shit, Shakespeare."

"Very good. I admire a sense of humor under trying circumstances. I suppose you think you were, according to the plan, supposed to have shot the President. This is untrue. It's much more complicated then that. Actually, you were set up by the Haney campaign to do exactly what you did."

"Rose Adams Haney?"

"Exactly. The point was to make the President look bad. It's easy to do in our red-state-blue-state nation because the majority of voters have become media sheep. It's not what really happens that's important. What's important is what the public perceives through the media. And then public perception goes through even wider swings because we are a nation divided. Suppose the Secret Service is viewed as overbearing? Especially against an apparently innocent man with a broom."

"But I had guns in my apartment. What if I really had been holding a gun? Wouldn't that have given the President sympathy votes?"

"Good point, Stanley. If the voters thought the President had been in danger some would rally around him. Especially if the would-be assassin was a maniac. In the end, it all depends what kind of person you are. You see? It's all perception, not reality. We can spin this thing any which way."

"What do you plan to do? It's over."

"Ah, but it's not over, Stanley. It's just begun. If I were to want to help the President in his re-election bid I can think of two ways to do it. Both involving you. One way involves your cooperation, the other, I'm afraid, your demise."

A car door clicked shut. Footsteps in the weeds. He turned and saw that the larger man was standing at his side. "It's finished," said the man.

"Good. I was just giving our friend Stanley his options. You see, Stanley, if you were to write a confession admitting that you really intended to kill the President but became frightened . . . chickened out, as they say . . . then everything would be fine. The President would regain his support and you'd still be alive."

"And the other option?"

"Yes, without a note. A bit more complicated, but just as effective. Let's assume your guilt in a heinous crime is revealed. Let's assume you become a murderer. If this were true I think the public might wonder themselves whether you really meant to brandish a rifle instead of a broom. Clever, don't you think?"

"Why would I murder anyone? Who would believe it?"

"Everyone. Your past reputation has set the stage for us. Dirty Old Man Stan, I believe you were called. When someone with a name like that commits rape, then murder, then suicide . . . well, I think homicidal maniac is the correct term."

There was something oddly familiar about this man. Something in the voice. He was being manipulated by a man who knew exactly who he was and who he had been. And if this man knew these things, then the phone calls and the dreams must have all been created by him. A dark angel, a nemesis.

"Who would I murder?"

"Why, Mrs. Delaney, your next door neighbor. You've spied her through your peephole in her sexy exercise outfit on previous occasions and you can't help yourself. She's young and attractive and you go berserk. You fabricate an elaborate plan to escape your guards for the night and go out with her under some pretense. Perhaps you ask her to drive you somewhere because your own vehicle is disabled. You force her to drive to a wooded area. Homicidal maniacs have been known to sever body parts and perform obscene acts, even necrophilia."

"But she said she wasn't Mrs. Delaney."

"Oh, the woman who brought you here? No, not her. Mrs. Delaney is in the trunk of the car. Would you like to see her?"

Mrs. Delaney was tied up. Although she was gagged and blindfolded, she raised her head and groaned when the trunk lid opened and the light went on. The larger man stood close to him, held his arm tightly. Mrs. Delaney wore tights and sneakers exactly like those worn by the woman who brought him here. He wanted to ask where the other woman was but he did not want Mrs. Delaney to hear anything. If she knew nothing, if he wrote the confession, perhaps they'd let her go.

He did not have to ask about the other woman. They showed him her body in the back seat of the car. Her head tipped out over the edge of the seat when the door opened and tiny double moons reflected from her dead eyes. Marge's eyes when he found her in the bathroom. Death an unending, unanswered question.

He was taken to the van and pushed into the back. After being out in the darkness, the overhead dome light was blinding. He could not see the faces of the two men who stayed outside the rear door of the van, their heads above the glare of the dome light. The back of the van was empty except for some paper and several pencils. He was told what to write by the man with the high-pitched voice, a voice that, though soft, seemed to grow in intensity occasionally as if he might begin to whine like a boy whose voice has begun to change. This is what the man told him to write:

A world dominated by men destroyed my family. The only good Presidents were Kennedy and Carter. We must put women in control. I know this because I am a man. We are violent and always have been. I wanted to destroy Montgomery, but failed. I pray that another advocate of liberty and justice succeeds.

They made him write the note again and again. He tried altering his handwriting in various ways, tried doing it in subtle ways because they were comparing each note by flashlight to something, probably a sample of his handwriting. He wrote slowly, trying to think of a way to escape. He had maneuvered his position enough to see that the key was not in the van's ignition, and to see that there was nothing—no tools, no jack handle—beneath the front seats.

As the man repeated the confession over and over, his voice became strained and higher-pitched. And, hearing the confession again and again, Stan knew that this was a suicide note as well. They would make it appear he had killed himself after killing Mrs. Delaney.

When he completed one of the notes he realized he had not altered the handwriting. So he added a line at the bottom, "It's all bullshit." When he handed this note over, the larger man threatened to hit him. But the older man restrained the larger man, told him to vent his anger upon Mrs. Delaney.

Stan was pulled from the van, dragged to the back of the car by the larger man, and made to watch as the older man slapped Mrs. Delaney several times with the back of his gloved hand, then used a pocket knife to tear open the front of her leotard, exposing her breasts. Back in the van he could still hear Mrs. Delaney's muffled groans coming from the trunk of the car.

And he could still remember the face of the older man.

A face seen in profile, an angry face, the face of a boy gone mad. It was as though the man were having a tantrum. The face familiar, especially at the chin, a small chin seemingly pushed inward like . . . like who? Like an angry boy in a junior high auditorium. An angry boy turning, looking away, trying to act like he doesn't give a damn about being made fun of, then turning back and, in the nightmare at the bridge, threatening Marge and Timmy and him as, in the background beyond the descending bridge, the school principal announces that John F. Kennedy has been shot in Dallas.

Johnny Tate!

The world—what he could see and hear and feel—backed away as if he were an observer. Time meant nothing because at any instant he could be a boy in an auditorium, or a young man beaten up and dragged into a car and driven into downtown Chicago where the whole world was watching. Or he could be a husband, then a father. All of this could be observed as if on a stage to which he had no access. Or a television screen. His hands trying to grasp at these moments as they float past like rushes of air. His breathing foreign, the air smelling foul. The inside of the van lit white by the overhead light. White enamel like the cold surface of the bathtub against which Marge is lying dead. The open back door of the van a huge television screen in negative where images are dark, where everything is dark. The world a dark place he would, if he had the power, smash into dust. The world a fiendishly evil place populated by millions of Johnny Tates whose goal is to destroy his life and make the undertaking of that destruction last so long. So long! Johnny Tate! Here!

He had friends once, in this other world. In junior high the friends gathered around him when Johnny Tate threatened him. The friends tended to his and Tammy's relationship that school year following the Kennedy assassination as if they were shepherds tending sheep. He hadn't asked his friends to do this, it simply happened. It happened because Stan lived with his aunt and uncle and his friends felt sorry for him. It happened because Stan's friends hated Johnny and wanted to get even with him. It happened because Tammy told Stan's friends secrets that Johnny confided to her, one secret being that the year before a boy who had threatened Johnny suddenly disappeared one day without a trace, the other secret being that Johnny's stepmother had had sex with him. Stan's friends believed the wild stories, even the one that Johnny's father was powerful enough to have the boy disappear. His friends embellished the stories, protected his and Tammy's relationship in order to foster what eventually became a legend at school, lasting all that year and into the following year in high school after Johnny returned from summer vacation.

As Stan wrote yet another copy of his confession—the copy that would most likely be acceptable because he was not altering his handwriting, the copy he had to write so that Mrs. Delaney would not be beaten again—as he wrote ever so slowly, he knew that whether he fought back or not, Johnny Tate was here and would kill him. Whatever else was happening, whatever effect this would have on the Presidential election, he knew Johnny Tate would kill him. But he also knew he had some time left. Revenge would not be complete until he was told all the facts, all the gruesome details.

Timmy and Marge.

The pencil lead broke under the pressure of his hand and he had to start again on a fresh sheet of paper with a fresh pencil. He struggled to maintain control. He had to maintain control if he was to uncover the truth. If

Johnny Tate was responsible for Timmy's and Marge's deaths, then *he* would have to become a killer.

The pencil, sharp enough to pierce skin. If only Johnny would come closer. If only the other man were not there. If only he had one of his guns he would fire endlessly into Johnny, fire again and again until there was nothing left. He trembled, took deep breaths trying to control himself.

When he finally handed the sheet of paper out the back of the van, he tensed his legs, made ready to lunge at Johnny's throat. But the distance was too great and the gun in the larger man's hand was pointed directly at him. He would die trying.

Die trying. He kept repeating it to himself. Used the words to steady himself. The larger man motioned him out of the van.

"Come," said Johnny.

The larger man pushed him from behind, bent his arm, pressed the gun into his back. They were taking him to the clearing in the woods again, the woods where he would most likely die if he did not do something to stop them. Die trying. Die trying for Timmy and Marge and the child whose head he'd found, and the dead woman in the back seat of the car and whoever else had been killed. Die trying but don't make it futile. And what of his neighbor? Poor Mrs. Delaney, a woman he once spied through a fisheye lens. A woman made to suffer because she happened to live next door to Dirty Old Man Stan.

He thought of Evie standing in the hall knocking on his door. She would smile at first, then her lips would press together, her forehead would wrinkle with concern. She would run outside the apartment, the two FBI agents out of their vehicle running toward her. He recalled how he had twisted Evie's arm after she Dutch-rubbed his scalp. He recalled his confusion, unable to distinguish between reality and nightmare. And, although he knew *this* was real, that Johnny Tate was indeed here, that he was not insane, what good would it do now?

Perhaps the police and FBI were already searching for him. Evie and the FBI agents calling out the alert after finding his apartment empty. Evie crying in Chief Jacobson's office, no one to comfort her, no one able to convince Evie he would be fine because she would know better. She would have seen the table set for two. It would have been better to let her think he was a criminal and that he had run away to do his evil, but it was too late for that.

As Stan stood in the clearing in the woods with the two men, the only sounds were an occasional muted whimper from the trunk of the car and the endless moan of distant traffic. Johnny had the gun again, told the larger man to let them speak privately. The man walked to the cars, stood next to the one containing Mrs. Delaney and the dead woman. Fifty feet away. If he could somehow disarm Johnny it would take only seconds for the man to come to Johnny's aid.

Johnny Tate. The thought of the name, the face, the boy, this man before him, brought tears to his eyes. He took deep breaths. In all his life things had happened to him. Except for that school year when his friends had rallied round him, he had never been in control. But he had to control what happened now. He had to talk to Johnny, look for a chance to attack. Or escape. Run like hell the way he'd tried to run the night the young man Johnny Tate had his thugs drag him downtown to be arrested with the anti-Vietnam War protesters.

Earlier the moon had been behind Johnny. Now the moonlight shone on one side of Johnny's face. A smile, Johnny trying to be recognized. Didn't the bastard realize he'd seen his profile against the lighted inside of the car trunk?

"So," said Johnny. "You've cooperated, perhaps not as rapidly or willingly as I would have preferred, but you've cooperated. And now you wonder about your future."

"Do I have one?"

A high-pitched laugh. "Of course you do. We all do. But the length of that future depends on you."

"You have my confession. What else do you want?"

"I want you to know who I am, Stanley."

"All right. What's your name?"

"I've had many names."

"What's your current name?"

"Jake. Jake Serrantino. Does it sound familiar?"

"No."

"I thought not. As a rule I keep a low profile. I've been the man in the background, behind the scenes. I have friends who count on me to do what needs to be done."

"I don't give a damn who you are."

"Then let's talk about others. Those in the distant past. Your wife and son, a girl named Tammy, a boy named Johnny."

Johnny's voice had gotten louder, still under control, but he knew Johnny was becoming angry. If nothing else, even if he died, at least he could make Johnny angry. And, as Dr. Todd said, anger leads to irrationality.

He glanced back, saw that the large man was still standing by the car, apparently not alerted by the change in Johnny's voice. Then he turned to Johnny and strained to speak in a calm-sounding voice. "I'm sorry. I don't know what you're talking about."

"Then you're a fool. You've always been a fool. My real name, my first name, was John. We met long ago in a grammar school not far from here."

Johnny stared at him, seemed to be waiting for a reaction. Then he smiled again. "I see. Very clever, Stanley. When did you guess who I was?"

Guessing. If he could keep Johnny guessing . . . "When I began getting those phone calls I knew you were behind it."

"Don't play games with me, Stanley. I know all about you. I know how you think. I know what you drink. I know everything. I've seen your psychiatrist's records. I've listened to you babble on at your kitchen table. You can't hide from me."

The dreams. The eagle and steer and pig and Jimmy Carter. Dr. Todd's accident. The junk mail. The phone calls. The man who admired his guns . . . Die trying. No. Not yet. He had to know.

"Did . . . did you kill Timmy?"

"Ha! You still don't understand. Do you really think I've acted independently all these years? Do you really think all of this has taken place simply to fulfill a childhood vendetta?"

"You shot Timmy. You poisoned Marge. You did it all. You drugged me, or hypnotized me. You made me insane with anger that should have been directed at you instead of the system. Was I supposed to have killed the President? Or was I simply supposed to wound him? What was the real plan?"

"You're not as stupid as I thought," said Johnny. "It didn't matter whether you shot the President or not. What mattered was to create an act that would turn the tide. In the media everything comes down to marketing. Call it a pre-election assassination event, if you like. What mattered . . . what still matters . . . is to have an effect on the future. The system is more important than any single individual. But martyrs still do make a difference. Look at what a martyr named Jesus did to the world. Why do you suppose Jesus was a man instead of a woman?"

"You're insane."

"Sanity is relative. And as for this so-called vengeance you seem to grasp so dearly to your heart, that was taken care of years ago when Tammy conveniently passed on in a drowning accident."

"You killed her?"

"No. I simply failed to save her. There is a difference. It's all in the timing. Sometimes we have to wait a long time for an opportunity."

Crazy. Everything meant to drive him crazy. Or to make everyone think he's crazy. Timmy kidnapped on election day. Timmy's body found the day Reagan was shot. Marge's apparent suicide. The child's head in the garbage. The phone calls, the junk mail, the dreams. As if everything that happens is nothing but a vast game of terror played by men like Johnny Tate who remain in the background, tapping on the shoulder of a world gone blind.

He knew he had to act. He knew he had to do something to ruin the plan, whatever the plan might be. How would it feel? How would the bullet feel when he died trying?

Without moving his head he searched the ground. A few feet away he saw a long shadow. A fallen branch like the one he'd imagined Timmy could have used to protect himself. If he fell, if he fainted . . .

But he had been silent too long. He could hear Mrs. Delaney moaning in the trunk of the car. Johnny on guard now. He had to keep talking.

"I can't believe it," he said.

"Believe what?" asked Johnny.

"All of this because of some schoolboy jealousy?"

Johnny laughed. "First you're smart, now you're not so smart. None of this has anything to do with jealousy. I had to pick someone. And you seemed as good as anyone else."

"But why children? Why my son and that child whose head was in the garbage?"

"In the past it was usually men who killed one another. But after the

Kennedy assassination all hell broke loose in this so-called society. Today, kids do most of the killing. Maybe your kid would have taken a gun to school and become a killer."

"What are you talking about?"

"I'm talking about carrying on the tradition of power. Others have fallen by the wayside, but not me. I learned from my father never to allow myself to fall by the wayside." Johnny stepped a little closer. "You want to talk about revenge? I'll give you revenge! They killed my father!"

"I thought your father died of a heart attack. I thought . . ."

"Stepfather. Not my real father. My real father was the one with power. My real father arranged for me to be brought up by the wealthy man who pretended to be my father. My real father was murdered to keep his mouth shut about another President who got his life fucked up by women. You remember that day in the auditorium when they told us about Kennedy's assassination?"

"Of course I do."

"Yes, of course you do. We all remember that day. And most of us think we know what happened because the Warren Commission told us what happened. But I'll tell you one thing. My father knew what really happened and they killed him to keep it out of the history books forever. Not then, not until 1975, but they did kill him. When men get older they sometimes talk too much. That's why high-profile men throughout history never have a chance to get old. That's why it's better to keep a low profile."

Stan felt a burning in his chest. To say what he was going to say would be obvious to Johnny, would probably do no good, but he had to say it. "My son was born in 1975, the day Ford was shot at. My son was kidnapped the day Reagan was elected. My son's body was found the day Reagan was shot."

Johnny laughed. "You give me too much credit. Do you honestly think I planned the date your son was to have been born?"

"No, but you planned the rest."

Silence.

"Tell me you planned the other dates. Tell me you had Timmy kidnapped on election day and made the anonymous call locating Timmy's body the day Reagan was shot!"

There was a pause, then Johnny spoke more softly. "Dates are relative. For you, your son was born in 1975. For me, my father was killed in 1975. Call it an even exchange. I was still living out my late stepfather's fantasy, running one of his businesses, when I found out who my real father was. Then, before I even got to know my real father, they killed him. It was then I decided life was too short to simply accumulate wealth. I decided then and there I wanted to *do* something. I wanted my birthright. And so I went into the background. Where before I'd had a high profile, I knew that the only way to reach my goals would be to drop out of sight. It's humorous in some ways, Stanley. My given name for instance. I took the name Jake from a computer programmer. Of course this was no ordinary computer programmer. This programmer held the distinction of having to be eliminated in order that I be able to go into hiding. There were only a handful who knew my lineage. And the computer programmer named Jake was among them. Ironic that I should take the name of someone who'd done his best to do me in, isn't it?"

The insanity of it was too much for Stan. Before he could stop himself, he said, "And so I guess now you should hand the gun to me and I'll kill you and take your name so we can keep all this wonderful irony going! I'll be reborn as you and we'll do it without any help from those fucking women! Is that what this is about?"

"As Ralph Kramden would say, 'You're a riot, Alice.' "

"You can't kill both of us."

"I can do anything I want, Stanley."

"But who would believe she'd go with me."

"You're the neighborhood Don Juan, aren't you? Besides, you might have had a gun at her back."

"I have no more guns."

"You might have hidden one. Perhaps a secret cubbyhole inside the wall of the maintenance shed for the apartment complex. Perhaps *this* gun I'm holding in my gloved hand has traces of fiberglass insulation on it. You see, Stanley, everything has been thought of. Every detail. Have you noticed this pistol is a .45 just like the one you kept in your dresser? I guess you'd be familiar with a .45."

He had to try. He would die where Timmy was found. They would kill Mrs. Delaney *and* him. But to look like suicide it would have to be at close range. In the head or chest. If he could get Johnny to shoot him in the back, what would happen then? Would they leave Mrs. Delaney's body here with the note and take his body away? Would the police believe he had run away? Would Chief Jacobson believe any of it? Had they really made a hiding place for a gun in the maintenance shed near the pool? A hiding place the police and FBI and Secret Service had failed to find?

He could not run away. Johnny was responsible for Timmy's death and Marge's death. He could not run away from that, could not let Johnny loose in the world. His regret was that he would not be able to explain it to Evie.

He felt faint, took deep breaths and decided he *would* faint. He would fall forward as quickly as possible, grab for the stick and, if it was not a root or a rotten piece of wood, use it on Johnny, get the gun. Kill him! But first he needed to drop Johnny's guard as much as possible.

"One more question, Johnny."

"Go ahead."

He made ready to fall because he knew the question he was about to ask would be the last. He took more deep breaths, spaced his words and strained so that Johnny would think he was about to faint. "It's . . . It's about your father."

"What about him?"

He shouted as loud as he could. "Did you and your stepfather fuck your stepmother at the same time, or did you take turns?"

Falling. Rolling. The stick coming loose. Dirt in his face. Waiting for the explosion that would blow him apart while he swings the stick at Johnny. Johnny falling. Johnny on the ground and him on top. Johnny swinging wildly with his fists. Johnny's neck stiffening. No time for the gun. Johnny's neck in his hands. Johnny hissing like a snake. Johnny's soul slipping toward hell and him along for the ride.

"Bastard! Goddamn bastard!"

Arms around his head and neck. Strong arms lifting him. The large man upon him, lifting him off, prying his hands free. Johnny coughing, breathing, alive. Johnny screaming.

"Don't hurt him! Not yet!"

He tried to turn on the man holding him but was thrown to the ground like a helpless, whimpering child.

CHAPTER 37

STANLEY JOHNSON

THE PRESIDENT'S NEMESIS

STAN WAS DRAGGED about on the ground, then pulled upright. They took off his jacket and used it to tie his arms behind him. Not at his wrists, at his elbows, his hands helpless at his sides as if he had no arms, his shoulders and back in pain as the large man tightened the knot wrenching his elbows behind him. He was thrown to the ground again, this time more violently. His sweatpants were pulled down and tied about his ankles. Then the large man dragged him about on the cold damp ground. During all of this Johnny Tate barked instructions.

"Don't break any bones!"

"Over here! Wipe out these footprints here!"

"All in the perception! Stay tuned to CNN for the latest updates!"

"That's enough!" Then, in a calmer voice, "Get the woman."

Stan lay panting on the ground on his back. The moon above was blurred. His exhales sent vapor into the night and his eyes burned. He blinked his eyes, tried to clear the dirt and realized how foolish this effort was. He turned on his side and tried to sit up but was shoved back down.

Johnny stood above him, one foot on his chest. Stan grasped at the foot with his hands but could not reach because of the way his arms were tied.

Johnny stooped down, pulled Stan's undershorts down to his ankles. "At our age, given two weeks notice we can still get it up. Is that the way the saying goes?"

The large man pulled Mrs. Delaney from the trunk of the car and removed her gag. She screamed as she was dragged along the ground in the moonlight and thrown down beside him, her leotard torn apart at her crotch, her tights pulled down to her ankles.

"No! Please don't! Don't hurt me!"

While she screamed, Stan alternately lifted one leg, pushed with the other, the sweatpants tied about his ankles coming loose. If only he could get loose and . . . and what? Run. Better to be shot in the back. But what of Mrs. Delaney?

Her arms were untied and she tore off the blindfold just as Johnny and the other man lifted Stan and placed him upon her.

She screamed in his ear, scratched his face, hit his ears, jabbed her knee into his groin. She began choking him, her hands cold and tight, killing him. He arched away from her grip.

"No! Not me! They're forcing me!"

He was being held down at the hips, pushed down upon Mrs. Delaney. Her knees forced down. He kicked out, felt his legs come loose. But what good would it do with this man pressing down on him? He wanted to apologize to Mrs. Delaney, explain the whole thing if that were possible. No. He must escape. It was their only chance. If he did not escape or get a gun, or do something . . .

Johnny was at his ear. "That's it, Stanley. Doesn't it feel great? Nice to have a younger one for a change."

He felt a sudden deflation of her chest, heard a gagging rushing sound deep in her throat. She heaved like a volcano, like a woman in the final throes of labor. Marge! Timmy! Then he realized what was happening and, with all his strength, turned his head aside and, at the same time, rolled himself and Mrs. Delaney toward Johnny.

When she vomited in Johnny's face, Johnny screamed like a wild animal.

No time to think. Twisting. Turning. The weight toppling off him. Johnny screaming. Mrs. Delaney pushing him off, crawling away. Then he was crawling, standing, following her as she pulled her tights up and ran.

A flash followed by an explosion tore through the night.

"Not in the back!" screamed Johnny.

Something pulled at Stan's ankle. All over. He would be caught, turned about, shot. But his ankle pulled free and he realized he was dragging the sweatpants and probably his undershorts behind him through the underbrush.

Footsteps all around, feet crushing dead leaves and branches. Moonlight split into shadows as he ran into the woods. Running with all his strength. Ahead, Mrs. Delaney like a gazelle leaping, sidestepping trees. When she veered to the right he continued straight ahead, almost ran into a tree.

Separate. Hide. Find a hole to hide in forever. A grave.

He tripped, fell to the ground and rolled among bushes. He lay still for a moment listening to thrashing in the woods. His arms. He had to free his arms. He sat up, bent forward and pointed his arms straight back behind him. Then, despite the pain, he brought his arms together behind his back and was able to grasp the sleeve of the jacket they had tied him with and pull it down toward his wrists. Just as he thought his arms would break, he had the jacket unknotted.

A car door slammed and the beam of a powerful flashlight strobed across the trunks of trees making them appear to jump. More thrashing, feet running, away from him, after her, after the gazelle.

He pulled the sweatpants from his ankle, untangled them and put them on. He quietly put on the jacket that had been used to tie his arms. The jacket was darker than the shirt he wore and he would be harder to see in the moonlight.

He began crawling slowly at a right angle to the chase. If only he could help. If only he could rescue Mrs. Delaney. If only he weren't so out of shape. As he crawled, his legs burned beneath the sweatpants because of the tumble into sharp branches. His arms threatened to collapse beneath him, feeling as though they *had* been broken during the struggle to get untied.

He looked behind, saw the momentary illumination of a pair of pink legs several hundred feet deeper in the woods. He struggled to his feet, walked bent over, kept going. The only way he could help would be to get away himself. To creep away into the darkness like a creature of the night.

"I've got her!" It was a deep voice. The large man had caught Mrs. Delaney, or wanted him to think he'd caught her.

He stopped, listened. He could hear childlike whimpering. Timmy! As if Timmy could be here again. He looked back just in time to see the flashlight go out. Johnny and the other man were mumbling. Mrs. Delaney was sobbing. Before the flashlight went out he could see that they had come out into the clearing some distance away, had backed out into the clearing and were facing the section of woods on the other side of the clearing. A horseshoe. The woods shaped like a horseshoe. Covered by all the noise Mrs. Delaney had made, he'd been able to circle the clearing. If he kept going, if he could get to the tip of the horseshoe without being heard, he'd be near the gravel road that led to the main road.

He moved slowly, bent over, testing the earth with his hands before stepping ahead. When he felt twigs he tried another spot. His progress was slow, the woods thick, one numbed hand ahead easing branches aside, the other testing the ground.

A light flickered through the trees ahead, then two lights. A car! A car on the main road! He was nearing the tip of the horseshoe and the gravel road that led to the main road. How far? A quarter mile maybe? Time going too fast. If he didn't get to the road soon they would begin circling the perimeter of the woods. They'd see him running in the moonlight. They'd chase him down in a car or the van and kill him. He and Mrs. Delaney found dead together. His note saying it all, telling everyone what a crazy bastard Dirty Old Man Stan had been.

I pray that another advocate of liberty and justice succeeds. Only an insane bastard like him would leave a note like that.

He stopped, looked back. Two figures standing in the moonlight, a swift movement, then a scream. Mrs. Delaney screaming in a high-pitched voice like . . . like a child. Timmy's scream returning to this woods after so long, after so many years.

The moon above the trees was like a light from another room. The door ajar, inviting him to escape the nightmare. But the light was far away. Looking up had made him dizzy and he felt as though he were floating outward into the vast chaos. Skeletal arms reached for him, brittle fingers scratched at him. He wanted to cry out, to make it all go away. He wanted to sit in a chair and watch all of this on television, then laugh at the ridiculousness of it during a commercial . . . a commercial for liquid drain cleaner.

The moon above the trees was like a computer screen at the far end of a huge dark room. The branches passing over the moon were like characters flashing across the screen.

You can't blame yourself for everything, Stan.

Why not, Dr. Todd? Why the hell not?

There was a thrashing in the woods behind him. When he looked back he saw the glare of a flashlight. The flashlight beam swept back and forth on the ground a few hundred feet back. The large man after him, coming his way, probably discovering his trail of broken branches and his footprints in the spongy undergrowth.

He moved forward, faster now because of all the noise behind him. He stopped when the man stopped, started again when the man began plowing through the woods like an elephant. If he got to the gravel road would he be able to outrun the man? Would he be able to outrun a bullet? Would they hesitate shooting him in the back now?

Suddenly, Johnny shouted to him. "Stanley! If you don't come out I'll kill the woman! And then I'll kill Evie! I know where she lives! I know everything! I'll just kill the fuckers!"

Something reflecting the moonlight to his left. The cars, the van. He was at the tip of the horseshoe. And he knew, now that he was here, that he could not run away. He knew that the imagined escape across the farm fields to the main road was simply a ploy, a trick he'd played on himself to keep moving. He would do what he had promised himself all along. He would destroy Johnny, save Mrs. Delaney if he could. Or die trying.

He stooped at the edge of the clearing and tried to catch his breath while he studied the two cars and the van. He knew the van did not have keys in it. But what about the cars? Had the woman who brought him here taken the keys out of the ignition? What about the other car? What about the car the man thrashing through the woods had waited in while he and Johnny spoke? No. The man would not leave keys in the car, would not leave open an escape route however improbable.

The Firebird. He tried to remember the arrival, tried to picture the woman driving. But he could not remember details. Only that, as she drove, the woman had been wearing gloves. All of them with gloves. The plan to make it look like he and Mrs. Delaney had arrived alone in the clearing. He could see details now, the way the van and the other car were parked out on the gravel road, the way the Firebird had been driven onto the dirt where it would leave tracks.

No time left. The large man coming closer. The flashlight beam arching across trees above him. They would have had to leave the keys here for the plan to work. And the woman, the woman who helped him escape from the apartment by hugging and kissing him, the woman who was now dead . . . If she had been with Johnny, if she knew Johnny, she would have sensed something. She would have left the keys for her own escape. She would have doubted Johnny and left the keys.

Then he remembered it. The jangle of keys dropped onto the Firebird's center console just before the large man opened the door and took him to meet Johnny. The keys dropped onto the console after he asked the woman if he could take off the hairpiece. She had said, "Sure," dropped the keys onto the console, and taken the hairpiece from him.

As soon as he made up his mind and ran into the clearing, shots exploded from the woods behind him.

CHAPTER 38

THE PRESIDENT'S NEMESIS

HE WAS AWARE of being cold, the air he breathed like icy liquid, his neck and torso invaded by the anticipation of the bullet that would kill him. He was aware of the moon and the man emerging from the woods behind him and Johnny and Mrs. Delaney watching him. He thought of Evie trying to help the police figure out where he could have gone. He thought of how Evie's face would look when she was told he had been found shot to death, that look of suspended emotion, that split second reaction of disbelief to all the possible tragedies that can be doled out in one lifetime.

He was in a state of suspension, a pitching, rocking state that lurched for-ward split second by split second. The not-knowing when the bullet would hit making time stretch out. The not-knowing where the bullet would hit straining his muscles, seemingly lifting him upward so that he might float above the ground.

Another shot from behind that did not hit him. The car ahead, low and sleek, its expanse of glass at the front and side so vulnerable. During the concentrated effort to study the door handle's position and decide whether to first lock the door or try to start the car, whether to try to run over the large man or Johnny, whether he could save Mrs. Delaney . . . during these last seconds before he reached the car, time sped up. And when another shot erupted he realized the man behind was shooting over his head.

Keys. A pile of them on a ring. Lights on. First two keys failing. Third key slipping in. Engine revving. Ahead, Johnny holding her in front of him. Car in gear, lurching ahead as the door opens and a hand tears at his arm trying to pull his hand free of the steering wheel that is alive in his grasp.

He held onto the wheel as tightly as he could, pressed down on the accelerator, dragged the man along, both the man and the Firebird growling, protesting. But the man's animal-like growl ended abruptly when the Firebird's acceleration slammed the door onto the man, then spewed him out onto the ground.

Stan steadied the wheel, slumped below the wheel, steered to aim the headlights at Johnny and the woman. As he approached he could see their faces side by side take on the same animal fear of death. Johnny's gun rose, aimed, fired through the windshield. Bits of glass stung his face.

He turned the car left following Johnny's run, Johnny pulling the woman along like a rag doll. He slowed, adjusted the angle, estimated the point of impact. The angle between the car and the runners became acute. And then he braked and the right fender nosed into Johnny's legs.

She was free, running back to his right. He reached, opened the door. "Get in! Get in!"

She was not crying. She kept repeating, "Hurry!" over and over as the shots began.

He spun the car around, ducked down and looked between the spokes of the steering wheel trying to find the way out. The van and car moved past and he realized he was circling. Glass hit his face and hands. The van and car came around again and he steered toward them, then veered right, onto the gravel road, the holes and ruts making the Firebird leap across the road as if it were trying to fly. By the time he reached the main road, two pair of headlights were plowing through the dust hanging above the gravel road behind.

"Who are you!" screamed Mrs. Delaney. "What's happening?"

Cold air buffeted the back of his head and the growl of the Firebird's exhaust came in through the opening where the back window had been. Except for two bullet holes and a maze of cracks on the passenger side, the windshield was intact.

"Johnny!" screamed Mrs. Delaney. "Johnny! Johnny!"

Johnny? No! Not Johnny Tate! Her husband. Sue and John Delaney. She was calling for her husband!

He gripped the wheel, steadied the Firebird as it rocked back and forth on the uneven crown of the road. He shouted, "It's okay! Everything's okay now!" even though he knew it wasn't.

When she reached for the controls on the dash he thought she might try to stop the car. But he felt warmth mixed with the cold air coming through the holes in the windshield and knew she had turned on the car's heater. Then she sat low in the seat with her arms folded about her. And he realized only then that, except for the tights she had pulled back on, and the remnants of the torn leotard about her shoulders, she was nude, her breasts and back and shoulders exposed to the cold.

Instead of turning east, back the way the other woman had driven him to the woods, he continued south, the Firebird's speedometer at eighty. A faster way, no slowing down for traffic or turns. Behind him the headlights were keeping up. Or were they catching up? He'd go south a couple miles and get on Interstate 80 eastbound, drive into downtown Joliet and right into the goddamn Joliet Police Headquarters garage. Ten or fifteen miles, no more.

Then he saw the gas gauge resting on empty. Mrs. Delaney had slid off the seat and was huddled on the floor. He shouted to her.

"Does the gas gauge work?"

"I'm so cold. So cold!"

"The gas gauge! Does it work?"

"Oh no! The gas! I didn't buy gas! It was my turn and I didn't buy gas! Johnny, please come! Please, Johnny! How much farther? Where are we going?"

"To the police if we can make it! Do we have enough gas?"

"I don't know! I don't know!"

Where were the police? Where was all the traffic? What time was it? The clock on the Firebird's dash said almost midnight. The car and the van were catching up. If he went faster would he run out of gas?

An all-night convenience store flashed by on his right. Telephone! He could telephone! He'd stop and run in and . . . and what? They'd run in behind him, kill him and anyone else in the store, make it look like he'd done it. Johnny making a plan out of any goddamn thing.

"Is there a phone in the car?"

"Johnny has it! Oh, Johnny!" she screamed.

"Mrs. Delaney! Listen! If I drop you off where there's a phone can you go in and call the police?"

"I . . . I don't know!"

"I'll give you my jacket! Can you do it?"

"I think so."

He braked hard and turned down a side street. He'd go in a block, double back to the convenience store they just passed, drop her off before they saw him, then get back on the road.

The street was dark, the Firebird's tires moaned as he turned a corner. Headlights a block back pursued him.

"Get ready! It's an all-night store! I'll give you my jacket. Don't take time to put it on until you get in the store!"

North two blocks, then another right, Firebird fishtailing, growling. Mrs. Delaney up off the floor, ready. He turned into the parking lot. "Now!" He stood on the brake, lifted himself off the seat, took off his jacket. "Here! The police! Describe your car!"

He did not wait for her to close the door. The Firebird's acceleration slammed the door shut and he exited the parking lot and was back on the main road heading south just as the car came into view behind him. Then, two blocks ahead where he had turned in to double back, the van backed out across the road, blocking him.

She would call the police. They'd get here just in time to find him dead. Or Johnny Tate and the large man would find Mrs. Delaney in the store, kill her, too. He could not stop. If he had to crash into the van that would be better than stopping. Maybe he could knock the van out of the way without killing the Firebird's engine that seemed now to be his own heart, the engine keeping him from death.

He turned left, slid the Firebird sideways, tires screaming, a clink like the clinking of glasses during a toast as he barely clipped the corner of the van. Then he saw Johnny, Johnny Tate in the driver's seat of the van aiming a gun at him, firing. Glass rained in upon him. He hunched down in the seat, pushed the accelerator to the floor. Tires spinning, rubber burning, him still alive and the Firebird doing a slow spin then breaking away from the van. He drove around the van, severed an outside mirror as he barely missed a telephone pole.

He was back on the road, but the car with the large man inside was directly behind him. Several shots tore through the Firebird. He felt something tap his shoulder. Like someone in the back seat tapping his shoulder. Then he felt the pain shoot down his right arm and screamed.

"No! Goddamnit! No!"

The Firebird pulled ahead. Pulled away from the car, but only a few feet away. The car then the van right behind him. Ahead, the lights above the Interstate 80 cloverleaf looked like champagne-colored moons.

He could steer only with his left hand now, his right arm dangling at his side, burning with each bump, with each beat of his heart. Would he bleed to death? Would he pass out before he could get to the police? Is this how Timmy felt before he died? No. Timmy shot through the heart. Didn't know what hit him. Didn't know!

As he sped onto the upgrade of the overpass he braced himself against the seat, put his left hand at the base of the wheel and prepared to take the cloverleaf beyond the overpass at high speed. A Firebird. A bird on fire. He'd outrun them on the cloverleaf and fly into Joliet, see how fast a bird can go. Better to die trying. Better to crash than to let them catch him. Even if he crashed the police might catch them. Mrs. Delaney's call getting through. Please God. Please!

Something was wrong. The car was right behind him but the van was breaking off. And as he leaned the Firebird onto the entrance ramp he could see the van on the other side of the interstate. The van on the westbound ramp while he was on the eastbound ramp. Going too slow now because the car was nudging him, threatening to spin him around.

He sped up, cut to the right, drove on the shoulder so the car could not cut to the inside. And as he drove down the circular ramp he imagined how it would be now. The large man killing him, Johnny Tate getting away. Or even if he had enough gas to get back to Joliet, even if the man in the car was caught, Johnny would be gone. Johnny heading west, going undercover, changing his name again. And then what? More killing? Killing children and Evie and anyone else who could be used or who got in his way.

I'll just kill the fuckers!

At the bottom of the ramp be braked hard, slid the Firebird sideways, U-turned left, headed west in the east-bound lanes, screamed out loud, "Johnny you bastard!" as a shot smashed through the side window just behind his head.

The first oncoming cars sailed by to his left as he hugged the lane adjoining the median. The third car left the highway, went into the median and skidded to a stop in a cloud of dust.

He was catching up to the van, the van on the other side of the median with Johnny inside, the van winding left and right as it passed several cars.

The wind coming in through the broken side windows shook him, his arm and shoulder on fire, his eyes threatening to close in the cold wind so that he had to blink repeatedly to un-blur his vision.

Ahead he could see the yellow marker lights above the headlights of trucks bearing down, trucks whose drivers sat above it all, protected. The Firebird just that, a bird to be squashed. The median deep here, but not ahead. It smoothed out ahead.

He looked in the mirror. The car with the large man at the wheel was on his bumper. Another shot. More glass. Ahead the truck in his lane flashed it lights. He pressed the accelerator to the floor. In the mirror he seemed to be dragging the car behind him.

A game. A child's playground game. Crack the whip. The truck's horn blared, smoke coming off its tires, driver pulling over to the side. He aimed the Firebird at the truck, then at the last second veered left, braked, then

356

veered right. The Firebird lunged into the median and he heard the crash behind as the truck smashed head-on into his pursuer.

His head jammed into the roof, thighs into the steering wheel. He hung on with his good hand, his right arm feeling like it was being torn away. The Firebird launched itself from the median, landed sideways, skidded across the westbound lanes and down the embankment. A speed limit sign appeared and seemed to leap over the car. He accelerated up the embankment back onto the road.

Now it was just him and Johnny. If he could not overpower Johnny he would take Johnny with him to hell. The Firebird, apparently having lost its muffler, roared its approval, its engine the chant of a million voices giving him strength.

The dash lights and headlights were out, but the Firebird ignored this and flew faster. Stan held on, made the same noise deep in his throat that the Firebird was making, chanted with the Firebird. The lights above the road flicked past, flashed on his hand faster and faster. The van rocked and swayed ahead.

Catching up. Catching up and going so fast Johnny would not possibly be able to aim his gun accurately. Catching up and now, in the rearview mirror, the minute pulse of a red light perhaps a mile back. He would keep up with the van until the police came. He would not stop until they stopped the van. Johnny would be caught. Johnny Tate would be caught!

But the Firebird died, caught again, died. Gas. Running out of gas!

Not now God. Not now!

He pumped the gas pedal again and again. Rocked back and forth. Saw the van beginning to inch away. The Firebird sputtered, came alive once more. Car lights flying over the road in the distance. An overpass ahead. Firebird pulling ahead. He passed on the left and could see Johnny in the driver's seat. Johnny Tate turning to look at him and smiling. Smiling!

The Firebird sputtered again, and just as the engine died, just as the van began to pull even in its eventual journey that would take Johnny ahead somewhere so he could kill again, Stan gripped the wheel with both hands, even his right hand despite the searing pain in this shoulder, and, with all his might, turned the wheel as hard as he could and rammed into the side of the van.

The rest was like a dream of falling. Falling from the bridge instead of driving under it. Liquid explosion as the van plunged head-on into the barrel barriers, as it upended and collapsed roof first into the concrete support of the overpass. The Firebird went beneath the overpass, careened off the concrete wall, slid across the road screaming as the air bag exploded. After that Stan screamed. A victorious scream. Though he could not see because of the air bag in his face, he knew he had killed Johnny Tate and he carried this thought with him as the Firebird emerged from the underpass, skidded sideways, and rolled in the median.

Then, after the air bag deflated, except for distant sirens, the long night was finally silent.

Inside a black Ford Expedition with darkly tinted windows, two men spoke as they sped toward the smoke rising from the highway in the distance.

"Sounded like a bad accident on the microphone pickup."

"Yep."

"If it's finished, what about the money?"

"Menendez is in L.A. He'll try to unearth some of it."

"Then what?"

"Back to sunny South America."

"Like in Nicaragua when it was nothing but babes, babes, babes?"

"Something like that."

"Don't we have business with Domenico in Washington first?"

"Menendez says Thorsen will take care of that. No need to hurry it. Thorsen knows the maintenance supervisor at Andrews."

"What if Domenico says something in the interim?"

"Lots of people say things. It's expected. If someone was completely silent, or had no theories, they'd be suspect. It's part of our Web-based world."

They arrived at the scene, the driver braking hard so that the Expedition skidded to a stop beside the wreckage of the van. The passenger jumped out, bent at the wreckage a moment, used a cigarette lighter to ignite a river of gasoline leaking from the wreckage, then ran back and got into the Expedition.

As the Expedition sped off, the lights of emergency vehicles bore down on the scene from both directions.

CHAPTER 39

THE PRESIDENT'S NEMESIS

STANLEY JOHNSON

THE DARKNESS WAS not expansive like the night sometimes seemed. At night, outdoors, there was always that feeling of others about. A train or the sounds of traffic in the distance. Or a dog barking, a dog that must be tied up and, therefore, must belong to someone, someone who might turn on a porch light and part a curtain to peer outside. But the darkness he experienced now was not like that, was not normal.

This darkness had boundaries, boundaries he could not see or touch. In school when the teacher spoke of the boundaries of the universe, he had imagined black walls beyond the stars. This made the universe seem, to him, a large room. Perhaps he was in bed in his attic room floating above a sea of sharks. Perhaps he was falling, had been falling for such a long time without points of reference that the sensation eluded him. Perhaps all that was left were thoughts. Perhaps he was dead.

But then there was a contrast and suddenly something dark moved against a blur of dim light. Something long and low, stopping, moving again, stopping. A long black car in danger, being fired upon. But the car had no roof. And on the trunk of the car . . . on the trunk! . . . bits of brain . . . thoughts! . . . were being sought after by a woman named Jackie. Somehow, as the darkness closed in again, it seemed important to remember this.

More movement. More cars. Dark cars in the night. No. Not long low cars with tail fins. Taller. Sport utes. Those damn sport utes that only get about three miles per gallon. Sport utes that should keep moving because of all their inertia, but stop instead beneath his window as if they are undertakers come to get him in the middle of the night. Dark figures, men exiting the sport utes, profiles turning to face him.

They know I'm here. Please God! Anything but this!

He was aware of his windpipe rushing air in and out. He was being carried. He could feel the movement, a gentle bumping from side to side, a gentle rocking of his head. He felt cold on his face, on his head. Then warmth as if he had been taken indoors.

When he opened his eyes he was blinded by light. A ceiling light was directly above him. A man, shadowed against the light, leaned over him. He could not see the face because of the bright light above the man. Only an outline, a man peering down at him as if . . . as if peering into a garbage bag in which he was trapped. Then he remembered the head of the child in the garbage bag and screamed.

The man above him bent closer. "Take it easy, pal. You'll be all right. Gonna get you to the hospital."

A door slammed, then a woman's voice shouting from somewhere. "You about ready?"

"Yeah."

"The other driver's fried, too hot to get near the body. State trooper wanted to know if one of our paramedics was at the scene first."

"What?"

"Says there was a black vehicle, thinks it was a Lincoln Navigator or a Ford Expedition."

"I don't know of anybody."

"Ready now?"

"Yeah, hit it."

When the man sat back against the near wall Stan saw a young face, mustached, earring in one ear. He recognized the close walls and ceiling of an ambulance. He took deep breaths, and when the ambulance began moving he closed his eyes.

Though his shoulder burned and his right arm ached, Stan was more concerned about his legs. Something was wrong with his legs. He could tell by the care with which arms lifted him after a furious rattling rush down a fluorescent-lit hallway. He could tell by the way messages were being sent through his thighs and hips, messages of impending pain. He could tell by the way he was made to lie still while scissors were used to cut away the sweatpants, while meetings of green-uniformed nurses and doctors convened below his waist.

Above his head an I-V bag dripped its contents into a tube leading to his left arm. He could only turn his head left because of a mass of bandages on his right shoulder where he'd been shot. He was rolled slightly, saw a male nurse inject clear liquid into an I-V port, then felt as though the needle of the I-V port had splintered apart and radiated outward in all directions.

He counted five drops from the I-V bag before his eyes closed. With great effort he opened them once more to see if Evie was there. But it was a pretty female nurse smiling at him. Then he slept, and after a while he dreamed.

He was in a voting booth. The curtain was closed behind him, but since the curtain did not reach the floor, he was aware that people outside the booth would be able to see his legs. And if there was a line of people, which he was certain there was because of all the time he was taking, then all of these people in line would be looking at his legs, at the backs of his legs in tight sweatpants, at his feet in sneakers.

He wondered if the people outside the booth knew who he was. He had the feeling that by looking at his legs beneath the curtain they could tell all about him. About his apartment and his wife and son and Evie and Chief Jacobson, and Johnny Tate.

His legs began to tingle as if the people outside the booth staring at his legs were sending rays into his calves and heels, as if their thoughts about him could leave their heads and penetrate his skin, as if their brains could send messengers out to scout the area, find out why the hell the guy in the booth is taking so long.

He was taking a long time in the booth because the places where there should have been names of candidates were blank. And he had the feeling they were blank because he had not adequately prepared, had not read the newspapers or listened to the radio or watched television enough to know anything about the candidates. If he left the booth without voting, the people outside would know he was a failure. An election judge would go into the booth to inspect the apparatus and make certain he had not tampered with it. If he left the booth without voting he had the feeling he would suddenly be naked.

So, he decided to vote. But it was an old voting machine with huge straight ticket handles. It was like nostalgia night at the Route 43 Drive-In. When he grabbed one of several straight ticket handles that was as large as a gear shift in a car, the handle broke loose and became a rifle. On the back wall of the booth a screen appeared, and on the screen a man in an overcoat stood alone next to a large black sport ute. The man had his back to him. But then the man turned slowly toward him and he could see that the man's face was that of a child, a child with mouth open and eyes in a dead stare.

Timmy!

He shouted, "Timmy!" and someone was there holding him down, a hand on his forehead as an electronic beep followed the heartbeat he could feel in his throat.

Then a woman whose voice was shaky as if about to weep said, "You'll be okay, Stan. You'll be okay."

The next time he awakened he felt a hand on his forehead again. And when he opened his eyes he saw Evie smiling down at him. The simplicity of it, Evie being there when he awoke, when he most needed her, made his eyes fill with tears.

"Don't cry, Stan. You're okay now. The doctor said."

"My legs?"

"Your legs are fine. Broken, but they'll be fine. Listen to me. Just broken. You'll have casts. Then your legs and everything else about you will be just fine."

"Are you sure?"

"Of course I'm sure. I talked to the big cheese herself. Head of orthopedics. Her name's Doctor Beth."

"Oh. Thank you. Thank you, Evie."

He had been in the hospital a day and a half. He had two broken legs—left a worse break than the right—a flesh wound in his upper right arm near the shoulder, a mild concussion, various contusions and scratches. Despite all this, his condition, because of the absence of internal injuries, was described as good. Doctor Beth, in telling him this, mentioned that he was lucky he had not been thrown from the car, but might have gotten off in even better shape and not been thrown around so much had he been wearing his seat belt. When he laughed at the absurdity of this, Doctor Beth looked puzzled, shook her head. He asked Doctor Beth about the condition of the other driver, and when she said she knew nothing of another driver, Stan began to worry. When Doctor Beth left he saw a uniformed guard just outside the door to the room. Then the questioning began.

First was Chief Jacobson asking how he felt, whether he thought he could answer some questions.

"Only if I can ask some."

"Go ahead, Stan."

"Where's Evie?"

"She's here in the hospital. You'll see her in a little while."

"What about the other men?"

"What men?"

"Don't give me that! The two men who were chasing me, the men who kidnapped Mrs. Delaney. I won't answer any questions until you tell me."

"Why is it so important to you?"

He did not answer. He turned his head away, stared at the wall, would have folded his arms to show his stubbornness if his right arm did not hurt so much.

Chief Jacobson left the room, then came back a few minutes later with one of the FBI agents who had questioned him at the hotel. He had forgotten her name but Jacobson introduced him to her. "You remember Agent Ross, Agent Myra Ross from Washington."

Agent Ross stood at the foot of the bed staring at Stan's left leg, which was encased in a cast and held up by some kind of ramp contraption. "Sorry we have to meet again under these circumstances, Stan."

"Yeah, sure. If the FBI had done its job I wouldn't be here."

"You're right," said Ross. "On the other hand, could it be you left something out when we spoke last week?"

"I . . . I don't know. Maybe. But I want to know about those two men first."

"Will we be able to talk then?" asked Ross.

"Yes."

"We'd like to record you."

"Fine."

While he waited for Ross and a man with her to set up the recorder, he wondered what he wanted to be told. The large man in the car who ran into the truck he didn't care about. But Johnny Tate . . . what did he want for Johnny? Severe injuries. Yes. And pain. But alive. Alive enough to be questioned. And in such pain that he wouldn't care anymore, in such pain that he would tell the truth.

But it was simply another dream, a wish for revenge unfulfilled. Despite the barricade of barrels in front of the concrete overpass support, the van, because of its excessive speed, had flipped forward, crushing Johnny, killing him instantly. The man and woman in the car that ran into the semi were also dead. Both the van Johnny drove and the car had caught fire after their separate collisions. All three bodies were burned beyond recognition. Of course they were all burned beyond recognition. What else did he expect? He would wait until later to tell them the female passenger was already dead back at the clearing in the horseshoe-shaped woods.

For now, all that mattered was that Johnny Tate was dead. They were all dead. And, although Mrs. Delaney would corroborate most of what had happened in the horseshoe-shaped woods, she had not heard his conversations with Johnny. Johnny had died and taken his secrets with him. All he could do now was try to remember everything Johnny had said.

He was asked to start at the beginning. He did this but hurried in the description because he wanted to be able to remember everything Johnny had said. Agent Ross and Chief Jacobson kept trying to slow him down, asked questions about details that seemed unimportant. Exactly what the woman who picked him up said, the make and year of the car and van, the type of pencils he used to write the phony confession, the exact wording of the confession.

Stan answered the questions as best he could. And when he finally got to his last conversation with Johnny, he blurted it all out. How Johnny had Timmy and Marge killed. How Johnny killed Tammy by letting her drown. How Johnny went under the name Jake Serrantino. How Johnny had used Stan's life in some kind of elaborate plan. How Johnny claimed to have friends in high places. How Johnny first said the plan had been to make the incumbent President look bad, then turned full circle and said the plan wasn't finished and it was really designed to help the President. How Johnny claimed that his stepfather was wealthy and that his real father was powerful. His real father, who he said was murdered in 1975. How Johnny said they—whoever they were—had hidden a .45 in the wall of the maintenance shed near the pool and that Johnny was going to use the gun to kill Mrs. Delaney and pin it on him.

Chief Jacobson and Agent Myra Ross did not interrupt him now. They positioned the microphone closer to his face, took notes, looked to one another. When he was finished, when he took a deep breath and began a coughing fit that brought in two nurses and a doctor, he knew he had sounded like a crazy man, a paranoid idiot seeing conspiracy and corruption in everything. Stanley Johnson the goddamn walking and talking . . . no, not walking . . . the talking white paper throwing out alleged facts to support yet another assassination theory. What the hell. Might as well drag everything into it. Might as well even drag sex into it. A plot to kill the male candidate orchestrated to help him defeat the female candidate.

As nurses and interns and doctors crowded around trying to calm him, he wondered how much of what had happened in his life was real, and how much was simply part of a vast, endless nightmare.

As the questioning went on, Stan began to feel more and more that Chief Jacobson and Agent Myra Ross were searching out flaws in his character rather than seeking the truth about Johnny Tate. They asked repeatedly whether he had ever taken drugs. Not sleeping pills or aspirin, real drugs.

Stanley Johnson the middle-aged junkie, so doped up he might have imagined the whole thing. No. He knew that wasn't true. Johnny and the large man and the woman were dead. A truck driver was injured. Drugs could not have created all that.

But drugs could make him feel like he was going crazy. Not now. Back in his apartment. Back when he was dreaming. He asked Chief Jacobson if he had been drugged.

"We're not sure, Stan."

"What do you mean you're not sure? They've taken enough goddamn blood samples."

"I know. But they're still not sure. The results take a while."

"Will anyone ever know about this?"

"What do you mean?"

"The whole thing. Sometimes I get the feeling the whole thing's being swept under the rug. Like making sure I don't say anything to the doctors or nurses. Like that guard always watching me."

"Not swept under the rug, Stan. Just kept quiet until we know what the hell went on."

"And how close are you to that?"

"I don't know. They don't tell me everything either. I just know they're working on it."

"Who are they?"

"The Feds. The FBI. The CIA. Probably ten other agencies and all of them with about a hundred people in unmarked windbreakers running around this town like rutting deer. I'm surprised they've allowed me here with Myra to question you. I guess they feel you trust me, and Myra. If anything, maybe you can take that as a sign they're not trying to sweep it under the rug."

369

During his recovery Stan was thankful for Evie. Evie was real while everything else was insanity. As the days wore on, Evie provided him with reasons to want to live, reasons to put the nightmare behind him.

At first he felt he had betrayed Evie, that he should apologize to her. But then he realized everything he had done in the past two months had been part of his struggle against a conspiracy—whether wide-ranging or not—that had done its best to absorb him. He had not used the gun because he had struggled. His obsession with pornography, his drinking, his encounter with Marion, his anger with Evie at the drive-in—all of it feeding his guilt so that he could struggle. But how could he explain to Evie that his guilt had made him aim a broom instead of a gun? How could he explain to Evie that his self-hatred had helped fight off the effects of manipulative drug-induced dreams?

He did not apologize to Evie because it seemed unnecessary. She was here, by his side, listening, talking, acting as though the world were being remade, the pieces being put back together so that soon everything would be clear.

"Who cares whether they believe you, Stan? What matters now is you don't have to worry about it anymore. We don't ever have to talk about it again if you don't want to. Or if you need to talk to someone, I'll listen. Lord knows I've always enjoyed a mystery. I admit it. And if you'd rather talk to Dr. Todd, that's okay, too. Who wouldn't need to talk to a professional after what you've been through? I think I'd like a few sessions myself. And anyway, it's too soon to give up on the FBI and the cops. They're not telling you everything. They never do until they're finished with their investigation. And, frankly, in this case I agree with you. It's unfair making you remember it over and over and not telling you a damn thing. I wouldn't be surprised if they've already figured out the whole mess and they're simply waiting until after the election to spill the beans. See, they probably can't release anything now with the election only two weeks away. It wouldn't be fair to the voters."

"Did they tell you not to say anything, Evie?"

"Yes. I feel like a real shit. They made me sign one of those Patriot Act oaths and everything."

"And that's why they've allowed you to visit?"

"Yes. And I'll tell you something else. They told me not to, but I don't give a damn."

"What's that?"

"They're recording us right now just in case you remember something."

"Yeah, Jacobson told me."

Evie leaned close, whispered. "But they can't hear everything."

She turned, her ear so soft, her hair smelling so good.

"Like what?" he whispered.

She put her lips to his ear. "Like kisses."

CHAPTER 40

WINTER. PRESIDENT MONTGOMERY has been defeated by a narrow margin and Rose Adams Haney has been inaugurated. During the inauguration parade, signs that said, "Rose Knows," were prominent. However, among all these signs, there was a sign with a photograph of former President Montgomery on it. A photograph in which the former President had been caught off guard and smiled weirdly. Beneath the photograph of the former President were the words, "Rose Knew." But Rose did not know everything.

Outside the townhouse window in the newly-opened gated community of Spring Hills, twelve miles northwest of Joliet, Illinois, it was just as sunny as it had been in Washington during the inauguration. And the streets and sidewalks had been cleared just as neatly as they had been in Washington. The television was off now. No need to follow the news, a wrap-up of the election and the intervening two months, the wrap-up saying among other things that the broom incident at the Joliet, Illinois, apartment complex had little if any effect on the election results. Chief Jacobson and FBI Agent Myra Ross had said as much back then, that it would not affect the election.

But who knew?

As for what happened following the broom incident, that, too, was already old news. The official story had been something to the effect that two men had kidnapped a woman from her Joliet apartment. The man living in the apartment next door—coincidentally, the same man involved in the broom incident—rather than ignore screams as the abductors dragged his neighbor down the stairs, had been a key player in saving the woman. Several brief interviews had already been given, contracts were in the works for two guest appearances, and a book deal was pending.

Of course, in the official story, Stan had quite a lot of help saving Mrs. Delaney, being that the FBI was, "Keeping him under guard for his own protection," and they were, "Alerted when Stan came running outside the apartment building calling for help." In the official story there was no mention of the fact that Sue Delaney's husband was home alone in the apartment next door, or of the woman who, disguised as Mrs. Delaney, convinced Stan to go with her, or of the meeting in the horseshoe-shaped woods, or of the names Johnny Tate or Jake Serrantino. Names had been made up for the man who had died after his van hit the overpass support, and also for the large man, who had died in the head-on collision with the semi.

Stan sat on the sofa near the two-story window in the living room of the townhouse. The sun had crept along the floor during the inauguration and now rested on his legs. After a while the warmth of the sun began to penetrate the oversized slacks and the casts, his legs like pies in an oven. Right leg would be out sooner, maybe a week more in the smaller cast. But the left leg, the one with the pins, the one enclosed all the way up to his groin giving him a rash like a baby, the one with the pant leg slit even though they were oversized slacks, would be in this cast for another month, then a smaller cast, then therapy. The itching on his upper right arm where he had been shot had gone away soon after the stitches were out. The itching had been a sign of healing, of renewal.

He felt more comfortable now that the leg casts were covered by the over-sized slacks. Before Evie got him the slacks he recalled thinking of his legs as two cylindrical stones excavated in an archeological dig. Two cylindrical stones with ancient writings on them. Actually, the writings had been the requisite autographs applied in the hospital by nurses, by the Delaneys, by Chief Jacobson, and even by Agent Myra Ross on the day she told him about the townhouse arrangement. The most elaborate autographs on the casts, complete with hearts and arrows, had been etched into his monolithic legs in red ink by Evie.

The sky was blue. In the distance the trees along the road were bare except for a few lonely leaves, the winter winds having taken their brothers and sisters down. The sod wouldn't go in until spring, but now that snow covered the ground, everything looked quite pristine at Spring Hills.

When he sat higher in the sofa, lifting himself up by his arms, he could see the cul-de-sac. He could see his new Toyota sport ute parked in his driveway. And he could see John and Sue Delaney's brand new red Corvette, which replaced the black Firebird he had wrecked, parked in their driveway. The red Corvette was probably about as red as his face had been after Sue Delaney gave him a big wet kiss during that initial visit to the hospital when she arrived with her husband John who'd wanted to shake his hand.

He and the Delaneys had taken up residence in their brand new town-houses at the FBI's request. Not exactly witness protection, Agent Myra Ross had said, but something like it. A free ride for at least a year, or longer if the investigation dragged on. There were no garbage dumpsters outside because here they had door-to-door pickup.

There was a stirring in his lap, at his groin, near the spot where the rash at the top of the left cast itched. He closed his eyes for a moment, took a deep breath, then opened them. He looked down and saw Evie staring up at him with her beautiful blue eyes.

"I thought you were asleep."

Evie yawned, covered her mouth with her hand, smiled. "I was."

"But you weren't walking in your sleep."

She pulled her pink robe more tightly about her. "Unlike you, I've never walked in my sleep. Especially not outside in this weather."

"Of course not. If you walked outside it would have to be much warmer. And then, being the lecher that I am, I'd want you to take the robe off and do a few turns up and down the sidewalk."

Evie gave him a mock punch in the nose. "Very funny."

"I guess I haven't walked in my sleep since we've been here. Or have I, and you haven't told me?"

"No," said Evie, smiling. "You haven't walked in your sleep." She knocked on his left cast with her knuckle. "I would have heard you if you tried to tromp around on these. I bet it was the drugs they gave you. Good thing it was nothing that would do any long-term damage."

"Maybe while we can, we should take advantage of that sexual arousal drug they found remnants of."

Evie gave him another mock punch in the nose. "I think we'll be fine without it, Stan. Besides, it's not funny what they did to you. Everything, all of it, even that guy who called saying things about child pornography, was obviously part of the setup to discredit the potential assassin."

"I'm glad Myra explained it all to Marion, and that Myra was also good enough to let me know someone wrote love notes to Marion and signed my name to them. And I'm especially glad you're so understanding."

Evie smiled. "Oh, so it's Myra now instead of Agent Ross."

"You bet."

"Yeah," said Evie. "I know what you mean about Myra being all right. But can we believe everything her superiors in Washington tell her to tell us?"

"I don't know. They only tell us what they want to tell us. But Jacobson's pretty sure, as I am, that when it comes to our well-being, they do level with us."

"Stan?"

"Yeah?"

"What do you think his agenda was?"

"Jake?"

"Yes. I didn't know if you wanted to call him Jake or Johnny. We've been jumping back and forth lately."

"Let's call him Jake in deference to Sue Delaney's husband."

"Okay. What do you think Jake's agenda was?"

Stan thought for a moment to pull it together, then said, "In a general way, I think it was to prove he could manipulate events and lives. His life had been manipulated and he wanted to do it to others. I think he'd been waiting in the wings for an ultimate cause. He'd spent half his life manipulating my life, he probably manipulated the lives of that man and woman who were in the other car, and who knows how many others there were. More specifically, I think when Rose Adams Haney threatened to defeat President Montgomery, and the polls were close enough, Jake felt he could kill two birds with one stone. Swing the election the other way, and have some fun getting back at me while he was at it."

"Do unto others," said Evie. "Unfortunately, no one had a chance to do unto him what he did to you and your family."

"I know. But I've convinced myself he didn't do it because of a single incident. He didn't do it because I took his girlfriend away back in 1963. It was deeper than that, his plans for the future were formulating all along the way. Then, when he was older and found out who he was and how much power he had, and what he could do with that power, I think only then did he begin to formulate the idea that he could manipulate my life."

"Do you think the child's head was real?" asked Evie.

"I'm not sure anymore."

"And all that pornographic mail?"

"Oh, that was real all right. I could tell by the questioning that the FBI was having a hard time figuring that out. I think a lot of it was decades-old material someone had saved, and it was re-sent to me. That ad I answered for a crank-operated film viewer looked like it was from the fifties, and Myra admitted she checked the box number, found it a dead end, and that my check for nine-ninety-five never cleared. That was one of the few things she let me in on during their questioning. She never said anything about the files stored on my computer. There's one thing I did tell her the other day that I haven't told you yet."

"What's that?

"That poor woman they killed. The one whose body burnt up in the car that hit the semi. I remembered that, when she came to my apartment, she looked familiar. I'd thought all along she resembled Sue Delaney. But the recognition came from somewhere else. I think hers was one of the photographs that showed up on my computer."

"You mean the nude women over forty?"

"Yeah."

Evie reached up, touched his cheek, smiled. "Are you sure I wasn't one of them? I *am* still in my forties, you know. Just barely, but I am."

He slid his hand beneath her robe. "I'm sure. I've seen enough of you to make a conclusive best-looking-babe-in-her-forties final judgment."

Evie tickled his ribs.

He reached deeper beneath her robe and tickled her ribs.

She sat up, faced him, opened her robe and pulled it around him as they embraced. He savored her warmth and her smell. They kissed. Then Evie stood and tied her robe.

"The windows in here sure are big," she said.

"Yes, they are."

"Should I get your wheelchair so we can go to the bedroom?"

"I'd like that."

The dream was a continuation of their lovemaking. There were no limos and sport utes, no dumpsters, no head of a child, no menagerie in his kitchen, no green fibers on the floor, no broom or gun nor anything else aimed out his apartment window. He no longer lived in the apartment. He no longer lived alone.

In the final part of the dream Evie had sat up in bed and pulled the covers up to his chin and kissed him, staring at him with her blue eyes until he finally fell asleep.

When he opened his eyes he saw Evie sitting up in bed beside him. Her robe was loosely draped about her shoulders, the covers were pulled up on her lap, and on top of the covers was her new notebook computer. He could see the phone wire draped across the covers and knew she was on the Internet. When he raised his head slightly he saw a Web site titled "Secrets They Don't Want You to Know," with a bunch of fine print that Evie was squinting at.

"What's that you've got there?" he asked.

She continued staring at the screen. "Boy, this is a new one, Stan.

Remember Montgomery's campaign manager, George Domenico? The one who was killed in that plane crash in Peru near the end of the campaign?"

"What about him?"

"It says here he was an ex-CIA and National Security Council official and that before he was killed he was a shoe-in for Montgomery's Director of Central Intelligence."

"Where are you going with this, Evie?"

"Wait, there's more. It says here the plane crash was not an accident. It compares it to that crash where Ron Brown was killed. You know, a mountainous region in a foreign country where the evidence can be conveniently covered up. It also wonders why the President's campaign manager would be flying off to South America on a military jet days before the U.S. Presidential election. It says here his wife didn't know about the trip, and had no idea what the purpose was. The plane crashed in a rugged region of the Andes and they didn't even find his body."

"Anyone can say anything they want on the Web."

Evie continued staring at the screen. "I know. I was just thinking about that other vehicle that was supposedly at the scene, the one that left while the paramedics were taking care of you. You remember that, don't you?"

"Yes, I remember them talking about it. The cops asked if they knew of another paramedic who had a Lincoln Navigator or a Ford Expedition. But how does that connect to George Domenico?"

"You have to use your imagination, Stan. How did Jake know the President would stop at the apartment complex? It was supposedly an unscheduled stop, but obviously it wasn't. Who would be able to set that up for Jake but the President's campaign manager? And now, like Jake, he's dead. The way I see it, either the Feds found out about the conspiracy and are eliminating the players, or some of the conspirators are still around and covering their tracks."

"Who says there had to be more to this than Jake and the man and woman killed with him?"

Evie turned toward him. "Come on, Stan. Have you forgotten about the men in the limo and sport ute? And what about those reports of prowlers around my house when we were dating? You know there's a lot more here than meets the eye."

He reached out and tugged her robe a few inches down her shoulder. "And there's a lot more here than meets the eye."

She laughed, pushed his hand away and pulled her robe back up. "Not so fast. Not until I finish my theory."

"Okay, theorize away."

"That's better. See, there's also a mention of the mob on this Web site. And of course you know the mob has come up in a lot of political conspiracies. Anyway, here's the picture. Jake was your age, born . . . What? Forty-nine or fifty?"

"Forty-nine."

"Right. Forty-nine. A damn good year. The war's been over a while, the mob runs Chicago and Las Vegas, they've got their vacation spots in Florida and California. Especially California where they party with celebrities like Sinatra and the rest of the rat pack. Anyway, when Jake said to you, 'I'll just kill the fuckers.' That's something a mob guy would have said."

"One site I was looking at yesterday said Tony Accardo was the boss in Chicago in forty-nine and that Sam Giancana took over in fifty-six. Here's the picture. These guys and their cronies dated lots of showgirl types. Somebody knocks one of them up and she doesn't want the kid and it's too late for an abortion and, low and behold, Jake is born."

"I'm listening."

"It could be a mob guy who's the father, or it could be a movie star. Anyway, no one wants the kid, but blood is blood so they decide to use one of their contacts . . . Jake's stepfather . . . to give the kid a good home. But here's the clincher. You said Jake told you his real father was murdered in 1975. Guess who was murdered in 1975."

"Who?"

"Sam Giancana. He was supposed to testify and someone needed to keep him quiet."

Evie stared at him wide-eyed and he closed his eyes and pretended to snore.

She poked his ribs. "Watch it, I'll tickle you awake."

He laughed, opened his eyes. "I'm awake. I was kidding. Actually I was thinking. How would Jake have known who his real father was? It's not like he would have done DNA testing or anything. I've seen pictures of Giancana and he didn't exactly look like Jake."

"Wait a minute!" shouted Evie her eyes open even wider.

"What?"

"Giancana!"

"What about him?"

"Jake wasn't his kid at all, but, like I said before, the father was someone who needed a favor. The father was someone whose career would have been ruined if anyone found out he'd had an illegitimate son."

"So, who was the father?"

"A Kennedy."

"What?"

"John or Joe Senior."

"You're kidding."

"Not at all, Stan. Joe was always known as a womanizer. Maybe this was his last fling and he screwed it up. Giancana and Joe were friends and so Giancana does Joe a favor.

"Or! John Kennedy's just gotten into public office, he hasn't met Jackie yet, and Joe gets Giancana to hide the kid away so his plans for making his son President don't get screwed up."

He stared at Evie, her excitement rubbing off, then he looked at the computer. "Maybe you'd better log off."

"Oh, sure."

After Evie logged off the Internet, she closed the computer and put it on the nightstand on her side. Then she lay down and faced him.

"Are you a mystery, Evie?"

"Huh?"

"I said, are you a mystery?"

She smiled. "Yes, I am."

As they embraced he looked toward the window where sunlight shown brightly through sheer curtains.

THE END

Also available from Medallion Press by Michael Beres:

GRAND TRAVERSE

"In his thrilling new novel, Michael Beres takes us into a future racked by environmental disaster. From the devastation he spins an exciting and very human tale of intrigue, revenge, and, ultimately, hope for our future."

—Carl Pope, Executive Director, Sierra Club

CHAPTER 1

A DEPARTMENT OF NATURAL RESOURCES sign at the public access ramp sloping down into the water announces that Wylie Lake is two-hundred acres in size and only electric motors are allowed. Other DNR signs, some of which are quite weathered, warn of various species contamination, including zebra mussels. Ripples from two boats in the center of the lake on this sunny, windless morning distort autumn leaves in the lake's mirror, creating a kaleidoscope of color.

A young man in his 30s rows an aluminum rowboat similar to dozens flipped upside down along the shore. The man wears a jacket and wide-brimmed hat that shades his light complexion as he bends at the oars. An old woman

— well into her 90s — maneuvers a pedal boat that lists to one side because of the lack of a second passenger. Rather than using the electric trolling motor mounted on the stern of the boat, and despite her age, the old woman pedals the boat. The woman has dark complexion and wears a brightly colored shawl over an ankle-length frock. The pedal boat's solar cell canopy is designed to shade two passengers, but the sun is low and it shines orange on its single occupant. The woman's dark complexion is accented by a coif of thinning gray hair through which her scalp is prominent.

As the bright morning sun rises above the tree line on the Michigan hillside, the ancestry of the two boaters is obvious: The old woman in the pedal boat is of African descent; the young man in the rowboat is of European descent.

The man stops rowing, picks up a fishing pole and casts a bobbered line as the rowboat's momentum diminishes. The woman stops pedaling and also picks up a fishing pole and casts. The two boats drift closer as if the center of the lake has a gravitational pull. Eventually the woman and the man are close enough to speak to one another.

"Lots of ashes in this lake," says the woman, her voice strong despite her age.

The young man answers. "Ashes? Is that some kind of fish?"

"People's ashes. They live down there. When they go fishing the bottoms of their bobbers are the tops of our bobbers."

The young man peers into the dark water for a moment, then looks back out to his bobber. A short stubble of thick facial hair is obvious on his white skin. Given a couple of weeks the man could have a fine beard.

The woman continues. "A lady friend of mine is down there." She chuckles. "When she died, I married her husband. Their daughter — my stepdaughter — has skin as white as yours."

A high-pitched whine in the distance interrupts their conversation. Something hidden by the brightly colored trees approaches the lake from the northwest, skirts the northern shore. It sounds like a winged insect with a tiny jet engine. Although they can see nothing but trees, cabins, docks, and upturned boats, the young man and old woman follow the sound, watching the shoreline attentively. Eventually the road nears the shore at a clearing and an electric cycle races past. Because of a wind-breaker suit, gloves, helmet, and face shield, it is impossible to determine the rider's sex or skin color. The whine of the cycle lowers in pitch as it climbs a hill where the road turns away from the lake. Once over the hill the whine diminishes and it is quiet again.

The old woman has one hand to her throat. "At first I thought it was a siren. Sirens used to scare my second husband to death."

"Why was he frightened of sirens?" *asks the young man.*

The old woman continues looking to where the electric cycle had disappeared. "You'd think it would be because of the terrorist attacks back then. But it wasn't. Nightmares did it, sirens coming down a lonely road. He used to sleep with his hand resting on the switch to the reading lamp. Said the energy waiting upstream from the switch calmed him. He used to call out his first wife's name — Jude — my best friend. Short for Judy. When I married him, sometimes he'd call out my name, sometimes he'd call out Jude's name. The nightmare was always the same. His daughter—my stepdaughter—and another girl playing in one of those backyard swimming pools. Both girls little and the other one wearing a big old sun hat like yours."

The young man tugs at the brim of his hat, suddenly realizing he's imitating a cowboy tipping his hat to a lady without removing it. As he does this he thinks perhaps the terrorists who started all the craziness at the beginning of the century should have worn cowboy hats during their attacks. Crazy cowboys because, after all, one of the definitions of cowboy is a reckless person who ignores risks and consequences.

The old woman leans to the side and looks down into the water. "Funny thing is, before my first husband died, he was in the dream, too. Who would've guessed one day I'd be sleeping in the same bed with a white man who had dreams about my first husband. Two little girls climbing into a backyard pool on a wobbly ladder, and my husband — a one-armed chemical waste troll who lives in backyard pools . . . See, my first husband was a veteran, got his arm blown off in Vietnam when he was just a boy. The chemical thing was because of a chemical waste dump . . . "

The old woman looks up toward the young man. "None of this is making sense. I already got a mess of bluegills. I should let you alone."

The young man begins reeling in his line. "That's all right. I'm not using bait. Fishing's simply an excuse to come out here in the morning." He holds his line up by the bobber and shows her the bare hook. "I also left my phone in the cabin so no one can interrupt me."

"I've interrupted you," she says.

"No. My uncle, whose cabin I'm staying at, told me about you. He's dead now, but the family still owns the cabin. Anyway, when I saw you out here . . . "

She looks at him a little warily. "You're not recording, are you?"

He puts down his pole, holds up both hands. "Absolutely not."

She nods. "Well, even if you were, what the hell difference would it make now? Want some breakfast?"

"Sure."

The old woman reaches over the side of her pedal boat and holds up a *stringer full of bluegills. "Nothing like fried fish for breakfast. The DNR's been stocking the lake with genetically pure pan fish for a couple years now. Catch them while they're young they're just fine."*

She lowers the stringer back over the side and begins reeling in her line, staring down into the dark water once again. "When I look back over the years it's hard to believe how much has happened. I never talked about it much back then. But now that there's not much time left for me, it seems all I do is talk. If you weren't here I'd be talking to the water, or singing to it."

She looks toward the horizon. "And now with another winter coming . . . " She hums a few bars of a song, then turns back to the young man. "My second husband used to play The Beatles singing "Hey Jude" when he and Judy made love. They recorded songs on tape back then. You've probably never used a tape machine."

"I've seen them," says the young man.

The old woman continues. "Anyway, my second husband played "Hey Jude" for him and Judy. Not for me. Not when we made love. It was my first husband who told me about my second husband playing "Hey Jude." See, way back then we lived in the same neighborhood and the boys went for walks in the morning. Anyway, you know the song, don't you?"

As the young man rows and she pedals, the old woman's voice cracks the quiet of dawn. She hums "Hey Jude" and even tries to sing a few words of the song. But the only part that comes out clearly is the chorus and the repeat of the song title.

When the old woman gives up on the song she coughs to clear her throat, wipes her nose with her sleeve, and as the young man rows slowly alongside her pedal boat toward a dock in the distance, she begins telling him about, of all things, a freight train crossing Illinois farmland.

Three Decades Earlier

The track was seamless, welded atop a recently refurbished track bed. It was dawn, patches of ground fog lingering in ditches. The railroad right-of-way, whose shoulders in days gone by carried steam-pulled troop trains, then diesel-pulled vista cars, then freights, now carried a train the media had dubbed the Dawn Patrol because it conveyed its cargo only at dawn when winds were calm and overhead aircraft were banned.

The Dawn Patrol headed east on its sparkling seamless rails toward the imminent sunrise. It was forty miles south of Chicago and would soon cross the state line into Indiana. So far that morning it had traveled eighty miles since leaving the Iroquois Nuclear Power Plant in northern Illinois. After crossing the state line it would turn northeast and travel another eighty miles to the Tri-State Nuclear Waste Disposal Facility near the Michigan state line. As usual it had left the Iroquois plant at one in the morning and would not arrive at the Tri-State facility until nine in the morning. The reason it took eight hours to cover the one-hundred sixty miles was because the Dawn Patrol traveled at exactly twenty miles per hour, no more, no less. The reason for shipping nuclear waste from Iroquois was because plants throughout the Midwest had shipped waste to Iroquois for many years while waiting for the Tri-State facility to be completed.

Thunderstorms were predicted for later that night, many hours away. By then the Dawn Patrol's radioactive cargo for the day would be safely put to bed.

Two men — one black, one white — out for a morning run, white man lagging behind. Black man shouts back to the white man.

"Here she comes, Paul. Where're the lazy bastard protesters who used to be out here?" Hiram's single arm swung in wide arcs as he made his way along the asphalt walkway.

"In bed," said Paul.

"Not very dedicated environmentalists."

Hiram's mention of environmentalists reminded Paul of his youth, back during the Reagan administration protesting when James Watt came to town. Environmental activism that introduced him to Judy and eventually led to their marriage. Environmental activism that turned out to be pretty damned ironic years later when their neighborhood in Easthaven was contaminated by Ducain Chemical. His daughter only two years old when it happened, his daughter who would later be called Chemical Jamie in grade school when legal appeals ran out for the chemical company and they finally put the senior Ducain on trial.

As Hiram set the pace in the wet-tipped dawn, his single arm twisting his stride out of balance as if sidestepping land mines, Paul wondered what Hiram would say when he told him about the dream. In the distant clearing, around a bend in the path, the

Dawn Patrol moaned.

"Come on, Paul!" shouted Hiram. "Got a train to meet!"

The track curved, giving the iron-clad cars the look of a thick snake. The train growled on its seamless rails, its flanks glistening in dawn light.

At the crossing, Hiram ran in place, massaging his stump with his right hand, while Paul stood still, rubbing a tender spot beneath his left rib. The vibration of the earth caused by the train reminded Paul of an acid trip years earlier when Marty Kaatz spiked his beer at a Sigma-Alpha-whatever house party. As the cars rolled past, Paul noticed that each set of wheel trucks gave off a slightly different pitch. He stared at the wheels imagining he had X-ray vision and could see the inner workings of machinery. See inside where a roller bearing, overlooked during final inspection, has flat-spotted and is, every few turns, pausing and heating up.

But the train passed without incident, the whisper of morning returned, and the two men jogged across the tracks, exchanging waves with a state trooper parked on the far side of the road where the path came out of the woods. Once off the asphalt path they boarded the sidewalk and began walking the final leg back to showers and breakfast tables and good-bye kisses as both their wives left for work and both of them did a few morning chores before leaving for their own jobs. They slowed, cooling down.

"I had a dream about you last night," said Paul.

"How romantic," said Hiram. "I thought you only dreamed about chemical dumps."

"The dream was about the chemical dump."

"What was I doing at the dump?"

"You were outside the dump. A neighborhood pervert exposing yourself in a backyard swimming pool."

Hiram wiped his brow in an exaggerated way. "Lordy, for a second I thought you'd made me into a chemical company president. What was his name? I keep forgetting it."

"Harold Ducain."

"Yeah, Ducain. Your ace of spades. But back to the dream. What was I doing in a backyard swimming pool?"

"You were trying to grab Jamie and another little girl who was sitting with Jamie on the pool ladder. But the dream, the whole point of it, still had to do with Harold Ducain."

"Really."

As they continued walking, the silence of morning became eerie. The cadence of the clickity-clack of the Dawn Patrol on that particular morning had triggered a feeling of déjà vu in Paul that he could not shake. He'd been here before, about to tell Hiram the whole story, only this time he really would tell the story. Why, after all the years they'd known one another — but why not? He had to tell Hiram about Ducain's daughter eventually. It was in the cards. It was déjà vu. The pressure to confess that morning was a technicolor pressure, insides exploding out, glistening in the morning sun if he didn't talk. *Just talk.*

"Anyway," said Paul, "in the past when I told you about Ducain I kind of left something out."

"Look, Paul, if you're trying to unload something, don't bullshit around. We're almost to my house and it's a work day."

"Okay, okay. See, Ducain's daughter's been in my dreams a lot lately and it's brought back memories. The trial never bothered me. What bothered me was Ducain's suicide. I always had the feeling he took the fall for someone else. It's not like he hauled those drums of shit out into that field on his back."

"How old was Ducain's daughter during the trial?"

"Eleven or twelve. Same as Jamie."

"And how old was Jamie when they chased you out of Easthaven?"

"Two."

"So, how can little girls two years old be sitting on a pool ladder?"

"In the dream Jamie and Ducain's daughter are the age they were at the trial. Ducain's daughter was a redhead and . . . anyway, it's just a dream."

"So you said. How many years has it been now?"

"Since the trial?"

"Since they chased you out of Easthaven."

"1989, that makes it twenty-three years."

"And so far everyone's still doing okay?"

"Everyone?"

"You, Judy, and Jamie. That's who you should be thinking about. Not a dead guy. A dead guy's a dead guy and you can't do a goddamn thing about him. What's important now is how your family's doing. So, the three of you, no new health problems?"

"Not since Judy's mastectomy."

"How long has that been?"

"Five years."

"If you can beat cancer for five years, the prognosis is damn good."

"Is this your Vietnam vet time-heals-all-wounds speech?"

Hiram stopped walking, turned toward Paul. "No," he said, sounding somewhat angry. "It's my dreams-are-bullshit speech. Best way to handle them is to get pissed enough to drive 'em the hell out. Think about what the chemical dump did to you and your neighbors. Ducain and his daughter didn't live next to his dump. You did!"

Paul turned to face Hiram, stared into his dark eyes. "How about slapping me around some?"

Hiram laughed and they continued walking.

"Yeah," said Hiram, "that's what Bianca used to do with me. When I'd wake up nights screaming about my arm, there'd be Bianca, who goes to Sunday church meetings with her girlfriends, slapping me around some, then holding me like a baby, saying over and over, 'It's all bullshit. It's all bullshit.'"

"Judy holds me when I wake up," said Paul.

As they walked into their neighborhood the sun was up and it was already hot. As if nudged from bed by the heat, the rest of the world had come alive. Doors slammed, cars backed out of driveways, the faint odor of coffee was in the air. But there was also the smell of decay, a smell Hiram sometimes commented on when reminiscing about his boyhood in the projects or his stint in Vietnam. It was garbage day, trash containers and recycling bins lining both sides of the street. As they neared Hiram's house, Paul thought about death and the shortness of life and remembered the invitation he and Judy had discussed but kept putting off, an invitation they had discussed again the previous night.

"Damn, I almost forgot."

"What?"

"We're going up to the cottage two weeks from Friday and we wondered if you and Bianca would come with us."

"Walden Pond, huh?"

"I don't think Thoreau ever made it to Michigan."

"Still planning to retire up there?"

"Judy wants to keep working a couple more years. I'd do it tomorrow."

"I'm with you, man. Tired of sitting in front of a computer all day. I'll ask Bianca about Michigan, let you know. And if there's any more of this chemical company lawsuit business you're holding back . . . "

"No, that's it, just some nightmares."

"Sounds like enough. See you tomorrow, man."

As he walked the last block to his house, Paul recalled the evening twenty-three years earlier when sirens sounded and lights flashed and squad car loudspeakers told everyone to leave as quickly as possible because of the mix of toxic chemicals that had been discovered seething in the field of drums behind the chainlink fence at the end of the block. The next day was to have been garbage day and he had been a younger, stronger man heaving the containers out to the curb in one trip. But the garbage wasn't picked up the next day because, by midnight, every man, woman, and child had been evacuated from the small town of Easthaven, Illinois, which, by the end of the century, had become a ghost town fifty miles from Chicago. A ghost town Rand McNally had long since taken off its maps.

Paul climbed the front porch steps and went into the house to get the garbage container and recycle bin. As he passed the downstairs bath on his way to the garage, he heard Judy singing "Angel of the Morning." It was a song Judy always sang in the shower, a song that had come out years earlier, long before she'd had her double mastectomy. A song she began singing in the shower back when they lived in Easthaven where, during that summer of 1989, she sang in the shower following a long swim in the backyard pool.

As always, the song brought tears to Paul's eyes. When he tried to wipe the tears away with the back of his hand, perspiration poisoned the tears and made his eyes sting like hell.

Grand Traverse
Michael Beres
ISBN#1932815341
Platinum
$24.95
Fiction
Available Now

For more information

about other great titles from

Medallion Press, visit

www.medallionpress.com